SIMPLICIUS
SIMPLICISSIMUS

The Library of Liberal Arts
OSKAR PIEST, FOUNDER

· ·

The Library of Liberal Arts

SIMPLICIUS
SIMPLICISSIMUS

JOHANN JAKOB CHRISTOFFEL
VON GRIMMELSHAUSEN

A modern translation, with an Introduction, by

GEORGE SCHULZ-BEHREND

Professor of Germanic Languages
The University of Texas

The Library of Liberal Arts

published by

THE BOBBS-MERRILL COMPANY, INC.
A Subsidiary of Howard W. Sams & Co., Inc.
Publishers • Indianapolis • New York • Kansas City

Johann Jakob Christoffel von Grimmelshausen:
ca. 1621-1676

SIMPLICIUS SIMPLICISSIMUS was originally published in 1669

· · · · · · · · · · · · · · · · · · ·

The "Phoenix Copper"

Frontispiece from the 1669 edition

Translator's Preface

Translation, like so many human endeavors, is never accomplished once and for all. An original has the dubious advantage of being unchangeable; translations must be redone every few generations.

The first English translation of *Simplicius Simplicissimus* appeared in 1912 and has been re-issued twice, most recently in 1962 by the University of Nebraska Press. Its maker, A. T. S. Goodrick, rendered the archaic German of Grimmelshausen into pseudo-antique English, as was the Victorian practice of translation. Fifty years later a second British translation appeared, Walter Wallich's *The Adventures of a Simpleton* (London: New English Library, Ltd., 1962). The Germans themselves have "translated" the novel; that is, there are any number of adaptations of *Simplicius,* and these editions in modern spelling have done their share in keeping the book a perennial favorite.

For the first five books of the present translation, I have used for my text the edition by J. H. Scholte, *Simplicissimus Teutsch* (1669) in the series "Neudrucke deutscher Literaturwerke des 16. und 17. Jahrhunderts" (Tübingen: Max Niemeyer, 1954). But I did not deliberately shut my eyes to the slightly less authentic later editions. For Book Six I used Scholte's edition of the *Continuatio des abentheurlichen Simplicissimi oder Schluß desselben,* in the same series (Halle: Max Niemeyer, 1939).

My translation is quite frankly a modern one. Grimmelshausen's language, aside from a few dialectal and personal peculiarities, is the stock-in-trade German of his day; I undertook to render it with contemporary American English. However, having made this arbitrary decision, I strove to retain as much of the original flavor as possible, rendering slang with slang, dialect with dialect, and often preserving imperfections of style. But where archaisms might have interfered with communication, I modernized and adapted. Though the scholar may frown at this practice, the cultural mediator will approve.

I have summarized or omitted passages when I was nearly sure that the present-day reader would be bored by the account *in extenso*. I admit that such assumptions are hard to defend, but I saw no reason to translate lengthy passages in which Grimmelshausen wanted little more than to prove to his learned contemporaries that his education, though autodidactic, was as good as theirs.

I hope that the readers of this edition are willing to risk the small loss inherent in the process of translation, rather than suffer a greater privation in not reading at all one of the masterpieces of world literature.

I wish to express my thanks to all those who helped me in the preparation of this translation, especially my good friend Professor W. F. Michael; and to the library of Yale University for use of the frontispiece.

G. S.-B.

Austin, Texas
June 1964

CONTENTS
. . . .

INTRODUCTION   xi

THE THIRTY YEARS' WAR   xxviii

SIMPLICIUS SIMPLICISSIMUS

Book One   3

Book Two   65

Book Three   132

Book Four   198

Book Five   263

Book Six: Continuation and Conclusion   330

Introduction

I

Johann Jakob Christoffel von Grimmelshausen was born in 1621 or 1622 in Gelnhausen. When this small Hessian town was ransacked in September of 1634, he lost his home and soon after became embroiled in the Thirty Years' War. In time he advanced from simple musketeer to regimental secretary. He married in 1649, and 1651 found him living in the Black Forest as administrator of his former colonel's family estates. In 1660 he became the innkeeper at Gaisbach, but two years later we find him as administrator of Castle Ullenburg, an estate acquired by a wealthy physician from Strasbourg. The doctor almost certainly put him in touch with a local coterie, the *Aufrichtige Tannengesellschaft* (Upright Society of the Fir) of which Grimmelshausen later made fun.

In 1665 Grimmelshausen returned to Gaisbach to take up innkeeping once more and to write. His first book, *The Satyrical Pilgrim or Black and White* (1667), seems not to have been very successful; and because his income from writing and innkeeping was insufficient to support his large family, he obtained the position of mayor of Renchen, a market town belonging to the bishop of Strasbourg. But once again war complicated his life. The French under Turenne were overrunning the country adjacent to the Rhine, and the bishop had no army to protect his subjects. In the midst of these turmoils Grimmelshausen died, on August 17, 1676. The parish register calls him an honest man of great learning and genius.

In spite of the "von" in his name, Grimmelshausen was of a middle-class family. Nothing definite is known about his education, but indications are that it was sketchy. Although he knew Latin and French only slightly, he was, for a man of his status, well read in German, and he had a retentive memory. He began writing in his late forties, and all of his literary activity was compressed into a few years, mainly from 1667 to 1673. Having first tried his hand at didactic writing, he also wrote courtly, fashionable novels; but success in these genres eluded him. When he turned to more popular entertainment by composing a kind of picaresque novel, he found himself the author of a best seller. The first edition of *Simplicius Simplicissimus* appeared pseudonymously in 1668 (but dated 1669) in Nuremberg, under a fictitious publisher's name and a misleading place designation. A second printing became necessary the same year. When a pirated edition came out soon afterward, Grimmelshausen followed it (in 1670 and 1671) by editions of his own. The 1671 edition added illustrations and took over certain dubious improvements of the pirated edition. The Continuation first appeared separately in 1669 and was later incorporated as Book Six.

Encouraged by this success, Grimmelshausen wrote a number of sequels: a life of the vagabond woman Courage (which in our day inspired Bertolt Brecht's *Mother Courage*), a life of John Jumpup, and several others. "Simplicius" had become a kind of trademark of entertaining reading, and several Simplician imitations appeared. Three editions of Grimmelshausen's collected works were published, the last in 1713. But soon thereafter his books were forgotten until, around 1800, the German Romanticists created a veritable wave of enthusiasm for Grimmelshausen, whose *Simplicius* had been available in adaptations since 1785. There followed criticism, modern editions, interpretation, and scholarship, all of which have done much to elucidate a work that contains many puzzles under a guise of utter simplicity.

II

When *Simplicius Simplicissimus* appeared, prose fiction in Germany was not concerned with the realities of the recent war, with the struggle for survival on the level of the lower and middle classes. Members of sophisticated circles, if they read fiction at all, read translations or adaptations of highly stylized, foreign courtly romances or novels of state. Works like d'Urfé's *Astrée,* Sannazaro's *Arcadia* and Sidney's novel of the same title, Montemayor's *Diana,* Madeleine Scudéry's exotic *Ibrahim Bassa,* and John Barclay's *Argenis* come to mind. Understandably, readers of the middle and lower classes found them dull and meaningless. Instead they enjoyed the picaresque (or rogue's) novel, which had originated in Spain with the anonymous *Lazarillo de Tormes* (1554). Critics in Grimmelshausen's day completely disregarded *Simplicius Simplicissimus,* for its author was not a learned man and he belonged to no literary group; the only indication of the novel's appeal to contemporary readers is those three editions in the very year of its appearance.

Since its rediscovery, numerous interpreters have regarded *Simplicius* as a novel of character development. While most critics have noted a certain resemblance to the opening of *Parzival,* a Middle High German epic by Wolfram von Eschenbach (*ca.* 1200), Friedrich Gundolf [1] was the first to draw a parallel between *Simplicius* and *Wilhelm Meister* (1829), Goethe's novel of character development. The heroes of both novels, Gundolf asserts, share the urge for personal fulfillment, and in both works the world is pictured as a realm of development through trial and error. In light of this interpretation, the adventures of Simplicius assume importance to the degree that they contribute to the maturing of the hero's personality. Accordingly Grimmelshausen makes use of outer events to unfold inner growth: Simplicius develops from a naïve child into a sophomoric fool; then he deteriorates into a show-off, a rake, and a gigolo. His illness serves as a turning point, after which his character improves until he retreats from the world and becomes, once more, as in childhood, a saintly hermit. The events of his life are shown to form a well-defined arc whose zenith of worldly success corresponds to a nadir of spiritual

[1] Friedrich Gundolf, "Grimmelshausen und der Simplicissimus," *Deutsche Vierteljahrsschrift für Literaturwissenschaft und Geistesgeschichte,* I (1923), 339–358.

depravity. Book Six, with its numerous extraneous episodes and Simplicius' second retreat from the world, does not readily fit into this scheme, and developmentalists point out that the Continuation was not a part of the first edition of the novel, that it constitutes an afterthought inspired by commercial rather than artistic considerations, and that it may almost be disregarded.

Recently, Günter Rohrbach [2] has maintained that Simplicius is not at all a character or individual in the modern sense. He is, rather, a "figure" whose purpose is functional. An *individual* arouses our interest through the growth of his personality; a *figure* does so because of the function he assumes in relation to the various elements of the work. Simplicius serves to unify the following themes and components of the novel: (1) a critical, moralizing attitude toward the world; (2) preoccupation with sin and repentance; (3) preoccupation with the inconstancy of the world; and (4) an episodic structure. While functioning to hold these elements together, Simplicius as an individual is not affected by them. Like an actor he slips into a role, soon to lay it aside for another. He has certain traits by which we recognize him, but they do not go beyond type characteristics. When viewed in this light, the story need not close with Book Five; it can be expanded without violating any preconceived plan or symmetry.

One might think that the developmental theory must exclude the figure theory, but at least one interpreter, Johannes Alt,[3] has combined the two into the "type-sequence" theory. According to Alt, Grimmelshausen started his story with a hero who was a folk character, a simple fool. However, realizing that such a story would have relatively limited appeal, he created diversity by introducing a different type as the central character of successive units of the story and surrounding him with other type characters. Because of the author's ingenious

2 Günter Rohrbach, *Figur und Charakter: Strukturuntersuchungen an Grimmelshausens Simplicissimus,* "Bonner Arbeiten zur deutschen Literatur," Vol. III (Bonn: H. Bouvier & Co., 1959).

3 Johannes Alt, *Grimmelshausen und der Simplicissimus* (Munich: C. H. Beck, 1936).

technique for concealing the seams of the various units, an unsuspecting reader gains the impression that development takes place, whereas, in reality, only type sequences are found.

In evaluating these three interpretations, one must observe that the developmentalists applied to *Simplicius* a nineteenth-century concept of unique personality development which was alien to seventeenth-century prose fiction. The German *Bildungsroman*, at its best exemplified by Goethe's *Wilhelm Meister*, portrays its hero in depth and lets him progress by way of manifold experiences from naïveté to his own *Weltanschauung* (personal philosophy of the purpose of life). It has been suggested that instead of calling *Simplicius* a *Bildungsroman* (novel of inner development) it might be called an *Entwicklungsroman* (novel of outer development). But this term is so general that it could be applied with equal justification to every biographical novel, inasmuch as every human being goes through the phases of childhood, youth, manhood, and old age. However, this sort of progress is far different from genuine *Bildung*, which implies growth of personality rather than merely chronological progress.

Alt's type-sequence theory is limited by its many compromises; it is too pat for complete satisfaction, and it might conceivably apply to any picaresque novel. The figure theory also oversimplifies; it fails to consider the many indications of character in Simplicius, for he does remember earlier events, he is careful to explain the reasons for his actions (not always, to be sure, but often enough), he emphasizes repeatedly that he wants his story to be complete; in these and other ways he exhibits at least the beginnings of being a character. Moreover, one must remember that the prose fiction Grimmelshausen knew was a far cry from the modern psychological novel that originated in England in the eighteenth century.

III

Neither these nor several other interpretations are wholly satisfactory, primarily because they stress one aspect of the novel while neglecting others, or because they are based on critical schemes that are inappropriate to the work. In order to gain a more adequate understanding of *Simplicius*, one must turn to the author himself, for Grimmelshausen has provided us with a number of hints as to the way in which he wanted his novel to be read and understood.

The most important of these indications are contained in the so-called phoenix copper, which appeared as the frontispiece of the original edition. This illustration, like many others throughout the Simplician writings, reflects the author's own ideas and is therefore of more than passing interest. The frontispiece shows, standing amid seven human masks, a most unusual emblematic figure. A human head with horns and the ears of a horse is set on a human trunk with arms; the human part is supported by an animal body with feathered wings and a scaly fish tail. The left leg is a goat's, while the right ends in a webbed foot. The creature wears a sword on a baldric and in his right hand holds a picture book on whose open pages are shown various objects: a crown, a cannon with a pile of balls, a tree, ointment jars, insects, a chalice, a baby in swaddling clothes, a drawn goose, dice and dice box, and so on. In the verses beneath the picture, the creature says that like the phoenix he was born from fire; that he flew through the air without being lost; that he traveled through water and over land; that in his wanderings he acquainted himself with much that was sad, and with but little that gladdened him; that he put all of it into his book, so that the reader, like the creature himself, may withdraw from folly and live in peace.

Although the grotesque creature possesses a horned head, a human trunk, and a goat's leg, he is clearly meant to represent the hero of the novel. The legend on the banner above him seems to confirm this. While the weirdly composed figure resembles no single creature on earth, its determining features are those of a satyr. We usually consider the satyr as the personification of unrestrained, particularly sexual, activity; but during the Renaissance and well into the seventeenth century the satyr was regarded equally as a wise being who, "under the abuse of that name [of satyr]," might guide human beings through the world without participating in its folly.[4] That is obviously the meaning here, but the satyr is also the symbol for satirical writing, and Grimmelshausen was aware of it.

Simplicius, then, is a strangely constituted being whose experience as a wanderer in various realms qualifies him as a guide for others. The verses beneath the figure allude more specifically to the fact that Simplicius was born a Christian through the fire with which the troopers burned his knan's house. He flew through the air to the assembly of witches and to Magdeburg without being lost. He traveled through the water of the Mummelsee to the center of the earth, and over land through many countries. Simplicius' adventures have been told not so much for entertainment as for guidance, particularly in achieving salvation of the soul. The pictures refer to various events in Books One through Five, and the masks on the ground signify the masks Simplicius pulled from the faces of persons and things, during his journey through the world.

The poem preceding Book Six, the Continuation, is also important to any consideration of the author's purpose. In it Grimmelshausen justifies taking Simplicius out of the quietude of his Black Forest retreat (to which he refers in the phoenix copper). Simplicius ponders the concatenation of events that made him suppose, wrongly, that he had found enduring rest. A fall, swift and unaccountable as death, has overtaken him, and, we may infer, the search for tranquility begins once more, for nothing except inconstancy is constant. The prefatory section of Book Six, chapter one, repeats Grimmelshausen's previously announced purpose in writing his novel: he wants to instruct, but not in the moralizing, theological style of the day. Rather, he wants to sugarcoat the bitter pill of his teaching so that the reader will continue to read and profit. He claims (rather conventionally) that his "satyrical" style scores general vices and not specifically personal ones. If a reader is satisfied

[4] Ellen Leyburn, *Satiric Allegory: Mirror of Men*, "Yale Studies in English," CXXX (New Haven: Yale University Press, 1956), 7.

with the husks of his story (the entertainment) when he might profit from the kernels of instruction, he has only himself to blame.

Finally, the title page of the first edition also gives us certain indications of the author's intentions. In the exuberant style of baroque titles, it summarizes the contents of the novel, explaining that "The Adventurous Simplicissimus [in] German" is "the biography of a curious rogue named Melchior Sternfels von Fuchshaim; where and how he came into this world; what he saw, learned, experienced, and suffered therein; and why he voluntarily quit it again. Exceedingly jolly to read and useful for everyone. Edited by German Schleifheim von Sulsfort." Once again the author, who hides behind two pseudonyms, insists that his book is not only entertaining but useful.

In an effort to find out how Grimmelshausen intended to fulfill the double function of entertainment and instruction, one may investigate the way in which Simplicius, our fictional autobiographical hero, communicates with the reader. At times he writes as if he were keeping a diary [5]—for example, in the scene in which he explains his identity to the hermit (Bk. I, chap. 8). At other times, but still using the first person and past tense, Simplicius tells the story of his life from the standpoint of the worldly-wise hermit of the island—for example, in the ironic description of the knan's farm, with remarks and references which a ten-year-old could not possibly make (Bk. I, chaps. 1–2). The two different views of reality are intermingled so that the reader often does not know which of the two chronologically distinct but personally identical reporters is writing. In addition, the author himself makes an occasional remark—for example, he asks how he could have transported Simplicius from near Hersfeld to Magdeburg so quickly without using the witches' ride (Bk. II, chap. 18).

Young Simplicius usually tells his entertaining stories in diary form while old Simplicius looks over his shoulder, mak-

---

[5] I am here following Lothar Schmidt, "Das Ich im 'Simplicissimus,'" *Wirkendes Wort,* X (1960), 215–220.

ing observations and offering evaluations. The retrospective attitude may be kept up throughout whole chapters, but often a retrospective comment is no longer than a single sentence or even a subordinate clause—for example, "If I had [by that time] read the heathen poets, I would have thought of the Eumenides" (Bk. II, chap. 6). The retrospective "I" is used to point out the lapse of time between the event and the writing, and it justifies moral reflections and admonitions (which usually come at the opening or the close of chapters). The "later ego" also gives the author: (1) the writer's omniscience; (2) the chance to impart miscellaneous information; and (3) the chance to make value judgments and to use satire. Naïve Simplex sees only the outer appearances, the masks of the world; the "satyr" Simplicius knows what is behind them, tears them off, and points out the discrepancy.

If the two egos are represented by two lines, their purely chronological progression may be indicated by straight, converging lines. But under the aspect of progression toward God, the mature ego is a straight line in relation to which the line of the younger ego fluctuates widely. Young Simplex in the woods with his father is certainly closer to the island hermit than are the Hunter of Soest or Simplicius in Paris. Resolutions of repentance, even if quickly forgotten, decrease the distance between the lines; and when, in Book Five, chapter twenty-three, Simplicius takes stock of his life and decides to become a hermit once more, the lines meet. But backsliding causes another divergence, which lasts until Simplex decides to remain on the island, where he praises God and lives a pious life.

Viewed thus, the novel presents a unified picture of one Christian's life. It tells of Simplicius' pre-Christian ignorance; his instruction in the essentials of Christian life; his fall at Hanau, where he accepts the parson's specious advice to go along with the world; his enthusiastic but essentially sinful involvement with worldly concerns during youth; the numerous ineffectual attempts at repentance—in France, in Einsiedeln, on the tree in the river, and so on; the self-appraisal induced by the realization that his life so far has been futile;

his interlude as a restless hermit who soon returns into the world; and his final contentment in a truly ideal life. Certainly the novel is meant to be an example for all Christians—and since Grimmelshausen was anything but narrowly sectarian, one might say for all religious people to follow. Nevertheless, *Simplicius* is entertaining, even if we fail to see or neglect to follow its message. (This is all the easier to do since for long stretches the author himself seems to have done so.) The novel constitutes good entertainment chiefly because Simplicius is the kind of man to whom all sorts of interesting adventures happen. He is, of course, a direct descendant of the Spanish *picaro,* and before stressing his peculiarly German traits, one should consider what he has in common with Lazarillo de Tormes, ancestor of all the picaros. Lazarillo, narrator and hero of his own story, is a talented fellow of humble origin who learns many of his tricks from a blind beggar. He soon develops into a social parasite, but he engages in his nefarious activities with tremendous gusto and *joie de vivre.* He has no high regard for the society on which he preys; he blames his misfortunes on bad luck and credits his successes to God and his own cleverness. Although Lazarillo is an antihero like Don Quixote, his outlook on life is more closely related to that of Sancho Panza, the realist. At the end of his story Lazarillo obtains a government appointment—"For nowadays nobody prospers except those who work for the government"; he becomes a town crier and shares his wife with the archpriest of San Salvador.

Translations and adaptations of Spanish picaresque novels had appeared in Germany, but Grimmelshausen mentions by name only the adaptation of Cervantes' *Rinconete y Cortadillo.* He specifically acknowledges indebtedness to a French adaptation, Charles Sorel's *Histoire comique de Francion,*[6] praising its jolly style and borrowing from it the figure of Mad Jupiter in Book Three.

Grimmelshausen modernized and Germanized his picaro by

[6] See Manfred Koschlig, "Das Lob des 'Francion' bei Grimmelshausen." *Jahrbuch der Deutschen Schillergesellschaft,* I (1957), 30–73.

making him the child of noble parents (though he is not allowed to benefit from his nobility), by letting him participate
in historical events, and, above all, by making him a searcher
for salvation. Like the author of *Lazarillo de Tormes*, Grimmelshausen adopted all sorts of literary and subliterary material, like folk tales and anecdotes, using his special knack of
narration to give them relevance and new life. In his enthusiasm for telling a good story Grimmelshausen was often carried
away and, forgetting his high purpose of furnishing instruction, created scenes that are unforgettably amusing. Many such
incidents could be mentioned—for example, the scene in which
Simplex steals the parson's bacon (Bk. II, chap. 31), and the
meeting of Heartbrother and Simplicius in Villingen (Bk. IV,
chap. 25).

Grimmelshausen is, furthermore, one of the first German
authors to capture the sweep and beauty of landscape; the
description of the view from his hermitage on the Black Forest
is justly famous (Bk. VI, chap. 1). His powers of observation
and association are such that he can highlight the salient fea-
ture of a person or an object by a striking comparison: his
aged knan is as chipper as a beetle; a pilgrim's staff is like a
Bohemian earpick; a lady is more *mobilis* than *nobilis;* and a
beard is shaped like a Swiss cheese. Nor is his observation only
visual; he has a fine ear for levels of speech, for dialects and
sounds: the peasants in the Black Forest speak broad Swabian
(Bk. V, chap. 17), while the blackamoor in the chest pleads for
his life in Westphalian Low German (Bk. III, chap. 8). This
flair for freshness and accuracy has deservedly earned Grimmelshausen the label of "realist."

Humor has undoubtedly contributed much to the enduring
popularity of *Simplicius*. Grimmelshausen's humor spans a
broad range from subtle irony (for instance, in the description
of the knan's farm in terms of knighthood, Bk. I, chap. 1),
through comic situations (the scene of Oliver and the cat, Bk.
IV, chap. 22), to homespun and even crude folksiness (Simplex' dilemma after his escape from the goosepen, Bk. II,
chap. 2).

Surprising as it may seem, Grimmelshausen was the only German writer with personal experience of the Thirty Years' War who made that war the setting of a novel. No one else appears to have had the ability or the courage for such an undertaking. Although his perspective is that of a simple trooper, his descriptions of the war are vivid, typical, and realistic. In addition to personal experience Grimmelshausen used published accounts of the war, but unless the reader consults a detailed source study he is unable to tell which passages are based on experience and which come from reading. Because Grimmelshausen stays remarkably close to historical fact, Germans have long used *Simplicius* as "readings in historical background." A comparison of the plot events with the facts of recorded history points up the close connection.[7]

Two days after the battle of Höchst, Simplicius' father appears at a country parson's home and is at first mistaken for General Mansfeld himself. Grimmelshausen is careful to explain that remnants of the defeated army were dispersed as far as the Spessart hills. Simplicius' mother also finds herself in the Spessart, where, a few days after the battle of Höchst, she gives birth to a boy. Thus the date of the hero's birth can be fixed as shortly after June 10/20,[8] 1622. The child stays in the forest until after the hermit's death; on his way into the world he passes by Gelnhausen, where he eats grain and sleeps in sheaves that the peasants could not harvest because the battle of Nördlingen had frightened them away. That was in the fall of 1634, and according to the chronicles winter came early that year and was unusually severe. James Ramsay, a Scotsman by birth, had been appointed commander of Hanau by Prince Bernhard of Weimar in 1634, and in January of 1635 Simplicius was present at the revels with which his uncle

---

[7] For a summary of the events of the Thirty Years' War, see p. xxviii.

[8] Although two dates are given, they are identical. The later date is that of the old style (or Julian) calendar used by the Protestants; the earlier date is from the new style (or Gregorian) reckoning used by the Catholics. Protestants did not change to the new and more accurate calendar until the eighteenth century.

celebrated the fall of Braunfels, while refugees inside Hanau were starving. The imperial colonel Corpus, whose men took Simplex with them, is mentioned in the annals of the war, as is the Hessian (Protestant) general Melander Holzappel.

The second siege of Magdeburg, where Simplicius was carried through the air, took place in 1635/6; the city fell to the imperials on July 3/13, 1636, and Simplicius stayed in the service of the cavalry captain's wife until after Werberschanze, Havelberg, and Perleberg were taken, in the fall of 1636. The two armies, the Saxon and the imperial, then allied, broke camp because the Swedish forces under Banér were approaching. The ensuing battle of Wittstock, on September 24/October 4, 1636, brings Simplicius welcome release from his arrest as a sorcerer and spy. After the winter of 1636/7, during which he is a servant of the imperial dragoon in Paradise convent, Simplicius as the Hunter of Soest harrasses the garrisons of Dorsten, Lippstadt, and Coesfeld, which Count von Götz had been unable to take from the Swedish. Count von der Wahl, mentioned as concentrating troops for an expedition to Meppen, Lingen, and other places, was in Westphalia in 1637. The commander of Lippstadt, where Simplicius is interned for six months during the winter of 1636/7, *was* a Colonel St. André. (Simplicius, only fifteen at the time, was at first addressed as "my child.") Several events mentioned only incidentally are authentic—for instance, a siege of Lippstadt was expected but did not materialize because Johann von Werth was defeated in the Breisgau and von Götz had to go to the upper Rhine to fight Bernhard von Weimar.

After his trip to Paris and his reluctant service in imperial Philippsburg, Simplicius joins the Merode Brothers until the day before the battle of Wittenweier, in which von Götz was defeated by Bernhard (July 30/August 9, 1638). On July 29, then, Simplicius is caught by the Weimarers and made a musketeer in Colonel Hattstein's regiment. He has to work with pick and shovel in the siege of Breisach, but receives permission to return to Lippstadt before Breisach capitulates on December 7/17, 1638. In Villingen he meets Heartbrother,

who calls himself Count von Götz's intimate friend and factotum. With Heartbrother Simplicius goes to Vienna in the
spring of 1640, and the two again become involved in the war.
Historically, von Götz was cleared in August 1640 of charges of
collaborating with the enemy. He was killed in the battle of
Jankau (March 1645), and although neither date nor place of
his death is mentioned in the novel, Grimmelshausen must
have been aware of the date, for in Book Five, chapter five,
Mad Jupiter asks Simplex about news from Münster. The
peace conference had convened there in December of 1644,
but six months were wasted in deciding who was to precede
whom into the meeting hall, and Simplex has nothing to
report.

The next definite date alluded to is the Duc d'Enghien's
expedition, from which the knan fled into the woods near the
Mummelsee (Bk. V, chap. 12). That expedition took place in
August 1644, and the Mummelsee episode must therefore be
dated after that time. The promises that Torstensson made to
the Swedish officer quartered in Simplicius' house must have
come before the autumn of 1646, when Torstensson retired.
Finally, Simplicius' return from his trip to Russia, after an
absence of three years and some months, is placed after the
German peace had been concluded, that is, after 1648.

Thus it is evident that the framework of historical facts and
dates is substantial and that Grimmelshausen has carefully
arranged the war experiences of his hero within the realm of
the probable. Simplicius' adventures in Russia are entirely
unhistorical, as is his life on the unnamed island in the Indian
Ocean. But those chapters will find a ready response in readers
familiar with the adventures of Robinson Crusoe. Exactly fifty
years before Defoe's classic was published, Grimmelshausen
created his island paradise by using a British pamphlet, *The
Isle of Pines* (London, 1668), which was a satire by Henry
Neville, and supplementing it with a description of the Dutch
island of Mauritius.

Fashionable baroque novels usually contained vast quantities of encyclopedic information. Hoping to satisfy this de-

mand, Grimmelshausen provided his readers with similar material—copied from handbooks. Such "learned" matter generally consists of references to the Bible, to Greek and Roman mythology, and to major and minor classical authors. But it also includes treatises such as the one on the influence of drugs on memory (Bk. II, chap. 8), or an essay on the life and customs of the Merode Brothers (Bk. IV, chap. 13), about whom Grimmelshausen was the first to write. In the present translation, much of this "scholarly" material is summarized or omitted.

Such embellishments, which were of considerable factual interest to contemporary readers, could be made to serve more than one purpose—for instance, in the episode of the Mummelsee (Bk. V, chaps. 12–17). Superficially, the adventure is a retelling of local folk tales, to which are added reminiscences from an essay by Paracelsus on nature spirits. But in addition the reader is given the length of the earth's radius, is told that lakes fasten the great bodies of water to the earth, is informed why some wells have medicinal qualities and why these waters are more effective when first discovered, and so on. Moreover, one becomes acquainted with the utopia of an intelligent race of little people who live happily in their appointed tasks except that they, being without souls, cannot participate in the benefits granted to mortals through the redemption of Christ. The sprites want to learn about life on earth, for when the earth is destroyed by fire because of human sinfulness, they too must perish. Simplicius assures their king that the sprites need not fear, for mortals are paragons of virtue and live according to God's commands. The king then awards Simplicius a magic stone; when placed on the ground it will produce a mineral well "which will enhance and advance you, [Simplicius,] to the extent that you have merited by revealing the truth to us." But Simplex has been lying, and therefore he loses the stone accidentally and barely escapes being beaten for causing a well to spring up where it is not wanted.

This episode, containing beautiful description, "scientific" information, satire on conditions on earth, and bitter irony, is an allegory with deep religious implications. Despite its seeming irrelevance, its fairy-tale quality, and its scientific inaccuracies, for seventeenth-century readers it carried the message that the soulless sprites envy us mortals the chance of looking upon the face of God and that we should exert ourselves harder to deserve that chance.

The satire of Mad Jupiter also has serious overtones, and even Simplicius' sober discourse with the parson in Lippstadt has a double purpose: Simplex discusses the various brands of Christianity with the minister, but his real purpose is to divert the man's attention so that Simplex can keep up his erotic activities. In this, as in other instances, one must distinguish between the "tongue-in-cheek" meaning and the true meaning of the passage.

For didactic purposes Grimmelshausen also makes extensive use of proverbs and maxims, and for admonition there is hardly a more impressive device than the litany, a series of prayerlike repetitions and invocations such as the one quoted from Guevara in Book Five: "Farewell, World!"

IV

Having considered a number of different interpretations, one may conclude that Grimmelshausen himself provides the best clues to an understanding of his major work. A perceptive seventeenth-century reader would have needed no lengthy introduction in order to understand Grimmelshausen's intentions, for he had an immediate relationship to the work, and he could hardly help being in sympathy with the author's goal. We, however, being children of a different age, are apt to view the novel in a different light. The modern reader, like his seventeenth-century counterpart, is perfectly capable of finding humor and entertainment in the novel; on the age-old problem of how to be a Christian in a world that makes the Christian life all but impossible, we must avail ourselves of what we can in *Simplicius,* even if we enjoy only the husks and do not penetrate to the kernel of the tale. Furthermore, if our religious concerns are somewhat different from those of an earlier age, the condition of the world is not. We may still see the historical relevance of *Simplicius* for our own uneasy times, in which war is no less a constant concern.

GEORGE SCHULZ-BEHREND

The Thirty Years' War

After the Reformation, a satisfactory relation between Catholicism and the two Protestant denominations, Lutheranism and Calvinism, had never been worked out in Germany, and much unresolved religious tension existed. But religion was not to be the only issue of a war that threatened even before the Protestant princes had formed a defensive alliance, the Union; and the Catholic princes had answered with one of their own, the League. In addition to harboring religious rancor and dissatisfaction resulting from the secularization of Catholic lands and other wealth, the German princes were jealous of the growing power of the House of Hapsburg, whereby their own increasing independence was threatened. From such accumulated resentment burst forth the Thirty Years' War (1618–1648). Its first phase was the Bohemian War (1618–1625).

In the Letter of Majesty (1609), Emperor Rudolph II had granted certain religious privileges to the nobles of his kingdom of Bohemia. When his less tolerant successor, Matthias, restricted these freedoms, the Bohemian nobles rebelled by electing their own king and, incidentally, throwing two high imperial officials out of the window of their meeting hall. The king they chose was the Calvinist Frederick V, elector palatine of the Rhine, leader of the Union, and son-in-law of England's James I. But the nobles of Bohemia and the princes of the Union failed to make adequate preparations for the approaching war, and in October 1619 Frederick's home territory, the palatinate with its capital of Heidelberg, was overrun by an army of allied Spain, whose general, Spinola, had marched up the Rhine from the Low Countries. About a year later, on November 8/18,[1] 1620, Frederick's army under General Mansfeld was decisively defeated in the battle of the White Mountain, not far from Prague.

Two North German princes then came to Frederick's aid, and with them Mansfeld was able to defeat the imperial general Tilly at Wiesloch, in April 1622. But since the army of Mansfeld had to scatter in search of food, Tilly was able to defeat the Protestant forces at Höchst, on June 10/20, 1622. The remnants of Mansfeld's army were dismissed, and the first phase of the war was over. King James, to whom the Protestants had looked for help, had sent no aid, but a considerable number of English volunteers under Captain Horace de Vere had been active in the Rhineland. Frederick, under the ban of the Empire for his rebellion, lost his lands, and his electorship went to the Duke of Bavaria. Lampooned throughout Europe as the "Winter King," Frederick retired to France as a picturesque and powerless exile. From that point on, foreign powers intervened in what had started as a domestic German quarrel.

In the second phase of the war, Christian IV, king of Denmark and a minor German prince, attempted to extend his power over the German seaports and at the same time to help the cause of Protestantism. While the Catholic forces were busy in Austria and Transylvania, Christian entered the war with a powerful army. In this emergency Emperor Ferdinand II found help in Wallenstein, an able new general who inspired his well-paid mercenaries with loyalty and enthusiasm. He defeated Christian decisively in the battle of Lutter am Barenberg, in August 1627. Discouraged, Christian withdrew from the war. At the height of his success the emperor issued the Edict of Restitution (1629), through which he restored by imperial fiat all lands seized from the Catholic church since 1555. While the outcry among Protestants was long and fierce, no one raised a hand. But then the Catholic princes, having become suspicious of the power concentrated in the

[1] Concerning the peculiarities of these dates, see Introduction, p. xxii, note 8.

House of Hapsburg, forced Ferdinand to dismiss Wallenstein, his chief instrument of power.

In the ensuing phase the Swedish king, Gustavus Adolphus, became the champion of the Protestant cause. Although he possessed a well disciplined army, trained in a war he had been fighting in Poland, the first significant event under his leadership was another Protestant defeat: Tilly took the stronghold of Magdeburg (1631) while Gustavus was still negotiating for passage of his troops through Saxony and Brandenburg. After Magdeburg had been sacked and burned with unprecedented cruelty, Tilly invaded Saxony, and her elector, John George, and Brandenburg belatedly rallied to the support of the cause. United, the Protestants won a brilliant victory at the battle of Breitenfeld. The Swedish army then proceeded to free the palatinate and to restore Protestantism there and in many other places. In 1632 Tilly was mortally wounded and the Swedish army swept deep into Catholic territory—as far as Augsburg and Munich. The elector of Brandenburg marched into Bohemia and took Prague without firing a shot; the Protestant armies appeared to be irresistible. Although Gustavus Adolphus was killed in the victorious battle of Lützen (November 1632), and Protestantism lost its ablest leader, the impetus of victory was not lost: Sweden carried on vigorously with Oxenstierna as the political leader and Generals Horn and Banér in the field.

At this desperate juncture the emperor recalled Wallenstein and gave him broad powers. Wallenstein quickly raised an army, cleared Bohemia of the enemy, defeated the Swedish and forced them out of southern Germany. While Wallenstein was holding out hope of a fair peace that would contain an amnesty for Saxony, rescinding of the Edict of Restitution, and granting of religious freedom, he was murdered—with the full connivance of the emperor.

Protestant leadership was then divided between the Swedish and the Saxons, with Elector John George as the political leader, and Generals Arnim and Bernhard of Weimar in the field. Wallenstein's death brought a resurgence of imperial initiative, and Horn and Bernhard were defeated by an army of imperial and allied Bavarian forces in the (first) battle of Nördlingen, Bavaria, in September 1634. Greatly to the chagrin of the Swedish leaders, Elector John George began to negotiate with the emperor. The result was the Peace of Prague (1635), a peace in which the emperor compromised on the Edict of Restitution, and a peace that was a reasonable basis for settling many of the grievances of the Protestant princes, but which, naturally, held no attraction for the Swedish.

The war then entered its last phase, the Swedish-French one (1635–1648). France had from the start subsidized Sweden; at this point, seeing an ever greater concentration of power in the family of Hapsburg, Cardinal Richelieu, the shrewd political leader of France, no longer refrained from bringing direct French influence to bear. He entered the war with an army of two hundred thousand men, more than had been previously used in this war. French policy and strategy were clear, and her resources were enormous, but even Richelieu and the riches of France were not adequate to the task he had undertaken. Soon French efforts bogged down in the Low Countries and in Italy, and France had to rely more and more heavily on allies whose war aims were different from hers. Prince Bernhard of Weimar joined the French and became the chief French general inside Germany. The Swedish had promised him a dukedom, but the battle of Nördlingen had put an end to the realization of such promises. Now he was trying to recoup his loss by conquering Alsace.

Even though military activity had slowed down inside Germany, the armies were not disbanded and continued to live off the land. Banér defeated the imperial troops at Wittstock, September 24/October 4, 1636, and Bernhard laid siege to the important imperial fortress of Breisach. Field marshal Count von Götz, who wanted to raise the siege, suffered defeat instead at Wittenweier, July 30/August 9, 1638. Bernhard died in 1639, the year after he took Breisach. The Swedish continued to score some successes against the imperial forces, but the French under the Duc d'Enghien (the later Condé), Turenne, and others were defeated by such men as Franz von Merci and the cavalry general Johann von Werth on the imperial side.

Peace negotiations had been in progress since 1644; they were hastened by the general exhaustion that had settled over all the armies. The Peace of Westphalia was finally signed with the French at Münster and with the Swedish at Osnabrück, in 1648. Never before had greater ravages been perpetrated in the name of religion, greater suffering been inflicted on soldiers and civilians—and all for such paltry results. The peace was dubious: for years groups of soldiers refused to disband, for many had never known a home, and they continued to live as marauders. The peace was also slow—the last foreign troops did not leave German soil until 1654—and it was unsatisfactory—both Catholics and Protestants denounced it as a betrayal of principles, and the clergy of more than one land had to be enjoined from preaching against it.

Nevertheless, the task of reconstruction could at last be undertaken. The population had diminished, energy and capital were insufficient, and the enormous job could apparently be accomplished only with the help of the local sovereign. Thus in Germany the foundation was laid for paternalism and planning from above by the local prince and his subservient bureaucracy. Germany became a collection of hundreds of practically independent political entities, each of which was governed by a more or less ambitious, more or less patriotic, more or less tolerant prince. The over-all government, the Holy Roman Empire, was weakened to the extent that the emperor retained his prestige almost exclusively as the ruler of Austria. Religion, having lost its importance as a cause for fighting, was determined by the ruler for his subjects.

SIMPLICIUS

SIMPLICISSIMUS

ℐ Book One

CHAPTER 1: *Simplicius' peasant origin and rustic education*

In our day and age, which some think to be the last, a disease is current among commoners, a disease which—once it has enabled its victims to put a few coins in their purses, to dress in the latest foolish fashion, in a suit with a thousand silk ribbons, or by some good fortune to gain valor and renown—makes them claim that they are knights and noblemen of ancient family, though it is often found out and diligent research reveals only that their forbears were chimney sweeps, laborers, hod-carriers, pushers of wheelbarrows, and that their cousins were mule-drivers, gamblers, vagabonds, and mountebanks, their brothers flatfeet and constables, their sisters seamstresses, laundresses, or even whores, their mothers procurers or even witches and, truth to tell, their whole families with their thirty-two ancestors as filthy and polluted as a gang of thieves and cutthroats. As a matter of fact, these would-be noblemen are often as black as if they had been born and raised in New Guinea.

I don't like to compare myself to these people, though—to come right out with it—I have often thought I must have some grand seigneur or at least an ordinary, run-of-the-mill nobleman for an ancestor, for by nature I am inclined toward the business of nobility, if only I had the necessary tools and investment capital for it. But joking aside, my origin and education might be compared to that of a prince (if only you don't stress the differences too much). My "knan"—that's what they call a father in the Spessart [1]—owned a palace as good as

[1] A sparsely inhabited, wooded hill country north of the Main and south of the Kinzig River.

the next man's. A king as mighty as the great Alexander himself would not have been able to build it with his own two
hands. It was well chinked with adobe, and instead of being covered with barren slate, cold lead, or red copper, it was thatched
with straw, on which grows noble grain. In order not to show
off his ancient nobility (which went back as far as Adam) and
his wealth, he had the wall about his castle made not of field-
stone picked by the wayside, or of indifferently manufactured
brick—no, he used oak planking, from a noble and useful tree
on which grow pork sausages and juicy hams, and which requires more than a hundred years to reach its full height.
Where is the monarch to imitate that? Where is the sovereign
wanting to do likewise? The rooms, halls, and chambers had
been tinted black by smoke—only because black is the most
durable color in the world, and paintings in that color need
more time to acquire perfection than even the most skillful
painters give their best work. The tapestries were of the most
delicate texture in the world, for they were made by a creature who in antiquity vied in spinning with Minerva herself.[2]
His windows were dedicated to St. Noglass for no other reason
than that he knew windows woven of hemp and flax took
more time and trouble than the most precious Venetian glass.
His station in life made him think that everything produced
with a lot of trouble was for that very reason more precious;
and whatever is precious is most becoming to nobility.

Instead of page boys, lackeys, and stable boys, he had sheep,
rams, and pigs, each neatly dressed in its own uniform. They
often waited on me in the fields until, tired of their service,
I drove them off and home. His armory was sufficiently and
neatly furnished with plows, mattocks, axes, picks, shovels,
manure forks, and hay rakes. He drilled and exercised with
these weapons daily; hoeing and weeding was his military
discipline, as in peacetime among the Romans. Hitching up
the oxen was his captaincy; taking manure to the field, his
science of fortification; plowing, his campaigning; splitting

[2] Arachne, a Lydian woman, was weaving in competition with Minerva
(Athene) and was changed into a spider.

fire wood, his troop movements and maneuvers; and cleaning
out the stables, his war games and most noble diversion. With
these activities he made war on the whole earth—as far as his
resources went—and thereby obtained rich harvest every fall.
I mention all this only by the way and without boasting, for
I don't think I was any better than my knan, whose residence
was situated in a pleasant spot, the Spessart Hills (a place
hardly anybody has ever heard of). Only brevity keeps me from
telling you about my knan's family, and mentioning his name
and ancestry here and now. Suffice it to say that I was born
in the Spessart.

Just as my knan's household was aristocratic, so my upbringing was similarly superior; in my tenth year I had already absorbed all the rudiments of the above-mentioned exercises, drills, and maneuvers. In book learning, on the other
hand, I was equal to the famous Amplistidus, of whom Suidas
reports that he could not count beyond five. My father was
much too bright for organized studies and observed herein
the usage of the times, that is, people don't think much of
useless knowledge, because you can hire flunkies for that kind
of drudgery. In addition, I was an excellent musician on the
bagpipes, on which I could produce splendid dirges. Musically
I equaled Orpheus, but I excelled on the bagpipes while he
handled merely the harp.

Concerning theology, there was no one like me in all Chris-
tendumb; I had heard of neither God nor man, heaven nor
hell, angel nor devil, and I did not even know the difference
between good and evil. You can easily imagine that with such
theology I lived like our first parents in paradise; they also
knew nothing of sickness, death, or dying, not to mention
resurrection. Oh, aristocratic (or asinine) life in which one
does not worry about medicine either! My studies in the law
(and all the other arts and sciences in the world) were similar.
I was so perfect and excellent in ignorance that I could not
possibly have known that I knew nothing at all. Once more
I say, Oh, happy life!

But my knan did not want me to enjoy such bliss any

longer. He thought I should live and act in accordance with
my aristocratic birth. So he started to draw me toward higher
things and to assign me more difficult lessons.

CHAPTER 2: *The first rung on the ladder of success which
Simplicius climbed, together with praise of
shepherds and appended excellent advice*

He endowed me with the office most dignified not only in
his household but in the whole world, namely, the ancient
appointment of herdsman. He entrusted me first with the
hogs, then with the goats, and finally with the whole flock of
sheep, and had me mind pasture and protect them from the
wolf, particularly with my pipes, the sound of which, according to Strabo, helped to fatten the lambs and sheep of Arcadia.
At that time I resembled David, but instead of bagpipes he
had only a harp; that was not a bad start for me, for I took
the omen to mean that in time I too might be world famous.
Since the beginning of time prominent men have started as
herdsmen; in Holy Writ we read of Abel, Abraham, Isaac, Ja-
cob and his sons, and Moses (who had to mind his brother-in-
law's sheep before he became the leader and legislator of six
hundred thousand Israelites).

Someone may object here that the aforementioned were devout and holy men, not peasant lads from the Spessart who
did not know God. I grant you it is so; but my innocence had
to make up for my other shortcomings. Examples can be
found among the ancient heathens as well; among the Romans there were noble families who without doubt were
called Bubulcus (ox herd), Statilius Taurus (bull), Pomponius
Vitulus (calf), Vitellius (baby beef), Annius Capra (goat), and
others who were so named because they handled such critters,
and probably herded them too.

But to get back to my own flock, you must know that I was
as unacquainted with the wolf as I was with my own ignorance. For that reason my father was all the more specific

with his instruction. He said, "Boy, pay attention! Don't let no sheep stray too far, and play on yer bagpipes so the wolf don't come and cause a lot of damage. He's a kind of four-legged rascal and thief who gobbles up men and animules. And if you don't watch good I'll tan yer hide." With equal graciousness I replied, "I ain't never seen a wolf." "Go on, ya muttonhead," he answered, "you'll stay stupid all your life. I wonder what'll become of ya. You're a big lunk already, not knowing that a wolf is a big four-legged rascal." He gave me some more instructions, and finally he got mad and walked off grumbling. He surmised that my crude understanding, which had not yet been sufficiently refined by his instruction, could not grasp his subtle teachings.

CHAPTER 3: *The sympathetic suffering of a loyal bagpipe*

I started to make such a hullabaloo with my bagpipe that you could have killed toads with it. That way I thought I was safe from the wolf. And as I remembered that my mother had often told me she was afraid her chickens would die from my singing, I started to sing, too, so that the remedy against the wolf would be all the more effective. I sang a song she had taught me, about us peasants and the valuable work we were doing.

I got as far as the tenth verse in my mellifluous melody when suddenly my flock and I were surrounded by a troop of heavy cavalry. They had lost their way in the woods and had been attracted by my music and herdsman's song.

Aha! I thought, what have we here? These are the four-legged rascals and thieves of whom your knan spoke, for at first I thought (as did the American Indians when they first saw Spanish cavalry) that horse and man were but one creature, and must be wolves. I wanted to chase them off like dogs and get rid of them, but I had hardly inflated my bagpipe when one of them picked me up by the wing and set me down so hard on one of the peasant horses they had liberated that I tumbled off and fell on my beloved bagpipe. It gave off a pitiful scream, as if it wanted to call upon the mercy of all the world. But although it used up all its breath to lament my fall, it did not a bit of good. I had to get back on. What troubled me most was that the soldiers pretended I had hurt the bagpipe by falling on it and that's why it had screamed so savagely. Well, like the *primum mobile,* my mare carried me in a steady trot to my knan's farm. Very strange notions and outlandish ideas were percolating in my head; I imagined myself transformed into one of the iron men (for the ones taking me with them were dressed in iron armor). But because the change did not take place, other notions entered my silly head. I thought these foreign creatures had come only to help me drive home the sheep, especially as none of them was devouring any sheep, but all were hurrying straight to my knan's farm. I was on the lookout to see if my knan and my mother were coming out to meet us and bid us welcome. But in vain. He and mother, together with Ursula, my knan's only and dearest daughter, had taken French leave by the back door. They did not want to wait for these ill-bred guests.

CHAPTER 4: *Simplicius' residence is taken by storm, plundered, and destroyed; warriors make a mess of it*

Though I hadn't intended to take the peace-loving reader into my father's home and farm along with these merry cavalrymen, the orderly progress of my tale requires me to make known to posterity the sort of abysmal and unheard-of cruelties occasionally perpetrated in our German war, and to testify by my own example that all these evils were necessarily required for our own good by the kindness of our Lord. For, my kind reader, who would have told me that there's a God in heaven if the warriors hadn't destroyed my knan's house, if they hadn't forced me to be among the people who taught me well enough? Shortly before this event I could neither

know nor imagine but that my knan, mother and Ursula, myself and the hired hands were the only men on earth, for no
people or habitations were known to me except my knan's
residence where I went in and out daily. But I soon found
out where people come from, and that they have no perma-
nent abode, but often have to move on again before they can
look around. I had been human in shape alone, and a Christian in name only; in reality I was an animal! But the Almighty looked upon my ignorance with forgiving eyes, and
wanted me to come to the recognition of both him and myself. And though he had a thousand different ways for this
purpose, undoubtedly he wanted to use as an example to
others the manner in which my knan and mother were punished for my negligent upbringing.

The first thing these horsemen did in the nice black rooms
of the house was to put in their horses. Then everyone took up
a special job, one having to do with death and destruction. Although some began butchering, heating water, and rendering lard, as if to prepare for a banquet, others raced through
the house, ransacking upstairs and down; not even the privy
chamber was safe, as if the golden fleece of Colchis might be
hidden there. Still others bundled up big packs of cloth,
household goods, and clothes, as if they wanted to hold a rum-
mage sale somewhere. What they did not intend to take along
they broke and spoiled. Some ran their swords into the hay
and straw, as if there hadn't been hogs enough to stick.
Some shook the feathers out of beds and put bacon slabs,
hams, and other stuff in the ticking, as if they might sleep
better on these. Others knocked down the hearth and broke
the windows, as if announcing an everlasting summer. They
flattened out copper and pewter dishes and baled the ruined
goods. They burned up bedsteads, tables, chairs, and benches,
though there were yards and yards of dry firewood outside
the kitchen. Jars and crocks, pots and casseroles all were
broken, either because they preferred their meat broiled or
because they thought they'd eat only one meal with us. In the
barn, the hired girl was handled so roughly that she was un-

able to walk away, I am ashamed to report. They stretched the hired man out flat on the ground, stuck a wooden wedge in his mouth to keep it open, and emptied a milk bucket full of stinking manure drippings down his throat; they called it a Swedish cocktail. He didn't relish it and made a very wry face. By this means they forced him to take a raiding party to some other place where they carried off men and cattle and brought them to our farm. Among these were my knan, mother, and Ursula.

Then they used thumbscrews, which they cleverly made out of their pistols, to torture the peasants, as if they wanted to burn witches. Though he had confessed to nothing as yet, they put one of the captured hayseeds in the bake-oven and lighted a fire in it. They put a rope around someone else's head and tightened it like a tourniquet until blood came out of his mouth, nose, and ears. In short, every soldier had his favorite method of making life miserable for peasants, and every peasant had his own misery. My knan was, as I thought, particularly lucky because he confessed with a laugh what others were forced to say in pain and martyrdom. No doubt because he was the head of the household, he was shown special consideration; they put him close to a fire, tied him by his hands and legs, and rubbed damp salt on the bottoms of his feet. Our old nanny goat had to lick it off and this so tickled my knan that he could have burst laughing. This seemed so clever and entertaining to me—I had never seen or heard my knan laugh so long—that I joined him in laughter, to keep him company or perhaps to cover up my ignorance. In the midst of such glee he told them the whereabouts of hidden treasure much richer in gold, pearls, and jewelry than might have been expected on a farm.

I can't say much about the captured wives, hired girls, and daughters because the soldiers didn't let me watch their doings. But I do remember hearing pitiful screams from various dark corners and I guess that my mother and our Ursula had it no better than the rest. Amid all this horror I was busy turning a roasting spit and didn't worry about anything, for

I didn't know the meaning of it. In the afternoon I helped water the horses and that way got to see our hired girl in the barn. She looked wondrously messed up and at first I didn't recognize her. In a sickly voice she said, "Boy, get out of this place, or the soldiers will take you with them. Try to get away; you can see they are up to no good!" That is all she could say.

CHAPTER 5: *How Simplicius uses his legs and is frightened by rotten trees*

Suddenly I began noticing the misery about me and started thinking about how to get out of it as soon as I could. But where should I go? My mind was much too shallow to give me a suggestion, but toward evening I succeeded in escaping to the woods and I didn't even leave my beloved bagpipe behind. But what now? I didn't know the roads any better than I knew the lanes through the frozen sea to Nova Zembla. There was some safety in the pitch-dark night that covered me, but to my dim wit it wasn't half dark enough. So I hid in thick bushes where I could hear the screams of the tortured peasants and the song of the nightingales, shut my eyes, and fell fast asleep. But when the morning star rose brightly in the east I saw my knan's house go up in flames, and no one was there to put out the fire.

In hopes of finding someone I knew, I crept out of hiding, but at once five cavalrymen saw me, and one shouted, "Boy, come here, or by God I'll drill you so the smoke will come out of your ears!" Since I didn't know what the soldier wanted, I stopped in my tracks, forgetting to shut my mouth, and stared at them as a cat looks at a new barn door. They wouldn't have become angry with me if a bog hadn't kept them from getting at me. One of them fired his carbine at me, and I was so scared by the flash and the noise (made more frightening by a multiple echo) that I fell to the ground and lay there for dead. As a matter of fact, I never moved a muscle. And when the horsemen rode off, thinking I was dead, I did not feel like sitting up or looking about me all day.

When night came around once more, I got up and walked a long way into the woods, until in the distance I saw a rotten tree sending out an eerie light. That frightened me again. I turned on my heels and kept walking till I saw another such tree, and I ran from this one too. I spent the whole night like this, running from one rotten tree to another. Finally daylight came to my aid by bidding the trees to stop being luminous, but this was no great help, for my heart was full of fear, my legs full of tiredness, my empty stomach full of hunger, my mouth full of thirst, my brain full of silly notions, and my eyes full of sleep. I kept on walking without knowing where I was headed. The farther I walked, the farther I went away from people and into the forest. At that time (though I didn't know it) I felt the effects of ignorance and unreason; if a dumb beast had been in my shoes, it would have known better what to do than I. But when night came a third time, I had enough sense to crawl into a hollow tree (taking good care of my beloved bagpipe, too), and I firmly resolved to sleep all night.

CHAPTER 6: *This chapter is short and so devout that Simplicius faints over it*

I had hardly made myself comfortable for sleeping when I heard a voice saying, "O great love shown to us ungrateful men! O my only solace, my hope, my treasure, my God!" and more in this vein that I could not altogether understand.

These words might well encourage, console, and gladden the heart of a Christian in the shape I was in at that time. But—oh, ignorance and simplicity!—it was all Greek to me and I couldn't make head or tail of it. But when I heard that the speaker's hunger and thirst would be appeased, my own unendurable hunger and my stomach, which from lack of food had become the size of a walnut, advised me to invite myself too. So I told myself to be courageous, crawled out of the tree, and approached the voice.

I saw a tall man with long grey and black hair that hung disheveled down to his shoulders; his tousled beard was the size of a cheese. His face, though haggard and sallow, was kind, and his long cloak was patched and mended with more than a thousand snippets of different materials. Around his throat and body he wore a heavy iron chain. To my eyes he looked so frightening and ghastly that I started trembling like a wet dog. But my fear was increased by the fact that he was hugging a crucifix about six feet high. Since I didn't know him, I could not but imagine that this old man must be the wolf of whom my knan had recently warned me.

In my fear I whipped out my bagpipe (which I had rescued from the cavalrymen as my only treasure), blew it up and started to make a horrendous sound to drive off this wolf. The anchorite was caught up in astonishment. No doubt he thought a devilish ghost had come to trouble him, like the great St. Anthony, and to disturb his meditation. As soon as he had recovered a little he reviled me, his tempter in the hollow tree (for I had retreated to it once more); he was even bold enough to come right up to me and rail at the fiend of men. "Hah!" he said, "you are just the one to trouble the godfearing. . . ." I did not understand another word, for his approach frightened me so much that I fainted dead away.

CHAPTER 7: *Simplicius is given a friendly welcome in a poor inn*

I don't know how I came to, but I was out of the tree, my head was in the old man's lap, and he had opened my jacket. When I had recovered a little, seeing the hermit so close to me, I screamed as if he were about to rip the heart from my chest. But he said, "Son, be still; I won't hurt you; calm yourself," and so on. But the more he comforted and soothed, the more I shouted, "You'll eat me!" "Now, now, my son," he said, "be quiet; I won't eat you." I carried on this sort of wrangling for some time until I managed to come with him into his hut. Here Poverty herself was marshal, Hunger was cook, and Want was the manager. Here my stomach was given some greens and a drink of water, and my mind, which was altogether confused, was straightened out and corrected by the old man's comforting friendliness. Soon Sleep tempted me to pay her tribute. When the hermit saw this he left the hut, for only one person could sleep in it. About midnight I awoke again and heard him sing the following song, which I later learned:

> Come, nightingale, O balm of night,
> Come, let your voice cheerful and bright
> Sing out in lovely rapture.
> The other birds have gone to sleep,
> But you a tuneful vigil keep,
> Your Maker's praise to capture.
> > Loudly raise your brilliant voice
> > And rejoice.
> > > Show you love
> > God who is in heaven above.
>
> Although the sunshine now has left
> And we of daylight are bereft,
> Yet we may now compete
> To praise his mercy, praise his might,
> Nor darkness hinder us nor night
> To offer praise replete.
> > Therefore raise your brilliant voice
> > And rejoice.
> > > Show you love
> > God who is in heaven above.
>
> True Echo with her wild reply
> Wants also to be heard close by
> When your praise is ringing.
> She bids us to avoid all sloth,

That we be active, never loth
She joins in happy singing.

    Therefore raise your brilliant voice, etc.

The stars which in the sky are found
In praise of God do still abound
And show their veneration.
The songless owl with ugly screech
Does yet a noble lesson teach:
Praise God in every nation!

    Therefore raise your brilliant voice, etc.

O come then, sweetest bird of night,
Inspire with your song's delight.
In bed let us not linger.
Instead let's sing to God in praise
Till Dawn the somber pall doth raise
From woods with rosy finger.

    Loudly raise your brilliant voice
      And rejoice.
      Show you love
God who is in heaven above.

While this song went on, it seemed almost as if the night-ingale, the owl, and Echo had joined in, and if I had ever heard the morning star sing, or could have imitated its melody on my bagpipe, I would have slipped out of the hut to join in, because this harmony seemed so lovely.

But I fell asleep again and did not wake up until late in the day. When the hermit stood in front of me and said, "Get up, little one, I'll give you something to eat and show you the way out of the woods, so you get back to your people in the village before night falls," I asked him, "What's that, 'people,' 'village'?" He said, "Have you never been in a village? Don't you know what 'men' or 'people' are?" "No," I said, "I've been nowhere but here; but tell me, what are 'people,' 'men,' and 'village'?" "God preserve us!" answered the hermit. "Are you foolish or bright?" "I am ma and pa's boy. My name is neither Foolish nor Bright." The hermit gave a sigh, crossed himself, and said, "My dear child, for God's sake I'd like to keep you here and teach you." The next chapter will tell of our dialogue.

CHAPTER 8: *How Simplicius uses elevated speech and thereby gives evidence of his excellent qualities*

Hermit. What is your name?

Simplex. My name is Boy.

Herm. I can see you're not a girl. But how did your father and mother call you?

Sim. I never had a father and mother.

Herm. Then who gave you that shirt?

Sim. My mither, of course.

Herm. How did your "mither" call you, then?

Sim. She called me "boy," also "rascal," "jackass," "clumsy lout," "stupid fool," and "jailbird."

Herm. Who was your mother's husband?

Sim. Nobody.

Herm. But with whom did your mother sleep at night?

Sim. With my knan.

Herm. How did your knan call you?

Sim. He called me "boy."

Herm. What was your knan's name?

Sim. Why, "knan"!

Herm. But how did your mother call him?

Sim. "Knan," and sometimes "boss."

Herm. Did she ever call him anything else?

Sim. Yes, she did.

Herm. What?

Sim. "Belch," "roughneck," "boozehound," and several other names when she was riled.

Herm. You are an ignoramus not to know your own name or that of your family.

Sim. Well, smarty, you don't know it either!

Herm. Do you know how to pray?

Sim. Naw, Annie and mither did all the praying at the house.

Herm. I'm asking you if you know the Lord's Prayer.

Sim. Sure.

Herm. Let me hear it.

Sim. Our dear father, who art heaven hallowed be name, kingdom come your will done heaven on earth, give us debts as we forgive debtors. Lead us never in no evil attempts, but save us from the kingdom and the power and the glory. Emma.

Herm. Didn't you ever go to church?

Sim. Sure. I'm a good climber and stole a whole shirtful of churries.

Herm. I didn't say *cherries* but *church.*

Sim. Ha, ha, you mean the little blue ones?

Herm. Heaven help me! Don't you know anything of our Lord God?

Sim. You bet! He hung in the corner behind the kitchen door. Mither brought him home from the fair and fastened him up there.

Herm. Oh dear Lord! Only now I see the great benefice of grace in thy presence and how man is nothing if he does not know thee. Listen, Simpleton—for I cannot call you anything else—when you say the Lord's prayer you must speak thus: "Our Father, who art in heaven, hallowed be thy name. Thy kingdom come, thy will be done, on earth as it is in heaven. Give us this day our daily bread."

Sim. Cheese, too?

Herm. Alas, dear child, be silent and learn. You need that more than cheese. Your mother was right when she called you clumsy. Boys like you should not interrupt an old man, but be silent, listen, and learn. If only I knew where your parents lived, I'd be glad to take you to them and teach them how to bring up children.

Sim. I don't know where to go. Our house burned down; my mither ran off and came back with Ursula; my knan ran off too; the hired girl was sick and lay in the barn. She told me to run away and not to hang around.

Herm. Who burned down the house?

Sim. Well, iron men came riding on animals as big as oxen, but without horns; these men stuck the sheep and cows and hogs, broke the windows and the oven; then I ran off, and later the house burned down.

Herm. Where was your knan?

Sim. Well, the iron men tied him up; then our old nanny goat licked his feet; this made him laugh and he gave the iron men lots of silver coins, yellow ones too, and nice shiny things and strings of white marbles.

Herm. When did this happen?

Sim. When I was supposed to herd the sheep. They wanted to steal my bagpipe too.

Herm. When were you supposed to herd the sheep?

Sim. Don't you get it? When the iron men came. Later our tousleheaded Annie told me to run away; otherwise the warriors would take me along. She meant the iron men, and I ran away and came here.

Herm. Where do you want to go now?

Sim. I sure don't know. I want to stay here.

Herm. It isn't good to keep you here, neither for you nor for me. Eat, and then I'll take you to some people.

Sim. Well, tell me what this "people" is.

Herm. People are humans like you and me. Your knan and mither and your Annie are humans. And when some of them get together, they are called "people."

Sim. Hoho!

Herm. Now go and eat!

This was the conservation we had together. The hermit often looked at me and sighed from the bottom of his heart; I don't know whether he pitied me in my excessive simple-mindedness, or for a reason I discovered only some years later.

CHAPTER 9: *Simplicius turns from a mere beast into a Christian*

I stopped chatting and started eating. This lasted only until I had had enough and the old man asked me to go away. Then I chose the tenderest words my peasant vocabulary afforded and used them all to persuade the hermit to keep me with him. Surely he thought it would be hard to keep me around, but still he decided to put up with me, more to instruct me in Christianity than to let me help him in his old age. His greatest worry was that my tender youth might not long endure his severe and frugal way of living.

My trial period lasted about three weeks. It was spring and I worked so well in the garden that the anchorite took a special liking to me, not so much because of the work I did (I was used to it), but rather because he saw I was eager to hear his instruction and my heart was apt to benefit from it.

He started his teaching with the fall of Lucifer. From there he proceeded to the garden of Eden, and when we with our parents were run out of it, he passed through the law of Moses and taught me, through God's ten commandments (and their interpretation) to tell virtues from vices, to do good and avoid evil. Finally he got around to the gospels and told me of Christ's birth, suffering, death, and resurrection. He concluded with doomsday and pictured heaven and hell as I could best grasp and understand it, clearly but not with too much detail. When he had finished one story he started another; my questions guided our progress, and he could not possibly have been a better teacher. I loved my teacher and the instruction so much that sometimes I couldn't sleep because of them. The hermit was successful in teaching me mainly because the smooth tablet of my mind was altogether blank; when he started writing on it, he did not have to crowd out or erase anything. Nevertheless, compared to other folks there still was plenty of simplicity in me, and for this reason the hermit called me "Simplicius," since neither of us knew my real name.

I learned from him how to pray, and when he had decided to let me stay, the two of us built me a hut. It was just like his, made of logs, brush, and dirt, and shaped almost like a soldier's tent or (to use a different comparison) like a turnip cellar on a farm, hardly big enough for me to sit upright. My bed was made of dry leaves and grass; it was the same size as the hut, and I can't decide whether to call this sort of shelter a covered bed or a hovel.

CHAPTER 10: *How he learned to read and write in a wild forest*

The first time I saw the hermit reading the Bible, I could not imagine with whom he was carrying on his secretive and, as I thought, very serious conversation. I saw his lips move and heard his mumbling, but I saw and heard no one with whom he was talking. And though I knew nothing of reading and writing, I noticed by his eyes that he was carrying on with something inside the book. I paid close attention to the book, and after he had put it aside I took hold of it, opened it, and happening on the first chapter of the Book of Job, with a beautifully colored illustration, I asked the picture some strange questions. But when no answer was forthcoming I became impatient and—just as the hermit came up behind me—I said, "You little rascals, can't you open your mouths anymore? Only a moment ago you were gossiping with my father." (That is what I had to call the hermit.) "I can see very well that you are driving the sheep home for your poor knan and that you too have set the house on fire. Wait, wait, I can still put out the fire so it won't do any more damage." With those words I got up to get a bucket of water, because I felt something had to be done. "Where are you going, Simplex?" said the hermit, whom I hadn't noticed behind me. "Oh, father," I said, "these soldiers have sheep and want to drive them off. They took them from the poor man you were just talking with. His house is on fire too, and if I don't help put it out it'll burn to the ground." And I pointed with my finger to what I saw. "Don't rush off," said the hermit, "there is no danger." I answered politely, "But are you blind? *You* see about the sheep and *I'll* get the water." "Boy," said the hermit, "these pictures are not reality. They are made to give us an idea of events long past." I answered, "But you were talking with them a while ago. Why shouldn't they be real?"

Contrary to his habit, the hermit laughed at my childish simplicity or simple-minded childishness and said, "Dear child, these pictures cannot talk. But I can tell from these black lines what they mean. It's called 'reading,' and when I read, you think I am talking with the pictures, but it's not so." I answered, "Since I am a human being like you, I should also be able to read the black lines. How am I to take your words? Dear father, tell me what to make of this." Then he said, "All right then, son, I shall teach you and you'll be able to talk with the pictures just as I can, but it will take time, and both of us will have to try hard."

On birch bark, he wrote the letters as they appear in print, and when I had learned them, I learned how to spell, then how to read and write; and since I imitated the printed letters I could write better than my teacher.

CHAPTER 11: *Of vittles, household utensils, and other things necessary for this life on earth*

I stayed in the forest for about two years before the hermit died, and a little longer than six months after his death.

Therefore, I think I should tell the curious reader (who often wants to know even the most minute details) of our activities and how we spent our life there.

For food we had all sorts of vegetables like carrots, cabbage, beans, peas, lentils, millet, and such. We did not turn up our noses at beechnuts, wild apples, pears, and cherries; even acorns often tasted good. Our bread (or perhaps I had better call it cake) of ground Indian corn was baked in hot ashes. In the winter we snared birds; in the spring and summer God kept us supplied with nests full of their young. We sometimes ate snails and frogs, and we didn't mind fishing with pots and line, since not far from our camp ran a creek with plenty of fish and crawfish. Its water was our drink. For a while we kept a wild pig in a pen and raised it on acorns and beechnuts; later we butchered and ate it. My hermit knew that it is no sin to use what God grants to man. We needed but little salt and no spices at all, for we did not want to stimulate thirst because we had no wine cellar. We received the necessary salt from a parson who lived about fifteen miles from us. I'll have to tell more about him.

We had a complete supply of household goods—a shovel, a mattock, an ax, a hatchet, and a Dutch oven for cooking; the iron kettle wasn't ours, having been borrowed from the parson. Each of us had a worn-down blunt knife. These things and nothing else were our property. As for the rest, we did not need dishes, plates, spoons, forks, skillet, frying and roasting pan, salt shaker or other table or kitchen utensils, for our Dutch oven also served as our dish, and our hands as forks and spoons. When we wanted to drink we used a pipe that ran into the well or we dipped our heads into the creek, like Gideon's warriors. Of all sorts of woven material, like wool, silk, cotton, and linen (for beds, table cloths, and drapes), we possessed nothing except what we wore. We thought we had enough as long as we were protected from the rain and cold. Our household had no special schedule except on Sundays and holidays. On these days we started walking at midnight in order to be on time for services in the parson's church before anybody else arrived. We always sat upstairs in the organ loft, where we could see the altar and the pulpit. The first time I saw the parson getting into his pulpit, I asked my hermit what he intended to do in the big tub! After services we went home just as secretly as we had come; and after we had returned, with feet and bodies tired, we ate bad food with good teeth. The rest of the time the hermit spent in prayers or in teaching me pious lore.

On weekdays we did what was most necessary according to the season. One day we'd work in the garden; the rest we spent collecting fertile soil in shady places or in hollow trees, in order to improve our garden even without manure. Another day, we wove baskets or fish pots, split fire wood, went fishing, or did anything else but loaf. And amidst all this activity the hermit did not cease instructing me in all good knowledge, and in such a severe life I learned to endure thirst, heat, cold, heavy work, and all kinds of trouble, but first of all to know God and how to serve him. And that was the most important. Beyond this, my hermit did not want to instruct me, for he considered it enough for a Christian to reach his goal through prayer and hard work. And that is why I stayed a simpleton, for when I left the woods I had been quite well instructed in spiritual matters, pronounced my German exactly as it is spelled, knew Christianity very well, and yet was such a plain idiot in worldly matters that I didn't amount to a hill of beans.

CHAPTER 12: *A pretty way of experiencing a blessed death and getting buried at next to no cost*

I had spent about two years and had just become used to my hard life when my best friend on earth took his mattock, gave me a shovel, and led me by the hand into the garden where we usually said our prayers. "Well, Simplex, dear child," he said, "since the time has come when I must depart the earth, pay my debt to nature and leave this world behind, and as I see the future events of your life approaching, know-ing well that you will not stay long in this lovely place, I have done my best to strengthen you in the way of virtue by giving you instruction. By means of this you are to guide your life as by a compass, to attain eternal life."

These words made my eyes water, and I said, "Dear father, do you want to leave me alone in this forest? Shall I. . . ." That is all I could utter; my heart was so troubled for love of the hermit that I fainted at his feet. He picked me up, con-soled me as best he could, and pointed out my mistakes by asking if I wanted to rebel against the order instituted by the Almighty. "Don't you know," he continued, "that neither heaven nor hell is able to do that? Nor you, son! Do you ask me to tarry longer in this vale of tears? Ah no, my son, let me depart, for I will be kept here in this misery neither by your tears nor by my own desire. I am called away by God's express will, and I prepare joyfully to obey his command. Instead of crying foolishly, pay attention to my last words. They are: Know yourself, the longer you live the more so. And if you grow as old as Methuselah, do not give up trying. Most men were lost because they did not know who or what they were, what they could have become or had to become." Then he ad-vised me to stay away from bad company, because the damage done by evil companions was inexpressible. He gave me an example of it by saying: "If you put a drop of sweet wine into a crockful of vinegar, the wine turns to vinegar, but if you put a drop of vinegar into sweet wine, the vinegar will go unnoticed." "Dearest son," he said, "most of all, remain stead-fast. Do not let the sweat of carrying the cross discourage you from finishing a good work, for whoever perseveres to the end shall be saved. But if against my expectation you should fall because of weakness of the flesh, do not stubbornly wallow in sin, but quickly arise through honest repentance!"

These three admonitions—to know oneself, to avoid evil companions, and to remain steadfast—this pious man con-sidered good and necessary because he had practiced them and he had not gone wrong. After he had come to know him-

self, he fled not only bad companions but the whole world;
he persisted till the end, and in his end he was doubtless
saved—how, I shall soon tell.

After he had finished speaking, he started digging his own
grave with the mattock. I helped him as best I could and as
he had requested, but I couldn't imagine his purpose. Then
he said, "My dear and only true son—for I have begotten no
creature but you to praise our Creator—when my soul has
gone to its resting place, pay your due respect to my body.
Cover me with the same dirt we have just now dug out of this
pit." Then he embraced me, kissed me, and pressed me much
harder to his chest than I thought a man like him could.
"Dear child," he said, "I commend you to God's protection
and die joyfully, for I think he will protect you." But I could
not help crying and bawling; I clung to the chains he wore
around his neck, thinking I might thus keep him from getting
away. But he said, "My son, let go of me so I can see if the
grave we have dug is long enough." He unfastened the chains,
took off his cloak, and, lying down in the grave like someone
going to sleep, he said, "Great God, take back the soul that
thou hast given me. Into thy hands, O Lord, I commend my
spirit," and so on. Then he gently closed his lips and eyes
while I stood there like a stick, not believing that his dear
soul had left the body, because I had seen him in such seizures
before.

As was my custom in these situations, I stayed a few hours
by him and prayed. But when my very dear hermit did not
make any effort to get out of the grave, I climbed down to
shake, kiss, and stroke him. But life had left him; grim, re-
lentless death had robbed Simplex of his company. I sprinkled
the lifeless body (maybe I should say I embalmed it) with my
tears and after I had run to and fro for some time and torn
my hair, I started to bury him, more with sighing than with
shovels of dirt. And when I had hardly covered his face, I
climbed down and uncovered it, to see it and kiss it once
more. I carried on like this all day, until I had finished the
funeral in this manner, altogether alone. Anyway, bier, coffin,

shroud, candles, pallbearers, mourners, and clergy were not available to help the dead man into his grave.

CHAPTER 13: *Simplicius lets himself drift, like a piece of reed on a pond*

A few days after my dear and worthy hermit's demise, I made my way to the parson mentioned above, reported my master's death to him, and asked his advice on how to act in this situation. Although he tried very hard to dissuade me from staying longer in the woods, and pointed out the obvious danger of doing so, I followed in my predecessor's footsteps bravely, and all summer long did as a pious anchorite should. But as time changes everything, the grief I felt for my hermit gradually lessened, and the severe cold of winter outside extinguished the ardor of my intentions inside. The more I began to waver, the lazier I became about my prayers, and instead of contemplating divine and heavenly things, I was overcome by a desire to look at the world. And since I wasn't much good anymore in the forest, I resolved to see the parson again and to find out if he would still advise me to leave the woods. To this end, I walked toward the village, and when I got there I saw it in flames; a troop of cavalry had just plundered and set it on fire, killed some of the peasants, run off many and captured a few, among them the parson. Oh, my God! How full of trials and tribulations is a man's life?! One misfortune hardly stops before another overtakes us.

The cavalrymen were about to leave, and the parson was led by a rope like a poor sinner and slave. Some were screaming, "Shoot the bastard!" Others wanted money from him. He raised his hands and begged them, for the sake of their souls, to spare him and treat him with Christian mercy—in vain, for one of them rode roughshod over him and hit him such a wallop over the head that blood trickled down; he fell, commended his soul to God, and lay there like a dead dog. The captured peasants didn't fare much better.

When it looked as if these horsemen had lost their minds in their tyrannical cruelty, an armed gang of peasants like an angry swarm of yellow jackets came charging out of the woods. They raised such a ghastly war whoop, attacked so furiously, and fired so savagely that my hair stood on end, for I had never attended this kind of free-for-all. Nobody's likely to make monkeys of our peasants from the Spessart—nor of the ones from Hesse, Sauerland, Vogelsberg, or the Black Forest! The horsemen made tracks, not only leaving the stolen cattle behind, but also throwing away the loot as they ran, giving up their prey lest they fall prey to the peasants. A few who were captured were given rough treatment.

This introductory entertainment almost spoiled my desire to see the world; I thought if this is the way things are, the wilderness is far more attractive. Still, I wanted to hear the parson's explanations, but he was rather faint from his injuries and the beating he had received. He admonished me that he couldn't help or advise me because in his present condition he would soon have to make a living as a beggar, and even if I wanted to stay in the woods, he wouldn't be able to give me any help, because, as I could see, his church and parsonage were at that very moment going up in smoke.

With these words I trotted sadly back toward the woods and my home. Since I had experienced little comfort on my journey (rather, I had become much more devout again), I decided never to leave the wilderness, but meant to conclude my life like a hermit, in contemplation of divine things. I was already figuring out how to get along without salt (which the parson had previously given me) and thus do without anybody's help.

CHAPTER 14: *A strange story of five peasants*

So that I might follow my decision at once and be a genuine hermit, I dressed in the late hermit's hair shirt and put on his chain—not because I needed to mortify my rebellious flesh, but to resemble my predecessor in appearance as well as in manner of living and also to protect myself better against the cold of winter.

The day after the village had been plundered and burned, I was just sitting in my hut, frying yellow turnips and praying at the same time, when some forty or fifty musketeers surrounded me. Although they hardly believed their eyes when they saw me, these boys turned my place upside down looking for something that absolutely wasn't there, for I had only a couple of books, and they threw them helter-skelter because they were no good to them. After a while, when they had taken a second look at me and seen by the feathers what kind of bird they had caught, they decided there was no hope of booty. Then they wondered about my hard way of living and took pity on my tender youth, particularly the officer in charge. He did me the honor of requesting me to show them the way out of the woods, in which they had been lost for some time. I did not refuse for a moment. To get rid of these unfriendly guests as soon as possible, I led them by the nearest road to the village where the parson had been manhandled. Truth to tell, that was the only road I knew.

But before we got out of the woods we saw about ten peasants, some armed with guns, the others busy burying something. The soldiers approached them and shouted, "Halt!" The peasants answered with their guns. And when they saw how many soldiers there were, they rushed off this way and that so that the musketeers (who were tired) couldn't catch any of them. Then the soldiers wanted to uncover what the peasants had covered up—an easy job because the spades and picks were still there. They had hardly started when a voice came up from below and said, "You bloody rascals! You dirty crooks! You damn bastards! Do you think heaven will let you go unpunished for your unchristian cruelty? There are plenty of stout fellows who will retaliate for your bestiality, so that nobody will come to lick your ass!" The soldiers looked at each other and didn't know what to do next. Some thought they were hearing a ghost, but I thought I was dreaming. Their officer told them to go on digging. Soon they struck a

barrel, opened it, and found inside a man whose nose and
ears had been cut off. But he was still alive. As soon as this
fellow had recovered enough to recognize some of the group,
he told how the peasants had captured six soldiers who had
been reconnoitering for feed. Only an hour ago, they had
shot five of these, standing them one behind the other; since
the bullet, having had to go through five bodies before him,
had not killed him, the sixth in the line, they had cut off his
ears and nose. But first they had forced him (I beg the reader's
pardon) to lick their asses. When he saw himself so degraded
by these dishonorable and dastardly knaves, he called them
the vilest names he could think of, hoping to trick them into
killing him, though they had vouchsafed his life, but in vain.
After he had embittered them, they stuck him in this barrel
and buried him alive, saying that since he tried so hard for
death, for reasons of spite they did not want to humor him.

While this man was telling of his misery, another group of
soldiers, infantry, came up out of the woods. They had captured five of the fugitive peasants and shot the others. Among
the captives were four peasants to whom the mistreated cavalryman had been forced to do as he was told. Now, when both
groups of soldiers discovered they were from the same army,
the horseman had to tell once more what had happened to
him and his comrades in arms.

You should have seen what happened to the peasants there!
Some of the soldiers in their first fury wanted to fill them full
of lead, but others said that these gay birds ought to be
tortured a little; they ought to get a taste of what they did to
our buddy. In the meantime, their ribs were being tickled
with musket stocks. Finally a soldier stepped forward and said,
"Gentlemen, since it is a crying shame to all soldiers that
five peasants abused this rascal (he pointed to the cavalryman), it is no more than fair for us to erase this blot and let
these bastards kiss our friend a hundred times." Another said,
"This rat is not worthy of the honor. If he hadn't been such a
numbskull he would have died a thousand times rather than
act in a manner unbecoming to a soldier."

Finally they resolved that each of the peasants was to re-
ciprocate on ten soldiers. Then they wanted to decide what
else to do to the peasants. But the peasants were so obstinate
that they could in no way be coerced. One soldier took the
fifth peasant aside and promised to let him go where he
pleased, if he denied God and all his saints. The peasant answered that he had never given a damn for the saints and his
personal acquaintance with God had been slight. He swore
he did not know God and wanted no part of his kingdom.
The soldier fired a bullet at his head, but it ricocheted as if
it had hit a steel wall. Then he pulled out his sword bayonet
and shouted, "Is that the kind you are? I promised to let you
go where you wanted, but since you don't want to go to
heaven, I am now sending you to hell!" And he split his head
apart down to the teeth. "This is the way to get revenge,"
said the soldier. "Send these villains to hell and keep 'em
there!"

Meanwhile the soldiers tied the other four peasants (the
same whose asses the soldier had had to lick) over a fallen
tree in such a way that their rumps stuck up. After removing
their trousers, they took yards and yards of fuse cord, made
knots in it, and neatly ran the knotted cord through the cleft
of their behinds until they drew blood. "This is the way to
dress their backsides," they said. The peasants screamed like
pigs, but a lot of good it did them! The soldiers didn't stop
until they struck the bone. I was sent back to my hut because
the second troop knew the way, so I didn't find out what else
they did to the peasants.

CHAPTER 15: *Simplicius is raided, and has a wondrous dream*
about peasants and how it goes in time of war

When I got back home, I found that all my firewood, my
household goods, and all the frugal food I had saved and
harvested in the garden all summer for the coming winter
were completely gone. "What now?" I thought. At that mo-

ment, need taught me to pray. I called on all my modest wit
to decide what would be best for me. But since my experience
was limited and indifferent, I could not reach a good decision. The best I could do was to commend myself to God
and to put my trust in him; otherwise I would surely have
despaired and perished. Moreover, the predicaments of the
injured parson and the five miserably wounded peasants
which I had witnessed that day were before me all the time,
and I thought not so much about food and survival as about
the hatred that existed between soldiers and peasants. But in
my simplicity I could not help thinking that since Adam's
creation there must surely be not one but two kinds of people on earth—wild ones and tame ones—who cruelly chase
each other like unreasoning animals. I was cold and troubled,
and with such thoughts I fell asleep, on an empty stomach.

Then, as in a dream, I saw how all the trees standing
around the place where I lived were suddenly changing and
taking on an utterly different appearance. On top of each tree
sat a cavalier; and instead of bearing leaves the branches were
decorated with all sorts of men. Some of these fellows had long
pikes, others muskets, pistols, halberds, small flags, and drums
and fifes. The sight was a pleasure to look at, for everything
was neatly divided by rank. The root was made up of lowly
people like day-laborers, craftsmen, peasants, and such, who
nevertheless gave the tree its strength and imparted vigor
anew when it had been lost. In fact, to their own great dis-
advantage and even peril they made up for the deficiency
caused by the fallen leaves. They were complaining about
those sitting in the tree; and they had good cause, for the
whole load rested on them and pressed them so hard that all
their money was being squeezed out of their pockets and even
out of the strongboxes which they had secured with seven
locks. But if money was not forthcoming, certain commissioners curried them with combs (a process called military
execution), and because of this there issued sighs from their
hearts, tears from their eyes, blood from their nails, and mar-
row from their bones. Yet among them there were some jokers

called funny birds who were little troubled by it all. They took
everything easy, and in their misery they came up with all
sorts of raillery so that they needed no consolation.

CHAPTER 16: *Omissions and commissions of modern soldiers,
             and how hard it is for a common soldier to
             get a commission*

The roots of these trees had sheer wretchedness to contend
with, but the men on the lowest branches had to endure even
greater trouble, hardship, and discomfort. And though the
branch-dwellers were jollier, they were also more defiant, tyrannical, and for the most part ungodly; and they constituted
at all times an unsupportable burden for the roots. About
them there appeared these lines:

> Hunger, thirst, and poverty,
> Heat and cold and tyranny,
> Whence, whatever, where the ache,
> Mercenaries give and take.

These words were all the less equivocal because they described the men's work perfectly; for their entire activity consisted of hard drinking, suffering hunger and thirst, whoring
and pederasty, rattling dice and gambling, overeating and
overdrinking, killing and being killed, harassing and being
harassed, hunting down and being hunted down, frightening
and being frightened, causing misery and suffering it, beating
and being beaten—in a few words, spoiling and harming, and
being despoiled and harmed in turn. And neither winter nor
summer, rain nor wind, mountain nor valley, fields nor
swamps, ditches, passes, seas, walls, water, fire, nor ramparts,
danger to their own bodies, souls, consciences, nay, not even
loss of life, heaven, or any other things of whatsoever name
kept them from it. On the contrary, they continued eagerly
in their works until after a while they gave up the ghost,
died and croaked in battles, sieges, storms, campaigns, and
even in their quarters (where soldiers enjoy paradise on earth,

especially when they run into fat peasants)—except only a few
oldsters who (unless they had stashed away stolen or extorted
goods) made the very best panhandlers and beggars. Right
above these troubled people sat some old chicken thieves who
had squatted and suffered a few years on the lowest branches
and who had been lucky enough to escape death till now.
These looked a little more serious and respectable than the
lowest bunch, for they had climbed up one level. But above
them there were some still a little higher, and they also
aspired to grandeur. Being the lowest in the chain of command, they were called jacket-dusters: they beat the pikemen
and musketeers and with their abuse and cursing dusted their
backs and heads. Above these, the tree had a kind of break or
separation, a smooth section without branches which was
greased with the soap of envy so that no one (unless he was of
the nobility) could climb up, no matter how smart or skillful
he was. This section was polished more smoothly than a mar-
ble column or a steel mirror. Above this place sat those with
flags or ensigns, some young, some older. The young ones had
been given a boost by their cousins. The old ones had climbed
up under their own power, either by means of a silver ladder
called bribery, or else by means of a rope which luck had let
them catch because there were no better men present just then.
A little further up sat still higher ones, and they also had
their afflictions, cares, and troubles. They did, however, enjoy
the advantage of being able to line their purses most con-
veniently with a liner they were cutting out of the roots; and
for this they were using a knife known as forced contributions. The situation became most pleasant, to the point where
a commissioner happened along and emptied a tubful of
money above the tree to refresh it. Then those on top caught
almost all of the rain as it dropped, while practically nothing
trickled down below. For this reason more of the lower squat-
ters died of hunger than were killed by the enemy. The upper
echelons were troubled by neither danger.

There was constant wrangling and climbing in this tree,
for every one wanted to sit in the highest, happiest place. And

yet, there were some lazy, devil-may-care louts who hardly
tried for a better position and who sleepily did what they had
to do. The lowest men were hoping for the fall of the uppermost so that they might sit in their seats. The struggle was
fiercest and least rewarding in the slippery section, for whoever had a good sergeant did not want to lose him through
promotion. So they found impoverished noblemen, ex-pages,
poor cousins, and other starvelings, and made ensigns out of
them, and these were taking the bread out of the mouths of
meritorious old soldiers.

CHAPTER 17: *Though in wartime noblemen are preferred over*
commoners (as is just and proper), many men
of low origin attain great heights

[In a discussion between an old sergeant and a nobleman
about the advantage of having only noblemen for officers, the
nobleman quotes the Bible, ancient writers, and a proverb in
order to prove his point. The sergeant asserts that hope of
promotion makes the soldier do his best; and the nobleman
admits that some men of lowly station have risen to be great
soldiers, for example, the imperial general Johann von Werth,
the Swedish Stalhans, the Hessian St. André, and a few others.
But as a rule, concludes the sergeant, noblemen keep the door
locked when commoners seek preferment.]

CHAPTER 18: *Simplicius takes his first leap into the world,*
and has bad luck

I did not feel like listening any longer to this argument;
and, turning to the trees again, I saw that they were moving
and colliding. The men came tumbling down lickety-split, and
the noise of falling and cracking up was all around me. One
man lost an arm, another a leg, a third even a head. While I
was still staring, it seemed as if all the trees were only one

tree and on its top sat Mars, the war god. He was covering all
of Europe with the branches of this tree; but seemingly he
could have covered the whole world, except that the sharp
north winds of envy and hate, distrust and jealousy, pride and
avarice were blowing through the tree and making it thin and
transparent.

Awakened by the roaring and raging of noxious winds and
by the destruction of the tree, I found myself alone in my hut.
Therefore I started thinking again, pondering inside my little
brainpan what in the world I was to do. To stay in the woods
was impossible, for I had been robbed of everything and
could maintain myself no longer. Nothing was left except a
few books that lay scattered pell-mell here and there. While
I was picking them up with tears in my eyes, and calling on
God to guide my steps where I was meant to go, by chance I
found a letter the hermit had written while he was still alive.
It read: "Dear Simplici, when you find this letter, leave the
woods at once and save the parson and yourself from present
hardship, for he has done me much good. God, whom you
should ever have before you and to whom you should pray,
will take you to the place most suitable for you. However, always keep him in mind and always try to serve him as if you
were still with me in the woods. Keep this always in mind and
follow these, my last words, and you will be able to live. Farewell!"

I kissed this letter and the hermit's grave many thousand
times, and without tarrying longer I started out to look for
people until I should find them. I continued walking straight
ahead for two days, and when night overtook me I looked
for a hollow tree to sleep in. My only food was the beechnuts
I picked up on the way. On the third day, not far from Gelnhausen,[3] I came upon a plain. There I enjoyed, as it were, a
meal like a wedding banquet, for everywhere in the fields lay
sheaves of wheat the peasants had not been able to carry off,
having been chased away after the important battle of Nörd-

---

[3] Grimmelshausen's birthplace, a town on the Kinzig River.

lingen.[4] Their loss was my gain. I made a bed of some of the sheaves, for it was cruelly cold, and rubbed out some grain and ate it. It was most delicious food, because I hadn't tasted anything like it in a long time.

CHAPTER 19: *How Hanau is conquered by Simplicius, and Simplicius by Hanau*

At daybreak, I fed myself on wheat again, and then walked toward Gelnhausen, where I found the city gates wide open. One or two gates had been burned; some still were barricaded with manure. I walked in, but though I saw no living people, the streets were littered with corpses, some stripped of all their clothes. This miserable sight frightened me, as you can well imagine. In my simple-mindedness I could not think what kind of disaster might have left the place in such a shambles. After a while I found out that imperial troops had surprised some of Prince Bernhard of Weimar's [5] men, and this is how they had been treated. I had hardly gone a stone's throw or two into town when I had seen enough of it. So I turned around, took my way through the fields, and came to a busy highway that took me to the lordly fortress of Hanau.[6] As soon as I saw the first guard I wanted to run like a rabbit, but two musketeers stopped me and took me to their guard-house.

But before I go on I must tell the reader about my droll appearance at that time, for my dress was very strange, and

[4] On September 6, 1634, the Swedish under Duke Bernhard of Saxe-Weimar and Count Horn were defeated by the imperial forces at Nördlingen.

[5] Duke Bernhard of Saxe-Weimar (1604–1639) was one of the most famous generals of the Thirty Years' War. When Gustavus Adolphus of Sweden was killed in the battle of Lützen, Bernhard took charge and saved the day for the Protestants.

[6] Located east of Gelnhausen on the Main River and not far from Frankfurt. The commander of the fortress, James Ramsay, a Scotsman in Swedish service, was a historical personage; he died in 1639.

wondrously disgusting; the governor later had me painted
that way. To begin with, my hair had not been cut in four
years, either in the Greek, German, or French fashion, nor
had it been curled or combed. Rather it reposed on my head
in its natural dishevelment, covered with more than a year's
dust for powder (*poudre* or puff-stuff or whatever the name
of this foolish material that's made for male or female fools),
and my waxen, pallid face peered out from under it like a
hoot owl about to light out at a mouse. And as I went bare-
headed all the time and my hair was naturally curly, I looked
as if I wore a Turkish turban. The rest of my outfit matched
my coiffure perfectly, for I wore the hermit's cloak, if cloak it
could still be called, since the original cloth from which it
was cut had altogether disappeared and there was nothing
left but the shape of it, barely held together by more than a
thousand snippets of multicolored cloth meticulously joined
and patched. Over this worn and multifariously mended cloak
I wore the hair shirt. In place of a shoulder wrap (because I
had cut off the sleeves and was using them for stockings), my
body was girded with iron chains crossing neatly in front and
back, as they usually paint St. William. I looked almost like
one of those persons who has been caught by Turks and goes
begging for his friends. My shoes were carved from a piece
of wood and tied on with ribbons of basswood bark; my feet
looked as red as if I wore a pair of red Spanish stockings or
had colored my skin with brazilwood dye. I think if at that
time some mountebank, quack, or vagrant had owned me,
and advertised me as a Mongol from Siberia or an Eskimo, he
would have found plenty of fools willing to pay a farthing to
see me. Though anybody with brains could easily see from
my lean and hungry look and my neglected exterior that I
had not run away from a cook shop or a lady's drawing room,
much less from some great man's household, still I was closely
questioned by the guard; and as the soldiers stared at me, so
I stared at the crazy attire of the officer whose questions I had
to answer. I did not know whether he was a "he" or a "she,"
for he wore his hair and beard long *à la française;* on either

side of his face long braids hung down like pony tails, and his beard was so miserably dressed and botched that between his mouth and his nose only a few scraggly hairs showed. I was no less puzzled by his wide trousers; to me, they looked more like a skirt than a pair of men's pants. I thought to myself, if he's a man he ought to have a regular beard, for this dandy isn't as young anymore as he pretends. But if he is a woman, why does the old harlot have so many hairs straggling about her face? Surely it must be a woman, I thought, for an honest man won't have his beard ruined in such a deplorable way. Even billy goats won't set foot in a strange herd when their beards have been clipped—they are that bashful. And though I was in doubt, not knowing the current fashion, I finally decided he was a man and a woman at the same time.

This male woman (or female man) had me searched thoroughly, but found nothing on me save a little book made of birch bark in which I had written my daily prayers; in it lay the slip of paper that the pious hermit (as reported above) had left me as a memento and a good-by present. He took it away. But since I did not want to lose it, I knelt before him, took hold of his knees and said, "Alas, dear Mr. Hermaphrodite, leave the prayer book with me!" "You fool," he answered, "who in hell told you my name was Herman Phrodite?" I had noticed right away that this joker couldn't read or write, and he gave the book to two soldiers and ordered them to take me to the governor.

Well, they led me through town and everybody came out to stare at me like a sea monster and made a big fuss over me. Some thought I was a spy; others, an idiot; still others, a bogey, a ghost, a spook, or an apparition of some kind of evil omen. A few thought I was a fool, and they might have been nearest the mark—if I hadn't had knowledge of God.

CHAPTER 20: *How he was saved from prison and torture*

When I was led before the governor, he asked me where I came from. I replied that I did not know. He continued,

"Where do you want to go? And what do you do for a living?" I kept answering, I didn't know. He asked, "Where's your home?" And when I answered again that I didn't know, his expression changed, whether from anger or astonishment I can't say. But since everybody likes to suspect the worst, especially when the enemy is close by (Gelnhausen had been taken only recently, and a regiment of dragoons had been lost there), the governor agreed with those who thought me a traitor and a spy. He ordered me searched. But when he heard from the soldiers who had brought me in that it had already been done, and that they had found only the small book they had handed over, he read a few lines in it and asked me who had given me the book. I answered that it had always been mine, for I had made it up myself and written it. He asked, "But why on birch bark?" I answered, "Because the bark of other trees won't do for the purpose." "You rascal," he said, "I am asking you why you did not write on paper." "Well," I said, "we didn't have any in the woods." The governor asked, "Where? In what woods?" I answered again, in the same vein, that I didn't know.

Then the governor turned to several of the officers in attendance and said, "This fellow is either a bad egg or a simpleton. Well, he can't be a simpleton because he can write so well." And as he thumbed through the book to show them my beautiful handwriting, the hermit's letter fell out. He had it picked up, but I turned pale because I considered this my dearest possession and treasure, and almost like a holy relic to me. The governor noticed and again suspected me of treason, especially when he opened the letter and read it, for he said, "I have seen this hand and know it was written by a famous soldier, but I can't remember who it is." The contents puzzled him, too, for he said, "This is undoubtedly some kind of code no one else understands except the one with whom it was arranged." Then he asked me my name and when I answered, "Simplicius," he said, "Well, well, I know your kind! Get him out of here and put his hands and feet in chains. Maybe he'll talk differently then." The two soldiers went with me to my newly appointed hotel, that is, the hoosegow, and there turned me over to the warden, who according to orders decorated my hands and feet with bonds of iron, as if it weren't enough to carry the hermit's chain I had around me.

This first reception was not enough for the world. Next came hangmen and executioners with their instruments of torture who (although I was satisfied with my innocence) made my miserable life altogether hell. "Oh, my God!" I said to myself, "this serves me right. Simplicius left God's service and joined the world so that this caricature of a Christian could get his just reward. I had it coming with my irresponsible actions. Oh, unhappy Simplici, where does your ingratitude take you? Behold, God had hardly got you into his service and cognizance when you quit him and turned your back on him. Couldn't you have kept on eating acorns and beans in order to serve your Creator without hindrance? Didn't you know that your faithful hermit and teacher fled the world and chose the wilderness? Oh, you bump on a log! You left the woods hoping to satisfy your shameful desires and see the world. But now look; while you think to feast your eyes, you needs must perish in this dangerous labyrinth. Could you not have imagined, you numbskull, that your late predecessor would not have exchanged the joys of the world for the hard life in the loneliness of the woods if he had been confident of obtaining true peace, real quiet, and the salvation of his eternal soul in the world? You benighted Simplici, now you get the reward for your vain thoughts and insolent foolishness! You can't complain of injustice and protest your innocence, because you rushed to this martyrdom and the death that's sure to follow, and all the misery ahead is of your own making."

Thus I accused myself, begged forgiveness of God, and commended my soul to him. Meanwhile we were approaching the jail for common thieves, and when my need was greatest, God's help was nearest. For when I was surrounded by police and stood waiting (together with a multitude of people) for the jail to open, the parson whose village had lately been robbed and burned wanted to see what was the matter. His lodging was close by and he too was under arrest. When he looked out of the window and saw me he shouted wildly, "Oh, Simplici, is it you?!" When I heard and saw him, I couldn't help raising both hands toward him and crying, "Oh, father! Oh, father! Oh, father!" He asked what I had done. I answered that I didn't know; they had surely brought me here because I had escaped from the forest. But when he found out from the onlookers that I was considered a traitor, he begged them to stop until he had reported to the governor. Such would be good for his and my release, especially since he knew me better than anyone else.

CHAPTER 21: *Fickle Fortune throws a friendly glance in Simplicius' direction*

He was permitted to see the governor, and half an hour later I, too, was summoned and told to go to the servants room, where there were two tailors, a shoemaker with a pair of shoes, a haberdasher with hats and hose, and someone else with all sorts of cloth to dress me up at once. They got me out of my ragged and patched coat, and took off the chain and the hair shirt so the tailors could measure me. Then a soldier barber came in with strong cleansers and scented soap, and just as he was about to start on me, another order arrived which scared me out of a year's growth. Though I worried, it didn't mean anything; it said I was to put my old weeds right back on, for a portrait artist was on his way with the tools of his profession—to wit, minium and cinnabar for my eyelids; lacquer, indigo, and azure for my coral-colored lips; orpiment and oxide of lead for my white teeth (which I bared from hunger); and carbon black and burnt sienna and lots of other colors for my weather-beaten coat. He also had a whole handful of brushes. This fellow now started squinting, drawing outlines, and putting the first coat of paint on; he tilted his head in order to compare his work exactly with my shape. Now he changed my eyes, now my hair, now my nostrils and everything he had not done right the first time, until in the end he had produced the spitting image of what Simplicius had once been, and I was quite shocked at my own ghastly appearance. Only then was the barber allowed to work on me. He washed my hair and snipped at it for at least an hour and a half. Finally he dressed it according to the latest fashion, for I had hair enough and to spare. After that he put me in a bathtub and scrubbed from my emaciated body the dirt accumulated over the last three or four years. He had hardly finished when I was given a white shirt, shoes and stockings, also a turndown collar and a hat with a feather in it. The trousers were beautifully finished, and trimmed with galloons all over. Now the only thing missing was the jacket, and the tailors were hurrying to finish it. The cook came in with a thick soup and the kitchen maid brought me a drink. There sat Mr. Simplicius like a young count, all dressed up and waited on. I enjoyed the food regardless of my uncertain future, for I had never heard of the hangman's meal! For this reason my magnificent beginning pleased me so much that I can hardly express it, let alone glory in it adequately. As a matter of fact, I don't think I've ever felt better, any time before or since.

When the coat was ready I put it on, but I made a pitiful appearance and looked like a scarecrow, for the tailors had intentionally made the coat too big, hoping I would soon grow in all directions, a hope I amply justified, for with the governor's good vittles I put on weight so fast you could almost see it. My rustic dress with its chain and other accessories was put in the museum among the rarities and oddities; my life-size portrait was hung next to it.

After supper my lord (that was me) was put into a bed the like of which I had never seen, neither at the hermit's or at home. But there was a roar and a rumble within me all night long so that I could not sleep, perhaps either because my insides did not know yet what was good for them or because they were upset about these newfangled vittles they had taken on. One way or the other, I stayed in bed (for it was cold) until the sun was shining again, and thought over the strange experiences of the last few days and how the good Lord helped me through and led me to such a good place.

CHAPTER 22: *The identity of the hermit whose generosity Simplicius enjoyed*

That same morning the governor's marshal ordered me to go to the preacher and find out what his master had decided about me. A soldier escorted me to the minister, who had me sit down in his study. "Dear Simplex," he said, "the hermit with whom you stayed in the woods is not only the governor's brother-in-law, but has been his dearest friend and protector in the wars.[7] As the governor deigned to tell me, this man never lacked the heroic courage of a soldier or the godliness and reverence of a monk, two virtues rarely found together. His religious sense and the late troubles so marred his worldly happiness that he disdained and gave up his nobility and great estates in Scotland (which was his home), for all worldly business appeared to him stale, vain, and reprehensible. To say it in a few words, he hoped to exchange his present high estate for an even brighter future glory, because his high mind was disgusted with all temporal splendor, and his thoughts and intentions were set on such a plain and pitiful life as you saw in the woods where you kept him company till he died. In my opinion, he was brought to this pass by reading too many popish books about the lives of the ancient hermits, or possibly also by his untoward luck.

"But I do not want to conceal from you how he happened to come to the Spessart Hills to fulfill his wish for a poor hermit's life, so you can tell others about it sometime. The second night after the bloody battle of Höchst [8] had been lost

---

[7] It is doubtful that Simplicius' parents, Captain Sternfels von Fuchshaim and Susanna, nee Ramsay, have historical prototypes.

[8] The battle near Höchst (now an industrial suburb of Frankfurt) took place on June 10, 1622. The imperial general Tilly defeated "Crazy Chris-

he came all alone to my parsonage, toward morning, when my wife and children had just dropped off to sleep. (We had been kept awake all of the previous night and half of this one by the commotion caused by refugees and their pursuers.) First there was a timid knock at the door which got louder until he awakened me and my exhausted servants, and when I opened the door after a short, polite exchange of words, I saw him dismount his steed. His costly dress was as much covered with the blood of his enemies as decorated with gold and silver. And since he was still brandishing his sword I became frightened. But when he put it in the scabbard, and uttered nothing but polite speech, I wondered why such a great gentleman was asking lodging of such a poor parson. Because of his splendid personal appearance, I addressed him as General von Mansfeld, but he answered that only as far as misfortune was concerned could he be compared to him, indeed take precedence over him. He complained of three things, to wit: (1) the loss of his highly pregnant wife; (2) the lost battle; and (3) the fact that, unlike other good soldiers, he had not been favored to give his life for his faith. I wanted to comfort him, but I soon saw that his magnanimity needed no consolation. So I shared with him what was in the house and had a soldier's bed made up of fresh straw, because— though he needed rest badly—he wanted to sleep in no other. The first thing next morning he gave me his horse and his money (of which he had quite a bit with him, in gold) and handed out precious rings among my wife, children, and the servants. I did not know what to make of him and could not adjust to him quickly, for soldiers usually take sooner than give. For that reason I was worried about accepting his precious gifts and insisted I had not deserved such of him, nor knew how to deserve them. Besides, I said, if such riches, and particularly the expensive horse (which could not well be hid-

---

tian," Duke of Braunschweig, who fought for Protestantism in the service of Frederick V, the erstwhile king of Bohemia. According to Bk. I, chap. 22, and Bk. V, chap. 8, some Mansfelders must have been involved in this battle.

den), were found at my place, many people would conclude I
had robbed or even helped to kill him. He said not to worry
about that; he would give me a letter of donation in his own
handwriting; he did not intend to wear his shirt, much less
the clothes on his back, when leaving the parsonage. And
then he acquainted me with his intention of becoming a
hermit. I did my utmost to dissuade him, for it seemed to me
such action smacked of popishness, and reminded him that
he could better serve the Gospel with his sword. But in vain,
for he talked so much and so long with me that he wore me
down, and I furnished him with the books, pictures, and
utensils you saw at his place, though he wanted in return for
everything he had given me, only the wool blanket on which
he had slept during the night. From this he had a cloak made.
I also had to exchange my wagon chain, which he wore from
then on, for a golden one on which he had been wearing his
beloved wife's picture; thus, he kept neither money nor valuables. My hired man took him to the loneliest spot in the
woods and helped him build his hut there. How he spent his
life there and how you helped him, you know yourself, and
better than I.

"When the Battle of Nördlingen was lost a while ago, and
I was stripped clean and robbed of my shirt, as you know I
fled to this place for safety because my most valuable things
were here already. And when my money was about to give
out, I took three rings and the gold chain with the picture on
it that I had received from the hermit (the ring with his
initials was among the lot) and went to a Jew to make them
into money. On account of their high value and good work-
manship, he offered them to the governor, who straightway
recognized the coat of arms and the picture, sent for me,
and asked how I got the jewelry. I told him the truth, showed
him the hermit's letter of donation (in his own hand) and
told him the whole story—how he had lived and died in the
woods. But he refused to believe me, and threatened to arrest
me until he found out the facts. While the governor was preparing to send out soldiers to look at the hermit's place and

to have you brought here, I saw you being led to prison. As the governor no longer has cause to doubt my words, because I referred to the place where the hermit used to live, to you, and to other witnesses, but especially to my sexton, who often let you and him into church before daybreak; and since the note he found in your prayer book gives excellent proof not only of the truth but also of the late hermit's holiness— the governor wants to do you and me as much good as he can, for the sake of his departed brother-in-law, and take good care of us. You have only to make up your mind what you want him to do for you. Do you want to study at a university? He will pay all expenses. Do you want to learn a trade? He'll apprentice you. Do you want to stay with him? He'll treat you like his own son, for he said that if even a dog came straying in from his late brother-in-law's, he'd take care of him too."

I replied that anything the governor wanted to do with me would be a pleasure, and I would be sure to like it.

CHAPTER 23: *Simplicius becomes a page. How the hermit's wife was lost*

The minister had me wait in his lodgings until ten o'clock before going with me to see the governor to tell him of my resolve. The reason was that then he might eat with him, since the governor was very hospitable. For at that time Hanau was surrounded, and the common man had a hard time of it, especially the refugees in the fortress; thus, a few of the better ones did not mind picking up from the streets some frozen turnip peels thrown out by the rich. The parson was lucky enough to get a seat opposite the governor. But I waited for food, plate in hand, as the major-domo told me to; I did it with the gracefulness of a jackass playing chess or a hog performing on the harp. But the preacher made up through his conversation what my own clumsiness jeopardized. He said I had been reared in the wilderness, had never been among people, and must therefore be considered excused because I

was ignorant of how to behave. My loyalty to the hermit and
my endurance of the hard life were admirable, so much so
that not only should my clumsiness be excused, but I should
even be given preference over the finest nobleman's son. He
further told how the hermit had thoroughly enjoyed my company, because—as he had often said—I was the very image of
his dearly beloved's face, and because he had often admired
my perseverance and unswerving intention of staying with
him, and many other virtues he had praised in me. In fine, he
could hardly stress enough how, shortly before his death, the
hermit had warmly commended me to him, the minister, and
how he had confessed he loved me like his own child.

This speech tickled my ears so well that it seemed to me I
had received from it reward and pleasure enough for all I had
ever endured at the hermit's. The governor asked whether his
late brother-in-law hadn't known that he was in command at
Hanau. "Certainly," answered the preacher, "I told him so
myself. But he took it (with a joyous face and a little smile)
as coldly as if he had never known a Ramsay. As I think of
it now, I still have to marvel at the man's constancy and firm
resolve, how he could endure not only renouncing the world,
but even forgetting his best friend, who was so close by!" The
eyes of the governor (who wasn't a bit effeminate, but rather
a tough heroic soldier) filled with tears. He said, "Had I
known he was still alive and where to look for him, I would
have had him brought here even against his will, that I might
repay his good deeds. But since luck was against me, I will
take care of his son Simplicius and thus show him my gratitude after his death." "Alas!" he continued, "the upright man
had good cause to mourn his pregnant wife, for she was captured by a band of imperial cavalry who were in pursuit.
That was in the Spessart Hills too. When I found out about
it, not knowing but that my brother-in-law had been killed
at Höchst, I immediately sent a trumpeter to the enemy to
inquire about my sister and to ransom her. But I found out
only that the group of cavalry had been broken up by peasants in the Spessart, and that my sister had been separated

from them and become lost. To this hour I don't know what
happened to her."

This and similar matters, concerning my hermit and his beloved, a lovely couple lamented all the more as they had been
married but a single year, were the table talk of the governor
and the preacher. But I became the governor's page boy, and
such a fellow as the people (especially the peasants, when they
wanted me to announce them) called Master Young, though
one seldom sees a young one who is a master (but many masters that used to be young ones).

CHAPTER 24: *Simplicius reproaches people; he sees many
idols in this world*

At that time, you could find in me nothing but a clear
conscience and a pious, upright mind, and this was accompanied and enhanced by noble innocence and simplicity. I
knew no more of vices than what I had heard or read about
them, and if I ran into one it seemed an awful and strange
thing to me, because I had been brought up to have God's
presence always in mind and to live seriously according to
his holy will; and because I knew his will, I was accustomed
to weigh men's actions and character against it. In doing this,
I thought I saw about me only vain corruption. My God! At
first, how surprised I was when I considered the law and the
gospel together with Christ's faithful warnings and—on the
other hand—the works of those who claimed to be his dis-
ciples and followers. Instead of an upright mind which every
righteous Christian ought to have, I found among the car-
nal-minded children of the world such hypocrisy and egregious foolishness that I was in doubt whether I saw Christians
or not. For I could easily notice that many knew the serious
will of God, but I noticed no seriousness in performing it.

Therefore, my mind was full of a thousand different whim-
sies and strange thoughts, and I fell into serious doubt concerning Christ's commandment that says, "Judge not, lest ye

be judged!" Nevertheless, the words of St. Paul, which he wrote to the Galatians, chapter five, entered my mind: "Now the works of the flesh are manifest, which are *these:* adultery, fornication, uncleanness, lasciviousness, idolatry, sorcery, enmities, strife, jealousies, wraths, factions, divisions, hatred, murder, drunkenness, revelings, and such like, of which I forewarn you, even as I did forewarn you, that they who practice such things shall not inherit the kingdom of God." Then I thought, almost everyone is doing these things openly; why can't I honestly conclude from the apostle's words that neither will everyone be saved?

Besides pride and avarice (and related vices), the wealthy indulged daily in gluttony and drunkenness, fornication and buggery. But what appeared worst to me was this abomination, that some, especially soldier boys (whose vices are usually not too severely punished), made a joke of their godlessness and God's holy will. For example, I once heard an adulterer who wanted to be praised for his deed say these ungodly words, "It serves that patient cuckold right to be wearing a pair of horns because of me, and, to tell the truth, I did it more to hurt him than to please her, that I might have my revenge on him." "Oh, barren satisfaction!" answered an honest fellow who heard it, "whereby one pollutes one's own conscience and acquires the shameful name of an adulterer!" "How so 'adulterer'?" was the sneering answer. "I did not break his marriage, I only bent it a little. The real adulterers are those of whom the sixth commandment speaks, where it says that nobody should climb into another's garden to reap the cherries before the rightful owner gets to them!" And to make his meaning clearer he explained the seventh commandment according to his diabolic catechism. He was so full of such explanations that I sighed and thought, Oh, cursed sinner, you call yourself a bender of marriages, and God a breaker of marriages because he separates man and wife through death! "Don't you think," I said from excessive zeal and chagrin, though he was an officer, "that you commit a greater sin by such godless talk than by adultery itself?" But he answered me, "Shut up, smarty, do you want to get hit?"

And I have no doubt I would have gotten a good-sized thrashing if the fellow hadn't been afraid of my master. But I kept silent, and later saw it wasn't at all unusual for single folks to hanker for married ones, and married folks to lust after single ones.

When I was still studying the way to salvation at the hermit's, I wondered why God had so strictly forbidden idolatry to his people. For I imagined that whoever had come to know the true, eternal God would never honor and adore another. In my simple mind I concluded that this commandment was unnecessary and superfluous. But alas, fool that I was, I knew not what I was thinking, for as soon as I came into the world I noticed that, regardless of this commandment, almost every worldling had a god besides God. Some even had more than all the ancient or modern heathens. Some had their god in a strongbox and found all their assurance and consolation in him; others had theirs at court, having put all their trust in a court favorite who often was a more despicable dullard than his worshiper, for his airy godhead consisted only in the prince's flibbertigibbet favor. Others had their idol in reputation and worldly glory, and imagined themselves demigods if only they had fame. Still others had theirs in their head—namely, those to whom the true God had given a healthy brain, making them clever in a few arts and sciences. These put the kind Creator on a shelf, and relied on this endowment in hopes of worldly welfare. Also, there were many whose god was their own belly, to which they daily delivered those sacrifices the heathens long ago offered to Bacchus and Ceres; and when the belly rebelled or other human frailty appeared, these deplorable ones made a god of their physician and took lodging, as it were, in a pharmacy, from which they were dispatched straight to the grave. Some fools made she-gods of slick wenches; they called them by different names, worshiped them day and night with a thousand sighs, and made songs praising them and humbly requesting that they take pity on their foolishness, and become she-fools even as they were he-fools.

On the other hand, there were wenches who had set up their beauty as a god. This one, they thought, will take care of me, let God in heaven say what he will. In lieu of other sacrifice, this idol was daily entertained and adored with grease paint, jellies, lotions, powders, and other toiletries. I saw people who considered houses in good locations their gods, for they said that, as long as they had lived there, they had had good luck, and money had, as it were, grown on the trees in the back yard. I marveled at this, for I saw the reason for their prosperity. I knew a fellow who never got a good night's rest worrying over his tobacco trade, for he had given it his heart, mind, and thoughts, which should be dedicated to God alone; by day and night he sighed a thousand times, for he was doing well by it. But what happened? This splenetic fellow died and was carried off just like tobacco smoke. Then I thought, Oh, you miserable man! If the salvation of your soul and God's honor had been of the same importance to you as your idol (who is pictured on your shop sign as a Brazilian with a roll of tobacco under his arm and a pipe in his filthy mouth), I would be very confident you'd be wearing a golden halo in the other world. Another fellow, named Jack Ass, I was told, had even more sleazy gods, for when it was told that he had not only survived but even got rich in time of famine and high prices, Jack said in so many plain words that snails and frogs had been his god. Without them he would have died. I asked him what he had thought of God himself, who at that time had provided him with these creatures for his survival? The simpleton didn't know what to answer, and I had to marvel all the more for nowhere had I read that either the old heathen Egyptians or the most recent Americans had ever proclaimed such vermin their god, as this fop did.

Once I visited a museum full of oddities. Among the paintings, I liked nothing better than an "Ecce Homo," on account of the sad expression that evoked such compassion in the beholder. Next to it hung a large sheet of paper painted in China, with the Chinese idols sitting there in all their majesty. Some looked like the very devil. The landlord asked me which piece in his museum I liked best. I pointed to the "Ecce Homo." But he said I was wrong; the Chinese picture was much rarer and hence more precious; he wouldn't give it up for ten such "Ecce Homo's." I replied, "Sir, is your heart like your mouth?" He said, "I try to have them agree." Then I said, "So the god of your heart is the one whose portrait you just now let your mouth declare to be the most precious thing." "Silly," he said, "I am talking about supply and demand!" I answered, "What is rarer and more admirable than that God's son suffered for us, as this picture portrays it?"

CHAPTER 25: *Everything on earth appears strange to Simplicius, and he seems strange to the world, too*

As much as these and other idols were honored, the majesty of our true God was held in contempt; though I saw no one who cared to keep his commandments, I saw on the other hand many who rebelled against him and outdid the publicans (who were open sinners in the days when Christ walked on earth) in meanness. Christ says, "Love your enemies; bless those that curse you; do good unto those that hate you; pray for those who insult and persecute you." But I found no one who obeyed these orders of Christ; on the contrary, they did exactly the opposite. One time I saw a soldier give another a good blow on the cheek, and imagined that now he would turn the other cheek. (I had never seen a fight before.) But I was mistaken. The victim whisked out his blade and cut the attacker on the head. I shouted at him, "Friend, what are you doing?" "I'd be an s. o. b.," he answered. "I'll get even, goddammit, or I'll croak. Only a bastard would take that lying down!" The noise between the two fighting cocks increased because each one's friends were fighting too. I heard them swear by God and their souls with such nonchalance that I couldn't believe they valued either above a penny. But that was only child's play. Pretty soon someone shouted, "May lightning strike me dead! Let hail and thunder strike me and a hundred thousand others!" The holy sacraments were poured out not by tens and scores but by thousands, by buckets, and barrelfuls and in whole rivers, and again my hair stood on end. I wondered what had become of Christ's commandment in which he says, "Do not swear, rather let your speech be, 'Yea, yea, nay, nay,' and whatsoever is more than these is of the evil one." What I had heard and seen prompted me to decide that these fighting cocks were not Christians, and I sought other company.

I wished everyone had been brought up and taught by my hermit. In my opinion, others would then have seen the ways of the world with the eyes through which I saw it. I was not so smart as to say that if there were only Simpliciuses in the world, there would be fewer vices; but one thing is sure, a Mr. Worldly who is used and inured to every vice and folly can least sense that he and his ilk are treading the primrose path to perdition.

CHAPTER 26: *An amazing new custom of welcoming people and wishing them good luck*

Being in serious doubt whether or not I was living among Christians, I went to my parson and told him all I had heard and seen, also my thoughts—namely, that I suspected people were only mocking Christ and his word, and that they were really non-Christians. I asked him to help me come out of this dream, that I might really know what to think of my fellow men. The parson answered, "Certainly they are Christians, and I wouldn't advise you to call them anything else." "My God," I said, "how can this be? If I remind someone of the sin he is committing against God, I am laughed at and made fun of." "Do not be surprised at that," answered the parson.

"I think if the early Christians, even the apostles themselves, were to rise and come back into this world, they would ask the same question as you, and everybody would consider them fools too. What you have seen and heard so far is common knowledge and only child's play in comparison with what else is being committed against God in this world, either secretly or publicly. But do not let it trouble you. You will find few such Christians as the late Mr. Samuel was."

While we were talking, some captured enemy soldiers were led across the square, and we interrupted our conversation to go and see the prisoners of war. Then I saw a crazy custom the like of which I never could have dreamed up. This was the new fashion of greeting and welcoming. One of our men knew one of the prisoners, who had previously served in this army and was now on the emperor's side. He went to him, shook hands with him, and shouted, full of joy and confidence, "Well, well, let lightning strike me! You still alive, old soak? Holy mackerel! How in hell did you get here!? I thought you had been rotting on the gallows since last year!" Then the other fellow would answer. "By God's potsticks, old soak, is it you or not? How in hell did *you* get here?! I never thought I'd see *you* again. Hasn't the devil taken you off yet?" And when they left, instead of "God be with you," they said, "Hell's bells, maybe we'll get together tomorrow and get good and drunk, and have a great time."

"Is that a Christian welcome?" I said to the parson. "If this is the way they speak to each other when they are friends, what will they say when they become enemies? Sir Parson, if these are Christ's sheep and you are their appointed shepherd, it is your job to lead them to better pastures." "Yes," replied the minister, "that's the way these soldier-boys are. May God have mercy on them. If I preached to them, it would do as much good as preaching to the birds—and what's more, these fellows would hate me."

I was astonished by this, kept on chatting a while longer, and finally left to call on the governor. At this time I had

permission to look at the city and to visit the minister, for
my master knew of my simple-mindedness and thought I'd
overcome it if I got around a little and was instructed by
others or, as they say, was cut down to size and polished up
a little.   `

CHAPTER 27: *A powerful stench stinks up the secretary's office*

My master's favor toward me kept increasing daily, for I
resembled not only his sister (who had been the hermit's wife)
but also the hermit himself; indeed, the resemblance improved the more our good food and lazy days made me sleek
and pleasant to look at. This favor was extended by others as
well, for whoever had something to do with the governor
showed favor toward me. This was especially true of the governor's secretary, who was supposed to teach me arithmetic
and who had a lot of fun with my ignorance and simplicity.

He had only recently graduated, and was still full of students' jokes and pranks, for which he had been famous at
school. (Some thought he had bats in the belfry.) He often
persuaded me that black was white, and white, black; that's
why at first I believed everything he said, and in the end,
nothing. Once when I reproached him for his dirty inkwell
he answered that was the best thing in the whole office, for he
could get out of it whatever he wanted—clothes or money; in
fact, he had fished a good many other things out of it. I did
not want to believe that such bulky and valuable goods could
come out of such a tiny glass. But he asserted the *spiritus
papyri* (that's what he called the ink) could do just that, and
the inkwell was called a "well" because it was deep enough to
hold everything. I asked how one could get them out, since
the well wasn't wide enough to stick in two fingers at the
same time. He replied he had an arm in his head that could
do it, and he had hopes of fishing out some rich and beautiful
girl; he was confident that if his luck held he could get real-

estate and servants out of it too. And this was nothing new; it had all been done before.

I was dumbfounded at this trick and wondered if other people knew how to do it, or might learn. "Sure," he answered, "all doctors, secretaries, managers, lawyers, commissioners, notaries, merchants, and innumerable others who commonly become rich if they fish diligently and look out for Number One." I said, "So the peasants and other hardworking people are stupid not to learn this trick instead of eating their bread in the sweat of their faces." He answered, "Some don't know how much good this trick can do, and therefore don't want to learn it. Others want to learn it, but don't have the arm in the head or something else they need. Some learn the trick, have the arm, but don't know certain little catches or gimmicks the trick requires if you want to get rich. Others know everything and can do everything they need, but they live on Failure Street and haven't the same chances I have to practice the trick."

While we were discussing the inkwell, a book on epistolary titles and salutations happened to strike my fancy. I said to the secretary, "All these people addressed are sons of Adam, all are dust and ashes! Why the big difference in salutation? Your Lordship, your Holiness, your Worship, your Grace, your Invincible Highness, your Majesty. Are these divine characters? And why 'Esquire'?" The secretary had to laugh as he explained these things to me, and while I was laughing about so much foolishness I couldn't help letting out such a fiendish fart that it startled both of us.

The smell spread through the office in no time. "Get out, you swine!" the secretary said to me. "Go to the other hogs in the pigsty, where you belong, instead of carrying on a conversation with educated people!" But he was forced to clear out, just as I was; the horrible stink was unbearable. That's how I messed up the good beginnings of a promising business training in the secretary's office.

CHAPTER 28: *Someone full of envy teaches Simplicius soothsaying and other gentle tricks*

I had gotten into this trouble through no fault of my own, for the unusual food and medicines I had to swallow every day, to straighten out my shrunk stomach and innards, raised many powerful storms inside me, and they bothered me when they urgently sought an exit. And since I did not think it at all bad to let nature take her course (it was impossible to resist her at length, my hermit had never instructed me in this matter, nor had my knan forbidden it), I let the wind pass—until the day I lost face with the secretary. Now, perhaps I might have done without his sympathy if I had not gone from bad to worse, for I fared like a pious, good man who comes to court, a place where Goliath tried to undo David; Minotaur, Theseus; Circe, Ulysses; *et al., et al.*

My master had another page, a smart aleck and sharp cookie, who had been there several years longer than I. Well, I chummed with him because we were of the same age. I thought, He is Jonathan and you are David. But he was jealous of my master's favor toward me, which grew daily. He worried that I might want to harm him; and therefore he thought secretly of ways to discredit me and through my fall prevent his own. But I, with the gentleness of a dove, confided all my secrets to him, and because these consisted only of childish simplicity and piousness, he could never get at me.

Once, in bed, we talked a long time before falling asleep and while we were talking about soothsaying he promised to teach it to me for nothing. He asked me to stick my head under the covers, this being part of the game. I did so eagerly, and watched closely for the arrival of the spirit of prophecy. Holy cow! It went in at my nose and with such concentration that I couldn't possibly stay under for the stench. "What is it?" asked my teacher. I answered, "You farted!" "And you," he replied, "are saying sooth and have caught on beautifully."

I did not think this was too bad, for at the time I was still too naïve to take offense. I only wanted to know how to let out quiet ones. My fellow page answered, "There's nothing to it. Just raise your left leg like a dog at the corner, whisper *je pète, je pète, je pète,* and push as hard as you can. Then when these travelers come out, they do so as quietly as thieves." "That's good," I said, "and even if there should be a slight smell, everyone will think it was one of the dogs." If I had only known about this in the office earlier today!

CHAPTER 29: *Simplicius picks up two eyes from a calf's head*

The other day my master gave a sumptuous party for his officers and other good friends. The occasion was the news that his men had taken Fort Braunfels without losing a single soldier. Like the other pages, my job was to help serve at the table, pour wine, and pass the food on a platter. First, I had to carry in a juicy calf's head. As it was well boiled, one eye hung out rather loosely; it looked pleasant and tempting to me. And because the smell of the broth and the ginger dressing made my mouth water, I suddenly felt an irresistible appetite. The calf's eye was smiling at my nose, my mouth, and my eyes, and almost begged me to incorporate it into my hungry stomach. I didn't break a leg fighting back, but, yielding to my desire, in the passageway I lifted out the eye with a spoon and swallowed it quickly. Nobody noticed until the calf's head reached the table and betrayed itself and me. When it was about to be carved up and one of its most delicate parts was missing, my master saw at once why the man with the knife hesitated. The cook was called in, and the runners were questioned closely. Finally it came out that I, poor fellow, had been given the whole head and that's as far as anyone could report.

With a frightful expression, as it seemed, my master asked me what I had done with the one eye. I didn't let him scare me, but whipped out the spoon and in a flash demonstrated with the other eye what they wanted to know. *"Par Dieu!"* said my master, "this trick tastes better than ten calves." The gentlemen present praised this bon mot and called my silly action a bright invention, a harbinger of future bravery and unflagging zeal. But the governor warned me not to try anything like that again.

CHAPTER 30: *How a person gets tipsy little by little, and how in the end he becomes plastered without being aware of it*

At this banquet, as at many others, people came to the table like Christians; they spoke a prayer quietly and reverently. During the soup and the first few courses, such reverence continued almost as if one sat in a Capuchin refectory. But hardly had they said, "God bless you," and, "To your health!" when more noise began. I can't describe how everyone's voice became louder as time passed. Perhaps the company could be compared to an orator who starts softly and ends like rolling thunder. There were foods called *hors d'oeuvres* to be eaten before the drink; they were well seasoned and salty, to make the wine go down more easily. Who knows but that Circe used these same foods when she changed Ulysses' companions into swine? I observed how the guests ate the courses like pigs, then drank like cows, acted like jackasses, and puked like dogs. They poured good wine like hock, Bacharach and Liebfraumilch down by the bucketful, and soon the effect in their brains became apparent.

I did not know where their unsteadiness came from, for I had never heard of drunkenness. I saw their strange movements, but did not know the cause of this condition. At first the glasses were easily emptied, but the job became harder as time passed and stomachs filled. I didn't know yet that they regurgitated in order to make room for more of the same. My parson was also present; since he was human, he had to step out, and I followed him. "Sir Parson," I asked, "why do these people act so strangely? Why do they walk unsteadily, as if they have lost their wits? They all have eaten and drunk their fill, and yet they are swearing by hell and damnation they want to drink more. Do they have to do this? Don't their bellies burst? Can they be in God's image and act like swilling swine?" "Shut up!" said the parson. "This is neither the time nor the place to preach. If it were, I'd do it better than you." Hearing this, I looked on silently as food and drink were wasted, while several hundred refugees, who had nothing in their larders, were starving at our doorstep.

CHAPTER 31: *How Simplicius fails in art and is beaten black and blue*

While I was thus waiting at table, platter in hand and mind full of thoughts and notions, my stomach informed me that there were winds demanding passage. Following instructions of the night before, I raised my left leg, put on the pressure, and would have mumbled the magic words *je pète*. But a tremendous, rumbling tornado passed out, and I was so embarrassed I felt like a condemned man, rope around his neck, on the way up the ladder to the gallows. I lost control of my muscles, and my mouth (unwilling to be outdone by the behind) started competing with it in noise. The worse the wind broke below, the louder came out the *je pète* above —as if the entrance and the exit were conducting a contest in decibels. This brought me a lot of inner relief, but it also incurred my master's disfavor.

Almost all of the governor's guests sobered up from the startling sounds of my mortars, trumpets, and bombs, and their reverberating echo. For my failure to control the winds, I received such a good licking that I can feel it to this day.

CHAPTER 32: *More on swilling, and how ministers are to be
kept away from it*

When the storm was over I had to resume serving at table.
My parson was still there and, like the others, was asked to
drink some more. But his mind wasn't on it, and he said he
didn't want to drink like a hog anymore. Then one of the
worst topers proved to him that the parson was drinking like
an animal, but he (the toper) and his pals, like men. Animals,
he said, drink only as much as they like, enough to quench
their thirst; they don't know what's good, and don't like wine.
But we humans know how to make use of liquor, and we let
the good wine infuse us, as our forefathers did. "All right,"
said the parson, "but it is also human to show moderation."
"Right you are," answered the toper, and had a glass filled
moderately full. "An honest fellow sticks to his word. Now
drink up!" But the parson fled, leaving the toper with his
bucketful.

After the parson left, things went from bad to worse. When
one was so full that he could not sit or walk or stand, the
others shouted, "We're even! You done me this way before,
now it's your turn!" and so on. Those who could last the
longest and drink the most boasted and considered themselves
to be great men. In the end, they were all reeling as though
under a spell. True, something strange had happened to
them, and yet no one was wondering about it except me. One
man sang, another cried; one laughed, another was sad; one
swore, one prayed; one hollered, "Courage!"; another couldn't
talk; one was peaceful and quiet, another wanted to fight the
devil; one slept, another chatted and would let no one else
get a word in. One told of his amorous exploits, another
spoke of warlike deeds. Some talked of church and theology;
others, of politics and world affairs. Some of them were restless
as quicksilver; others lay like lead and could not lift a finger,
let alone stand upright. Their actions were so droll, foolish,

strange, and sinful, and ungodly, too, that the bad smell I
produced, and for which I had been beaten, was a joke in
comparison. Toward the end serious fighting broke out; they
were throwing glasses, tumblers, plates, and dishes, using their
fists, chairs and chair legs, swords, and other handy objects to
strike at each other, and a few were wounded. But my master
soon quelled the riot.

CHAPTER 33: *How his honor the governor shot a horrible fox*

When peace had been restored, the master topers, together
with musicians and ladies, promenaded into another building whose hall had been selected for and dedicated to another
foolishness. My master reclined on a lounge, for he wasn't feeling well, because he was too full or too angry. I was about to
leave the room to let him rest and sleep, but when I reached
the door, he tried to whistle for me and couldn't do it. He
called, and it came out "Simpls!" I ran to him and found him
with eyes rolling like a stuck hog. I stood there like a smoked
fish, not knowing what to do. He pointed to a washstand and
stammered, "Br, bra, bring me the . . . you louse, pass the
basin. I have to. . . ." When I got back, he had cheeks like a
trumpeter. He grabbed me by the arm and maneuvered me in
such a way that the basin was right in front of him. His
mouth burst open and let such a mess escape into the basin
that I almost fainted from the smell, especially as my face got
splattered. I would have joined him, but when I saw how
pale he turned, I gave up that idea for fear he might die; for
he broke out in a cold sweat, which made his face look like a
dying man's. When he recovered, he asked me to bring him
some water to wash out his wineskin.

CHAPTER 34: *How Simplicius spoiled the dance*

I followed the governor into a large house where I saw men
and women, married and unmarried, moving so quickly and

confusedly that my head swam. They were so lively and
shouted so loudly that I thought they had all gone stark mad;
I simply couldn't imagine what they meant by this raving and
raging. When I came closer I saw that they were our guests
who had been quite rational in the forenoon. My God, I
thought, some madness must have come over them. Now I
thought it might be spirits of hell mocking the human race
in this pretentious manner, with monkey movements and foolish runs. Would human souls and the images of God act so
inhuman?

When my master came on the floor, the music just stopped,
but there was more ducking, swashbuckling, and scraping of
feet as if they wanted to erase the tracks made in their rage.
By the sweat running down their faces and the huffing and
puffing, I could see they had been working hard; but the joy
in their faces showed they hadn't minded in the least.

I wanted to know what it was all about, and asked my comrade and fellow page, who had taught me how to soothsay a
few days ago. He told me (for honest truth) that those present
had agreed among each other to break down the floor of the
hall. "Why else would they carry on so? Didn't you see how
they broke the windows awhile ago? It will be the same with
the floor," he said. "My God!" I replied, "we'll fall down in
the cellar and break our necks." "Yes," said my friend, "that's
what they intend to do and they don't give a damn. You will
see that each man who exposes himself to this danger will
grab a pretty girl. They say that couples who cling to each
other don't get hurt when they fall." Since I believed all I
heard, I was greatly frightened, and when the music started
again and the boys ran toward the girls, as soldiers do to their
guns at the sound of the alarm, I already felt the floor giving
way, and every bone in my body breaking. But when the
music played the latest tune and everyone started jumping I
thought, This is the end. Now, Simplex, you have been a man
for the last time. I thought the whole structure would col-
lapse momentarily, and in my fright I grabbed a lady of the
highest nobility and most excellent reputation, who was just
conversing with a gentleman. I held her by one arm like a

bear, and hung on like a burr. When she drew back, not knowing what sort of fool notions filled my head, I went berserk and started screaming as if they were about to kill me. But that's not all. By chance I also soiled my underwear, and the smell was terrific. The musicians suddenly broke off, dancers and their partners stopped, and the good lady to whose arm I clung felt insulted; she thought my master had ordered me to do all this to offend her. The governor gave orders to administer another licking and lock me up, because I had been up to more mischief that day. The soldiers given the order not only felt sorry for me, but didn't want to stay with me because of the smell. They dispensed with the beating and locked me in a goose-pen under a stairway.

End of the First Book

✐ Book Two

CHAPTER 1: *How a goose and a gander copulated*

In my goose-pen, I formulated those thoughts about dancing and swilling which I have already laid down in the first
part of my book called *Black and White;*[1] therefore to report
further on them here is not necessary. Still, I can't deny that
at that time I was in doubt whether the dancers were really
raging so furiously in order to break down the floor, or
whether I had only been fooled into thinking so.

Now I want to tell how I got out of the goose jail. I had
to sit and stew in my own juice for a full three hours—that is,
until the honorable dance was over—before someone sneaked
up and rattled the latch. I listened as hard as a hog that's
peeing in a puddle, but not only did the fellow open the gate,
he even slipped in as gladly as I would have slipped out. In
addition, he dragged a girl in by the hand, just as I had done
at the dance. I did not know what he was up to, but since I
had run into various adventures on this foolish day and was
getting used to them, so to speak, I decided to await with
patience and in silence what fate would send my way. Expecting the worst, I slunk toward the door.

Now between the two intruders there arose a whispered
conversation, of which I could make out only that one party
was complaining about the rank odor of the place (but it
was mainly my trousers). The other party was trying, in turn,
to comfort the first. "Fair lady," he said, "I regret with all
my heart that an unhappy fate will not grant us the use of a

[1] The author here creates the misleading impression that he and the
character of Simplicius are identical. Grimmelshausen's *Satyrical Pilgrim
or Black and White* had appeared in Leipzig in 1667.

suitable locality wherein to enjoy the fruits of our love. However, I can assure you that your gracious presence makes this despicable corner more lovely than the most pleasant nook of paradise itself." At this juncture I heard kisses and noticed strange postures, the meaning of which I did not know. So I kept quiet as a mouse. When a remarkable noise arose, and the goose-pen (which was only knocked together from some boards, under a stairway) gave off a rhythmical racket, and the wench moaned as if she were being hurt, I thought, These are two more of those raging lovers who helped to destroy the floor, and who have come here now to do the same and to kill you. As soon as these thoughts poured into my head, I rushed over to the door, to escape destruction. I raced out screaming, exactly as I had screamed before I got in, but I had enough sense to bolt the door behind me and to dash out of the wide-open front door.

Well, this was the first time in my life that I attended a wedding, though I had not been invited. But then, I didn't have to give a present either, though the bridegroom later added up quite a bill for me, and I had to pay every penny of it.

Gentle reader, I'm not telling this story only for laughs, but to make the tale complete and to show you what dancing can lead to. This much is sure: at dances some bad, feather-brained bargains are made, of which, later on, the whole family has to be ashamed.

CHAPTER 2: *When it's a good time to take a bath*

Though I luckily escaped the goose-pen, I still was very much aware of my misfortune, for I didn't know what to do about my trousers. In my master's quarters everyone was asleep and I didn't dare approach the guard on duty before the house; in the guardhouse they wanted none of me because of my aroma; it was too cold to stay in the street—and

so I didn't know what to do. Long after midnight, it occurred
to me to take refuge once more with my parson friend. I was
rash enough to knock at the door until the maid let me in,
but she didn't like it. When she smelled me (her long nose
picked up my secret at once), she became still angrier. She
started making a scene and her master, who had almost finished sleeping, heard it. He called the two of us to his bed,
almost as if he wanted a good noseful too. As soon as he
noticed the trouble, and had twitched his nose at me a little,
he said this was an excellent time for bathing, never mind
what the calendar said. He ordered the maid—or rather,
gently begged her—to wash my trousers and hang them up
in front of the stove, before daybreak. I was to go to bed, for
he saw I was practically stiff with cold.

I had hardly warmed up a little when dawn broke, and the
parson came to my bed to hear how I had been doing and
how my affairs were coming along. (On account of my wet
trousers and underwear I couldn't go to him.) I told him
everything, starting with the trick my friend had taught me
and how *that* had turned out. Then I reported that the guests
had gone stark mad after he, the minister, had left, and how
they had tried to break down the floor of the house, and how
I had become frightened; how I had wanted to escape annihi-
lation and had been locked in the goose-pen; what words and
works I had noticed in the two who had let me out; and how
I had locked them in instead of me. "Simplici," said the parson, "your situation is rotten. You had a good thing, but I'm
afraid it's all off! Hurry, get up and out of the house, or I too
will incur your master's anger when they find you here." So,
in my damp clothes, I had to move on, and for the first time
I found out how fortunate is a person who has his master's
favor, and how people look the other way when your favor
starts limping or you lose it.

I went to my master's quarters. Everyone was dead asleep
except the cook and a couple of maids. They were cleaning
the rooms used yesterday for drinking, and the cook was
fixing a breakfast—more a snack—from the leftovers. I went

to the maids who were working among broken glass and big puddles of spilled and vomited wine and beer. The floor looked like one of those maps picturing various oceans, islands, and continents. The room smelled much worse than the goose-pen, and I didn't stay long. In the kitchen, while I dried my clothes before the fire, I awaited with fear and trembling what fate might have in store for me when my master finished sleeping. I also pondered the foolishness and senselessness of the world and thought about everything that had happened to me during the last day and night, and what I had seen, heard, and experienced elsewhere. Such thoughts caused me to consider as happy the poor and miserable life my hermit had led, and to wish that he and I might be back in our old place.

CHAPTER 3: *The other page gets his comeuppance, and Simplicius is chosen to become a fool*

When my master arose, he sent his orderly to fetch me out of the goose-pen. The fellow brought him the news that he had found the door open and a hole behind the latch cut with a knife, and that the prisoner had sprung himself. But before the news reached him, my master heard from others that I had recently been seen in the kitchen.

Meanwhile, the servants had to run to and fro fetching yesterday's guests for breakfast. Among these, of course, was the minister, who had to come earlier than the others because my master wanted to discuss me with him before they sat down to eat. First of all he asked the minister if he thought I was smart or foolish, simple-minded or mischievous. He told him how scandalously I had behaved the previous day, before table as well as at the dance; how many of the guests (who thought it had been arranged to mock them) had resented this; how he had me locked in the goose-pen to prevent further mischief; how I had escaped and was now parading in the kitchen like a young squire no longer required to wait on him. In all his born days he had never seen the like of such disrespect—and that in front of so many good and honorable people. All he could think of was having me flogged and sending me clear to hell, because I was just too stupid.

While he was still busy complaining, the guests arrived one after another; and when the governor had finished, the parson answered that, given the chance, he might tell many a lively story about me, not only to prove my innocence, but also to calm the angry mood of those disgusted by my behavior. This was accepted, provided he told his stories at table, so that all the company might hear and enjoy them.

While they were talking about me upstairs, the mad ensign whom I had penned up in place of myself drove a bargain with me downstairs in the kitchen. By threats and a thaler which he secretly slipped in my pocket, he got me to promise to keep my mouth shut about his doings.

The table was set and the guests sat down as they had the day before. Various concoctions of wine with vermouth, sage, empecampane, quince, and lemons, as well as a cordial called "hippocras," were on hand to clear up the heads and smooth out the stomachs of the topers, for all of them were martyrs of the devil. Their first topic of conversation was themselves—how they had managed to get each other drunk yesterday. And yet, not one wanted to admit that he had been really pickled, though the night before they had sworn by all hell they couldn't drink another drop. A few admitted they had been a bit elevated; others asserted that nobody got *drunk* any more since getting *high* had been invented. When they tired of being told or telling their own folly, poor Simplicius was made to suffer. The governor himself reminded the parson to begin the stories he had promised.

First he begged their pardon for having to use a few words that might not be exactly becoming to him as a man of the cloth. Then he told about the natural causes of the winds bothering me; about the mishap I had had in the secretary's office; and about the trick I had learned for controlling the wind—along with soothsaying—and how badly I had fared trying it out. Next he told how outlandish the dance had appeared to me, since I had never before seen one; what my friend had told me about it; why I had grabbed the aristo-cratic lady and had been goose-penned for it.

He told all this in such a pleasant and humorous way that the company couldn't help laughing heartily. Thus he man-aged to make excuses for my ignorance and simplicity in such a modest way that I regained my master's graces and was again permitted to wait on table. But the parson did not want to mention my experiences inside the goose-pen and how I escaped from it, because he was afraid some saturnine old sourpusses would take offense, thinking a minister must al-ways wear a long face. Instead, to amuse his guests, my master asked me what I had given my friend for teaching me such useful tricks. When I answered, "Nothing," he said, "I'll pay him for you." He was given the same licking I got the day before.

My master had now heard enough of my foolishness. He asked me why I had cut the door open and escaped from the pen. I replied that perhaps someone else had done the cutting. "Who?" he asked. "Maybe the one who came inside." "Who came in?" "I dasn't tell anybody." But the governor saw at once how to fool me, and asked who had forbidden me to tell. Without hesitation I answered, "The mad ensign." The laugh that went up told me that I must have pulled a boner. The ensign, who was there at the table, blushed like a red-hot coal, and I said I wouldn't speak another word unless I first got permission from him. My master motioned the en-sign to grant permission, and I was free to tell what I knew. Then the governor asked me what the crazy ensign had been up to in the goose-pen. I answered, "He brought a girl with him." "What then?" said my master. I answered, "I thought he wanted to make water." My master asked, "What about the girl? Wasn't she ashamed?" "Heavens no, sir," I replied. "She raised her skirts as if to keep him company by (may the gentle, honorable, virtuous reader pardon my impolite pen for writing down so coarsely what I said then) shitting." At this point such laughter arose among all the people present that my master could no longer hear me, let alone ask me any more questions. It wasn't necessary, either, unless they had wanted to drag the "good" girl through the mud too.

Then the major-domo said that recently I had come in from the ramparts and told him I knew where thunder and lightning came from. I had seen big hollow tree trunks on half a wagon each. They were filled with onion seed and an iron turnip with the tail cut off. When the trunks were tickled a little with a jagged stick, smoke, thunder, and hellfire came out. There were more stories of this kind, and it seemed that the conversation and laughter throughout the whole breakfast was about me. They finally decided to keep me well befuddled and in time I'd make a capital jester, one who could be given to the world's mightiest sovereign and who would make even the moribund smile.

CHAPTER 4: *About the man who provides the money, the military service that Simplicius rendered to the Crown of Sweden, and how he received the name "Simplicissimus"*

While they were all having a good time and were about to continue yesterday's celebration, a guardsman handed a letter to the governor and announced that a commissioner, sent by the Swedish war council to inspect the garrison and look over the fortress, was at the gate. This spoiled all the fun, and the diners' enjoyment collapsed like a bagpipe when the air escapes. Musicians and guests dispersed like clouds of tobacco smoke that leave only a faint smell behind. My master, with his adjutant (who carried the keys) and a committee of officers (carrying lights), trundled toward the gate to let in the so-and-so of an inspector. My master wished Old Nick would break the visitor's neck in a thousand pieces before he ever entered the fortress! But when he let the commissioner in, welcoming him at the inner drawbridge, he almost held his stirrup to show his sincere devotion. In fact, the respect mutually displayed soon grew so monstrous that the inspector dismounted and walked to his lodgings. Each of them wanted to show his politeness by getting on the left side of the other, etc. Alas, I wondered, what is this strangely false spirit that rules men by making a fool of either one through the folly of the other?

As we approached the main guard, the sentry shouted, "Who goes there?"—though he saw it was the governor. He didn't answer because he wished to allow the commissioner the honor of replying. So the sentry shouted a second time, twice as loud. Then the inspector answered, "The man who pays you!" As we passed, I, being one of the last ones, heard the sentry (who was a green recruit, a well-to-do young farmer from the Vogelsberg) mutter these words, "I'll bet you are a liar. 'Man who pays!' A filcher and a robber who grabs my money, that's what you are. You've stolen so much money from me, I wish lightning would strike you dead before you leave this town."

At this point, I got the notion that our gentleman in the velvet jacket must be a holy man, not only because curses did not harm him, but also because even the people who hated him showed him honor, love, and respect. That same night he was entertained like a prince, made blind with drink, and put into a magnificent bed.

The inspection on the following day was a crazy affair. Even I, so simple-minded, was smart enough to hoodwink and outwit our smart inspector (and for this sort of job they don't usually employ innocent children). I was too small to pass for a musketeer, so I took about an hour to become a drummer boy. They gave me a borrowed uniform (my page-boy pantaloons would not do for this) and a borrowed drum—probably because I was borrowed myself!—and that is how I passed the inspection. But since they didn't think I could remember an assumed name to which I could answer at roll call, I kept "Simplicius." To this the governor himself added the family name and had me mustered in as "Simplicius Simplicissimus."

He made me the first of my family, like a harlot's child, though in his own opinion I greatly resembled his sister. I later kept this name—until I found out the correct one—and under it I played my role quite well, doing a considerable favor to the governor and only slight harm to the Crown of Sweden. And that's all the military service I ever rendered the Crown, and its enemies have no cause to hate me for it.

CHAPTER 5: *Simplicius is taken to hell by four devils and treated to Spanish wine*

When the commissioner had left, the minister secretly asked me to come to his rooms. He said, "O Simplici, I take pity on your youth, and your future misfortune moves me to sympathy. Listen, my child, and find out for certain that your master has decided to rob you of your reason and make you into a fool. He has already ordered you a costume. Tomorrow you will have to attend the kind of school in which you are to lose your reason. They'll probably grill you in such a way that you become a buffoon, unless God and natural means prevent it. But since being deprived of reason is a dubious and troublesome matter, I have decided to help you with advice and other good and necessary remedies and therapies—all for faithful Christian charity and the sake of the hermit's piety and your own innocence. Therefore follow my advice and swallow this powder. It will strengthen your mind and memory, that you may overcome every attempt without hurting your reason. Here I also give you an ointment. Put it on your temples, the nape of your neck, and your nostrils. And use these remedies before you go to bed, for you may be gotten out of bed at any hour. But look out and be sure that no one discovers anything about my warning or these remedies; otherwise both of us might be the worse for it. And when they give you their damnable treatment, don't believe everything they want you to believe but act as if you do. Don't talk much or your teachers will find out they are sawing deadwood and they'll make your troubles worse, though I don't know what they will do to you. When you have put on the fool's cap and bells, come back and we'll discuss your situation again. Meanwhile I will pray to God that he save your health and your mind." Then he gave me the powder and the ointment, and I walked home.

The matter proceeded as the parson had said. I was in my first sleep when four big fellows, dressed up like frightful devils, came into my room and stopped before my bed. They jumped around like mountebanks and Shrovetide fools. One had a red-hot poker, the other carried a torch; the other two whisked me out of bed, danced with me awhile, and forced my clothes on me. I acted as if I thought they were real, natural devils, let out some piteous wails, and made gestures of fear, but they announced I would have to leave with them. They tied a towel around my head, that I might not see or hear or scream. By various roundabout ways, upstairs and down, they led me, trembling like an aspen, into a cellar where a big fire was burning. After they had taken off the towel they began toasting me in Spanish wine and malmsey. It wasn't hard for them to persuade me I had died and gone to the pit of hell, because I purposely pretended to believe everything they were making up. "Go right on drinking," they said, "for you'll be with us forever anyway. But if you don't want to be a regular fellow who joins in, you'll go into that fire!" Those poor devils tried to disguise their voices so I couldn't recognize them, but I noticed right away that they were the governor's quartermaster sergeants. Of course I didn't let on I knew; rather I laughed up my sleeve that these bruisers, who wanted to make a fool out of me, instead must be my fools.

I drank my share of the Spanish wine, but they outdid me because such heavenly nectar is seldom given to such fellows, and I swear they got full before I did. When the time seemed right, I staggered about as I had recently seen my master's guests do. Finally I no longer wanted to drink, only to sleep, but with the poker that was always kept in the fire they chased and pursued me into all the corners of the cellar. They seemed to have become foolish themselves, for they wanted me to drink, not sleep. And when I fell down in the chase (as I did often, on purpose), they picked me up and made as if to throw me into the fire. They kept me awake like a falcon in training, and it was a great trouble and hardship to me.

I might have outlasted them in drinking and waking, but they took turns, and in the end I would have come out the worse for wear. I spent three days and two nights in this smoky cellar, which had no light but that shed by the fire. My head started to hurt and throb as if it was about to burst, and I had to think of something to rid myself of these tortures and torturers. I did as does the fox who urinates in the dogs' eyes when he sees no hope of escaping them. When nature urged me to defecate, I stuck three fingers down my throat, and filled my pants and beslobbered my clothes all at the same time. The stench was so unbearable that even the devils could stay with me no longer. They wrapped me in a bed-sheet and beat me so miserably that my innards and my soul almost left me. From this treatment I fainted and lost the use of my senses. I lay there like a corpse and don't know what else was done to me, I was so far gone.

CHAPTER 6: *Simplicius goes to heaven and is changed into a calf*

When I came to again, I was no longer with the devils in the cellar vault but in a beautiful room, in the hands of three of the ugliest old women the earth has ever seen. At first, when I opened my eyes, I thought they were natural spirits of hell. (If I had read the heathen poets, I would have thought of the Eumenides.) One of them had eyes like two will-o'-the-wisps and between them a long bony hawk nose whose tip reached her lower lip. I saw only two teeth in her mouth. They were so long, round, and thick that either could compare with a ring finger in shape, and with gold in color; there was bone enough for a whole mouthful of teeth, but it was badly distributed. Her face looked like Spanish leather and her hoary hair hung strangely disheveled about her head, for she had just been hauled out of bed. I don't know how to compare her two long breasts, except maybe with two cow bladders about half blown up. At the end of each dangled a dun-colored plug half a finger long. Truly, this was a frightening sight that might have been, at best, a good remedy for the mad love of lustful bucks. The other two were just about as ugly; they had flat monkey noses and their dresses weren't quite so sloppy. When I regained my senses a little more, I saw that one was our dishwasher; the other two, the wives of the two quartermaster sergeants.

I acted as if all my limbs had been cut off so that I couldn't move. As a matter of fact, I didn't feel like dancing. These three old hags undressed me naked as a grape and cleansed me of all filth like a little baby. This did me no end of good, and during their work they showed much patience and sympathy. I almost revealed to them how well I had caught on to everything.

But I thought, No, Simplici! Do not confide in an old crone. Rather remember you will have glory enough if you, a child, can pull the wool over the eyes of three experienced old hags with whose help one might catch the very devil in an open field. Let this be a sign of your future success.

When they had finished with me they laid me in a marvelous bed where I fell asleep without being rocked. They left, taking the dirty clothes and the washtub with them. As I figure, I slept more than twenty-four hours without interruption, and when I woke up two beautiful winged boys stood by the bed. They were magnificently dressed in white nightshirts, taffeta sashes, pearls, jewels, golden chains, and other precious jewelry. One carried a gold-plated washbasin full of cookies, candy, marzipan, and other goodies; the other held a gold-plated cup. They claimed to be angels and wished to convince me that I was now in heaven, since I had happily gotten out of purgatory and escaped the devil and his dam. For that reason I was to ask for whatever I wanted; everything I wished either was on hand or could be sent for. I was bothered by thirst and when I saw the cup before me I asked only for a drink, which was gladly given to me. However, I drank not wine but a sleeping potion, and fell asleep again as soon as the potion got warm inside me.

The next day I awoke—otherwise I'd be sleeping yet!—and found myself no longer in bed, or in the previous room, or with my angels, or in heaven—but in my old goose-pen. It was as dark and scary as the previous cellar; moreover, I wore a suit made of calfskin with the rough side out. My trousers were in the Polish (or Swabian) style and the jacket was even crazier. On my head was a cap like a monk's cowl; it was pulled way down and had a large pair of donkey's ears. I had to laugh at my misfortune, for I saw by the nest and the feathers what sort of bird I was to represent. Only then did I begin to take stock and to think of my welfare. And as I had reason to thank God for not letting me lose my mind, I also ardently begged him to keep, rule, lead, and guide me. I determined to play the fool as much as I could, and at the same time to bide my time and see what else fate had in store for me.

CHAPTER 7: *How Simplicius behaved in this bestial state*

I could have escaped from the pen by means of the hole the crazy ensign had cut in the door. But because I wished to seem a fool, I didn't, but acted like a hungry calf calling for its mother. My mooing was soon heard by those who were supposed to watch me, for two soldiers came and asked who was in the goose-pen. I answered, "You fools, don't you hear it's a calf?!" They opened the pen, took me out, and acted surprised to hear a calf talking. (But they did this like an actor newly hired and clumsy, who has trouble impersonating the character he is supposed to act. I felt like helping them get into the spirit.) They wondered what to do with me and agreed to give me as a present to the governor, who would give them more for me, since I could talk, than would the butcher.

They asked me how I was doing. I said, "Badly enough." They wanted to know why, and I said, "Because it seems to be customary here to put honest calves in goose-pens. You boys ought to know that if I am to become an honorable ox I must be raised like a respectable critter." After this brief discussion they took me across the street toward the governor's quarters. A mob of boys followed me; they all took to mooing just like me, and a blind man would have thought, judging by the noise, that a herd of cattle was being driven by. But on sight it looked like a bunch of fools, some younger than others.

Well, the two soldiers presented me to the governor as if they had just captured me in a military raid. He gave them a tip and promised me the best treatment ever. I had my own thoughts about it—namely, "All that glitters isn't gold"—but I said, "Sir, do not have us calves confined in goose-pens if you want us to grow up into regular critters." The governor comforted me, thinking he was terribly bright to have made such a cunning fool of me. But my thoughts were, Just wait! I've passed the baptism of fire and have been hardened by it. Now we'll see who can best act the other fellow's part.

Just then a peasant who had been run off his farm by soldiers drove his cattle to the watering trough. When I saw him, I left the governor and rushed mooing and bawling to the cows, as if I wanted to suck. But when I got close, the cows were frightened by me worse than by a wolf. In fact, they stampeded as if a nestful of hornets had gotten loose among them, and their owner couldn't keep them together anymore. It was lots of fun. In no time at all, a mob of people gathered who were all looking at my foolishness, and when my master managed to stop laughing a little, he said, "One fool makes a hundred more!" I thought, Pinch yourself, sir, for it is yourself you are talking about.

Since from then on everyone called me the Calf, I in turn gave everybody a special nickname or mock name. Most people (but especially my master) thought them very suitable, for I named everyone as his character seemed to require. To put it in a nutshell, many people thought I was a witless fool, and I thought of people as foolish nitwits. As I see it, this is still the way of the world; everyone is content with his brains, and imagines he is the most intelligent of all. But as the Latin saying goes, "All the world is full of fools."

My pastime with the peasant's cows helped to make the short forenoon even shorter, for it was the time around winter solstice. At the noon meal I waited on table as usual, but I also had a little fun. When I was supposed to eat, I would take no human food or drink. I demanded grass—which was not available at that season. My master sent to the butcher's for two calfskins and ordered them slipped on two little boys. He seated the boys with me at the table and asked us not to be bashful when the food came. Our first course was a tossed green salad. The governor even had a real calf brought in and it was given lettuce sprinkled with salt. First I put on a cold stare as if to express surprise, but under the circumstances I thought I had better join in the game. When some onlookers saw me so disconcerted, they said, "It is nothing new to see calves eat meat, fish, cheese, butter, and other foods. Why, calves even get drunk now and then! These critters know a good thing when they taste it. It's even reached the point where there is hardly any difference between calves and humans. So why should you be the only one to hold out and not join in the fun?"

I was persuaded the more quickly to start eating because I was hungry, and not because I had seen men more piggish than swine, fiercer than lions, more lecherous than billy goats, more jealous than dogs, more headstrong than horses, more stubborn than jackasses, more given to drink than cattle, slyer than foxes, more voracious than wolves, sillier than monkeys, and more venomous than snakes and toads. All of these ani-

mals enjoy human food. Yet men differ from them in shape
and do not often retain the innocence of a calf.

So I fed myself, along with my fellow calves, as my appetite
required, and if a stranger had chanced to see us together
at the table he would surely have thought old Circe had returned to change men into animals, an art my master knew
and practiced.

My dinner was exactly like my lunch, and as my fellow
calves had to eat with me, so they had to sleep with me—unless my master allowed me sleep in the cow barn. I insisted on
this because I wanted to fool those who thought they were
making a fool of me. And I concluded that God, who is full
of loving kindness, provides each man with enough intelligence for self-preservation, whatever job he has been given;
and the notion many folks have, that they alone are smart, is
foolish, for there are people living on the other side of the
mountain too, and the doctor's degree is no one's monopoly.

CHAPTER 8: *Of some people's retentive memories and of
others' forgetfulness*

When I awoke in the morning my two vealified companions
were gone. So I got up, and when the adjutant went for the
key to open up the town gate, I sneaked out of the house and
went to the minister. I told him everything, how I had survived hell as well as heaven. When he saw that I felt guilty
about deceiving so many people, particularly my master, by
playing the fool, he said, "That is something you must not
worry about. The foolish world wants to be fooled. Use what
intelligence they have left you; use it for your own advantage
and thank God you came out on top—that's not given to
everyone. Imagine you have been reborn like the phoenix,
through fire, from unreason to reason and thus to a new life.
But keep in mind that you aren't out of the woods yet. At
the risk of losing your mind, you slipped into this jester's

outfit, but the times are so strange that no one knows if you can slip out of it without risking your life. Anybody can dash into hell, but to get out again takes sweat and toil. You aren't half the man you think you are, when it comes to escaping imminent danger. For that you'll need more brains and caution than you had when you couldn't tell bright from foolish. Put yourself into God's hands, pray diligently, remain humble, and await future changes with patience."

His lecture was purposely much different in tone, and I thought he had seen by the size of my head that I considered myself quite a big shot because I was so good at tricks and tomfoolery. In turn I read in his face that he was put out with me—and what good *was* I to him? Accordingly, I changed my tune and thanked him heartily for giving me such wonderful remedies for preserving my mind, and made an impossible promise to repay him everything. This tickled him and changed his mood. He praised his remedies and told me that Simonides Melicus had invented a technique (perfected by Metrodorus Sceptius) by which people could repeat word for word everything they had heard or read. This could not have been done, he said, without mind-building drugs of the kind he had given me.

Well, dear parson, I thought, in the books you lent the hermit I read it quite differently—but I was smart enough not to say so. For to tell the truth, it wasn't till I was supposed to have turned foolish that I became careful in my speech. The parson droned on about how Cyrus had been able to call any of his 30,000 soldiers by name and gave many other examples of mnemonics. Finally he said, "I am telling you all this so that you will really believe a man's memory can be improved and strengthened by drugs, just as it can be weakened or even erased by them." And he launched into at least a dozen more examples.

Then he gave me some more medicine and instructions. When I left the house, about a hundred boys again followed me, all bellowing like calves. My master, who had just gotten

up, came to the window, saw all these fools in a drove, and
had a good laugh.

CHAPTER 9: *Cockeyed praise of a beautiful lady*

As soon as I got home I had to go up to my master's, for
some aristocratic ladies were there, and they wanted to see
and hear his new jester. I came in and stood there like a mute.
After a while the lady I had grabbed at the dance spoke up,
remarking that she had been told this calf could talk, but
now she saw it wasn't true. I piped up with, "Well, I heard
monkeys couldn't talk, but now I see it isn't true." "How so?"
said my master. "Do you think these ladies are monkeys?" I
answered, "If they aren't now, they soon will be. Who knows
how it all comes out? I never thought I'd be a calf, and yet
I am one." My master asked how I could tell that the ladies
might be monkeys soon. My answer was, "A monkey is bare
behind. The ladies are already bare in front. The girls I've
seen cover up better." "You jackanapes, you are a foolish
calf, and you talk like one. These ladies show what's worth
seeing, but monkeys are bare by necessity. You had better
make up in a hurry for putting your foot in your mouth, or
I'll have you whipped or get the dogs to run you into the
goose-pen, as happens to calves that don't behave. Let us hear
how you can praise and compliment a lady." Well, I looked
at this lady from tip to toe and up again, and finally I said,
"Sir, I see what's wrong. It's the tailor's fault. He used the
material that was to cover neck and breast in the skirt; that's
why it drags so behind. If the fellow can't tailor better than
that he ought to have his hands cut off." "Lady," I said to
her, "get rid of that tailor and use my knan's. His name was
Master Littlepaul and he made such pretty pleated skirts for
my mither and our Annie and Ursula. They were the same
width up and down, and they never dragged in the dirt like
yours. You have no idea how he dressed up those cute
wenches." My master asked if Annie and Ursula were prettier

than this lady. "Heck, no, sir!" I said. "This lady has hair the color of baby dirt and her hair is as straight and white as if hog bristles had been slapped on her head. And her curls are so well rolled they look like hollow pipes, or a dozen candles or sausages hanging on either side of her head. Just look at her nice smooth forehead, isn't it curved more attractively than a backside? And it's whiter than a skull that's been out in the open for years and years. But what is this in comparison with her delicate body, which I can't see at all? Isn't it as tender, slim, and graceful as if she had had the skitters for eight weeks running?" At this they all started laughing and could hear me no longer, nor could I speak anymore. So I took to my heels laughing, letting others make fun of me only so long as I was pleased to put up with it.

CHAPTERS 10–13: *Telling exclusively of notable heroes and artists. On the troubled and perilous lives of rulers. Concerning the judgment and understanding of some brute animals. Containing all sorts of information; if you want to find out, read it yourself or have someone else read it to you*

Then came lunch and I did a lot of talking again, for I had decided to discuss all foolishness and punish all vanity, and my job at that time gave me an excellent excuse for it. No one at table was too great to escape my tongue. And if there was one who wouldn't stand for it he was either laughed at by the others or he was told by my master that no wise man should ever get angry at a fool.

Once my master said, "I don't know what I have in you. For a calf you are too reasonable. I almost think under your calfskin you are covered with a rogue's hide." I pretended to be angry and answered him, "Do you humans suppose we animals are all fools? You ought not to, for I imagine if the older animals could talk like me they would really tell you off. I might almost say you humans have learned your arts and crafts from us. You eat and drink yourself into the grave; not so with us animals. In the springtime who tells the summer birds to come here? And in the fall, to fly to warmer lands? Who leads them or shows them the way? Or do humans lend them their compasses, so they don't lose the way? No, dear people, without you they know the way, how long they must travel, and when to leave one place and the next. They don't need your compass or your calendar. If you lived among us animals and saw what we do and don't do, you would find that all of us have our own abilities and virtues. Hence, many ancient philosophers were not ashamed to ask if dumb animals have reason. Even wise King Solomon, in Proverbs 30, bids you pay attention to us."

After this speech, my master's table companions delivered diverse opinions about me. The secretary thought I should be considered mad because I regarded myself as a dumb animal. Still, he said, lads who have bats in the belfry, and yet considered themselves wise, make the very best and most amusing jesters. My master said he thought me to be a fool because I told everyone the unvarnished truth, and yet my discussions were altogether unlike a fool's. (They said all this in Latin, so I shouldn't understand them.) He asked me if I had been a student while I was still human. I said I didn't know what "student" was and asked if one needed a stud to stude with. The mad ensign thought the devil spoke through me. Then my master asked me whether I was still accustomed to praying like people, and whether I was looking forward to going to heaven. "Sure," I said. "I still have my immortal human soul, and it doesn't long for hell, especially since I didn't get on very well in that place awhile ago. I have only been a little transmogrified, and hope in time to become human again." "I join you in that hope," said my master, and sighed. From this I concluded that he was sorry he had dared make a fool of me. "But let me hear," he continued, "how you pray."

I kneeled down, raised my eyes and hands toward heaven as the hermit had done, and because my master's repentance comforted me, I couldn't hold back my tears. After the Lord's Prayer, I prayed for all Christendom and for my friends and enemies, and I asked that the good Lord might enable me to live according to his will, and that I might become worthy of praising him through all eternity. This prayer was full of reverently composed words the hermit had taught me. Some of the more softhearted listeners almost started crying, for they were full of sympathy for me. There were tears in my master's eyes, too, though he seemed not to want to show them. He said his heart was about to break at seeing such a sad person who so much resembled his own lost sister.

After the meal, my master sent for the parson, told him everything I had said, and hinted that he was afraid things might not be as they ought to be and that perhaps I was in league with the devil. Not long before, I had been altogether simple-minded and ignorant, but now I was discussing things that made one's hair stand on end. The parson replied that he should have thought of this before making a fool of me. Human beings, he said, were made in God's image and no one ought to fool with them as with beasts, especially not with one so young. But he did not think the evil one had gained an entrance, for I had always commended myself to God in fervent prayer. But if, contrary to his expectations, I had been lost to the fiend, those who were responsible for it might see how they answered God for it. Surely it was one of the greatest sins to rob a man of his wit, for it made him incapable of God's service and praise, and it was chiefly for these ends that man had been created.

"I assured you," said the parson, "that he had intelligence enough. But he could not adapt himself to the world because he was educated in simple-mindedness by his father, a crude peasant, and by your brother-in-law in the wilderness. A little patience in the beginning would have let him prove his worth. He just happened to be a pious, simple child who didn't know the wicked world. But I have not the least doubt he can be set straight if only one could get him to give up the illusion that he is a calf."

"I am worried," answered my master, "because though at first he was so ignorant, now he gives out all sorts of information without the least hesitation—things someone better read and more experienced could hardly know. Why, he told me many characteristics of animals, and has described my own person as charmingly as if he had always been a man of the world. His talk astonishes me, and I should perhaps consider it as a hint from the Lord."

"Sir," replied the parson, "this might be explained naturally. I know he has read a lot; he and the hermit read through all my books, and there were quite a few. And since the boy has a good memory and his mind is idle now, he can dredge up what he previously stored away. Oh, I am sure he can be restored."

With these words, the parson left the governor dangling between hope and fear. The upshot was that a wait-and-see period followed. The parson had given his advice more for his own sake than for mine, because by pretending to be worried about me and taking a lot of trouble he gained the governor's favor and had himself appointed chaplain of the garrison. In those evil days, that was nothing to be sneezed at, and I was glad for him.

CHAPTER 14: *How Simplicius continued to lead the life of Riley; how the Croatians robbed him of that, too*

From this time on, I was in my master's favor, grace, and love, and I was completely happy except that I had too much calfskin and too few years—but I didn't know that yet. The parson did not want me to be normal again, as the time for that seemed not to have come yet. When my master saw that I liked music, he had me instructed by an excellent lutist, whom I soon surpassed because I could sing better than he. Thus I provided entertainment for my master. All the officers showed me their good will, the richest burghers honored me,

the servants and soldiers wished me well because they saw
how much my master liked me. I got presents here, there, and
everywhere, for people knew that jesters and fools have more
influence with their masters than straightforward people, and
their gifts were meant that way; some gave them that I
mightn't tell on them, others to have me do just that, and thus
I picked up a pretty penny. I gave the parson much of it because I didn't know what it was good for. As no one dared
to look at me askance, so I had no tribulations, troubles, or
cares. I put all my mind to my music and to how I might
skillfully reproach someone for his shortcomings. So I grew
up like a fool in fairyland; my face got sleek and my muscles
grew strong, and anybody could see I was no longer mortify-
ing myself, as in the woods, on water, acorns, beechnuts, roots,
and herbs. Instead, Rhine wine and the stout of Hanau
washed down my rich food, all of which in those poor times
was truly a great gift of God; for in those days all of Germany
was wholly seared by the flames of war, hunger, and pesti-
lence, and Hanau itself was surrounded by enemies. But
none of this bothered me in the least.

My master decided that, after the siege was lifted, he would
give me either to Cardinal Richelieu or to Duke Bernhard of
Weimar. Besides wanting to earn much gratitude through me,
he let on that he couldn't stand the sight of me in jester's
garb because in face and mien I reminded him so much of
his lost sister, whom I resembled more every day. The parson
advised him against getting rid of me. He thought the time
had just about come to perform a miracle and change me
back into a reasonable human being. He suggested that the
governor have some calfskins put on other boys, and then
have on hand a third person, in the guise of a doctor, prophet,
or traveling showman, who should undress these boys with a
lot of hocus-pocus, pretending he could turn animals into
men and vice versa. That way I might be straightened out
without too much trouble and made to think I (like others)
had turned human again.

When the governor had accepted this suggestion, the parson told me of the agreement and easily persuaded me to go along with him. But jealous Fortune was ready neither to let me slip out my fool's dress nor to let me enjoy my fat, fulsome life any longer.

While the furrier and the tailor were preparing the clothes that went with the act, I was roving with some boys on the ice just outside the fortress. Someone—I don't know who—led a raiding party of Croatian soldiers who rounded us up, sat us on farm horses they had just stolen, and trotted us off. To be sure, they were in doubt for a moment whether or not to take me along. Then one of them said in Bohemian, "Mih weme daho Blasna sebao, bo we deme ho gbabo Oberstowi." Another replied, "Prschis am bambo ano, mi ho nagonie possadeime, wan rosumi niemezki, wan bude mit Kratock wille sebao." [2] So I was forced to get on a horse and found out that a single unlucky hour can deprive one of all well-being, happiness, and salvation, and one's whole life is changed.

CHAPTER 15: *Simplicius' life in the cavalry; what he saw and learned among the Croats*

Although the alarm was sounded at once in Fort Hanau, and cavalry sent out, that bothered the Croats but little and hardly retarded their getaway. Our men retrieved nothing, for the Croats were very mobile and made for the forest near Büdingen, where they could forage, trade off the Hanau children who were to be ransomed by their parents, and sell their stolen horses and other "liberated" goods to the burghers. Before it had become really dark, they started up again, and quickly crossed the forest toward the monastery of Fulda, everywhere taking along whatever they could carry. Robbing and plundering did not delay their rapid movement the least little bit, for they were just like the devil who, they say, can

---

[2] Less than perfect Bohemian: "We'll take this fool along and give him to the colonel." "Gad, yes. We'll put him on a horse. The colonel knows German. He'll have fun with him."

run and crap at the same time. In the evening we arrived at
the monastery of Hersfeld, where their quarters were. Their
large loot was shared evenly, and I was given to the colonel.

Everything here seemed strange and disgusting to me; I
had to trade my Hanau delicacies for coarse black bread and
lean beef, or for a flitch of stolen bacon—but this was only
when times were good. Wine and beer had turned to water,
and instead of sleeping in a bed I had to be content with
straw in the horse barn. Instead of playing the lute for everyone's delight, I often had to crawl under the table like our
other boys, howl like a dog, and take my chances on getting
wounded by spurs while looking for food, and that was no
fun. Instead of taking walks in Hanau, I could go along on
foraging raids, curry the horses, and haul the manure out of
the stable.

Foraging is defined as riding out to the villages and, with
danger to life and limb, threshing, grinding, and baking, grabbing and stealing whatever is handy, maltreating and abusing
peasants and even ruining their women, daughters, and hired
girls. (But I was still too young for such work.) And when the
poor peasants object to this treatment or get bold enough to
rap some forager's knuckles while he is at his work (and there
were plenty of such thieves in Hessia at that time), then you
strike them down—provided you can—or at least make their
houses go up in smoke.

My new master had no wife (this type of soldier doesn't
usually take his wife along because any female can fill her
place), no page, no manservant, no cook, but he did have a
swarm of hostlers and boys who waited on him and his horses,
and he was not at all ashamed to saddle and feed his own
horse. He regularly slept on a straw pallet or on the bare
ground, covered only with a fur coat, and that's why lice were
sometimes seen wandering all over his clothes. He was not
embarrassed about it and laughed when somebody picked one
off him. He wore his hair short and had a wide beard like a
Swiss; this served him well when he disguised himself in peasant clothing and went reconnoitering. Though he never kept

a luxurious table, he was honored, loved, and feared by his men and all who knew him. At that time we were never quiet or in the same place for long, but now here, now there. Now we were raiding, now being raided. But we hadn't enough strength to defeat the Hessians, whose lieutenant general, Melander by name, gave us no rest. He captured many of our men and sent them home to Cassel.

I didn't like this unstable life one bit and often wished I were back at Hanau. My greatest trouble was that since I couldn't really talk with these fellows, I got pushed from pillar to post and had to take beatings and abuse. The colonel's greatest fun was having me sing in German and play on the trumpet, but that seldom happened. Mostly I got boxed on the ears so hard that blood came out of my nose and I didn't come back for second helpings. Since, on account of my youth, I wasn't very useful on raiding parties, I took an interest in cooking and keeping my master's guns clean. He liked this so much that I gained his favor and he had a new jester's suit made for me. It was of calfskin again and had ears much larger than the old one. Since my master was not a gourmet, I did not need much skill in cooking. But I really got tired of my job when I was short of salt, fat, and spices (as often happened), so I lay awake nights and thought how I might get away, especially when spring came around. About this time I made it my job to remove the entrails of butchered sheep and cows, which had been smelling up the camp. The colonel approved. Each time I dragged them farther away, and one fine day, after dark, I escaped into the nearest woods.

CHAPTER 16: *Simplicius picks up a rich loot and becomes a thieving forest-dweller*

My situation, to judge by appearances, gradually became worse—so bad, as a matter of fact, that I imagined I had been born only to suffer misfortune. Only a few hours after I escaped from the Croats, some highwaymen picked me up. No doubt they thought they had made a good catch; it was night

and they couldn't see my jester's suit. Two of them were ordered to take me to a certain spot far inside the woods. While
it was still pitch dark, one of these demanded money from
me. He laid down his gun and gloves and started frisking me
and asking me who I was and if I had money.

As soon as he felt my furry suit and the long donkey ears
on my cap (he thought they were horns), and saw the brilliant
sparks that came from my fur when he stroked it, he was
frightened and became edgy. I noticed this, and before he
could recover, I rubbed my suit with both hands so that it
glowed as if I were full of burning sulphur. In a frightening
voice, I answered, "I am the devil, and I'll wring both your
necks!" This scared the two of them so much that they made
off through shrubs and bushes as if hellfire was after them.
The darkness of night did not slow them down; when they
fell over sticks, stones, stumps, logs, or even each other, they
jumped up again and continued running. They ran until I
couldn't hear them anymore. But I laughed so loud that the
woods echoed, and that too was awful to hear in such a lonely
place.

As I was about to leave I stumbled over a blunderbuss,
which I picked up and kept, for I had learned from the
Croatians how to handle guns. Continuing on, I ran into a
knapsack made, like my suit, of calfskin; I looked it over and
found dangling from it a pouch containing powder, lead, and
everything else I needed. I strapped it on, shouldered the gun
like a soldier, and hid nearby in a dense thicket, hoping to
get a little sleep. But at daybreak the whole raiding party
came back to the place looking for the lost gun and knapsack. I pricked up my ears like a fox and kept quieter than
a mouse. When they found nothing they laughed at the two
who had run away from me. "Oh, you cowards!" they said.
"You ought to be ashamed—scared by a single man, running
away and leaving your gun!" But one of them swore the devil
should fetch him if I hadn't been Satan himself; had he not
touched the horns and the rough skin? The other fellow got
cross and said, "Hell! I don't care if it was the devil or his
dam. I want my knapsack back." One of them—one of the

better ones, I thought—answered, "Why do you think the devil wanted your knapsack and gun? I'd bet my neck, the chap you ran from took both with him." Another replied that it might well have been some peasants who had passed by, found the gun, and picked up the things. They all agreed this might have been the case, and everyone allowed the devil in person had been in their midst, especially because the one who had searched me swore frightful oaths it had been so and made the most of my horns and sparkling skin. I think if I had suddenly appeared, they would all have run again.

Finally, after they had been looking in vain for a long time, they moved on. I opened the knapsack, looking for something for breakfast. The first thing I found was a purse with 360-odd ducats in it. No one need ask if I was pleased, but let me assure the reader that I liked the knapsack even better when I saw it well stocked with food. And since among common soldiers ducats and their like are much too scarce to be lugged around on raids, it occurred to me that this fellow must have just gotten them and secretly slipped them into the knapsack, so as not to share them with his companions.

I ate my breakfast joyfully, soon found a pleasant spring to quench my thirst, and then counted my ducats. But to save my life I couldn't say where this happened. I stayed in the woods as long as my food lasted (and I used it very sparingly). But when the knapsack was empty, hunger drove me to the homesteads of the peasants. By night I crawled into their cellars and kitchens, and took what food I found and could carry off. I dragged it with me into the wildest parts of the woods. Here again I led an altogether hermitlike life—except that I stole much and prayed little, and had no settled home but kept moving about widely. Fortunately, summer was on its way.

CHAPTER 17: *How Simplicius rode to dance with the witches*

Occasionally on my travels through the woods I met some peasants, but they always ran away from me. I don't know if

the war had made them fearful, had perhaps robbed them of
their homes, or whether the raiders had broadcast their encounter with me, so that the peasants who saw me thought
the fiend himself was walking in their part of the woods.

Once when I had been lost in the forest for several days
and was afraid my rations would run out, I was glad to hear
two woodcutters. I followed the sound of their axes, and
when I saw them I took a handful of ducats out of the purse,
sneaked up close to them, showed them this attractive gold,
and said, "Gentlemen, if you will take care of me I'll give
you this handful of gold." But the minute they saw me and
my gold they took to their heels, leaving behind them axes,
wedges, and hammers, as well as their lunch of cheese and
bread. This I picked up, put it in my knapsack, and got lost
in the woods again, almost despairing of ever getting back
among people.

After much thinking I reached this conclusion: Who knows
what will become of you? But you have money, and if you put
it in a safe place with reliable people, you can live on it for a
long time. Thus it occurred to me that I should hide it. From
the donkey's ears that made people run I made two arm-
bands, combined all my ducats, sewed them inside the arm-
bands, and fastened them on above my elbow. When I had
thus secured my treasure I again entered a peasant's house
and took from their supplies what I needed and could lay my
hands on; and though I was still quite simple-minded I had
enough sense never to return to a place where I had once
stolen the least bit. For this reason I was very lucky in my
thefts and never got caught.

Once, toward the end of May, I again wanted to get some
food in my usual (though forbidden) manner. I had made my
way to a farmstead and gotten into the inner sanctum of the
kitchen. When I heard people were still up, I opened wide a
door leading out to the yard, to provide a way out in case of
necessity. (N.B. I never went where they kept dogs.) I was waiting quietly for everyone to go to bed when I noticed a slit
in a little serving window to the next room. I sidled up to it,
to see if the people were going to bed. But my hope came to

nothing, for instead of undressing they had just gotten dressed, and instead of a candle they had a bluish flame burning on a bench. They were greasing sticks, brooms, forks, chairs, and benches, and, one after the other, were riding out the window on them. I was greatly surprised and rather horrified. But since I was used to greater horrors and had neither heard nor read of ghosts, I did not worry too much.

When everyone was gone and it was quiet, I went into the room to look for whatever I could take along. I sat down astride a bench and had hardly touched the wood when I rode—no, whizzed—on this bench straight out the window. My gun and knapsack stayed behind as carfare! Sitting down, taking off, and landing took place in one instant, it seemed, and all at once I was in a big crowd of people who were all doing a strange dance, the like of which I had never seen. Holding each other by the hand, they had formed many circles, one within another, their backs toward the center, as the three graces are sometimes pictured. The innermost ring consisted of seven or eight persons; the second had twice as many; the third more than the first two, and so on, so that there were over two hundred people in the outer ring. Since one circle danced clockwise and the next counterclockwise, I could not distinguish exactly how many circles there were, or what occupied the center around which they all revolved. The way the heads all reeled past one another looked awfully funny.

And the music was as weird as the dance. I think everyone was singing the tune while dancing, making an extraordinary harmony. The bench that took me there set me down by the musicians who were standing outside the circles. Instead of clarinets, flutes, and whistles, they were busily playing on vipers, asps, and chicken snakes. Some were holding cats and blowing in their bungholes; when they fingered the tails, the sound was like a bagpipe. Others ran a bow across a horse's head as if it were a fiddle, and still others played on a cow's skeleton (like you sometimes find in a pasture) as on a harp. An old gaffer was holding a bitch, cranking her tail, and fin-

gering her tits! Then there were devils using their noses for
trumpets, and the echo resounded through the woods. When
this dance came to an end, the whole hellish mob started
racing, shouting, reeling, roaring, howling, raging, and raving
as if everyone had gone stark mad. It is easy to imagine how
frightened I was.

While this noise was going on, a chap came toward me,
carrying on his hip a giant toad, big as a drum. Its entrails
hung out the rear and were stuffed in at the front again. It
looked so repulsive that it just about turned my stomach.
"Lookee, Simplex," he said, "I know you are a good lute-
player. Let's hear something!" I practically keeled over when
I heard him address me by my name. I could not answer
and felt as if I were in a deep dream. In my heart I prayed
to God Almighty that he help me out of my dream and let
me wake up. The chap with the toad looked me straight in
the eye and flicked his nose in and out like a turkey; then
he struck me such a blow on the chest that I couldn't breathe.
I started shouting to God, "Jesus Christ!"

This strong word was no sooner out of my mouth than the
whole army disappeared. In no time at all it was pitch dark,
and I felt so bad I crossed myself at least a hundred times.

CHAPTER 18: *Why it is unlikely that Simplicius is telling tall
tales*

Since there are people—some of them learned and influential—who don't believe that witches and ghosts exist, let alone
fly through the air, there are bound to be those who will say
at this point that Simplicius is pulling the wool over their
eyes. Well, I don't want to argue with these people. Nowadays four-flushing is a very common practice, and I don't
deny that I know how, for otherwise I would be something of
a stick-in-the-mud.

But people who doubt that witches ride through the air
should remember that Simon Magus was raised on high by

an evil spirit and did not fall down until St. Peter had prayed. In Book III of his *History of Northern Nations* (chapter 1, p. 19), Olavus Magnus tells us that Hadingus, king of Denmark, who had been expelled from his kingdom by rebels, returned home on the spirit of Othonus, who had disguised himself as a horse. It is well known from the *History of Doctor Faustus* that he and others (though they were not sorcerers) traveled through the air from one place to another. I myself knew a woman and her maid (both are dead now); this maid was polishing her mistress' shoes, and when she had finished one and set it down by the fire to do the other, the polished one slipped up the chimney in no time. But this story was kept quiet.

I have reported all this only because I want to let you know how witches and wizards have at times actually traveled to their conventions, and not because I want you to believe that *I* traveled that way. It's all the same to me whether you believe it or not; but whoever prefers to be skeptical, let him figure out a better way to get me from Hersfeld or Fulda—I don't know myself exactly where in the woods I was hanging out—to Magdeburg in such a short time.

CHAPTER 19: *Simplicius becomes a fool, just as he had been before*

But to resume my story: I assure the reader that I lay still on my stomach till daylight, for I hadn't the heart to sit up. I was in doubt whether I had dreamed what I have been telling. Though I was rather frightened, I was bold enough to fall asleep, for I thought at worst I might find myself in a wild forest; but even that wouldn't have been too bad, for since leaving home I had spent most of my time there and was quite used to it. About nine o'clock in the morning some foragers came and woke me up. Only then did I notice that I was in the middle of an open field.

The soldiers took me to a windmill and, when their feed

had been ground there, to the camp outside of Magdeburg. I was assigned to a colonel of the infantry, who asked me where I came from and to whom I belonged. I told everything, down to the smallest detail; since I didn't know the Croatians' name, I described their clothing, gave examples of their speech, and told how I had escaped from them. I carefully neglected mentioning my ducats. The tale of my trip through the air and the witches' dance was considered foolishness and tall talk, especially since the rest of my story was also a little mixed up.

Meanwhile a mob of people collected about me, for one fool makes a thousand more, and among them was one who had been a prisoner of war in Hanau last year; he had joined the forces there, but afterward had gone back to the imperial troops. He recognized me and said immediately, "Ho-ho, this is the commander's calf at Hanau!" The colonel asked for particulars, but the chap knew only that I was good at lute-playing, that the Croatians had taken me away, and that the governor had hated to lose me because I was a good fool and jester. Now the colonel's wife sent to another colonel's wife, who could play the lute quite well, and therefore always carried one with her. She asked for this instrument, and when it was brought I was told to show what I could do. But it was my opinion I should be given something to eat first, because my empty stomach was no match for the bulging belly of the lute. This was done, and after I had eaten my fill and had swallowed a good stein of brown beer, I sounded both my own and the lute's voice, talked thirteen to the dozen, and without any trouble got everyone to believe I was what my calf's clothing seemed to indicate.

The colonel asked me where I wanted to go now, and when I answered that it was all the same to me, we soon agreed that I should stay with him and become his page. He wanted to know what had become of my donkey's ears. "Well," I said, "if you found out where they are I should still be wearing them." I kept mum because all my riches were contained in them.

In a short time I became acquainted with most of the high officers in the Saxon as well as in the imperial camp, and with the ladies, too, who dressed up my cap, sleeves, and cut-off ears with silk ribbons in gay colors. I almost suspect some of today's fancy dressers first got the idea from me. The money I received from the officers I charitably shared with others, for I drank up every last penny of it in the good beer of Zerbst and Hamburg—two varieties that agreed well with me, though I had enough to eat and drink, without it, wherever I went.

When my colonel got a lute for my own use (he thought I'd stay on forever), I was no longer allowed to buzz back and forth between the two camps. He hired a tutor for me, who was to look after me and whom I was to obey. The tutor was a man after my own heart, for he was quiet, understanding, learned, of good conversation but not too talkative and—to mention the most important thing last—pious, well-read, and full of all sorts of arts and sciences. At night I had to sleep in his tent, and by day I was not to get out of his sight. He had been very wealthy, the counselor and official of some prince, but since the Swedes had robbed and utterly ruined him, and his wife died and his only son been forced to give up his studies because of poverty (he had become a regimental clerk in the Saxon army), he stayed with this colonel as a stable master, in order to have something to do while waiting for the war to end and hoping that the sun of his former good fortune might shine on him again.

CHAPTER 20: *This chapter is rather long and deals with throwing dice and what goes with it*

Because my tutor was on the old side he couldn't sleep through the whole night. This was the reason for his finding out during the first week that I wasn't such a fool as I pretended to be. In fact, since he was an expert in physiognomy,

he had noticed it right away, in my face. One time I awoke
at midnight and made all sorts of remarks about my life and
strange experiences; then I got up and rendered to God Almighty thanks for all the benefices he had shown me and all
the dangers from which he had saved me, commended my further commissions and omissions to his love, and prayed not
only for the forgiveness of my sins (committed in my condition as a foolish jester), but also that he might please to take
me out of my fool's clothing and let me be counted among
reasonable human beings. After this, I lay down again with
a heavy sigh and went to sleep.

My tutor, who had heard everything, pretended to be fast
asleep. But when the prayer was repeated several nights in a
row, he felt quite sure I had more sense than many an oldster
who thinks he is quite important. But he did not discuss it
with me in the tent because, he said, the walls were too thin,
and, for reasons of his own, he did not want anyone else to
know my secret just then—before he himself was sure of my
innocence.

One time I went for a walk behind the camp; he did not
mind because it gave him a chance to look for me and talk
to me alone. He found me in a lonely place and said, "My
dear young friend, because I want only what's best for you,
I am glad to be able to talk with you here alone. I know that
you are not a fool, as you pretend, and that you do not wish
to live in this lowly and despicable condition. If your welfare is dear to you, and you wish with all your heart what you
ask of God every night, and if you will put your trust in me
as an honest man, then tell me about yourself and I shall
try in every way to help you get out of your fool's suit."

At this I embraced him and in my joy acted as if he were
an angel or at least a prophet come to save me from the fool's
cap. And then we sat down in the grass and I told him my
whole life's story. He looked at my palm and was quite taken
with my unusual past and future. He advised me not to take
off my fool's clothing in the next few days, for he could tell

by palmistry that I would be a prisoner of war and in mortal
danger. I thanked him for his good will and advice, prayed
that God might reward his help, and begged him to be my
true friend and father because I was forsaken by all the world.

Then we got up and went to a gambling place, where a
contest with dice was going on and every throw was accompanied by a thousand curses. The place was about as big as
the Old Market in Cologne; coats lay on the ground, tables
stood everywhere, and gamblers were milling around. Each
group had three bones of chance to which they entrusted
their luck in splitting and reapportioning their money. Each
table had a supervisor (or croupier, who reaps the crops!)
whose job it was to be umpire and see to it that no injustice
was done. He also lent coats, tables, and dice, and from the
winner collected a fee for it in such a way that he usually
came out best. Yet these operators don't prosper, for they also
gamble and lose; or if they invest their money well, the can-
teen keeper gets it, or the surgeon, for after a fight they often
have to have their heads dressed and bandaged.

While I was standing there, looking at the place and all the
gamblers and their foolishness, my tutor asked what I thought
of it. I answered, "I don't like their taking God's name in
vain; but as for the rest, I let it stand on its own merit
or lack of it, as something strange to me, which I do not yet
understand." My tutor replied, "You must know that this is
the most wicked and abhorrent place in the whole camp. The
people here covet their neighbor's money and lose their own
over it." I asked, "Dear sir, if gambling is such a horrid and
dangerous matter, why do the people in charge allow it?" My
tutor answered, "I shouldn't like to say it's because the officers
themselves join in, but rather because the soldiers don't want
to do without it, or can't do without it. For whoever has
yielded to gambling once (or who has once been possessed by
the gambling devil) gradually becomes so ensnared that he can
give it up no more than he can give up sleeping." I crossed
myself and wondered why such inventions of the devil should
be permitted in a Christian army.

CHAPTER 21: *A bit shorter and livelier than the preceding one*

As time passed, my tutor and I became more and more devoted to each other, and yet we kept our closeness a secret. I was still acting the part of the fool, but my jokes had become more thoughtful than foolish. When our siege of Magdeburg [3] made no progress, I suggested having a big rope made and wrapping it all the way around the town. Then all the men and draft animals in camp should pull on it and thus raze the town in a single operation. Every day I thought up plenty of such foolish jokes and gags and always had a handy supply of them. My masters's secretary (who was quite a joker and prankster) gave me a lot of material that kept me going along the road of foolishness.

Once I asked him what kind of fellow our regimental chaplain was, and why he dressed differently from other people. The secretary said, "He is Mr. Dicis-et-non-facis. That means a guy who ties the knot for other men but doesn't take a wife of his own. He dislikes thieves because they don't tell what they do, but *he* never does what *he* says. Thieves don't like him, either, because the only time they associate closely with him is at their hanging." Later when I called our good chaplain by that Latin name, he was laughed at, and I was called an evil-minded fool and birched for it.

The tutor, on the other hand, entertained me, whenever he was with me, with utterly different matters. He told me a lot about his son, the above-mentioned regimental secretary with the Saxon army. His abilities were much greater than those of our colonel's secretary. Thus our colonel not only liked him but tried to get him released and to make him *his* secretary.

This secretary (who, like his father, was called Ulrich Heartbrother) and I became such good friends that we swore

[3] This is not the important siege of May 1631, but a second one of 1635/6. Simplicius' suggestion goes back to the Bible; see II Samuel 17:13.

each other eternal brotherhood, by virtue of which we would never forsake each other, in good luck or misfortune. And since this was done with the knowledge of his father, we kept our union all the better. After that we cared only for getting me honorably out of my fool's cap, so that we might serve one another better. But the elder Heartbrother, whom I honored and respected as a father, did not approve; he said in so many words that changing my status now would bring imprisonment and grave danger upon me. And because he could predict some great trouble for himself and his son, he thought we had good reason to live all the more carefully and warily. He did not want to be involved with the affairs of a person whose future danger he clearly foresaw; he was afraid that if I revealed myself my bad luck might strike him too, for he had known my secret right along and known me inside and out, as it were; but he did not tell the colonel about it.

Shortly afterward I noticed that the colonel's secretary was clearly green with envy of young Heartbrother, fearing that my friend would be promoted ahead of him, and he would lose his job. I saw how worried he was; envy made him sigh whenever he looked at either the older or the younger Heartbrother. From all this I guessed that he was planning to trip them and make them fall. Through a sense of affection and duty, I communicated my suspicion to my heart's brother, that he might look out for this Judas. But he made light of the matter, for he was far superior in pen and sword, and in addition had the colonel's love and favor.

CHAPTER 22: *A roguish thieves' trick to wear each other's shoes*

It is customary to choose military constables from among the older, more experienced soldiers, and we also had some like that in our regiment. One of them was a crafty gallow's bird and archrogue, far more experienced than was necessary

for the job, for he was also a necromancer, alchemist, coscino-
mancer,[4] and sorcerer. He was as bulletproof as steel, made
others bulletproof, and could put whole squads of cavalry into
the field. His face looked very much like painters' and poets'
representations of Saturn. Now, although some poor, unfortunate soldiers who got nabbed felt very much downhearted
because of him, there were others who were glad to have this
creepy character as a friend. One of these was Oliver, our
secretary, and the more his jealousy of young Heartbrother
grew, the more intimate he became with the constable. I soon
concluded that the conjunction of Saturn and Mercury would
be dangerous to the ingenuous Heartbrother.

About this time the colonel's wife gave birth to a son, and
the christening was celebrated in high style. Young Heartbrother was asked to serve on table, and because my friend
was glad to do a favor, Oliver took this opportunity to per-
petrate a piece of villainy that he had long contemplated.
For when all the guests had left, the colonel's large gold-
plated cup was missing. It had definitely been used after certain strangers had left, and the colonel wasn't too keen about
losing it. The page said he had seen it last in Oliver's hands,
but Oliver said he must have been mistaken. They summoned
the constable to enlist his aid, asking him to use his magic to
regain the cup, and, if possible, to arrange that the thief
become known only to the colonel. (He did not want to ruin
any of the officers of his regiment if by chance one of them
had stolen it.)

Since everyone knew himself to be innocent, we all gathered
in the colonel's big tent, where the necromancer was about to
perform. Everybody looked at everyone else, wanting to know
where the cup had gone and what would come of it. When
the constable had mumbled a few words, several young dogs
crawled out of one person's pants pockets, another's sleeves,
and still another's boots, fly, and any other openings in his
clothes. These pups ran all over the tent; they were very

4 A person able to discover hidden objects by looking through a sieve.

pretty, of different colors and each differently marked. It was lots of fun. My own tight Croatian calfskin trousers were filled with puppies, too, and I had to pull them down. During my stay in the woods, my drawers had rotted on me, and I stood there stark naked, all I had before and behind appearing in plain sight! Finally a doggie jumped out of Heartbrother's fly; it was the jolliest of the lot and wore a golden collar. This one swallowed up all the other puppies (there were so many you couldn't put a foot down without stepping on one). When it had gobbled them all up it gradually shrank, but the collar grew until it changed into the colonel's loving cup.

The colonel and everyone else concluded that young Heartbrother, and no one else, had stolen the cup. Therefore the colonel said to him, "Look, you ungrateful guest, is this theft your thanks for all the good turns I've done you? Tomorrow I wanted to make you my secretary, but instead you ought to be hanged, as of today. And it would be done, too, if it weren't for your honest old father. Hurry up, get out of my camp, and don't let me see you as long as you live!"

Heartbrother wanted to explain, but since his theft was so obvious to everybody, he was not heeded, and when he went out his father fainted and we had quite a time bringing him to and comforting him, saying that a good father is not responsible for what a bad child has done. This is how Oliver, with the devil's help, got what he wanted, which he had been unable to get by honest means.

CHAPTER 23: *Ulrich Heartbrother sells himself for a hundred ducats*

As soon as young Heartbrother's captain found out about the theft, he dismissed him, despising him so much that others too began to despise him, and even the dogs practically peed on him. For this reason he often wished he were dead. His father was so worried about him that he fell ill and prepared for death. Since he had predicted that he would have to go through mortal danger on the twenty-sixth of July (which day was drawing near), he got permission from the colonel to see his son once more in order to talk about his will. I was the third person at this sad meeting. Well, I saw that the son needed to make no excuses to his father, who knew his character and upbringing well enough and was sure of his innocence. As a wise, understanding, and thoughtful man, he gathered from the circumstances that Oliver had been out to get his son and had schemed with the constable to get him in trouble. But what could he do against a sorcerer? He might be in worse trouble if he avenged himself. Furthermore, he was aware that he might die; yet he could not die in peace so long as his son lived under a cloud of shame. As for the son, the less he relished living under these conditions, the more he wished to die before his father. Surely the suffering of these two men was so pitiful to witness that I had to cry from the bottom of my heart. Finally they decided to be patient and to put their affairs into the hands of God. The son was to think of a means of getting away from his company and seeking his fortune elsewhere. But when they thought it over, he lacked funds to buy himself free of the captain. And while they pondered and commiserated over the straits in which poverty kept them, cutting off all hope of improving their lot, I remembered the ducats which were still sewn up in the donkey ears. I asked how much money they needed in this emergency. Young Heartbrother answered, "If someone came along and gave us a hundred thalers, I would be fairly sure to get out of trouble." I answered, "Brother, if this will do it, lift up your heart, for I will give you a hundred ducats." "Alas, brother," he answered in turn, "are you really a fool, or are you heartless enough to play with our grief?" "No, no," I said, "I'll produce the money for you." Taking off my jacket, I peeled one donkey ear from my arm, snipped it open, and let him count out a hundred ducats. I kept the rest and said, "With this I will take care of your sick father if he needs it." At this they embraced me, kissed me, and were beside

themselves with joy, calling me an angel whom God had sent
for their comfort. They wanted to give me a promissory note
and to assure me that I would share in old Heartbrother's
inheritance equally with the son, or (if God helped them to
their estate again) that they would gladly repay me this
amount with interest. I would have none of this but their
friendship. Then young Heartbrother wanted to swear that he
would have his revenge on Oliver or die trying, but his father
forbade it, assuring him that whoever killed Oliver would be
done in by Simplex. "Yet," he said, "I am sure neither will
kill the other, because you are not fated to die by weapons."
After that he made us swear to love and assist each other in
trouble.

Having commended his father to my care, young Heartbrother bought himself free with thirty thalers and the captain gave him an honorable discharge. Then he went to
Hamburg and with the rest of the money bought two horses
and equipment and joined the Swedes as a volunteer cavalryman.

CHAPTER 24: *Two prophecies in a row come true*

None of the colonel's men was better suited than I to care
for old Heartbrother in his sickness, and because the sick man
was more than satisfied with me, I was put in charge by the
colonel's wife, who also did much good for him. And since
he was in such good hands and reassured about his son, he
improved from day to day so that he recovered almost completely before the twenty-sixth of July. Yet, he wanted to
bide his time and play sick until this fateful day, of which
he was truly afraid, should pass.

Meanwhile he was visited by many officers, from either
army, who wanted to know their fortunes, and since he was
a good astrologer, physiognomist, and chiromancer he was
seldom wrong. He even named the day on which the future
battle of Wittstock took place, for many came to him who

were threatened with violent death. He assured the colonel's wife that she would have her baby in camp, because Magdeburg would not be surrendered before the end of the week. He expressly told Oliver (that snake-in-the-grass who tried to curry favor with him) that he would have to die a violent death, and that I would avenge his death and kill his murderers. For this reason Oliver was my friend for a while.

He told me my own future life in so much detail that it seemed it had already been completed and he had always been by my side. But I did not pay much attention, and only afterward, after many things had happened, I remembered he had mentioned their coming. He especially warned me of water, for he feared I would perish by it.

Now when the twenty-sixth of July came, he told me and a soldier whom the colonel had assigned to him for his protection, repeatedly and with emphasis, to let no one enter his tent. He was its only occupant, and he prayed constantly. Toward afternoon a cavalry officer came riding up and asked for the colonel's stable master. He was presented to us and was refused admission. But he insisted; he importuned the soldier and promised him a reward if he could see the stable master; he *had* to see him this evening. Because this got him nowhere, he started swearing, calling down the Lord's wrath and asserting he had come many times at the stable master's bidding and yet had missed him every time. Now that he'd arrived, he'd be damned if he would be refused. He dismounted and could not be prevented from opening the tent flap. I bit his hand, but he hauled off and hit me in the face.

As soon as he was inside and saw the old man, he said, "Sir, I beg you to excuse the liberty I am taking, but I must talk to you." "All right," said the stable master, "what is it?" The lieutenant said, "I only wanted to ask you to cast my horoscope." The stable master answered, "I hope, most honored sir, you will forgive me and excuse my refusal because of sickness, for my thick head cannot at present do the work, which requires many calculations. If you will be patient until tomorrow I hope to be able to satisfy you." The lieutenant shouted, "Sir! Just read my palm then." "Lieutenant," replied old Heartbrother, "this art is unreliable and deceptive. For that reason, may I insist that you put off your request until tomorrow, when I shall be glad to be of service."

The lieutenant was reluctant to be turned away. He stepped up to Heartbrother's cot, stretched out his hand, and said, "Sir, I only ask you to tell me a few words concerning the end of my life; I assure you if that it should be violent, I shall interpret your words as a warning from God to take better care of myself. Therefore I beg you for God's sake to come right out and not conceal the truth from me." The good old man answered him in a few words, "All right then. Look out or you'll be hanged within the hour." The lieutenant (who was drunk as a lord) shouted, "You rascal! You talk this way with a gentleman!?" He drew his blade and killed my dear old Heartbrother on his cot. The soldier and I immediately raised the alarm, and everyone ran for his gun. The lieutenant was on his mount in no time and would have escaped if the Elector of Saxony and his entourage had not come by just them. He had the lieutenant arrested and when he heard what had happened, he turned to our general, von Hatzfeld, and said only, "If a sick man in his bed is not safe from murderers, we certainly have rotten discipline in an imperial camp!" That was a severe sentence and enough to cut short the lieutenant's life. Our general immediately had him hanged by his precious neck, and that procedure choked off his breath.

CHAPTER 25: *Simplicius is metamorphosed from a youth into a virgin and acquires several wooers*

This true story proves that one cannot reject all predictions, as do some smart alecks who think they know everything and believe in nothing. It also shows that a man can hardly avoid the end that was set for him, even though his downfall is foretold by prophecy. As to whether it is necessary, useful, and good to have one's horoscope cast, I only say this: Old Heart-brother told me so many things, but I have often wished, and still wish, that he hadn't. I have never been able to avoid the bad things he predicted, and the ones still ahead are turning my hair grey—and all in vain, for presumably, like all the rest, they will happen whether or not I look out for them. Concerning the good forecasts, I hold that they are more deceptive and will not help a person as much as the bad predictions.

What good did it do me that old Heartbrother swore to high heaven I was the son of noble parents, while I knew of no other parents than my knan and mither, who were crude peasants in the Spessart? Or, to cite another example, what good did it do Wallenstein, Duke of Friedland, to be told he would be crowned king while violins played? Everybody knows how *he* was rocked to sleep at Eger.[5] Let other people ponder these matters. I'll get back to my story now.

When I had lost both my Heartbrothers, as I have told, I became disgusted with the camp at Magdeburg; I grew sick and tired of my jester's garb and my foolery, and I no longer cared to be the butt of everyone's jokes. I wanted to be free of all this, even if it cost me life and limb. And because there was no better opportunity, I went about it in a thoroughly irresponsible way.

Oliver, who had become my tutor when old Heartbrother died, allowed me to go foraging with the soldiers. Now, when we came to a large village and everyone went into the houses to see what he might take along, I sneaked off to see if I could find some peasant clothes I might slip into. But what I was looking for did not turn up and I had to be satisfied with a woman's dress. Finding myself alone, I changed into it, threw my suit into a privy, and imagined that now I was out of trouble. In my new outfit I started walking across the

---

[5] Albrecht Eusebius Wenzel von Wallenstein (1583–1634), the greatest general on the Catholic side, was murdered in the town hall of Eger, Bohemia, on February 25, 1634. In his drama *Wallenstein,* Schiller presents the last few days of his life.

street toward some officers' wives; I was very careful to take little steps. But I had hardly left the house when some of the foraging party saw me and I speeded up my gait. When they shouted, "Stop!" I ran all the faster and reached the officers' wives before they did. I implored the ladies, for the sake of honor and virtue, to save my virginity from these lusting goats. Not only was my wish granted, but a captain's wife hired me as her maid and I stayed with her until our men had captured Werberschanze, Havelberg, and Perleberg.

The captain's wife, who was no longer a spring chicken, though she wasn't too old either, took such a liking to my pretty face and straight body that finally, after much hemming and hawing and beating vainly about the bush, she told me in plain language where the shoe was pinching her. But at that time I was still very conscientious; I acted as if I had not understood and gave no indications but those from which one might conclude that I was a shamefaced maiden.

The captain and his man were sick and confined to the same hospital. He asked his wife to have me dressed better, so that they need not be ashamed of my ugly peasant dress. Doing more than she had been told, she dressed me up like a French doll, and this fed the fire in all three of them. In fact, the ardor of the captain and his man grew so that they hotly begged of me what I could not give them and what I was most elegantly refusing the lady.

Finally, the captain determined to create a situation that would enable him to get by force what he couldn't possibly have. His wife got wind of it, and because she hoped ultimately to wear down my scruples, she blocked his every move so that he thought he'd go crazy. The one I really felt sorry for was our man, the poor fellow, for master and mistress could cool their ardor with each other, but this poor chap had nobody. Therefore, one night when man and wife were sleeping, the hired man stood by the wagon where I slept, with fiery tears poured out his love for me, and asked for my pity. But I proved harder than any stone and let him know that I intended to keep my virginity until I got married.

When he offered marriage a thousand times and yet heard only that it was impossible for me to marry him, he despaired (or at least acted that way), pulled out his sword, put the point to his chest and the handle against the wagon, and let on he wanted to kill himself. I thought, The devil pushes a man to suicide. I comforted him and said I would give him my decision in the morning. This satisfied him and he went to sleep. But I stayed awake all the longer and contemplated my dilemma. I sensed that my situation would come to no good end; the captain's wife was becoming more and more impatient, the captain more daring in his approach, and the man more desperate in his love. I did not know what to do.

Often I had to help my mistress catch a flea, but of course this was to get me to see and touch her lily-white breasts and her whole body. And because I was flesh and blood, this sort of thing was getting more difficult for me. If the woman left me in peace, the captain pestered me, and if I had a night of peace from these two, the manservant was after me. Thus my female clothing was much harder to wear than the fool's cap. At that point (but much too late) I thought of the deceased Heartbrother's prophecy and warning, and I imagined I was right in the middle of that danger to life and limb he had predicted for me. The dress held me captive; I could not escape in it, and the captain would have crushed every bone in my body if he had surprised me catching fleas on his pretty wife. What was I to do? I decided to make a clean breast of it to the manservant next morning. I assumed his ardor would cool, and if I gave him some of my ducats he might help me back into men's clothing and thus out of trouble. This would have worked well if luck had been with me, but it wasn't.

My foolish lover got up right after midnight in order to hear my consent. He started rattling and rocking the wagon just after I had fallen into a deep sleep (for I had lain awake worrying for some time). In a loud voice he called out, "Sabina, Sabina, get up and keep your promise!" But he woke up the captain before me because his tent was close to the wagon. Undoubtedly the captain was livid and green with

envy, but he did not come out to interfere; he only got up in
order to see how the deal would come out. The manservant
woke me up and urged me either to come out of the wagon
or to let him in. I gave him a scolding and asked if he thought
I was a whore; my promise was based on marriage and without that he could never have me. He asked why I didn't get
up; it was beginning to get light and I could make an early
start with the breakfast. He would fetch water and firewood
and make a fire for me. I answered, "If you want to do that,
I can sleep that much longer. You go ahead. I'll be there
soon." But since the fool would not leave me in peace, I got
up, more to do my work than to be kind to him, especially
since yesterday's mood of despair seemed to have left him. I
could easily pass for a soldier's hired girl, for I had learned
from the Croats how to cook, bake, and launder, and no finer
work was required. Whatever I could not do, like arranging
the captain's wife's hair, she gladly overlooked, for she knew
very well I had never learned it.

When I climbed out of the wagon my lover became so en-
flamed by the sight of my white arms that he could not re-
frain from kissing me, and I didn't put up much resistance.
The captain, who was looking on, could not stand it and came
running with drawn sword to dispatch my lover. But he took
to his heels and forgot to come back. The captain said to me,
"You bloody whore! I'll teach you. . . ." He couldn't say *what*
because of his anger. He started beating me as if he were insane. I began screaming and he had to stop to avoid causing
an alarm, for the Saxon and the imperial armies were en-
camped close to each other since the Swedes, under General
Banér, were approaching.

CHAPTER 26: *How Simplicius is considered a traitor and a
warlock*

When daylight came and both armies began to break camp,
my master abandoned me to the stable boys. They were a

bunch of brutes and the trouble I had with them was bad
enough. They chased me toward a clump of bushes where
they hoped to satisfy their animal lust, as is the custom of
these children spawned by the devil when a woman is turned
over to them. Many other lads ran out just to watch this
pitiful sport, and among these was John, the manservant. He
had kept an eye on me, and seeing that things were getting
rough, he wanted to save me by main force even if it cost his
head. He got some help by saying I was his fiancée. His friends
felt sorry for both of us and wanted to do what they could.
But the stable boys, who claimed prior rights and did not
want to give up their quarry, took a different view and set
force against force. So a fight started and help came running
to either side; the situation almost resembled a tournament
where everyone does his best for the sake of a beautiful lady.

The riotous noise brought in the constable, who arrived
just as they were dragging me back and forth and tearing the
clothes off me. And then they saw I was no woman. The appearance of the constable calmed everybody, for he was feared
worse than the devil, and those who had been fighting evap-
orated. He got the essential information quickly, and while I
was hoping he would get me out of distress, he arrested me
because it was most unusual and highly suspicious for a man
in women's clothing to be found inside an army camp. On
the way to the general provost marshal, the constable and one
of his men led me past the different regiments (who were all
ready to march). But when we passed my colonel's regiment
he recognized me, talked to me, and gave me some clothes,
and I was handed over to our old provost who put me in
handcuffs and chains.

I found it hard to walk that way, and I would have starved
if Oliver, the secretary, had not given me something to eat. I
did not dare show my ducats, which I had managed to conceal until now, for surely I would have lost them and drawn
even greater suspicion on myself. In the evening Oliver told
me why I was given such severe treatment. Our regimental
magistrate had received orders to question me at once and to

communicate the results to the provost marshal. They thought not only that I was a scout or a spy, but also that I knew witchcraft, for shortly after I disappeared from the colonel, some witches had been burned, who had confessed (and died for it) to seeing me at one of their meetings, at which they had deliberated about drying up the river Elbe so that Magdeburg could be captured sooner.

The regimental magistrate was given a list of seven questions to ask me, but I wanted to tell him my whole story so that the strange circumstances of my life might explain everything neatly and put my answers to the questions in proper context. But the magistrate was not that curious; he was tired and grouchy from marching and wanted only brief answers. When he had finished writing them down he said, "Hm, yes, you are the kind whose tongue needs loosening on the rack." My thought was, "May God help me if things go his addlepated way." Early next morning the provost marshal sent our constable an order to keep me under arrest because he intended to examine me personally, as soon as the armies stopped moving. Doubtless I would have been tortured if God had not destined it differently. While under arrest I thought constantly of the parson at Hanau and of the late Heartbrother, for both had predicted my fortune after my escape from the fool's cap. I also pondered how difficult—maybe downright impossible—it was for a poor girl to go on living in these military times and keep her virginity.

CHAPTER 27: *How the provost weathered the battle of Wittstock*

We had hardly pitched camp that night when I was taken to the provost marshal. He had my previous answers in front of him and started examining me. I told him how things had come about, but he did not believe me. It *was* hard for the provost marshal to tell whether he was dealing with a fool or a clever scoundrel, for although questions and answers came tripping off my tongue, the whole business was most strange. The provost marshal asked the constable whether anything unusual, like written documents, had been found on me. The constable answered, "No, why bother to frisk him? The camp police brought him in almost naked." But, alas, that wasn't good enough. The provost had to frisk me in everyone's presence, and since he did this most thoroughly, he found the two donkey's ears that were wrapped around my arms and contained my ducats. Then they said, "Do we need any other proof? This traitor undertook some big job. Why else would a man put on fool's clothing or a woman's dress? It's best to put him on the rack tomorrow or, as he is probably guilty, burn him; since he admits keeping company with sorcerers, he doesn't deserve anything else."

You can easily imagine how I felt. I knew I was innocent and trusted in God, but I also saw the danger, and deplored the loss of my ducats, which had disappeared into the provost marshal's pockets. But before they could give me the third degree, Banér's army and ours started fighting. First they fought for position and then for the heavy artillery, which we promptly lost. Our constable, that clever puppy-maker, stayed pretty far behind the battle lines, with his helpers and the prisoners, and yet we were so close behind our own brigade that we could recognize the individual soldiers by their clothing. When a Swedish squadron clashed with ours, we were in danger of death no less than the fighters, for the air was so full of whizzing bullets that you might think they were fighting exclusively for our personal benefit.

Those who were afraid ducked and cringed, but those with experience and courage let the bullets pass without turning pale. In the battle itself each man tried to prevent his own death by killing the man approaching him. An awful music was performed by the cruel shots, the clashing of armor plates, the splintering of pikestaffs, the screams of the attackers as well as the wounded, by the blare of trumpets, the roll of drums, and the shrill sound of fifes. Heavy dust and dense smoke covered the scene, as if to hide the ghastly sight of the wounded and dead. From the darkness one heard the pitiful moaning of the dying and the joyful shouting of those still full of courage. As time went on, even the horses seemed to become more energetic in the defense of their masters. A few of them fell down dead beneath their riders. They had received wounds through no fault of their own and in recompense for faithful service. For similar reasons, others fell on their masters, and thus, while dying, enjoyed the honor of being supported by those whom they had carried while alive. Still others, in rage and anger, ran away, leaving mankind behind, and for the first time sought their freedom in the open fields. The earth that is accustomed to covering the dead was, herself now covered by corpses. In one place lay heads that had lost their masters, and elsewhere lay bodies without heads. Out of some bodies entrails hung in a cruel and ghastly manner. The heads of others had been crushed and the brains spattered all over. Here one saw lifeless bodies robbed of their blood; there, some still alive and gory with the blood of others. Here lay severed arms with the fingers still twitching as if they itched to get back into the melee. There some fellows who had shed or spilled not one drop of blood were taking to their heels. In one place lay thighs separated from the burden of their bodies; yet they had become heavier than ever they were in life. In another place mortally wounded men were praying for speedy death, while others were begging for mercy and asking quarter. To sum it all up: it was one pitiful, miserable sight.

The Swedes soon drove our people before them and scattered them in quick pursuit. On this occasion our Mr. Constable and his prisoners also decided to flee, though we—never having fought—did not deserve any hostility; but the constable threatened to kill us if we didn't join him. At that moment young Heartbrother came galloping up with five other horsemen and greeted the constable with a shot from his pistol. "Look at you, you old son of a bitch," he shouted. "Do you still feel like producing puppies? I'll repay you for your trouble!" But the shot didn't hurt the constable any more than it would a steel anvil. "Ho-ho!? Is this the kind you are?"

shouted Heartbrother. "I don't want to have made this trip
for nothing. You puppy-maker, you'll die even if your soul
is sewed to your guts." Then Heartbrother ordered one of the
constable's own soldiers to kill him with an ax, if *he* didn't
want to get killed.

This is how the constable got his comeuppance. When
Heartbrother recognized me, he took off my chains and handcuffs, put me on his horse, and had his man take me to safety.

CHAPTER 28: *Concerning a great battle in which the trium-
phant conqueror is taken prisoner in the very
act of being victorious*

Though my savior's man removed me from further danger,
his master rode into it, for reasons of honor and a desire for
spoils. He was surrounded and taken prisoner. When the
victorious Swedes had divided their loot and buried their
dead, and Heartbrother was missing, his captain inherited me,
the horses, and the man. I had to become the captain's stable
boy for no other pay than the promise that he would "set me
up," i.e., buy me a mount and an outfit, if I did well and
when I had grown a little older. For the time being, I had to
be content and patient.

Soon after that my captain was promoted to lieutenant
colonel. It was my job to do what David did long ago for
King Saul; I had to sing and play the lute. On the march I
had to carry his cuirass for him—a job I hated. Though this
piece of equipment was invented to protect against the enemy's thrusts, I found the very opposite to be true, for under
the protection of the cuirass the little crawlers that fed on me
could persecute me all the better; beneath it they had free
passage, fun, and frolic. It seemed I was wearing this piece
of armor for *their* protection, not mine, because I couldn't
possibly get at them with my hands. I thought of all sorts of
strategic devices for eradicating this armada, but I had neither
the time nor the opportunity to stamp them out by fire (as is
done by baking them in an oven), water, or poison (mercury

would do it!). Nor did I have the money to get rid of them by buying all new shirts or a set of new clothes. I had to live with them at the expense of my life's blood. When they were nibbling and irritating me too much, I'd whip out my pistol as if to exchange shots with them, but I only took the ramrod and pushed them away from their food. After a while I put a piece of fur on the end of the rod, tied it with sticky tape, and, reaching under the cuirass with this louse-catcher, I nabbed them by the dozen and hurled them to the ground from high on horseback. But still, it didn't really help.

One time my lieutenant colonel was ordered to ride to Westphalia on a special mission. If he had then had as many men as I had lice, he would have frightened the whole world. But since he hadn't, he had to proceed carefully and hide in a forest between Hamm and Soest.[6] At that time my pedicular enemies had reached the height of their glory. They were plaguing me so much with their undermining tactics that I thought they would soon take up quarters between my skin and flesh. No wonder the Brazilians eat lice—anger and the spirit of revenge drives them to it! One time, when part of the cavalrymen were feeding their horses, while others slept or kept a lookout, I could no longer stand the annoyance and stepped aside under a tree to do battle with my enemy. Though others put on their armor when they fight, for this battle I took mine off and started such a murder and massacre that my swords (both thumbs) were dripping blood, and corpses (or dead skins) fell everywhere. The ones I didn't kill I chased out into the cold world and let them take a walk under the tree. I thought of a ditty I had heard:

And when the slaughter started, my nails they all got red.
One louse said to her neighbor, "O lousy, we'll be dead!"

[6] Westphalia, a district in northwestern Germany, is partly hilly, partly good, level farmland; as a class its farmers are well to do. Various industries flourished there even in the seventeenth century. The towns mentioned were centers of military activities. Soest has one of the finest examples of church architecture in the Catholic cathedral of St. Mary-on-the-Height.

When I think of the slaughter my skin still itches. I continued so furiously that I did not notice some imperials charging my lieutenant colonel until they were close upon me, relieved the poor lice, and captured me. My manly courage, with which I had lately slain many thousands, did not impress the imperials. I was given to a dragoon and the best thing about me that he got was my lieutenant colonel's cuirass; he sold it to his commander at Soest (where they were quartered) for a stiff price. I had to be the dragoon's stable boy, and he became my sixth master in this war.

CHAPTER 29: *How, before his death, a pious soldier lived well in Paradise; and how the Hunter took his place after his death*

Because our landlady did not want me to populate her and her whole house with my pedicular multitudes, I had to get rid of them. She didn't fool around, either, but stuck my ragged clothes in her oven and roasted the lice alive until dead. I began living as if in a rose garden; in fact, no one can believe what a relief it was to be rid of this torment, which had been like living in an ant hill.

But having gotten out of one kind of trouble, I ran into another. My master was one of those soldiers who are sure they'll go to heaven. He was satisfied with his pay and wouldn't hurt a fly. All he owned he had saved from his weekly wages and extra guard duty. Though this was little enough, he treasured it more than Oriental pearls; every two bits he sewed up in his clothing, and his poor horse and I had to help him save. That is why I had to subsist on dry pumpernickel and water or, if prosperity was rampant, on small beer. But I had no taste for this because my throat became rough from the coarse bread, and my body frightfully emaciated. If I wanted better food I had to steal it—but secretly, so that he could not be blamed.

As far as he was concerned, there was no need for gallows,

the wooden horse, hangman, bastinadoes, or for surgeons, or tavern-keepers, or the musician who plays taps; his whole life was far removed from gluttony, swilling, gambling, and dueling. When he was ordered on convoy duty, raiding, or some such special job, he straggled along like an old lady on a cane. I am convinced that if it hadn't been for this good dragoon's heroic and martial *virtues* he would never have caught me. He wouldn't have paid any attention to a lousy boy but would have pursued my lieutenant colonel instead. There was no use in looking forward to any secondhand clothing he might give me, for the chap wore clothes that were almost as well patched as my hermit's. His saddle and other gear were hardly worth three bits; his horse was so weak with hunger that neither Swede nor Hessian need fear being pursued by him.

All this persuaded his captain to place him as a guard in a convent at Paradise, near Soest—not because he was so good for the purpose, but rather to give him a chance to get ahead and to buy a new mount, and particularly because the nuns had asked for a pious, conscientious, and quiet man. Well, he rode there and I walked along, because unfortunately he had only one horse. Along the way he said, "Tarnation, Shrimpy" —he could never remember "Simplicius"—"we're going to Paradise and how we'll gorge there!" I answered, "The name is a good omen. May God grant that the place lives up to it." "Sure," he said (and he hadn't understood me), "even if we could drink an 'Ohm' of beer—that's forty gallons—every day or two, I'm sure they wouldn't mind. You just be a good boy. I'm going to have a brand new coat made for myself and let you have the old one. It'll make you a nice piece of clothing yet."

We found Paradise as we wanted it or even better; instead of angels it was full of pretty young women who treated us so well with food and drink that after a while I put on weight. There they had the richest beer, the best Westphalian ham and knockwurst, and very tender and well prepared beef. I learned to put half an inch of salted butter on pumpernickel, and cheese on top of that, to make it slide down better. And when I sat over a leg of mutton (well seasoned with garlic!) and had a stein of beer by my side, soul and body were refreshed and I forgot all my hardships. This Paradise did me as much good as if it had been the real thing. My only concern was that it wouldn't last forever and that I had to walk around in rags, so tattered and torn.

But just as bad luck had before come to me by the jugful, so good luck came now by the tubful: when my master sent me to Soest to get the rest of his baggage, I found on the way a package, and in it were several yards of red cloth, with red velvet for lining. I took it along and exchanged it at a woolen-draper's for enough common green cloth for a suit, together with the buttons. The man also agreed to have the suit made up for me and to give me a hat into the bargain. Since now I needed only a pair of new shoes and a shirt, I gave the haberdasher the silver buttons and the braid that went with the red cloth, and for these he gave me the shoes and shirt; and so I had a complete new outfit.

When I returned to Paradise and my master, he was hopping mad because I hadn't brought the package to him first. He even talked of whipping me and taking the suit away from me (and he would have done it if it had fit him and if he hadn't been ashamed). I thought I had done right all the time!

Now this niggard and tightwad had to be ashamed that his boy was dressed better than he. For that reason he rode to Soest, borrowed money from his captain, and bought himself a whole new outfit. He promised to repay from his special weekly wages, which he did. Of course he had the money himself, but he was too smart to use it; for if he had done so, he might have lost the lazy man's job of safeguarding Paradise that winter. This way, if the captain wanted his money back he would leave him in this sinecure.

From now on we had the laziest life on earth, and bowling was our most strenuous sport. When I had curried, fed, and watered my dragoon's nag, I carried on like a rich man's son

and went for a walk. The convent was also watched over by
the Hessians, who had sent a musketeer from Lippstadt. He
was a furrier by trade and a good singer and fencer. In order
not to get rusty, he practiced fencing with me and I soon
got so good at it that I held my own against him. My dragoon
bowled with him, but only for who would have to drink the
most beer with the next meal; thus the convent was the loser
however we came out.

The convent had its own game forest and employed a
keeper for it. Since I was clad in green, I associated with him,
and that winter I learned all the tricks of his trade, particularly those concerning small game. For this reason, and because the name "Simplicius" is a little unusual and not easy
to pronounce, everyone called me "Hunterboy." I got to know
all the roads and trails, and this came in handy later. When
I couldn't go out because of the weather, I read all sorts of
books that the steward lent me. But when the noble ladies of
the convent noticed that I could play the lute and a little on
the clavichord, besides having a good voice, they started paying more and more attention to me. Since I was well proportioned and my face wasn't hard to look at, they all thought
my demeanor and bearing were that of a nobleman and altogether becoming to a well-liked young man. Before I knew it,
I became popular, and everyone wondered why I was working
for such a slovenly dragoon.

In spring, having spent the winter in this pleasant manner,
my master was relieved of his job. He took it so hard that he
fell ill. A severe fever and some old troubles then set in, and
three weeks later I had to bury him. I wrote this inscription
for his grave:

> John Starveling lies here, a soldier good and brave.
> He ne'er spilt human blood & now he's in his grave.

By custom and legal usage his captain should have inherited his horse and gun while the sergeant got the rest of his
possessions. But since I was an up-and-coming young man
who would in time be a good soldier, everything was offered

to me if I wanted to join the army in place of my late master. I accepted with enthusiasm, because I knew that my master had left behind quite a number of ducats he had scraped together and sewn into his old breeches. When I gave my name —Simplicius Simplicissimus—to the clerk (and his name was Cyriacus) he couldn't spell it and said, "There must be a devil in hell by that name!" When I asked *him* if there wasn't one by the name of Cyriacus, he didn't know what to say, though he thought he was smart. My captain, who heard this conversation, liked me from the beginning and set great hopes by my future military exploits.

CHAPTER 30: *How the Hunter prospered when he began soldiering. Any young soldier can learn a lot from this chapter*

Because the commander at Soest needed a stable boy and I seemed to be the kind he liked, he was reluctant to see me become a soldier. He said he'd get me yet, for I wasn't old enough to pass for a man. Then he argued with my captain about it, sent for me, and said, "Listen, Hunterboy, you ought to be my servant!" I asked what I was to do in this position. He answered, "Help wait on the horses." "Sir," I replied, "we are far apart in this matter. I'd rather have a master in whose service the horses wait on me; but since I can't have that kind of a job, I'll stay a soldier." He said, "Your beard is too soft yet." "Oh no," I said, "I feel strong enough to outdo a man of eighty. It's not the beard that kills another man; otherwise billy goats would sell at a higher price." He said, "If your courage is as good as your tongue, I'll let it pass." I answered, "This you can find out in the next battle"; and so I let him know I wished to be a stable boy no longer.

Next I performed an autopsy on the dragoon's old pants. With their contents I bought a good horse and the best pistols I could find. Everything had to be spick-and-span, and because I liked the name "Hunterboy" I also had a new green suit made. I gave the old one to my stable boy, for I had outgrown it. So my boy and I rode side by side, and no longer could anyone consider me poor stuff. I was bold enough to decorate my hat with an outrageous plume, like an officer's, and soon I had plenty of enemies who were jealous of me. We exchanged angry words and finally came to blows. But as soon as I had shown a few of them what I had learned from the furrier in Paradise, and that I could repay every thrust in kind, they not only left me in peace but even sought my friendship.

I frequently volunteered to go raiding, either on foot or on horseback, for I was well mounted and faster on foot than many others. When we got involved with the enemy, it was neck or nothing with me, and I always wanted to be one of the first.

This activity soon made me well known and so famous among friend and foe that both sides reckoned with me, especially since the most dangerous tasks were given to me and I was put in charge of whole groups of raiders. About that time I started helping myself to everything, and whenever I got hold of something special I gave my officers such a big share of it that they helped me out and looked the other way when I raided off limits. General Götz [7] had left three enemy garrisons in Westphalia, one each at Dorsten, Lippstadt, and Coesfeld. I annoyed them no end, for I was at them with small groups of raiders almost every day, now here, now there; and I took valuable loot. Because I came out on top everywhere, the people grew to think I could make my-self invisible and was bulletproof, like iron or steel. Therefore, I was feared like the plague, and thirty of the enemy's men were not ashamed to run like rabbits when they knew me to be nearby with only fifteen men. It got to the point that I was sent to exact "contributions" from towns or to see that they paid what they owed. This benefited my purse and my name; officers and fellow soldiers loved their Hunterboy; the

[7] Count von Götz, an Austrian (imperial) field marshal who died in 1645.

most prominent enemy raiders shook in their boots, and the peasants were kept on my side by love or fear. I punished my enemies and richly rewarded those who had done me the least favor; I spent almost half my plunder on rewards and information.

For this reason no enemy raiders proceeded, no convoy or expedition by the enemy took place that I didn't know of. I then guessed their intentions and made my plans accordingly. And since, with a little luck, I had for the most part anticipated well, everyone was surprised at my youthful success, and many officers and experienced soldiers, even on the enemy side, wanted to see me. Furthermore, I treated my prisoners with great consideration so that they often cost me more than I gained through them; and whenever I was able to show some courtesy to an enemy, especially to officers, I always did so, if it could be done without violating my duty and loyalty.

With this sort of behavior I would soon have been commissioned as an officer if my youth hadn't prevented it. For if one wanted to command a squadron at my age one had to be of ancient nobility; moreover, my captain could not promote me because at the moment there were no positions vacant in his company. He did not want to lose me, for in me he would have lost more than a milch cow. But he did make me a sergeant.

The honor of being preferred over older soldiers—though it was a slight thing—and the praise I received daily encouraged me to even greater achievements. I lay awake at night thinking of what I could do to make myself even greater, more renowned, and more admirable. I worried over lack of opportunity to show my skill with weapons, and often wished for the Trojan War or the Siege of Ostend, but, fool that I was, I did not consider that every grey goose gets caught at last. But when a rash young soldier has luck and pluck and money, that's how it goes. Pride and arrogance are sure to arise in him. Because of my arrogance I kept two hostlers instead of a stable boy. By giving them expensive clothes and horses, I incurred the envy of all the officers who begrudged me what they lacked the energy to go out and get.

CHAPTER 31: *How the devil stole the parson's bacon, and how the Hunter got caught in his own trap*

I want to tell a story or two about the time before I joined the dragoons. These events are not of world-shaking importance, but they are entertaining; for I didn't undertake only big things—I didn't scorn the little ones either, if I could just make a name for myself and arouse admiration among the people.

My captain was ordered to proceed with some fifty men to the fortress of Recklingshausen, there to execute an assignment. Because we thought we might have to hide in the woods for a few days, each of us took along a week's rations. But when the convoy we were awaiting did not come in time, we ran out of food, and we couldn't steal it without giving away our presence and ruining the plans. We were starving and it hurt. Unfortunately in this place I had no helpers (as I had in most others) who might secretly bring me and my men vittles and information. So, unless we wanted to return empty-handed, we had to think of something. My comrade, a student who had only lately flunked out and joined the army, was longing for the good oatmeal his parents used to provide and which he had scornfully left behind. And while he was thinking about breakfast he remembered his studies. "Oh, brother," he said, "isn't it a shame I didn't study how to feed myself. . . . Hah! If I went to the parson over in the village he'd give me something to eat." I thought about this awhile and then spoke with the captain about using the student. Our situation was so bad and his trust in me so great that after some hesitation he consented.

I traded clothes with another soldier and then my student and I, taking the long way around, trotted toward the village, which was only half an hour away as the crow flies. We recognized the minister's house because it was close to the church, and because it looked somewhat citified and was built against a wall that enclosed the whole parsonage. I had already instructed my comrade what to say. He was still wearing his threadbare school clothes; I pretended to be a painter's journeyman. (I did not think I'd be called on to paint, because few peasants have painted houses.) The parson was polite, and when my pal addressed him in well-turned Latin phrases and told him (like a seasoned liar) that soldiers had robbed him and taken all his food and money, he was given a sandwich and a pot of beer. I pretended we did not belong together and said I would have a bite to eat at the inn and then come back and holler for him, so that we could travel some distance before nightfall. So I went toward the inn, more to see what could be picked up at night than to satisfy my hunger. On the way I had the good luck to spot a peasant sealing his oven; it was full of pumpernickel and they are baked for twenty-four hours! I thought, "Go right ahead sealing! One way or another we'll get at this good stuff."

I didn't stay long at the inn, because now I knew where to get bread, but I bought a few rolls to take to my captain; and when I got back to the parsonage the "student" had already finished eating and had told his host I was a painter on my way to Holland, where I wanted to continue studying art. The minister welcomed me cordially and asked me to accompany him inside the church where he had some art objects he wanted repaired. To avoid spoiling the plans, I had to go along, and when he opened the locked door that led to the churchyard—oh, marvelous sight!—I saw the heavens full of black stars—I mean hams, sausages, and sides of bacon hanging in a chimney that we passed. I looked at these hopefully, thinking that they were smiling back at me. But *wishing* them off the hooks and into the hands of my comrades in the woods did not move them. Well, I thought of ways and means of associating them with the bread previously mentioned, but nothing good occurred to me right away; the parsonage was enclosed by a wall, with all windows protected by iron bars, and two monstrous dogs were cavorting about the yard—and they probably would not be sleeping at night if a person tried to steal what they would ultimately gnaw on if they guarded it well.

Inside the church, while the parson and I discussed the repair and restoration of some paintings, and I made all sorts of excuses, including my present journey, for not wanting to work on them, the sexton or sacristan said, "Hey you, you look more like a ragged soldier than a painter." I wasn't used to such talk any more, and yet I had to take it; I only shook my head and answered, "Oh you rascal, if you'll give me a brush and some colors I'll paint you a jackanapes that looks just like you." The parson took it in fun and warned us that it wouldn't do to tell each other off in this holy edifice. He meant that he didn't trust either of us, but he offered the student and me one more drink and let us go. My heart stayed with the sausages!

Before nightfall we were back in camp, changed clothes again, told the captain of our experiences, and chose six stout men to help us carry the bread. We got to the village about midnight and quietly liberated the bread (we had a man along who could sweet-talk the dogs into silence). When we passed the parsonage I just could not go on without some bacon. I wondered how to get into the parson's kitchen, but I saw no other entrance than the chimney and thought it might, on this one occasion, substitute for a door. We hid the bread inside the charnel house in the cemetery and got a ladder and a rope from a barn. Since I could climb in and out of fireplaces like a chimney sweep (I had learned it in hollow trees as a child), I climbed on the roof with another fellow, and having tied my long hair in a knot, lowered myself down to the supplies, and then tied one ham after another onto the rope. They were hauled to the roof and taken to the cemetery. But dammit! Just when I was ready to quit, the rail on which I was standing broke, and I fell down head over heels and was caught as if in a mousetrap. My friends on the roof lowered the rope, but it also broke before they could lift me off the floor. I thought, "Well, Hunterboy, now they'll chase you, and you may get your skin torn." My fall had awakened the minister, who asked the cook to make a light. She came into the kitchen in her nightshirt, with a housecoat over her shoulders, and stood so close that she touched me. She reached for a live coal, held a candle to it, and blew on it. I blew harder than she, and that frightened the poor biddy so badly that she shook and trembled, dropped coal and candle, and retreated to her master. This gave me a chance to think how I might get out of my predicament, but nothing occurred to me. My comrades wanted to get me out by main force, but I wouldn't let them. I asked them instead to look to their firearms, to leave only one man on the roof, and to wait and see whether I could get away without a big commotion, so that our assignment—the surprise attack—should not be betrayed. If this couldn't be done, they were on their own and had to act as best they could.

While the parson was striking a light, the cook told him that there was a ghastly two-headed spook in the kitchen. When I heard this, I quickly rubbed soot and ashes all over my face and hands so that I certainly did not look like an angel (as some of the ladies at Paradise had occasionally said). If the sexton had seen me, he would have had to admit I was a very fast portrait painter! Then I began making a fearful racket by banging pots and pans together; I hung a stove ring around my neck and picked up a poker with which to defend myself in case of necessity. But none of this impressed the pious parson. He and the cook came in like a procession. He dressed in his black gown and stole, book in one hand, aspergillum in the other. The cook held a wax candle in either hand and a kettleful of holy water slung over one arm. He started exorcising me, asking who I was and what I was doing there. Since he thought I was the devil himself, I thought I might appropriately act like him. So I lied and said, like the devil, "I am the devil and I want to wring your neck—and your cook's." He continued his exorcism and reproached me for bothering him and his cook, who had done nothing to deserve this. He adjured me to go back where I came from. In an atrocious voice I answered that I couldn't, even if I wanted to. Meanwhile the fellow on the roof, who could imitate animal sounds and was not stupid, caught on to what was needed below and hooted like an owl, barked like a dog, whinnied like a horse, bleated like a billy goat, and heehawed like a jackass; he sounded down the chimney now like a bunch of cats mating in February, now like a cackling hen, and finally like a pack of hungry wolves. This rather frightened the parson and the cook, but I worried that I was being exorcised because the parson had heard or read that the devil likes to wear green.

In the midst of these troubles, which surrounded all of us (but particularly the poor cook), I luckily noticed that the night latch on the door to the cemetery was not locked, only bolted. I quickly snapped it back and rushed out the door into the cemetery (where my friends awaited me with pistols cocked) and let the parson exorcise all the devils he wanted. After my friend on the roof had handed down my hat and we had put the vittles in sacks, we went back to our camp, for we had nothing more to do in the village, except perhaps to return the rope and ladder.

We tarried two more days in the woods, waiting for our convoy. When it finally came we lost not a single man, took thirty prisoners, and found richer spoils than I had ever shared. On account of my courage and meritorious conduct I received two shares—namely, three beautiful Friesland stallions loaded with all the merchandise we could pack on them in a hurry. If we had had time to locate and secure the loot, everybody would have gotten rich on his share. As it was, we had to leave more behind than we could carry off. We retreated to Rehnen, where we fed the horses and divided the plunder.

There I got to thinking again about the parson and how I had carried off his bacon. The reader can imagine what an ambitious and arrogant chap I was. Not only had I robbed the pious minister and frightened him nearly out of his wits, now I wanted to feel proud of it, too! Therefore, I took a gold ring with a sapphire, which I had liberated on the same raid, and sent it by messenger to the parson. I also sent this letter:

Your Reverence,

If lately in the forest I had not run out of food, I should have had no cause to steal your Reverence's bacon. I hereby assure you that I frightened you against my will and hope for your pardon. Concerning the bacon itself, it is only fair to pay for it, and in lieu of cash I am sending you this ring, furnished by the parties for whose sake the smoked pork had to be carried off. I hope your Reverence will accept it. Moreover, I assure you that I shall be your faithful and humble servant in all emergencies, even though your sexton doesn't think I am a painter.

Your devoted,
Hunterboy

The farmer whose oven had been emptied of pumpernickel was sent sixteen thalers out of the raiders' common kitty, for I had taught my comrades that they ought thus to get the farmers on their side, because in a pinch they can either help you out or give you away and sell your neck. A few days later I received this answer from the parson:

Honored Hunter,

If the victim of your bacon raid had known you would appear in devil's guise, he would never have wished to see the famous Hunterboy. But inasmuch as the "borrowed" bacon and bread have been overpaid, the fright you gave us will be more easily forgotten, especially as it was inflicted reluctantly and by such a famous person. All is forgiven, and when you pass through here again, do not hesitate to look in at the house of one who is not reluctant to exorcise the devil. Farewell!

This is how I carried on everywhere. I became very famous, and the more I spent and wasted, the more plunder came to me. I thought I had invested the ring well, though it was worth around a hundred thalers. And that's the end of this book.

End of the Second Book

✐ Book Three

CHAPTER 1: *How the Hunter begins to stray from the path of righteousness*

In the previous book the gentle reader learned how ambitious I had become in Soest, and how I sought and found honor, glory, and favor through behavior which in other men would be considered punishable. Now I want to tell how I allowed my foolishness to mislead me further into extreme danger. As I have mentioned, I was so eager for honor and glory that I could hardly sleep, and when I lay awake many a night thinking up new tricks, some curious notions came to me. For instance, I invented shoes one could wear hind end front, with the heels under one's toes. I had made some thirty pairs of these, of different sizes; I gave them out to my companions, and when we went raiding, it was impossible to track us, for we wore now these, now our regular shoes, carrying the other pair in our knapsacks. When an observer came to a place where my men had changed shoes, the tracks would lead him to think that two parties had met and disappeared again. But if I kept wearing my backward pair, one would think I was going where I had already been or had come from a place to which I was just then going. Thus my tracks were more confusing than a maze, and those who wanted to capture me by tracking me could never find me or catch me in their net.

Often I was very close to the enemy, who was supposed to look for me far away, and even more often I was miles from the woods they were surrounding and combing through to catch me. And as I managed the raiding parties on foot, so did I those on horseback; I thought nothing of getting off at a fork or crossroads and having the mounts reshod with the irons pointing the other way. The common tricks that are used on raids, if one is weak and yet wants to be judged strong from the tracks left behind, or if one is strong and wants to be considered weak, were such an everyday matter that I don't want to tell about them here.

Besides, I invented an instrument by which, on calm nights, I could hear a horn signal three hours away, a horse neighing or dogs barking two hours away, and human beings talking at an hour's distance. I kept this invention very secret and I derived much glory from it, because everyone considered such reception to be downright impossible. The instrument (which I usually carried in my breeches along with the telescope) wasn't very practical by day, unless it was used in a lonely and quiet place, for otherwise everything, from horses and cows down to birds and frogs, became as audible as if one stood in a market square surrounded by crowds of people and animals.

When I could not go raiding with a party, I went out stealing by myself, and then neither horses, cows, pigs, nor sheep were safe. I collected them from their stables for miles around. I put shoes or boots on cattle and horses until I got them to a busy road where no one could trace them. Then, too, I reversed the shoes on the horses or, in the case of cows or oxen, put reversed boots on them, and so spirited them to safety. When I brought my booty home I shared it honestly with my comrades and officers. And that is why they let me go out time and again, and if my theft was betrayed or found out, they covered up for me. As for stealing from poor people, taking chickens or other trifles, I considered myself above that.

Eventually I began to lead an Epicurean life, eating and swilling, for I had forgotten the precepts of my hermit, and there was no one who would tell me off or whom I'd have to mind. The officers joined me in malfeasance by enjoying my payoffs, and those who should have punished and corrected me encouraged me in further vices. Finally I became so godless, bold, and despicable that there wasn't a piece of roguery

I wouldn't have tackled. As time went on, I was secretly en-
vied by my comrades for having a luckier hand at stealing
than anyone else, and by the officers for carrying on in grand
style, raiding and getting more famous than any of them. I am
sure if I hadn't been so generous someone would have turned
me in before this.

CHAPTER 2: *How the Hunter of Soest gets rid of the Hunter
of Werle*

While I was carrying on this way, being about to have some
devil's masks made, plus frightful clothes with horse and oxen
feet to go with them, so that I could scare the enemy and also,
in this disguise, take loot from my friends, I heard of a fellow in Werle, a renowned raider, who was wearing a green
suit and, under my name, committing all sorts of monstrosities
like robberies and attacks on women, especially among people contributing to our maintenance. Extremely insistent complaints came in about my conduct, and I should have lost face
if I hadn't clearly shown and proven that when *he* was pulling
a job under my name *I* was somewhere else. Having informed
the commander in Soest, I invited the stranger to swords or
pistols in an open field. But when he hadn't the heart to appear, I sent word that I wanted to avenge myself, even if I
had to do it in the castle of the commander at Werle, who
did not punish him. I also let him know that if I caught him
on a raid, I would treat him as an enemy. For this reason, not
only did I not use the devil's masks, for which I planned something important, but I even chopped up all my green suits
and had them publicly burned in Soest, disregarding the fact
that the clothes alone, without the feathers and harness, were
worth more than a hundred ducats. In my rage, furthermore,
I swore that the next man calling me a hunter would have
either to kill me or to be murdered by me, even if I'd hang
for it. And I would not lead any more raiding parties (not
being an officer, I didn't have to), until I had avenged myself

on the phony hunter in Werle. So I stayed home and did
nothing more military than stand my watch, and if I received
orders I carried them out very indifferently, like any other
sleepyhead. This soon became known in the neighborhood,
and the enemy raiders became so cocksure and daring that
they practically camped on our turnpikes, and I couldn't
stand this either. I found hardest to bear the fact that the
Hunter of Werle continued to operate under my name and
to take rich booty.

Meanwhile, when everyone thought I had gone to sleep on
my laurels and wasn't about to get up, I scouted my opponent's activities and found out that he was not only imitating
me in dress and name but also, at night, stealing anything
he could get. Then I awoke to the challenge and made my
plans accordingly. In the course of time I had gradually
trained my two hired men like bird dogs, and both were so
devoted to me that in case of need they would have walked
across red-hot coals for me because I gave them plenty to eat
and drink, and plenty of loot.

I sent one of these men to Werle to my enemy. My man pretended that since I had promised never to go raiding again
and was beginning to live like a lazybones, he didn't want
to stay with me but had come to offer his services to him who
had assumed his former master's hunting dress. He hoped he
might be employed as a regular trooper. He knew all the high-
ways and byways, could tell him many tricks for getting
plenty of booty, and so on. This good simpleton believed my
man and was talked into hiring him. Then my man persuaded
him and his fellows to go to a sheep farm to pick up some
fat rams. But I and John Jumpup,[1] with several others, were
already lying in ambush. We had bribed the sheepman to tie
up his dogs and let the arrivals go into the barn for their

[1] Simplicius' boon companion John Jumpup had been a sort of husband
to the "lady" with whom Simplicius becomes acquainted in the spa (see
Bk. V, p. 278 and note 3). Jumpup received his nickname from his "wife."
In one of the "Simplician Writings," Grimmelshausen tells of the adventures of this *seltsame Springinsfeld*.

nefarious work without interference. I promised to bless their
mutton. When they had broken a hole in the wall, the
Hunter of Werle wanted my man to climb in first. But he
said, "No, someone might be watching inside and brain me
as I came in. I see you are still inexperienced at filching. Let
me look around a little first." He drew his sword, put his hat
over the point, advanced the hat a few times into the hole,
and said, "This is the way to find out if the boss is home!"
After this the Hunter of Werle himself crawled in, but right
away Jumpup caught him by the arm that held the sword
and asked if he wanted quarter. His pal heard it and started
to rush off. But since I didn't know which one of them was
the Hunter and since I was faster than the fugitive, I caught
up with him and grabbed him after a few steps. I asked,
"What army?" He answered, "Imperial." "What regiment? I
am imperial too; only a rascal denies his colors." He answered,
"We are dragoons from Soest who have come to get some
mutton. If you are imperial, I hope you'll let us pass." I asked
again, "Who are you from Soest?" He answered, "My friend
inside the barn is the Hunter of Soest." "You are rascals!" I
shouted. "Why do you rob your own people? The Hunter of
Soest isn't a fool who gets caught in a sheepfold." "Oh, I
mean from Werle," he answered in turn. And while we were
arguing, my man and Jumpup came up with my enemy.
"Look at him, the jailbird," I said. "Is this where we meet?
If I did not respect the imperial arms you took up against our
enemies, I'd fire a bullet through your head! Until now *I*
have been the Hunter of Soest, and I call you a dirty dog
until you take up one of these swords and fight with me." My
man (who, like Jumpup, wore a ghastly devil's mask with
ram's horns) laid two identical swords before us and let the
Hunter of Werle choose one. But the poor Hunter did exactly as I had done in Hanau when I spoiled the dance, for
he spoiled a good pair of pants and no one could stand him
for the smell. He and his comrade trembled like two wet dogs;
they got down on their knees and begged for mercy. But John
Jumpup hollered, in a voice that sounded as if it came out of
a rain barrel, "You'll have to fight or I'll twist your neck!"

"Oh, my dear devil," answered the Hunter, "I didn't come here to fight. If you'll excuse me, sir, I'll do whatever you want." Amid such confused babble my man put one of the swords in his hand and the other in mine. But the Hunter shook so hard that he couldn't hold his. The moon shone brightly, and the sheepman and his help could see and hear everything. I called him closer so that I'd have a witness to this affair. When the sheepman approached he acted as if he didn't see the two men in devil's clothing and asked why I was having an argument on his place and why I didn't go elsewhere. Our troubles, he said, were none of his business; he was paying his monthly "counter-bution" and he wanted only to live in peace. He asked the other two why they were taking all that gaff from me instead of knocking me down? I said, "You knave! They wanted to steal your sheep!" The farmer answered, "I wish you'd kiss my backside—and those of my sheep, too," and went away.

I insisted on fighting, but the poor Hunter could hardly stand on his feet for fear, and I really felt sorry for him. In fact, he and his friend spoke such moving words that finally I pardoned him and forgave him everything. But Jumpup wasn't satisfied; he made him kiss the rears of three sheep— as many as they wanted to steal—and scratched his face so that he looked as if he had tried to steal food from a cat's dish. I let it go at that. Soon the Hunter of Werle disappeared, because he was too ashamed. My friends spread the word and asserted with many juicy curses that I owned two real devils who were waiting on me. For this reason I was feared more and loved less,

CHAPTER 3: *The great god Jupiter is caught and discloses the designs of the gods*

I soon found this out, and I changed my former ungodly life and strove for pious virtue. I went on raids as before, but I was so kind and discreet to friend and foe alike that everyone I dealt with thought me different from what they had

heard of me. Then, too, I stopped throwing away my money
and collected many pretty ducats and jewels, some of which I
cached in hollow trees near Soest because that's what the
famous lady soothsayer of Soest suggested. She said I had
more enemies in my own regiment and in town than outside
or in the enemy's garrison, and that they were all after my
money. And while the news was spreading that the Hunter
had skipped the country, I was right on the backs of those
who were tickled about it. And before one place really found
out that I had struck at another, that same place had reason
to feel I was still present, for I got around like a whirlwind,
was now here, now there, and more rumors spread about me
than had in the days when the other fellow impersonated me.

One time, near Dorsten, I lay in ambush with twenty-five
shooting irons and waited for a convoy of several carts. According to my custom I was on lookout because we were close
to the enemy. Who came along but a single man, neatly
dressed, talking to himself and carrying on a strange argument with his fancy walking-cane. He seemed to say, "Unless
the great Numen interposes, I'll punish the world." From this
I suspected he might be a great prince, traveling incognito,
who wished to learn how his subjects live and who had resolved to punish those that did not live according to his
wishes. I thought, if this man is of the enemy, he'll fetch a
good ransom; if not, I ought to treat him so politely and impress him so favorably that I'll have a friend in a high place
for the rest of my born days. So I jumped out of the bushes,
with my gun cocked, and said, "You will please walk ahead
of me into the bushes, sir, unless you want to be treated as an
enemy." He answered very seriously, "I am not accustomed
to such treatment." I urged him on politely and said, "You
will not regret doing the inevitable just this once." When I
had taken him to my men and replaced the lookout, I asked
who he was. He answered very magnanimously that it would
probably matter little to me, if I didn't know already that
he was a great god. I thought he might perhaps know me
or be a nobleman from Soest pulling my leg, for the Soesters
are sometimes kidded about the great god and his golden

apron, a huge crucifix they have in their church. But I soon caught on; I had caught not a nobleman but an arch-nut who had studied too many things too hard and had gone off the deep end particularly on the subject of poetry. When he warmed up a little, he claimed to be Jupiter.

By now I wished I hadn't made this catch, but since I had the fool I had to keep him until we moved on. And as time hung heavy on my hands anyway, I thought I'd tune up this instrument and enjoy the sounds it made. So I said to him, "How is it, my dear Zeus, that your divinity leaves its heavenly throne to descend upon us here? Forgive my question, O Jupiter; you might consider it frivolous, but we too are related to gods, being sylvan folk born of fauns and nymphs, and you can speak frankly to us." "By the river Styx," answered Jupiter, "if you were Pan's own son you wouldn't find out a thing about this, but since you resemble my cupbearer Ganymede to a T, I'll tell you that a big hue and cry about the viciousness of the world has penetrated through the clouds to me, and the council of the gods has given me permission to destroy the earth by flood, as in the days of Lycaon.

"But since in my heart I harbor an unaccountable love of the human race and prefer to use kindness rather than severity, I am presently perambulating here in order to explore human behavior. And though I find everything worse than I had expected, I am not about to terminate the human race unconditionally and peremptorily; rather, I'll punish the guilty and try to educate the rest."

I had a hard time keeping a straight face, but I said, "Alas, exalted Jupiter, your care and trouble will presumably be in vain if you don't annihilate people as before, by water or even fire. For if you send a war, all the bad, refractory rascals will get busy killing the peaceable, pious people; if you send hard times, it will mean good business for usurers and wholesalers who have a corner on the market; if you send sickness and death, the misers and survivors will have their heyday since they'll inherit a lot. You will have to eradicate the whole rotten bunch if you want to punish them."

CHAPTER 4: *Concerning the German hero who will overcome the whole world and make peace among all nations*

Jupiter answered, "You speak of this problem like a human, forgetting that we gods can devise means to punish only the bad and to preserve the good. I shall create a German hero who will accomplish all with the edge of his sword. He will kill all the bad people and preserve and foster the good."
I said, "Such a hero would need soldiers; where soldiers are involved there is war, and where there is war the innocent must suffer with the guilty!" "You terrestrial gods are just like people on earth; you understand practically nothing! I shall send a hero who needs no soldiers and yet can reform the world. In the hour of his birth I shall give him a body stronger and more handsome than that of Hercules; he will be equipped with abundant foresight, wisdom, and understanding. Venus herself will give him an ingratiating face so that he will surpass Narcissus, Adonis, and my own Ganymede; she will endow him (in addition to all his virtues) with a peculiar charm, grace, and personality so that he will become popular with everybody. Mercury will present him with incomparable sense and reason, and the inconstant Moon will encourage rather than hinder him, for he will give him great speed. Pallas Athene will raise him on Parnassus, and at the astrologically right time Vulcan will forge his weapons, particularly the sword with which to strike down the godless and subdue the whole world—without the help of a single person fighting as a soldier. He'll need no help. Every large city will tremble at his presence and every fortress that is otherwise impregnable will fall to his power in the first quarter of an hour. Ultimately he will rule over the greatest sovereigns on earth and set up such a government over land and sea that men as well as gods will love it and praise it."
I said, "How can destruction of the godless and power over

the whole world be achieved without strong-armed action? O Jupiter, I frankly confess that I can understand these matters even less than a mortal." Jupiter answered, "I'm not surprised, for you don't understand the wondrous power the hero's sword will have. Vulcan will make it of the same material of which he makes my thunderbolts, and he'll give it such virtue that my magnificent German hero can deprive whole armadas of their heads with one stroke through the air, although the men may be behind a mountain and an hour's distance away. The poor fellows will have to lie down headless before they even know what hit them. Whenever he comes to a town or a fortress, he'll use one of Tamerlane's tricks,[2] raising a white flag as a sign that he comes in the interests of peace and the common welfare. If the people come out, well and good; if not, he'll draw his sword, and by virtue of its special power he'll cut off the heads of all warlocks and witches in that town and display a red flag. But if no one presents himself after that, then in the same manner he'll dispatch all murderers, usurers, thieves, rogues, adulterers, whores, and pimps and run up a black flag. Finally, if the ones still left in town don't come to him and act repentant, he'll want to eradicate the whole city as disobedient and obstinate. But he will execute only the ones who kept the others from yielding sooner. Thus he will go from one town to another, giving to each the countryside around it, to be governed in peace. From each town in all of Germany he will summon the two wisest and most learned men, make a parliament of these, unite the towns forever, abolish serfdom and tariffs, imposts, interests, mortgages, and dues throughout Germany, and take such measures that all memory of servitude, contribution, confiscation of money, warring, or onetime special taxes will be lost among the people, who will be more blessed than the inhabitants of the Elysian fields.

"Then," Jupiter continued, "I shall descend frequently with the whole crowd of the gods to revel among the Germans and

[2] Tamerlane, or Timur (*ca.* 1336–1405), a renowned Mongolian conqueror, usually pictured as the incarnation of deceitfulness and atrocity.

their vines and fig trees. I shall relocate Helicon inside Germany and transplant the Muses there. The three Graces will awaken a thousand merriments in the Germans. I shall bless Germany more abundantly with all sorts of luxuries than Arabia felix, Mesopotamia, and the country around Damascus. I shall forswear use of the Greek tongue and speak only German, and, in a word, prove such a Germanophile that I shall yield to them (as previously to the Romans) dominance over the whole world."

I said, "Your Highness Jupiter, what will the masters and princes say when the future German hero illegally takes away what is theirs? Won't they resist by force or at least protest to men and gods against this seizure?" Jupiter answered, "My hero will bother very little with them. He will divide all the mighty into three groups. Those who live in sin and evil he will punish like commoners, for no earthly power can resist his sword. The others will be given the choice of staying in the country or leaving it. Those who love their land and elect to stay in it will have to live like other common people. But the private life of the Germans will become much happier and more enjoyable than is the life of kings at present. All Germans will be like Fabricius who refused to share the kingdom of Pyrrhus because he loved his fatherland and his virtue and honor too dearly.[3] Those will constitute the second group. The third group, the ones who want to stay rulers, our hero will lead by way of Hungary and Italy into Moldavia, Wallachia, Macedonia, Thrace, Greece, and even across the Hellespont into Asia. Having obtained these countries for them, he will there deposit and make into kings all the military cutthroats of Germany. Then he will capture Constantinople in one single day, will lay in front of their behinds the heads of those Turks who won't convert to Christianity, and re-establish the Roman Empire.

[3] Gaius Fabricius Luscinus was regarded as a model of ancient Roman simplicity and integrity. After the defeat of Heraclea (280 B.C.), he had been sent to negotiate with Pyrrhus for the release of Roman prisoners and had spurned the enemy's bribes.

"Returning to Germany, he (with the two members of parliament summoned from each of the German cities, who will be called the leaders and fathers of the German fatherland) will construct a city right in the middle of Germany. This city will be larger than Manoah in America, contain more gold than Jerusalem in the days of Solomon. Its ramparts will compare to the Tyrolean Alps; its moats, to the straits between Spain and Africa. In the city he will build a temple of diamonds, rubies, emeralds, and sapphires; and in the museums that will be built he will collect the rarest objects from all over the world and the rich gifts that will be sent him by the kings of China and Persia, the Great Mogul of the East Indies, the Great Khan of Tartary, Prester John in Africa, and the Great Czar in Moscow. The Turkish emperor would send him even more—if our hero hadn't taken his realm away from him and given it as a fief to the Roman emperor."

I asked Jove what the Christian kings would do in this emergency. He answered, "The ones in England, Sweden, and Denmark (because they are of German blood and family), and the ones in Spain, France, and Portugal (because the ancient Germans once conquered and ruled these countries) will volunteer to receive their crowns, kingdoms, and lands as fiefs from the German nation. Then there will be a constant and everlasting peace among all nations of the world—as in the days of the Emperor Augustus."

CHAPTER 5: *How the hero will unite the religions and mold them into one*

Jumpup, who had been listening, provoked Jupiter and almost ruined the whole game by saying, "And then Germany will be like the land of Cockaigne, where it rains muscatel and six-inch pies grow over night like mushrooms, where I'll have to chew with both cheeks full like a thrasher and guzzle malmsey wine until my eyes start watering." "Sure, sure," Jupiter answered, "particularly when I strike you with eternal

hunger like Erysichthon, because it seems to me you are making fun of my majesty." To me he said, "I thought I was
among good fauns, but I see I ran into ridicule personified.
One should not reveal the counsels of heaven to such traitors,
nor throw precious pearls to the swine. Well, shit on his back
and let him use it for a scarf!" I thought, What a curious and
foul mouthed idol is this, who, besides the sublime, handles
such filthy matters? Sensing that he disliked laughter, I sup-
pressed it as best I could and said, "Kindest Jove, just because
of one rude and immodest faun, please don't conceal from
your Ganymede how things will be in Germany." "Oh, no," he
said, "but order this godling to hold his tongue hereafter, lest
I transform him into a rock." Then he said, "Dear Ganymede,
.the making of gold will be as common in Germany as any
other trade—pottery, for instance—and every stable boy will
carry the philosophers' stone in his pocket." Then I asked,
"How can Germany have an enduring peace with our different religions? Won't the various priests incite their people
and provoke one new war after another?" "Oh no," said
Jupiter, "my hero will wisely anticipate this matter, and
above everything he'll unite the Christian denominations
throughout the whole world." I said, "Miracle of miracles,
that would be a great and unsurpassable deed! How could it
be done?" Jupiter answered, "I'll be glad to reveal that to
you. After my hero has created universal peace in the world,
in moving words he will address the spiritual and worldly
leaders and heads of the Christian peoples and particularly of
the churches; and he will eloquently point out to them the
harmfulness of the prevailing discord in matters of faith.
Through the most reasonable, incontrovertible arguments he
will lead them to the point of desiring a general union and of
handing the whole matter over to his direction. He will then
assemble the wisest, most learned, and most pious theologians
of every denomination and assign them a quiet, serene place
where they can cogitate without being disturbed; he will fur-
nish them with food, drink, and all other necessities, and
order them first to compose the differences among their various religions and then to put down in clear wording the cor-

rect, true, holy Christian religion according to Holy Writ, the ancient traditions, and the opinions of the holy fathers. About that time Pluto will scratch his head long and hard because he'll be worried about a diminution of his realm. In fact, he will initiate all sorts of quibbles, conspiracies, evil, and deceit; he'll advance one amendment after another and try to kill the matter or at least prolong it *ad infinitum* or *indefinitum.*

"He will undertake to point out to each theologian, in glowing colors, his vested interests, his status, his peaceful life, his wife and children, his reputation, and whatever is most likely to make him insist on his own opinion. But neither will my brave hero be idle; as long as this council lasts, he will ring the churchbells to admonish all Christians to pray ceaselessly to the highest Numen to send the spirit of truth to the council. But if he notices that one or two are perhaps yielding to Pluto's blandishments, he will torture the whole conclave with starvation, and if they won't work to complete the great cause he'll speak to them of hanging or show them his marvelous sword; first with kindness, later with seriousness, terror, and threats, he will bring them to the point at issue, so that they will no longer mislead the world, as they used to, with their obstinacy and false doctrines.

"When unity has been reached, he will have a great celebration and publish the refined and improved religion to all the world. He'll make a bloody victim of anyone who is against it, tar and feather him, and send him to Pluto for a New Year's present. Now, dear Ganymede, you know all you wanted to know. Now tell me the reason for your leaving heaven, where you used to pour many a precious cup of nectar for me."

CHAPTER 6: *What the ambassador of the fleas effected with Jupiter*

I thought to myself that the fellow might not be a fool after all, but rather that he might trick us as I had tricked others at Hanau in order to get off more easily. For that reason I tried to provoke him, because you can always tell a fool by the way he acts in anger, and I said, "The reason I left heaven is that you weren't there. I took the wings of Daedalus and flew to earth to look for you. But wherever I inquired I found that your reputation had suffered among people and that you and the other gods had lost credit among men. They called you an adulterous whoremonger full of crab lice and denied you the authority to punish others for such sins. Vulcan, they said, was a pitiful old cuckold who had been forced to accept the adultery of Mars without any particular revenge; they were wondering what kind of armor such a lame-brain might be forging. Venus herself was called a most hateful strumpet because of her lack of chastity, and men wondered what manner of charm and grace she might bestow on others. Mars was called a murderer and a robber; Mercury, an idle gossip, thief, and procurer; Apollo, a presumptuous harlot-chaser; Priapus, a filthy swine; Hercules, a crazy madman. In short, the whole crowd of gods was esteemed so despicable that they ought to be given no other lodging than the stinking Augean stables."

"Ach!" said Jupiter, "would it surprise you if I forgot my customary kindness and smote these hopeless character assassins and ungodly detractors of gods with thunder and lightning? What do you think, my dearest Ganymede?" And while he was grumbling and threatening, Jupiter shamelessly pulled down his breeches, in front of me and my whole party, and chased the fleas out. His splotchy skin showed how cruelly these insects had been troubling him. I couldn't imagine what he was driving at until he said, "Shoo! Begone, you little pests! By the river Styx I swear you shall never have what you solicit so eagerly!" I asked him what he meant by these words. He answered that the tribe of fleas, when they heard that he had come down to earth, had sent their ambassador to transmit their compliments. The fleas had indicated also that, though they had all been assigned to dogs, at times some of their number found their way into the pelts of women, either because they liked it there or because they had gotten lost. But these out-of-bounders, they complained, were treated badly by the women, captured, and not only murdered but, before death, horribly martyrized and mauled between their fingers, so that a stone might cry out and take pity on them. "As a matter of fact," Jupiter continued, "they presented their cause in such moving and piteous words that I had to have compassion for them and assure them of my assistance, but with the proviso that I was to hear the women too. However, the fleas replied that the women, if allowed to contest the matter, would either prey on my pity and kindness with their poisonous, bitching tongues or would outshout the fleas, bribe me with beauty and lovely words, and seduce me into a false judgment, disadvantageous to the fleas. They prayed, more-over, to be rewarded for the humble devotion and loyalty they had always shown and would continue to show, for they had always seen at close range what had been going on with Io, Callisto, Europa, and several others, and had never passed the news to Juno, though they were very close to her too. But if I should permit the women to hunt and kill them on the premises, they petitioned to be granted a heroic death, to be killed with a cleaver like oxen or shot like game. I answered, 'You boys must be awfully hard on them, or they wouldn't be so hard on you.' 'That is so,' they said, 'but the ladies won't let us live in our own territory. Some of them take care of their lap dogs with brushes and combs, washing them with soap and lotions, so that we are forced to quit our fatherland and look for homes elsewhere.' I then allowed them to take refuge on my human body so that I might know of their ac-tivities at close range and pronounce my sentence accordingly. Well, this rabble started to pester me, so I have to get rid of them, as you have seen. I will defecate my charter right on their noses and let them trouble and tribulate the women all they like."

CHAPTER 7: *Once more the Hunter tracks down honor and booty*

We couldn't really laugh because, first, we did not want to give away our position by making too much noise; secondly, our hallucinator didn't like it. But Jumpup almost exploded. Just about that time our lookout in a high tree let us know something was approaching in the distance. Having climbed up, I saw through my telescope that it was the draymen we were waiting for. For protection they had some thirty-odd cavalrymen with them. I could easily figure that they would not drive through the woods where we were but would go around it, across the open field where we could do nothing to them, though the open road was in very poor shape. I hated to have lain in wait for nothing, with only a fool as our prize, so I quickly made another plan.

From our campsite a creek bed ran toward the field; one could ride along in it on horseback. Twenty men and I placed ourselves at the point where it left the woods, and I ordered Jumpup to keep himself in reserve at the campsite. Then I ordered each of my men to pick some one man in the convoy and told each man whether to fire or hold his shot in reserve. Some experienced hands asked me if I thought the convoy would come here, where they had no business. Others who thought I could work magic spells expected me to deliver the convoy into our hands by magic. But I did not need any devilish tricks for it, only my well trained and clever Jumpup; for when the convoy, which proceeded in strict grouping, was about to pass us, Jumpup, following my orders, started bawling like a heifer and whinnying like a horse so that the woods echoed with the sound, and anyone would have sworn there were droves of horses and cattle in it.

As soon as the convoy heard these sounds, they decided to do a little stealing and collect some items that were rare in these parts, for the countryside had been pretty well picked over. All of them rushed helter-skelter into our ambush, as if they were racing for the privilege of being gunned down first. Thirteen saddles were vacated by the welcome we gave them, and we squeezed a few more empty soon afterward.

Then Jumpup ran down the creek shouting, "Cavalry this way! Cavalry this way!" This so confused and frightened the horsemen that they could ride neither forward nor sideways nor back; they dismounted, hoping to take off on foot, but I

managed to capture all seventeen survivors plus the lieutenant who was in charge. Then I rushed to the freight wagons
and unhitched twenty-four horses. But I got only some bolts
of silk and some Dutch cloth. There wasn't enough time to
rob the dead, let alone search the wagons thoroughly, because
the drivers had galloped off as soon as the action began. They
were sure to sound the alarm at Dorsten, and everything
might be taken away from us. When we had packed up,
Jupiter came running out of the woods wanting to know
whether Ganymede was about to leave him. I said, "Yes"—
unless he gave the fleas their charter. "I'd rather see them all
in Cocytus first!" he answered. I had to laugh, and because
I had several horses free, I asked him to get on one. But since
he could stay in the saddle no better than a nut, I had to
have him tied to the horse. He said the skirmish reminded
him of the battle between the Lapithae and the Centaurs at
Peirithous' wedding.[4]

Now when everything was over and we were hurrying off
with our prisoners as if someone were breathing down our
necks, the captive lieutenant got to thinking about the big
mistake he had made in delivering the cavalry troop reck-
lessly into the hands of the enemy and sending thirteen good
men to the slaughter. He became desperate and wanted to
force me to have him killed. He thought this dereliction was
a blot on his name and would block his future promotion—if
he ever got that far and wasn't shot first. I tried to cheer him
up by pointing out that fickle Fortune often shows her meanest side to soldiers; yet I had never seen a man downhearted
or even desperate on that account. His attitude, I told him,
was a sign of faintheartedness. Bold soldiers always tried to
make up for losses next time; he would never get me to
violate my word of honor and military custom by harming
him. When he saw that I was not about to kill him, he started
cursing me, in hopes of arousing my anger. He said I had

4 Intimate knowledge of classical mythology used to be the mark of an
educated gentleman. "Jupiter" has it.—Peirithous was a Thessalian prince
who also ruled over the Lapithae. At his wedding he and his friends had
to subdue the Centaurs, who threatened to carry off the bride.

fought with him not honorably but like a highwayman and a cutthroat; I had deprived his men of their lives; I was a rascal and a murdering son of a bitch. His own men were greatly startled when they heard him talk this way, but mine got so angry they would have riddled him like a sieve if I had let them, and keeping them from it required considerable effort.

Personally, I didn't even get excited about his talk. I called on friend and foe alike to witness what had taken place, and I had the lieutenant tied up and guarded like a madman. I promised, if my superiors permitted it, to let him have his choice among my own horses and weapons and to prove to him, in a duel, that it is fair in war to practice deception on an enemy. Both friend and foe then said that among a hundred raiders they had never met anyone who would not, after such derogatory remarks, have shot the lieutenant and dispatched the other captives as well.

Early in the morning I brought my booty and prisoners safely to Soest, and I got from this raid more honor and glory than I had ever received. Everyone said, "We'll have a second Johann von Werth in him!" [5] and that tickled me greatly. The commander wasn't in the least inclined to have me fight a duel with the lieutenant. He said I had overpowered him twice before and that was enough. The more my reputation increased, the greater grew the envy of those who were jealous of my good fortune.

CHAPTER 8: *How the Hunter finds the devil in a trough, and how Jumpup comes by some fine horses*

But I just couldn't get rid of Jupiter. The commander didn't want him, and said he was giving him to me because

[5] Johann von Werth (*ca.* 1595–1652) was a famous general of cavalry. He had won his reputation as a swift and terrible leader of forays from about 1633 on. In France he was called Jean de Wert, and his name was used to frighten children into submission.

he could earn no ransom. Thus I got a personal fool and
didn't have to buy one, though only a year ago I had been
forced to be one myself. Well, that's the way luck and the
times change! Only a little while ago lice were eating me
up, and now I had the lord of fleas in my charge. Six months
ago I was the stable boy of a lousy dragoon; now I employed
two men who called me "master." It wasn't quite a year ago
that the gang of boys was running after me to make a harlot
of me; now the girls were turning silly because of love for me.
Thus I discovered early that nothing in the world is more
constant than inconstancy. And I was beginning to worry
that Luck, once she vented her spite on me, would really show
me a rough time.

Just about then Count von der Wahl, governor general of
the Westphalian district, was collecting troops from the various garrisons to lead a campaign through Münster across the
Vecht river toward Meppen, Lingen, and such places. He particularly wanted to smoke out two companies of Hessian cavalry at Paderborn that had been giving our men trouble. I
was included among the dragoons; and, some troops having
been assembled at Hamm, we rode quickly toward the cavalry garrison, a badly fortified town, and waited for more of
our men to arrive. The enemy tried a sally, but we chased
them back into their nest and offered them retreat without
horses and arms but with everything their belts encompassed.
They refused and fought us with carbines and muskets.

Thus it came about that I had to try my luck in capturing
towns, for the dragoons were advancing for that purpose. I
succeeded excellently and Jumpup and I were among the
first inside. We soon emptied the streets because whoever
among the citizens carried a gun was cut down, and they did
not want to fight anyway. Then we went inside the houses.
Jumpup said we should pick the house with the biggest pile
of manure in front of it, because that meant the richest codgers lived there and officers would be quartered there. Well,
we attacked such a house. Jumpup went into the stables and
I into the house itself, our understanding being that each

would divide with the other what he had liberated. Each lit
a candle. I shouted for the master of the house; receiving no
answer (because the people were hiding), I stumbled into a
room in which I found only an empty bed and a locked chest.
I forced it open, hoping to find something precious, but when
I lifted the lid a pitch-black something rose up, and I thought
it was Old Nick himself. I swear I was never in all my life
so scared as when I came on this devil unawares. After a second of hesitation I shouted, "I'll beat your brains out!" and
raised the hatchet with which I had opened the chest. And—
I didn't have the heart to strike.

Then he kneeled down, raised his hands, and said, "Dear
suh, Ah begs uv you fer God's sake, lemme live!" I knew he
was no devil because he had mentioned God and was begging
for his life. Accordingly I told him to hurry and get out of
the chest. He did, proving to be as naked as God created him.
I cut a piece off my candle and let him show me the way. He
did so, taking me to a room where the owner of the house
waited. He and the domestics were amused at the incident,
but they still feared for their lives and begged for mercy. I
reassured them; that was easy because we had orders not to
harm the civilians. Then the master turned over to me a
cavalry captain's belongings (among which was a heavy, locked
traveling bag) and said the captain and all his men, except
the blackamoor and one other, had gone to their posts to fight.

Meanwhile Jumpup had caught one man and six beautiful
horses in the stable. We put them in the house, locked it,
asked the Negro to dress, and told the owner what to tell the
captain. After the city gates had been opened and the guard
had taken their places, our general of ordnance, Count von
der Wahl, was admitted; he took lodgings in the very same
house we occupied. For that reason, in the middle of the
night we had to move and look for other quarters. We found
them with our comrades who also had come into town with
the attack. We had a good time and spent the rest of the
night eating, drinking, and carousing, after Jumpup and I
had shared our loot. My share consisted of the blackamoor
and the two best horses. One of these was a Spaniard on

which a fellow wouldn't be ashamed to be seen by his enemy; later I used it to show off. From the contents of the traveling bag I received various precious rings and, in a gold casket studded with rubies, the miniature portrait of the Prince of Orange. These things, valued at no more than half their worth, along with the horses amounted to over two hundred ducats. The darky who had scared the daylights out of me I gave to the general and got a mere two dozen thalers for him.

From there we moved quickly to the Ems river, where we achieved little. As it happened that we were passing by Recklinghausen, Jumpup and I got permission to visit the parson whose bacon I had once stolen. We had a good time reminiscing. I told him that the blackamoor had repaid him and his cook by frightening me the same way I had scared them. I gave him a nice pocket watch that rang the hours—another piece of loot from the captain's bag—and so everywhere I made friends of people who otherwise would have had occasion to hate me.

CHAPTER 9: *An unequal struggle in which the weaker is the stronger, and the victor is vanquished*

My pride increased with my luck, and the upshot of it was bound to be my ultimate downfall. We were camping about half an hour from Rehnen when I and some of my friends sought and obtained permission to go to town in order to have our guns repaired. But we really intended to have a good time together, and we turned in at the best inn and asked for musicians to play some tunes to help us down the beer and wine we were drinking. We lived it up and left out nothing that might hurt our pocketbooks. I even bought drinks for fellows from another regiment and acted like a young prince who owns land and serfs and has money to burn. Therefore, we were served better than a group of cavalrymen that weren't spending quite so lavishly. This made them mad and they started quarreling with us.

"Why is it that these foot-sloggers throw around their

money?" (They thought we were musketeers, and, in fact, there is no animal in the world so much like a dragoon as a musketeer; when a dragoon falls off his horse, a musketeer gets up.) Another shouted, "That milkface is sure to be a clodhopper whose mother sent him some of the milk money. He's spending it on his comrades so they'll help him out of the lurch sometime—or maybe the ditch." These words were meant for me, for they thought I was a young nobleman. The waitress told me this, but since I hadn't heard it myself I couldn't do much about it. Immediately after that I ordered a big beer glass filled with wine and let everyone drink to the health of all good musketeers, and with each toast we made such a racket that no one could hear his own words. This displeased them even more and one of them said, to no one in particular, "What a life these foot-sloggers are leading!" Jumpup answered, "What's it to you, bootblacks!?" That hit home, but he looked so ugly and made such a cruel and defiant face that no one dared cross him. And yet they resented us, and one of them, a clean-cut fellow, said, "If these town-crappers couldn't show off on their own dunghill, where would they show off?" (He thought we were garrisoned here, for our clothes looked fairly clean.) "Out in the field we'd pick 'em off as a falcon picks off doves." I answered him, "We capture cities and fortresses and they are handed over to us to guard. But you horsemen, you don't even rouse the dogs in the meanest crossroads town. I don't see why we shouldn't enjoy ourselves in a place that's more ours than yours!" The cavalryman answered, "The master in the field takes the fortresses. And that we are the masters I'll prove by not being afraid of three such gun-toting babies as you. Two of 'em I'll stick behind my hatband and the third I'll ask if there are any more like you. And if I were sitting over your way, my young squire, I'd hit you over the head."

I answered, "Although I am not one of your cavalrymen, but only a hybrid between them and the musketeers, I think my pistols are as good as yours. But this baby is brave enough to face a horsy blowhard like you with nothing but a musket

and on foot." "Huh, you son of a bitch," said the guy, "I consider you a rascal if you don't live up to your words like a
nobleman." I threw a glove at him and said, "Look! If I
don't get that back from you, in the open field, on foot, and
using only my musket, you can call me what you called me
just now." We paid our bill and the horseman readied his
pistols and carbine, and I my musket. As he rode off to the
place we had agreed on, he advised Jumpup to go ahead and
order my funeral. Jumpup told him to have his friends order
his own. But he reproached me for my cockiness and said he
was afraid my number was up. I only laughed because long
ago I had figured out how to deal with a well-equipped cavalryman if one were to attack me.

When we came to the place where this jolly meeting was to
take place, I had already loaded my musket with two balls,
put on fresh priming, and smeared the cover of the pan with
tallow, as careful musketeers do in rainy weather. Before we
engaged, our friends on either side agreed that we should
attack each other in an open field. One of us was to enter a
fenced-in field from the east, the other from the west, and
then each was to do his best, like a soldier in the face of the
enemy. No one was to help his friend, nor was anyone to
avenge the death of either. When all had promised this, my
opponent and I shook hands; each forgave the other his own
death, and each hoped to prove the superiority of his branch
of the army in this stupidest of all stupidities in which a
reasonable person ever engaged.

With my priming lighted on both ends, I entered the field
on the side assigned to me. When I saw my opponent, I acted
as if I were throwing off the old priming as I walked. But I
was only pretending. My opponent thought the musket had
misfired. Eagerly, pistol in hand, he rushed toward me, thinking to pay me for my sins and send me to hell. But before he
could say Jack Robinson I had the pan open and the fire
going again, was aiming, and welcomed him in such a way
that my blast and his fall were one and the same thing.

After this I retreated to my friends who received me almost

with kisses. His comrades took him out of the stirrup, behaved honorably toward him and us, and returned my glove with words of praise. But when I thought my honor was at its highest, there came twenty-five musketeers from Rehnen who arrested me and my friends. I was put in chains and sent to headquarters, for all duels had been forbidden on pain of death.

CHAPTER 10: *The general of ordnance restores the Hunter to life and encourages him*

Since our general of ordnance was used to keeping strict discipline, I was afraid I might lose my head. I only hoped to get off easy because I had always been a good soldier though still very young, and I had gained a great reputation for bravery. But this was an uncertain hope, for the daily occurrence of such brawls required exemplary punishment.

Meanwhile, our men had attacked a strong redoubt and demanded surrender, but had not obtained it because the enemy knew we had no heavy artillery. For that reason the general, Count von der Wahl, moved up his whole force, let a trumpeter once more demand surrender, and threatened to storm the place. There came a polite letter to the effect that only the eloquence of force would induce the commander to surrender.

While everyone was wondering what to do next, it occurred to me to take this opportunity to get out of jail. So I racked my brain and set my mind to work thinking about how to deceive the enemy, because all we needed were the big guns. And because something occurred to me immediately, I let my lieutenant colonel know I had an idea how the place could be taken without great trouble or expense, if only I were pardoned and set free. Some old, experienced soldiers laughed and said, "The fellow thinks he can talk his way out of jail. Well, no harm in trying." But my lieutenant colonel himself, and some others who knew me, accepted my words like articles of faith, and went to the general to report concerning my intention and other details they knew about me. Because the count had heard of the Hunter, he ordered me to his house, where I was free of my chains for the duration. The count and my lieutenant colonel were just at table when I came in.

When the general asked what I wanted, I answered, "Your Excellency, although my life is forfeit because of my crime and your Excellency's orders, allegiance to our Imperial Roman Majesty impels me to show how the enemies of our Majesty can be harmed and the armed might of our Majesty strengthened." The count interrupted my speech and asked if I hadn't recently given him the blackamoor. I said I had. Then he continued, "All right, your diligence and faithfulness might possibly suffice to save your life. But what's your plan?" I answered, "Since the place can't hold out against heavy artillery, I think the enemy will be ready to negotiate as soon as they *believe* we have big guns." "Any fool could have said that," answered the Count. "But who will persuade them to believe it?" I answered, "Their own eyes. I saw their lookout with my telescope. We can fool them by loading logs, like wooden pipes, onto wagons and taking them into the field with heavy teams. They'll think these are guns, especially if your Excellency will order some excavations as for gun emplacements." "My dear young fellow," answered the count, "those men are not a bunch of children. They won't believe this nonsense—unless they hear the guns. And if the trick doesn't come off," he addressed the officers about him, "we are the laughing stock of the world!" I answered, "Dear sir, let me make those guns sound in their ears. Just let me have a few double-barreled muskets and a fairly large barrel. There will be nothing there except the proper sound. But if, contrary to expectation, the thing goes wrong and we get laughed at, then I—who must die anyway—as the author of it all, will take the mockery with me and erase it with my life."

Although the count wanted none of my scheme, my lieutenant colonel persuaded him by saying I had a lucky hand in such things and he didn't doubt I'd succeed this time too.

Therefore, the count ordered him to arrange everything as could best be done. And he promised jokingly that all the honor gained by this trick would go to the lieutenant colonel.

So three of the hollow logs were prepared and twenty-four horses hitched to each—though two would have been plenty! Toward evening we took these out where the enemy could see them. Meanwhile I also had obtained three double-barreled muskets and a huge cask, which we got from the wine cellar of a castle. I arranged these things to suit myself and at night had them taken out to our mock artillery. I loaded the muskets with twice the normal charge of powder and fired into the cask, the head of which had been removed. This simulated three trial shots. The report was such that anyone would have sworn on stacks of Bibles that we had ten or twelve-and-a-half-pound cannons. Our general of ordnance could not help laughing at this elaborate trickery, but once more he offered the enemy terms, adding the information that if they did not surrender tonight they'd have to pay for it tomorrow. Both sides sent hostages, the articles of surrender were signed, and that same night we moved through one of the gates. This benefited me considerably, for not only did the count grant me the life I had forfeited by violating his orders, but he also set me free that same night, and in my presence ordered the lieutenant colonel to make me an ensign at the first opportunity. But this was inconvenient, for he had many cousins and in-laws on the waiting list, and they were all watching to be sure I wasn't promoted ahead of them.

CHAPTER 11: *Containing all sorts of things of slight importance but of great imagination*

In that campaign nothing more that was remarkable happened to me. But when I got back to Soest, the Hessians from Lippstadt had captured my man, whom I had left behind in my quarters with the baggage; moreover, they had taken one of my horses from the pasture. The enemy learned from this

man about my exploits, and they thought more highly of me
than before, for until now common report had persuaded them
to think that I could work magic. He also told them he had
been one of the devils who had so frightened the Hunter of
Werle in the sheepfolds. When the "Hunter" found this out,
he was so ashamed that he took French leave once more and
went from the Hessians to the Dutch. But my man's being
captured turned out to be the greatest stroke of luck for me;
this will become clear from a later part of my story.

I started to live a little more respectably than before, for I
had great hopes of soon becoming a junior officer. Gradually I
began to associate with the officers and young noblemen who
were waiting for exactly the same thing I imagined I would
be getting before long. For this reason they were my worst
enemies—except that to my face they acted like my best
friends. The lieutenant colonel didn't particularly like me
either, because he was under orders to advance me ahead of
his relatives. My captain disliked me because I kept better
horses, clothes, and weapons than he, and moreover, I no
longer came across with gifts for the old miser. He would have
preferred that they chop off my head instead of promising me
a troop, for he had hoped to inherit my fine horses. And my
lieutenant hated me because of *one* word that had slipped
out recently.

It happened like this. On our last expedition he and I had
been ordered to keep watch together at a difficult post. It had
to be done lying down, though it was pitch dark, and when
my turn came, he came crawling up to me on his belly like a
snake and said, "Sentry, do you notice anything?" I answered,
"Yes, sir, lieutenant." "What is it? What is it?" he asked. I
answered, "I notice the lieutenant is scared."

From that time on he didn't like me, and I was ordered
to go where the situation was most risky. In fact, he was looking high and low for opportunities to "get me" before I became an ensign—that is, while I could not defend myself
against him. All the sergeants were my enemies, too, because
I was preferred. Even the common soldiers started to waver

in their love and friendship for me, because it appeared that I despised them since I kept company with the big wheels— who didn't like me any better. Worst of all, not one solitary person told me how everyone felt about me. I didn't notice anything because to my face each man played up to me, though he would rather have seen me dead. So I kept on living blindly in false security, and as time passed I became more and more conceited. Even though I knew that some people were disgusted when I outdid the nobles and the officers of rank with my showing-off, I did not stop doing it.

After I had become a corporal, I was bold enough to wear a leather collar worth sixty thalers, scarlet-red trousers, and sleeves of white satin embroidered all over with gold thread— all of which were worn at that time by the highest officers. Of course, everyone took notice. But I was a frightfully stupid fool to manage things this way, for if I had used the money I squandered on clothes for bribes in the right places, I would have gotten my command and not made so many enemies. But that wasn't all: I dressed up my best horse (the one Jumpup had gotten from the Hessian captain) with saddle, bridle, and arms, so that when I sat on him I might well have been mistaken for St. George. I hated it that I wasn't a nobleman and couldn't dress my man and the stable boy in my personal uniform.

I reasoned that everything had to have a beginning; once I had a coat of arms I could have liveried servants, and when I became an officer I would have a seal even though I wasn't a nobleman. I had not entertained this thought very long when an imperial count palatine gave me a coat of arms. It had three red masks on a white field, on the crest the bust of a young jester in calfskin with a pair of rabbit ears, and bells in front. I thought this matched my name perfectly, for I was called "Simplicius." So I properly became the first of my lineage, family, and coat of arms, and if someone had tried to make fun of this, I would have been quick to unsheath my sword or to pull a pair of pistols on him.

Although I did not care much for women yet, I went along

with the nobles whenever they called on ladies, of whom there were many in town. I wanted to be seen and show off my precious wardrobe, my well-groomed hair, and the plumes on my hat. I must confess that I was preferred to all others because of my good figure, but I also heard that the spoiled females compared me to a handsome, well-carved wooden statue that has little to recommend it besides its beauty. Except for playing the lute I could not produce anything to please the ladies, for as yet I knew nothing of love. But when the men who were popular with ladies twitted me for my wooden manners—mostly in order to show off their own eloquence—I said that, for the time being, it was enough for me to enjoy a bright sword and a good musket. The ladies approved of this speech, and this so enraged the ladies' men that they secretly swore to kill me, though there was no one who had the heart to challenge me or provoke me to challenge him—for which a slap in the face or some insulting words would have sufficed, and I had laid myself wide open for that. From this behavior the ladies inferred that I must be a resolute youth; they said publicly that my appearance and resoluteness spoke louder than all the lisping compliments Cupid had ever invented, and that enraged the gentlemen even more.

CHAPTER 12: *Fortune fortuitously grants the Hunter a noble honorarium*

I had two fine horses, and at that time they were all the joy I had in the world. Every day I was free I rode them on bridle paths and in the riding school. Not that the horses could have learned anything more than they knew—I did it so people would see that these beautiful creatures belonged to me. When I was prancing through the streets, or rather when the horse was dancing along with me on it, the silly people looked at me and said, "Look, that's the Hunter! What a beautiful horse! What a panache!" or "God Almighty, what a guy he is!" I cocked my ears and enjoyed it as if the Queen of Sheba had compared me to the wise King Solomon in all his glory. But, fool that I was, I did not hear what prudent and experienced people thought of me or what my detractors said. In a word, the wisest doubtless considered me a young puppy whose extravagance would necessarily be of short duration, because it was built on a weak foundation and maintained by uncertain loot. And if I am to confess the truth, I must admit that the latter were right, although at that time I did not understand it, for the situation was this: I was able to make an enemy sweat and could pass for a good plain soldier, but I was still only a child. The reason for my greatness was that then, as now, the snottiest stable boy could shoot the bravest hero in the world. But if gunpowder had not been invented, that would be an apple off another tree.

While riding around, it was my habit to memorize all roads, paths, ditches, swamps, bushes, hills, and watercourses in order to use my knowledge of the locality later on, either in offense or defense, if the occasion arose. One time I passed a ruined building not far from town and thought this might be an ideal place for a retreat or a lookout, especially for us dragoons if we were chased or outnumbered by cavalry. I rode into the yard, the enclosing walls of which were nearly ruined, to see if a horse could be accommodated there in case of necessity and if one could defend the place on foot. As I rode past the cellar my horse balked and couldn't be made to move either by force or by kindness. I gave him the spurs till I felt sorry for him, but all for nothing. I dismounted and led him down the stairway, but he jumped back, and when I tried to coax him down, I noticed he was sweating from fear and had his eyes glued to one corner of the cellar. As I looked at the trembling horse, I got scared myself and felt as if someone were pulling me up by the hair and pouring a bucket of ice water on me. But I could see nothing. Then I thought that perhaps the horse and I had been hexed and would have to die in this cellar. When I tried to get out, the horse refused

to follow and that made me even more frightened and confused, so that I didn't know what I was doing.

Finally I took up my pistol, tied the horse to a sturdy elder-
berry bush that had grown in the cellar, and as I was about
to look for help in getting my horse out, it occurred to me
that perhaps a treasure was hidden in the ruin and *that*
might make the place so eerie. I became convinced of this and
looked around more closely, particularly in the area where my
horse did not want to go at all. In the corner I noticed a
section of the wall about the size of an ordinary strongbox
where the masonry was different in color and texture. But
when I was just about ready to investigate I again felt as
if all my hair were standing on end, and this seemed to confirm my hunch that a treasure-trove must be hidden there. I
would have preferred an exchange of bullets in a duel ten—
no, a hundred—times more than being in this frightful situation. I was troubled and didn't know by whom, for I could
see and hear nothing. Having taken the other pistol as well, I
moved to get out, leaving the horse behind, but I couldn't
get up the stairs; a strong air current seemed to keep me
down. At that point cold shivers started running down my
back. Finally I had a bright idea: I would fire the pistols to
alarm the peasants who were working in the fields nearby,
and they would help me. There was no other way of getting
out of the haunted place. But I was so desperate and mad
that in firing I aimed at the exact area of the wall where I
thought the cause of my strange experience lurked. The bullets made two holes in the masonry as big as a good-sized fist.

After the shots my horse whinnied and perked up his ears,
and that made me feel good. I don't know whether the monster or ghost disappeared at that instant or whether the poor
horse was glad to hear the shots. My courage returned; I
walked up to the place unhindered and started enlarging the
holes in the wall. There I found a treasure in silver, gold,
and jewels so rich that I should still be enjoying it—if only
I had known how to keep and invest it. There were six dozen

old-fashioned silver cups, a large, gold loving cup and several plated ones, four silver salt cellars and one of gold, an old golden chain, several diamonds, rubies, sapphires, and emeralds, some of them mounted in rings and other jewelry, and a whole boxful of large pearls (but all old and no longer of the highest quality); then, in an ancient moldy leather bag, I found eighty of the oldest Joachimsthalers of the purest silver, and 893 gold pieces with the French coat of arms and an eagle. No one could identify these because, as they said, the inscription was illegible. I put the coins, rings, and jewels in my pockets, boots, and saddlebags; and since I didn't have a sack with me on this pleasure ride, I cut the blanket off the saddle and put the rest of the silver vessels between the blanket and the lining. I hung the gold chain around my neck and rode happily toward my quarters.

But as I was leaving the yard I noticed two peasants who were about to run away when they saw me. I easily caught up with them because I had three pair of legs and level ground. I asked them why they feared me and wanted to run away. They told me that they thought I was the ghost who lived in the deserted farmhouse and usually mistreated anyone who got close to it. When I asked for additional information, they told me that, from fear of the specter (or rather monster), no human being had come there for years on end, except perchance a stranger who had lost his way. Rumor had it that in the cellar lay an iron trough full of money, guarded by a black dog and an accursed maiden; as their grandparents told it, a strange nobleman who knew neither his father nor his mother would some day arrive to save the maiden, unlock the iron trough with a fiery key, and take the hidden money with him. They told me lots more of such silly things, but because they sound too tedious I won't go into them. Then I asked them why they came, since they dared not enter the ruin. They answered that they had heard a shot and a loud scream. When I told them that I was frightened and had fired a shot hoping to summon help, but that I had not screamed, they replied that in this ruin lots of shots might be heard before anybody in the neighborhood would investigate. "For in truth, it is so haunted that we would not believe your Lordship when he said he had been there, had we not seen him with our own eyes when he rode out."

Now they wanted to hear from me whether I had seen the maiden with the black dog and the iron trough. If I had wanted to, I could have told them the worst cock-and-bull story, but I said nothing at all, not even that I had found the treasure. I rode home and looked over my find and was glad all over.

CHAPTER 13: *Simplicius' strange notions and castles in the air, and how he kept his treasure-trove*

Those who see the value of money and consider it their god know what they are talking about. If anyone learned the power, the almost divine virtue of money, it was I. I know the feelings of a person who has a good supply of the stuff, and I've found out more than once how it feels to have not a single penny. I venture to prove that money possesses all the virtues, and more, of precious stones: money removes fear and makes people jolly and happy, as the ruby does. It often robs you of sleep, like garnets; on the other hand, it also induces repose and sleep, like the hyacinth. Like the sapphire and amethyst, it strengthens the heart, drives out fright, and makes people joyful, wide-awake, moral, and mild-mannered. It dispels bad dreams, quickens the wit, and if one quarrels makes one win, like the carnelian—especially if one bribes the judge with it. Money allays lecherous and adulterous desires, because one can buy pretty women. In short, one can hardly overstate what money is able to accomplish (as I have already shown in my book, *Black and White*) if only one knows how to use and invest it.

My money—what I had amassed of it by robbery and finding the treasure-trove—was of a strange kind. In the first place, it made me more cocky than I had ever been before, so much that I hated from the bottom of my heart being called just plain "Simplicius." Like amethyst, it kept me from sleeping, for I lay awake many a night worrying about how to invest it and thereby get more. I made myself a perfect arithmetician, for I added up how much my unminted gold and silver might be worth and added this to the total of cash hidden here and there or still in my purse. This came to a considerable amount even without the precious stones. It also tempted me with its peculiar trickiness and evil nature, by jolly well interpreting the proverb, "He who has a lot wants more," and making me so stingy that everyone would have been glad to become my enemy. I considered quitting the army, buying a little place somewhere, and twiddling my filthy thumbs all day long. But, in view of the free life I was leading and my hope of becoming a big shot, I soon rejected that plan. Next I thought, Simpli, get a patent of nobility; at your own expense, recruit a company of dragoons for the emperor, and you are sure to become a young lord who in time will go places. But as soon as I considered that a single unlucky skirmish or the end of the war might be *my* end too, I no longer favored this.

Next I wished to be of age, a grown man. If I were, I'd take a beautiful, rich, young wife. I'd buy an estate in the country and lead the quiet life of a gentleman farmer. I would specialize in animal husbandry and have a good income honestly obtained. But since I was much too young for this scheme, I had to give it up too. I had plenty of ideas like these until I finally resolved to put my most valuable possessions in the hands of a wealthy man in a well-defended city and let him administer them until Fortune decided what to do with me.

At that time my Jupiter was still with me, for I could not get rid of him. At times he was altogether rational and talked very sensibly for weeks on end. He liked me because I had done a lot for him. When he saw me walking around in deep thought, he said, "Son, your dirty money, your gold and silver —give it away." I asked why. He answered, "That way you'll acquire friends and get rid of unnecessary worries." I told him I'd rather have more than give it away. He said, "Then get more, but you will never have peace of mind or friends."

I thought about it and came to the conclusion that what Jupiter said was indeed sensible, but lust for money had such a hold on me that I wouldn't dream of giving anything away. Yet after a while I gave the commander a couple of silver and gold-plated cups, and my captain a pair of silver saltshakers. But these rare antiques only served to whet their appetites for more. I gave twelve silver thalers to my dearest friend, Jumpup. He advised me to dispose of my wealth or be prepared for trouble over it, because officers didn't like a common soldier's having more money than they. He had heard rumors going around about my wealth. If he were in my shoes he'd retire from the wars, go to some quiet place, and let God provide.

I said, "Listen, brother, how can I so easily give up the prospect of having my own troop?" "Ah!" said Jumpup, "don't you see many a good sergeant become old and grey, who should have had a troop before a lot of others—even you?" I had to keep silent because Jumpup was telling the truth and he meant well with me. But secretly I resented it, for I was awfully conceited at that time.

I considered this advice and that of my Jupiter very carefully, and I remembered I had not a single natural-born friend in the world who might assist me in trouble or avenge my death. Yet neither my greed nor my ambition nor my desire for greatness would let me quit the army and seek peace. But I stuck to my first plan, and when I had a chance to go from Münster to Cologne with a convoy of a hundred dragoons, several merchants, and their freight wagons, I wrapped up my treasure-trove and handed it over for safekeeping to a prominent merchant, in exchange for an itemized legal receipt. There were 74 marks of unminted fine silver, 15 marks of gold, 80 Joachimsthalers, and in a sealed box, various rings and jewelry, which with gold and precious stones weighed altogether eight and a half pounds; there were also 893 an-

tique gold coins, each valued at one and a half florins. I took
Jupiter along because he had well-to-do relatives whom he
wanted to join. He praised me to the skies for all I had done
for him, and therefore his kinsmen treated me with much
consideration. But he kept advising me to invest my money
better, to buy friends who would do me more good than gold
in a strongbox.

CHAPTER 14: *How the Hunter is caught by the enemy*

On the way home I thought about arranging my life from
now on so that I might regain everyone's favor, for Jumpup
had put a busy flea in my ear by persuading me to believe
everyone was jealous of me—and in truth, that's how it was.
I also remembered what the famous fortuneteller of Soest had
told me some time ago and then I was even more disturbed.
With these thoughts I sharpened my wits: I noticed that a
man who lives without care from one day to the next is really
almost like a dumb beast. I tried to find out why this or that
person might hate me and concluded that my pride had made
more enemies than anything else. For that reason I decided
to act humble again (even though I wasn't), to associate once
more with the common soldiers, to take off my hat to the
higher-ups, and to diminish my wardrobe, until perhaps my
status improved.

From the merchant in Cologne I had brought along a
hundred thalers, which I was to repay with interest when I
returned to claim my treasure. I thought that on the way I'd
spend half the money among the soldiers of the convoy, for I
had learned by now that greed makes no friends. I had resolved to change and to make a new start on this trip. But I
had reckoned without the host, for when we were passing
through the duchy of Berg eighty muskets and fifty horsemen
ambushed us at a very favorable spot, just when I had been
sent ahead with four other men and a corporal to reconnoiter
the road. The enemy kept quiet while we rode into their trap,

letting us pass so as not to warn the convoy until it got into
their line of fire. But they sent a cavalry officer with eight
men who watched us until their group had attacked the convoy and we turned around to join our men at the wagons.
Then they pounced on us and asked if we wanted quarter. I
for one was well mounted and rode my best horse, but I did
not care to run. I swung around to a small plain to see what
could be done. Meanwhile the volley our men received told
me what we were up against, and flight suddenly appeared
attractive. But the ensign had it all figured out; he had cut
off retreat, and while I was trying to fight my way out, he—
mistaking me for an officer—once more offered me quarter.

I thought that getting off with my life was better than
risking it and asked if he would keep his promise of quarter
as an honest soldier. He answered, "Yes, honestly." So I
handed over my sword and was taken captive. He asked right
away who I was, for he thought I was a nobleman and therefore an officer. But when I replied that I was called the
Hunter of Soest, he said, "It's your good luck not to have
fallen into our hands a month ago. At that time I could not
have given you quarter because we considered you a sorcerer."

This ensign was a bold young cavalier and not more than
two years older than I. He was overjoyed at the honor of
capturing the famous Hunter and for that reason he kept his
word—even in the Dutch manner. (It's their custom not to
take from their Spanish enemies anything under a man's belt.)
In fact, he was even so considerate as not to have me searched;
I, in turn, was generous enough to hand him the money in my
pockets. When the time came to divide the loot, I told him in
secret to make sure he got my horse with saddle and bridle,
for the saddlebag contained thirty ducats, and to find another
horse like mine would be hard. For that the ensign liked me as
if I were his own brother. He immediately mounted my horse
and let me use his. Of the convoy only six were killed and
thirteen captured (eight of whom were wounded); the others
fled, not having the guts to recapture the enemy's spoils, as
they could have, for they were all mounted.

In the evening, after the loot and the captives had been parceled out, the Swedes and Hessians (who had come from various garrisons) left for home. The ensign kept me, the corporal, and three other dragoons, all of whom he had captured. We were taken to a fortress located somewhat less than ten miles from our garrison. Because I had harassed that place quite a bit, my name was well known there, but my person was feared rather than revered. When we came in sight of the town, the officer sent a cavalryman ahead to announce his arrival to the commander and to let that gentleman know how the ambush had turned out and who the captives were. When the word got around there was nearly a riot, for everyone wanted to see the Hunter who could supposedly work miracles. Then some said this and others that about me, and it was just as if a great potentate had come to town.

We captives were taken straight to the commander, who was greatly amazed at my youth. He asked where I came from and if I had ever served on the Swedish side. When I told him the truth, he asked if I didn't want to stay on his side again. I answered that it didn't make any difference to me, but since I had sworn on oath of loyalty to the emperor I thought I ought to keep it. He then ordered us taken to the provost marshal, but the officer, at his own request, was allowed to invite us for the evening, since I had formerly entertained my prisoners, one of whom had been his brother.

That night several officers, soldiers of fortune as well as born noblemen, convened at the officer's and he sent for me and my corporal. To tell the truth, I was extremely well treated by them; I acted as if I had never lost a thing, was the life of the party, and carried on not as one captured by the enemy but as if I were among my best friends. For all that, I behaved as modestly as possible, because I guessed my behavior would be reported to the commander—and it *was*, as I later found out.

Next day we prisoners of war were taken one after the other to the regimental judge advocate, who examined us. The corporal went first; I was next. When I entered the room he was surprised at my youth, and in order to reproach me he said, "My child, what have the Swedes done to you that you fight against them?" That riled me, especially since I had seen soldiers just as young among them, and I answered, "The Swedish soldiers took away my prettiest marbles and I wanted to get 'em back."

Hearing me pay him back, some of the officers present were ashamed, and one said in Latin that he should ask me serious questions, for I was clearly no child. That's how I found out the judge advocate's name was Eusebius, for that's how the officer addressed him. Then he asked me my name, and when I told him he said, "There isn't a devil in hell by the name of Simplicissimus." I answered, "Probably there isn't one named Eusebius, either," and repaid him in kind. But this didn't go over so well with the officers, for they told me to remember that I was a prisoner and hadn't been brought here to make wisecracks. I neither blushed nor apologized, but replied (since they were holding me for a soldier and wouldn't let me get off as a child) that I had answered as I had been asked; I hoped that I was not to blame for that. Then they asked about my home, family, and connections, and whether I had served on the Swedish side; they inquired, furthermore, about conditions in Soest, the strength of the garrison there, and other items like that. My answers to all their questions were brief and to the point; I said no more about Soest and the garrison than I thought I could justify. I kept altogether mum about having been a jester, for I was ashamed of it.

CHAPTER 15: *Under what conditions the Hunter becomes free again*

Meanwhile, in Soest, they had found out how the convoy had fared, that the corporal, myself, and several others had been captured, and where we had been taken. The next day a drummer was sent to come and get us. The corporal and the three others were turned over to him, with a letter the commander let me read before dispatching it. It went approximately as follows:

Monsieur, etc.,

Your letter was handed me together with the ransom by your drummer, who is returning with the corporal and the other three prisoners. As concerns Simplicius, the Hunter, because he served on our side before, he cannot be released. If I can be of any service in which duty does not interpose, I am and remain,

Your humble servant,

N. DE S. A.

I did not half like this document, but still I had to seem grateful for it. I asked to see the commander but was told he would send for me after the drummer had been dispatched the next morning. Until then I would have to be patient.

I had waited longer than the appointed time when, around noon, the commander sent for me and for the first time honored me by inviting me to his table. During the meal he drank to my health but did not indicate by even one word why he wanted me, and it was not becoming for me to mention it. But after the table had been cleared and I felt quite content, he said, "Dear Hunter, you saw from my letter what pretext I used to keep you here. Now, I don't intend anything unreasonable, dishonest, or contrary to the rules of war. You yourself told the judge advocate that you used to serve on our side in the main army. For that reason you will have to make up your mind to join my regiment. If you do, and you serve to my satisfaction, in time I shall advance you further than you could hope for on the imperial side. Otherwise I hope you won't mind if I return you to the lieutenant colonel from whom the dragoons took you."

I answered, "Honored Sir Colonel, since I never swore allegiance to the Crown of Sweden or to its allies, and since I was only the lieutenant colonel's stable boy and never swore allegiance to him, I do not feel bound to go into Swedish service or to break my oath of allegiance to the Holy Roman Emperor. For this reason I humbly beg you to excuse me for refusing this request." "What?" said the colonel. "Do you despise Swedish service? Remember that you are my prisoner, and I'll show you a thing or two before returning you to Soest so you can serve the enemy, or maybe I'll let you rot in jail. Now think that over."

To be sure, these words frightened me, but I did not yield and said I hoped God would protect me from such treatment and keep me from perjury. As for the rest, I'd leave it to the colonel's well-known discretion to treat me like a soldier. "Sure," he said, "I know how to treat you—if I wanted to be severe; but you had better think it over. And don't give me cause to teach you a lesson." After this I was put back in the stockade.

It isn't hard to imagine that I didn't get much sleep that night but instead had all sorts of ruminations. Next morning several officers, including the one who had captured me, appeared, on the pretext of entertaining me, but in truth to bring news that the colonel was about to accuse me of sorcery, since he couldn't get me to comply in any other way. They meant to frighten me and see what I would do, but because I had a clear conscience I reacted rather coldly. Even though we talked little, I noticed that the colonel's main concern was to keep me from going back to Soest. He could easily figure out that I wouldn't leave a place where I was hoping for advancement and where I still had two beautiful horses and other valuables.

Next day he sent for me again and once more questioned me if I had changed my mind. I told him, "I have decided to die rather than commit perjury. But if you will let me off without forcing me into Swedish service, I solemnly promise not to bear arms for six months against either Swedes or Hessians." The colonel was downright pleased with this offer; we shook hands on it, and he forgave me the ransom and ordered the secretary to make out a document in duplicate, which both of us signed. In it the colonel promised me freedom and protection so long as I stayed in the fortress which was entrusted to him. I, in turn, pledged to do nothing harmful to the garrison so long as I stayed in the fortress. The colonel kept me for lunch again and showed me more honor than the imperials ever had done or would do. That's how he gradually won me over, so that I wouldn't have gone back to Soest even if he had set aside my promise and let me go. And that is how, without spilling a drop of blood, he did considerable damage to the enemy, for from this time on, having lost me, the reconnoitering of the Soesters was not at all effective. Yet, I don't want to depreciate them or brag about myself.

CHAPTER 16: *How Simplicius becomes a free lord*

If something is to happen, everything shapes up for it. I thought I was practically married to Lady Luck (or at least was so close to her that even the worst must turn out to my advantage), when at the commander's dinner table one day I heard that my stable boy had come over from Soest with my two beautiful horses. However, I didn't consider (but later learned) that in the beginning fickle Fortune raises whom she wants to destroy all the higher, in order to dash him so much lower in the end.

Because I had done him much good, this servant (whom I had captured from the Swedes) was very devoted to me. Every day he had saddled my horses and ridden out of Soest to meet the drummer who had been sent to bring me and the others back. He had taken my best clothes along, that I might not come back naked or in rags (for he thought I had been stripped bare). When he did not see me and heard I had been asked to accept service with the enemy, he dug his spurs into the horses and shouted, "Farewell, drummer! Farewell, corporal! I'm going where my master is!" Thus he fled from Soest and arrived just as the commander had freed me and was honoring me. The colonel put up my horses at an inn until I should find myself lodgings. He thought me lucky to have such a faithful man and such excellent horses while I was still so young and only a common dragoon. When I took his leave, he praised one of the horses so highly that I thought he would

have liked to buy it from me. And since he was too discreet
to ask the price, I said I would be honored to offer it as a gift.
But he roundly refused, mostly because I was in my cups, and
he did not want it said that he had talked a drunken man out
of something he might have refused while sober.

That night I got to thinking about how I would arrange
my future life. I decided to stay my six months where I was,
that is, to spend the winter, which was approaching, in peace
and quiet. I had enough money for this without using any of
my treasure at Cologne. I thought it would be a good time to
finish growing and to reach full strength. In the spring I could
all the more courageously join the imperial army.

Early next morning I did an autopsy on my saddle, which
was in much better shape than the one the ensign had received from me. After that I had my best horse taken to the
colonel's quarters. I told him that since I had resolved to
spend my six warless months here under his protection, my
horses would be worthless to me. To let them be ruined would
be a shame. Therefore, he'd do me a favor by giving this martial nag a place alongside his own, and I'd be happy if he
would accept it as a token of my gratitude for all the favors I
had received from him. The colonel thanked me very courte-
ously and, through his steward, sent me a fattened live steer,
two fat hogs, a barrel of wine, four barrels of beer, and twelve
loads of firewood. He had all these things delivered to the
lodging I had just rented for half a year. He sent word along
that these housewarming gifts were to provide a little help
in getting my household started.

Seeing that my generosity earned me much credit with the
colonel, I wondered how I could enhance my reputation with
the common people. So I sent for my man and, in the presence of my landlord, said to him, "Dear Nicholas, you have
shown me more loyalty than a master can require of a servant.
But now that I have no master of my own and no war in
which to obtain the means of paying you as I'd like, and since
I won't need a man in the quiet life I intend to lead, I am
giving you as your wages my second horse together with the

saddle, pistols, and other gear; and I am asking you to be content for the present to find another master. If I can be of service to you in the future, be sure to let me hear from you at any time."

My good Nick kissed my hands. He could hardly speak for tears. He didn't want to accept the horse but thought I should sell it and use the money to support myself. Finally, after I had promised to take him back in my service as soon as I needed someone, he was persuaded to accept it.

This farewell scene so moved my landlord that he could not keep from crying; and as my man praised me among the soldiers, so the landlord praised me to the skies among the citizens. The commander thought I was a prince of a fellow because not only had I kept faithfully the oath I had sworn to the emperor but also I had given up my excellent horse, servant, and weapons—all the better to keep my oath to him. To myself I was a great master—like any beggar who is subject to no one. In this manner everything gets turned around in this topsy-turvy world: some have to swear an oath when they enter military service; I had to do it when I quit.

CHAPTER 17: *How the Hunter plans to spend six months, and an encounter with the prophetess of Soest*

I don't believe there is a person in this world who hasn't a screw loose somewhere, for we all come from the same place and when my pears are ripe the other fellow's aren't far from it. But someone might answer, "Ah, you coxcomb, do you think because you are silly others are too?" I don't say that, but I do think that some are better than others at hiding the fool within them. A person with foolish notions isn't necessarily a fool; when we're young we all have such notions. But he who acts them out is thought a fool, for some people show none of their foolishness, and others, only half of it. Those who suppress it altogether are regular sourpusses. But those who give a little indication of it when time and occasion permit—those I consider the best people and the most under-

standing. Since I was quite independent and had money in
my pocket, I probably let my own foolishness show a little too
much, for I hired a boy, dressed him like a page in the most
outrageous colors—purple, violet, and yellow, no less—and
declared these to be *my* colors because I liked them. This
youngster had to wait on me as if I were a prince of the realm
and had never been a dragoon—or, half a year before that, a
poor stable boy.

This was my first folly in that town. And though it bulked
large, it was not even noticed, much less was I reproached for
it. But what's the difference? The world is so full of foolishness that nobody pays attention to it any more, or laughs at
it, or is surprised—they're all so used to it. I was reputed to be
a smart, professional soldier, not a fool still wearing children's
shoes. I made arrangements with my landlord for boarding
myself and the page and I gave him as a down-payment the
meat and wood the commander had sent me in exchange
for my horse. My boy had to have a key to the wine cellar, for
I was pleased to serve wine to my company. And since I was
neither a burgher nor a soldier, and therefore had no one of
my own kind to keep me company, I made friends in both
groups and had daily visitors whom I did not want to leave
unwined. The organist became a good friend of mine, and
since I may say, without bragging, that I loved music and had
a good voice, which I wanted to keep from getting rusty, he
taught me how to compose, and to play the organ as well as
the harp. As I already played the lute masterfully, I bought
one of my own and had a lot of fun with it every day.

When I was tired of music, I sent for the furrier who, in
Paradise, had taught me the art of self-defense. I practiced
it with him in order to become even more perfect, and I
persuaded the commander to have one of his artillerymen
teach me, for a fee, the art of aiming and firing a cannon
and the use of gunpowder. As for the rest, I kept very quiet
and to myself, so that people were amazed when they saw me
poring over books like a student—me, who had been used to
robbery and bloodshed.

My landlord was the commander's watchdog and my keeper;

he reported everything I did or didn't do. But that suited me well enough, for I hardly gave a thought to soldiering, and if the conversation got around to it I never let on I'd been a soldier. I acted as if I were here only for my daily lessons and exercises. I wished my six months were over, but no one could tell where I'd take service after that. As often as I called on the commander he kept me for lunch or supper, and sometimes we got into conversations meant to probe my thoughts and intentions. But I answered so carefully that no one could tell what my plans were, and no one could suspect anything but good in me.

One day the commander said, "How about it, Hunter? Don't you want to become Swedish yet? Yesterday one of my ensigns was killed." My answer was, "Honored sir, a wife is not expected to remarry immediately after her husband's death. Why can't you let me wait my six months?" With such repartee I always escaped a definite answer and gained more and more of the colonel's favor. He even permitted me to walk around freely inside and out of the fortress. In time I was allowed to hunt rabbits, quail, and other birds—a privilege not given his own soldiers. Moreover, I fished in the river Lippe and had such good luck that I seemed to be catching fish and crayfish by magic. Then I had a hunter's suit of middling quality made; dressed in this, I tramped by night all over the countryside around Soest, where I knew every road and pathway. Occasionally I collected the treasures I had hidden in various places, hauled them into the fortress, and let on I wanted to spend the rest of my life with the Swedes.

Once I ran into the fortuneteller of Soest, and she said to me, "Look, son, didn't I advise you well to hide your money outside the town of Soest? I assure you, it was the greatest stroke of luck for you to have been taken prisoner. If you had come home, certain fellows who swore to kill you because you deprived them of a lady's favor would have strangled you while you hunted." I answered, "How can anyone be jealous of me when I care nothing for girls and their favors?" She replied, "Surely you will not remain long of this opinion, or the

ladies will run you out of the county on a rail. You always
laughed at me when I foretold events. Do you again not want
to believe me when I tell you more? Don't you find people
friendlier to you here than in Soest? I swear, they love you
only too well, and such excessive love will harm you if you
don't accommodate yourself to it." I asked her why, if she
knew so much, she didn't tell me more about my parents and if
I'd ever see them. But she should have spoken up in clear
language instead of using abracadabra. She said I should ask
about my parents after I'd accidentally met my foster father
leading the daughter of my wet nurse by a rope. She laughed
violently and assured me that she had told me, voluntarily,
more than she had revealed to others who had begged her.
From now on I would hear little from her, and as a parting
gift she advised me to use plenty of bribes and to love weapons
instead of women if I wanted to fare well. "Old blabber-
mouth," I said, "that's just what I am doing!" She answered,
"Yes, sure, but soon you will be different." Then I gave her a
few silver thalers, and when I started kidding her she left
hurriedly. Just then the coins were heavy in my pocket, and I
also had many precious rings and other jewelry. These valuables were constantly screaming at me that they wanted to cir-
culate among people again and that I should let them go if I
wanted to be popular. I obeyed them willingly, for as I was
quite a show-off I paraded my wealth and let my landlord see
it without reserve. He reported even more than he had seen!
People wondered where I had acquired it, for word had got
around that I deposited my treasure-trove in Cologne, because
the cavalary officer had read the merchant's I O U when he
captured me.

CHAPTER 18: *How the Hunter begins courting and makes an
occupation of it*

My plan to learn the mastery of firearms and fencing during these six months was good, and I made excellent progress,

but it wasn't enough to keep me occupied, and boredom is the devil's workshop, particularly when you don't have a boss. Diligently I studied all sorts of books and learned a lot from them. But there were some that helped me like the grass eaten by a sick dog. The incomparable *Arcadia*,[6] from which I hoped to learn polite conversation, was the first that diverted me from wholesome stories to books of love and from true history to heroic fiction. I picked up books of that sort wherever I could, and when I had found one I didn't stop until I'd finished reading it, even though it took me all day and all night. Instead of eloquence, these books taught me how to pitch woo. But at that time my affliction was not so strong or violent that one could have called it a divine frenzy or an oppressive malady, for whenever my love happened to alight, I received what I wanted easily and without special effort, and I had no cause to complain like other wooers and lechers who are full of fantastic thoughts, troubles, desires, secret suffering, anger, eagerness, revenge, rage, tears, bragging, threats, and a thousand other manifestations of foolishness, and who in their impatience die a thousand deaths. I had plenty of money and did not mind spending it; I had a good voice and practiced daily on various musical instruments. Instead of dancing, which I never liked, I exhibited a well developed, supple body when fencing with the furrier. Moreover, I had a fine, smooth face and was acquiring a graceful pleasantness of manner so that the ladies ran after me even though I did not particularly trouble about them.

As the approach of Martinmas (when we Germans start the swilling and stuffing that goes on until Lent), officers and civilians invited me to various places to help eat the Martinmas goose. And that's when things began to happen, for on these occasions I met some ladies. My singing and my lute made them look at me, and when they did, I made such graceful eyes and gestures—in addition to the love songs I had com-

---

[6] The *Arcadia* (1502) of Iacopo Sannazaro is the outstanding pastoral novel of the Renaissance; however, Grimmelshausen probably means Sir Philip Sidney's *Arcadia* (1590), for it was available in German translation.

posed myself—that many a pretty girl fell for me and was in love with me before she knew it. Lest I be considered a tight-wad I, in turn, gave two parties, one for the officers, the other for high society in town. Thus I gained favor with both sides and entrance to their houses, for my food and drink was of the best. I really cared only for the company of the ladies, and though I might not get what I wanted from one or two (there were still a few who could withhold their gifts), I treated them all alike, so as not to bring suspicion on those who showed me more favor than virtuous maidens should. I made each of them believe that I merely made conversation with the others and that *she* alone enjoyed my love.

An even half dozen loved me, and I them, but none alone had me or my heart. In one, I liked only her dark eyes; in another, her golden hair; in the third, her lovely charm; and in the fourth, something else that the first three did not have. If I called on still others, I did so because they had something new or strange, and in any case I refused or despised nothing, since I did not intend to stay in the same place long. My page, who was an archrascal, was always rushing around with love notes and messages; on the side, he received a lot of favors from the *Fräuleins* and knew when to keep quiet, all of which cost me a pretty penny, since I wasted a fortune by doing this and might well have said, "What's gained by the drum is lost by the fife." In all this I kept my affairs so secret that not one in a hundred knew what a lover-boy I had become, except perhaps the parson, for I didn't borrow half so many theology books as I used to.

CHAPTER 19: *How the Hunter wins friends, and the sermon the preacher delivers*

If Fortune wants to cast one down, she first raises him high, and the good Lord always sends a warning before the fall. He sent one to me, but I refused to accept it. In my own mind I thought my present happy state so firmly established that no misfortune could touch me, because everyone, especially the commander, wished me well. "What a friendly man the Hunter is," I heard them say. "He speaks with the children in the street, and he is everyone's friend."

I often visited the oldest of the town's ministers, from whose library I borrowed many books, and when I returned one, he discussed all sorts of subjects with me and we got along well. When the Martinmas goose and the Christmas holidays were past, I gave him, for the New Year, a bottle of Strasbourg brandy, which he sipped with rock candy, as all the Westphalians do. When I stopped off to call on him he was just reading a book called *Joseph,*[7] which I had written and which my landlord had lent him behind my back. I blanched and was ashamed that such a learned gentleman should be reading my attempts at writing, especially as it is well established that a man is best known by what he writes. But he invited me to sit down with him, and although he praised my imagination, he upbraided me for going into so much detail on the amorous adventures of Potiphar's wife. "Out of the abundance of the heart the mouth speaks," he added. "If you did not know from experience how a lover feels, you could not have told so much about this woman's passion." I answered that what I had written was not my own invention; I had copied and extracted it from other books in order to gain practice in composition. "I am willing to take your word for it," he said, "but you may be sure I know more about your love than you think!" This sent a shudder down my spine, and I wondered if the devil himself had told him about it. When he saw me blushing he admonished me to consider what a dangerous road I was taking. He mentioned the proverb, "Young soldiers make old beggars," and warned me against squandering my money on women and in other useless ways. I wasn't used to such talk and became very impatient, but I let on that I was grateful for his paternal concern and promised to think it over. In my heart I thought, "What business is it of yours, how I man-

7 Grimmelshausen, not Simplicius, wrote the novel *Joseph the Chaste.* See p. 65, note 1, for a parallel.

age my life?!" And as I had become used to the pleasures of love, I did not want to do without them. Such warnings count for nothing when a young man is no longer used to the bridle and spurs of virtue, and he runs headlong into his undoing.

CHAPTER 20: *How Simplicius pulls the wool over the preacher's eyes, so that he forgets to look at Simplicius' life of pleasure*

I was not yet so stupid or so drowned in lusts of the flesh that I neglected to keep up my friendships with everyone so long as I was staying in the fortress, that is, until the end of the winter. I also recognized what trouble a man may have if he incurs the hatred of the clergy, for they have great influence among all nations, regardless of creed or denomination. So I racked my brain and returned on the next day to the parson and, using learned words, lied atrociously about how I had resolved to follow his advice. From his reaction I could see how pleased he was. "I feel how much I need an angelic counselor and have needed him for some time—in fact, even in Soest; now I am happy to have found one in your Reverence, learned sir. If only the winter were over or the weather improved so that I could leave." I asked his further advice, particularly about a college where I might enroll. He answered that his alma mater was Leiden, but for me Geneva would be just the place. "Holy Mary!" I answered, "Geneva is farther from home than Leiden." "Alas," he said, considerably shaken, "it seems you are a popish Catholic. My God, how you've pulled the wool over my eyes!" "Why, Reverend?" I said. "Because I don't want to go to Geneva?" "Not at all," he said, "but because you are calling on the Virgin Mary." I replied, "Isn't it becoming for a Christian to call on the mother of his Saviour?" "Certainly," he answered, "but I beg of you to tell me what denomination you belong to." I answered, "You have heard, Reverend, that I am a Christian, for if I were not, I would not be in church so often. But I confess that I am a follower neither of St. Peter nor of St. Paul.[8] I simply believe what is contained in the twelve articles of the common Christian faith, and I will decide when one of the three denominations can persuade me with sufficient reason and proof that *it* has the only true and saving religion. For only one of them can be right; the other two must be wrong. If I were to embrace one without sufficient deliberation I would be eternally sorry. No, I'd rather stay off the road altogether than go astray. If your Reverence will be my guide, I will follow you with deep gratitude and accept that religion which you yourself profess."

He then said, "I see you are caught in pernicious error, but I hope God will enlighten you and help you out of the slough. To this end, I will shortly prove to you from Holy Writ the truth of our faith, so that it will prevail even against the gates of hell." I answered that I was eagerly looking forward to such proof; but secretly I thought, "I won't mind your faith if only you don't nag me about my love affairs!" From this the reader can see what an ungodly and evil rascal I was at that time, for I caused the good parson a lot of futile trouble just so he would leave me alone in my life of vice; and I thought, "When you finish with your proofs, I shall have flown the coop!"

CHAPTER 21: *How the Hunter contracts an unexpected marriage*

Across the street from my lodging there lived a retired lieutenant colonel with an exceptionally beautiful daughter who always looked like a lady. I had long wanted to meet her, though at first she didn't seem the kind of girl for whom I would give up the others that I might love her alone and cleave to her forever. Yet I often went walking in hopes of

---

[8] The followers of St. Peter are Catholics; those of St. Paul, Protestants. Since the Protestants were divided into Lutherans and Calvinists, Simplicius refers to three denominations.

meeting her, and many times I made amorous eyes at her. But she was so well chaperoned that I could never talk to her alone. Moreover, I had to be on my best behavior because, for one thing, I was not acquainted with her parents, and for another, the family had a much higher social position than I considered myself to have. I got closest to her when we chanced to meet on the way to or from church. Making good use of my chance, I sighed piteously—something I could do perfectly, though it was all pretense. But she reacted so coldly that I was forced to believe she could not be seduced as easily as the daughter of a common burgher. And while I was beginning to doubt that I could ever have her, my desire for her grew violent.

The lucky star that helped me to make her acquaintance was the one children carry on a stick ahead of the procession around Christmas to commemorate the fact that the three wise men were guided to Bethlehem by a star. In the beginning I took it as a good omen that a star guided me to her house. When her father summoned me, he said, "Monsieur, I have sent for you because of your position of neutrality between soldiers and citizens. I need an impartial witness for an affair in which I am about to mediate between the groups." I was beginning to think he had something of awesome importance in mind because there were pens and paper lying on the table. But it was nothing more than an invitation to a "royal" party (since the Eve of the Three Kings, or Twelfth-night, was at hand) for which the guests are given various titles, and I was to see that no favoritism was shown and that the offices were distributed by lot without respect to person. His secretary was helping too, and because the lieutenant colonel was something of a merry drinker and it was after supper, he sent for wine and snacks. The secretary was writing the names down, I was reading them off, and the lady my heart longed for was drawing the slips of paper. Her parents were looking on and complaining about the long winter evenings. That was their way of hinting that I was welcome in their house to help them pass the time after the lamps were lit, since they were not occupied with anything special. This was exactly what I had been hoping for. After this night (when I showed only a moderate interest in the lady) I was trying once more to catch my sweet bird and to make a big fool of myself so that the girl and her parents couldn't help thinking I had swallowed hook and all, though in reality I was only half serious. My aim was, rather, to act like a husband without bothering to get married first. Like a witch, I dressed up only at night when I went to call on her, and throughout the day I kept busy with love stories. From these I copied love notes to my sweetheart, as if I were a hundred miles away or wouldn't see her for years to come. After a while, since her parents encouraged rather than prevented my billing and cooing, I offered to teach her the lute and thus had free access to her, by day as well as by night, and I had to change the ditty—

> The bat and I,
> By night we fly,

which I had made up, into one in which I congratulated myself on my luck at seeing her by day after many a beautiful evening. I continued the song by complaining that now my nights were made unhappy for lack of daytime pleasures. Though the verses turned out to be somewhat too free, I sang them for my beloved to a sensuous melody and with many deep sighs. In addition, the lute seemed to ask, in my behalf, that the maiden please cooperate in making my nights as happy as my days. But her answer was rather chilly. She was an intelligent girl and had ready answers for all my inventions and conceits. I was careful not to mention marriage, and when the matter came up in conversation I spoke of it vaguely and ambiguously. My lady's married sister noticed this, and, seeing that her sister loved me from the bottom of her heart and that the affair would at length end badly, prevented me from meeting my beloved alone as often as previously.

It isn't necessary for me to go into the details of my courting, because love stories and novels are full of that sort of

information. It is enough if the gentle reader knows that I
was first permitted to kiss my beloved doll, and after a while
to continue from there. I pursued such advances with all the
incitements I could think up until I was finally admitted by
night into my sweetheart's bedroom. I lay down beside her in
bed as if I belonged there. Now, because everybody knows
what usually happens next, the reader might surmise that I
did something improper. Not me! All my entreaties were in
vain and all my promises fell on deaf ears. Such resistance as
I encountered I would not have thought possible in a woman,
for she was intent solely on honor and marriage, and though
I promised her the latter with a thousand sanguinary oaths
she wanted to do nothing until after the wedding. But she
did let me lie next to her in bed and, worn out by arguing
and chagrin, I dozed off. But I was awakened with a venge-
ance. At four in the morning the lieutenant colonel stood by
the bed with a torch in one hand and a pistol in the other.
"Croat!" he shouted to his man, who was standing next to him
with a drawn sword, "Croat, run and bring a parson." I woke
up and saw the danger I was in. "Golly," I thought, "he
wants you to make your peace with God before he makes war
on you." There were green and yellow spots before my eyes
and I wasn't quite sure whether to open them or keep'em closed.
"Irresponsible rascal, you want to dishonor my house?!" he
said to me. "It would serve you right if I broke your neck
—and that of this slut who has become your whore. Hold me
or I'll tear your heart out, you beast, and throw it to the dogs
for mincemeat." He rolled his eyes and gnashed his teeth like
a rabid dog. I did not know what to reply and my corespond-
ent, who also received a terrific tongue-lashing, could do nothing but cry. When I recovered my senses a little, I wanted to
defend our innocence, but he ordered me to shut up and I had
to let him talk.

Meanwhile his wife came in, and she started a brand new
sermon, so that I wished I lay somewhere in a briar patch. I
don't think they would have stopped for the next two hours if
the Croat and the minister hadn't arrived. Before they came I

tried several times to get up, but the lieutenant colonel threatened my life and made me lie down again. That's how I found out that a man who is caught in an evil deed has no courage at all, and how a thief feels when he's nabbed breaking into a place, even though he has stolen nothing yet. I was thinking of occasions when I would have chased off the lieutenant colonel with two of his Croats, but now I lay there like any coward and hadn't the heart to open my mouth, much less use my fists.

"Look at this fine spectacle," he said to the parson, "to which I had to call you to make you a witness of my own shame." He had hardly uttered these words in an ordinary tone of voice when he started raving again and losing his sense of proportion. He ranted about breaking my neck and spilling my blood with his own hand, and so on, and I thought he might shoot me in the head any minute. The parson did his utmost to keep him from a rash deed that he might later regret. "Lieutenant colonel," he said, "use your God-given reason and consider making the best of a bad bargain. This handsome pair isn't the first or the last to be overcome by the irrepressible force of love. The crime they have committed—if it is to be called a crime—can be easily remedied by them. To be sure, I don't approve of this approach to marriage. Still, our couple deserves neither the gallows nor the wheel, and you will derive no shame from their action if you forgive them, keep this peccadillo secret, consent to the marriage, and let them confirm their intention by the customary church ceremony." "What?" he answered, "I am to forgive them, praise them, honor them, instead of punishing them? I'd rather tie them up and drown them in the river before daybreak! You must marry them this moment—that's why I sent for you—or I'll wring their necks like chickens."

Seeing I'd have no choice in the matter, I considered that I would not have to be ashamed of the girl; as a matter of fact, in view of my family and background, I was hardly worthy of sitting down where she kept her slippers. I swore up and down that we had done nothing sinful together. But I was told we should have behaved so that no one could suspect

anything evil; this was no way to remove the suspicion we had
raised. Then, sitting up in bed, we were joined in matrimony
by the parson, and thereafter we were requested to get up and
leave the house together. At the threshold the lieutenant
colonel told his daughter and me never to darken his door
again. Having recovered a little and having my sword by my
side, I answered almost in jest, "Dear father-in-law, I don't
know why you do everything topsy-turvy. When others get
married, their relatives lead them to their bed. You, on the
other hand, not only chase me out of bed, but also out of the
house after the wedding; instead of wishing me luck in my
marriage, you don't even want me to have the pleasure of
seeing my dad-in-law's face and of serving him. If your attitude were to spread, the institution of marriage would make
few friends in this world."

CHAPTER 22: *How the wedding goes, and what the Hunter
plans now*

The people at my lodgings were surprised to see me bring
home this girl who—even greater surprise—went to bed with
me without batting an eyelash. And even though the trick
played on me put perplexing notions in my head, I wasn't so
foolish as to scorn my bride. Now I had my sweetheart in my
arms, but my head was full of a thousand thoughts of how to
manage and improve my situation. One minute I thought I
deserved my fate; the next, that I had suffered the most
grievous disgrace on earth and would have to avenge myself
for it. But when I considered that revenge would necessarily
hurt my father-in-law and therefore also my innocent, kind
wife, all my plans came to nothing. I was so ashamed that I
decided to keep to myself and show myself to nobody, but
then I realized that that would be the greatest foolishness of
all. Finally I resolved to regain my father-in-law's confidence
and, as for the rest, act as if nothing untoward had happened
and everything about my marriage was all right.

Over such thoughts daylight came, and I got up, although

I would have liked to stay in bed longer. First I sent for my brother-in-law and informed him of how closely we were now related. I asked him to send over his wife to help us with plans for entertaining at our wedding celebration; and I asked if he would please try to patch things up with my in-laws. Meanwhile I would invite guests who would promote peace between us. He agreed willingly to do what he could, while I went to see the commander and invited him with clever phrases. He promised to come, sent me a deer and a barrel of wine, and said he'd try to bring my father-in-law along. I had a meal prepared that was good enough for princes and had plenty of fine guests, who not only had a good time but even reconciled the parents-in-law with me and my wife in such a way that they wished us as much luck and happiness as they had cursed and sworn at us the night before.

I didn't mind the unusual procedure after all, for if the vows had been said in church, I fear there would have been some members of the fair sex who might have made trouble for me, for among the burghers' daughters there were at least half a dozen who had known me only too well and who were in trouble now.

On the day following, it was my father-in-law's turn to entertain the wedding guests; but since he was on the miserly side, he did not have as much to offer as I. Then he told me how to arrange my life and how to keep house, and I noticed that I had lost my noble freedom and was about to go into bondage. I played the obedient son, as if I really wanted to hear my father-in-law's advice and, if possible, follow it. This attitude pleased the commander, and he said, "Since you are a promising young soldier, it would be foolish for you to take up anything but soldiering in these martial times. Nowadays it is far better to put a horse in someone else's stable than to feed somebody else's horse in your own. As far as I am concerned, you can have a troop any time."

My father-in-law and I thanked him, and I no longer rejected the offer as I used to. Then I showed the commander the merchant's I O U and informed him that I had to go and

get the valuables before joining the Swedish service; for if anyone found out that I had gone to the enemy they'd keep my
fortune and give me the raspberry in Cologne. This made
sense to them, and it was agreed that I should leave for
Cologne in a few days, return to the fort with my treasure,
and accept my troop. My father-in-law also was to get a
lieutenant-colonelcy and a company in the commander's regiment. Since Count von Götz was in Westphalia at that time
and had his headquarters at Dortmund, the commander expected a siege next spring and was looking for good soldiers
(though this was all for nothing, because von Götz had to quit
Westphalia and face the Duke of Weimar on the upper Rhine
the next spring).

CHAPTER 23: *Simplicius comes to a city, which he calls*
Cologne (because it has to have a name), in
in order to retrieve his treasure-trove

Things have a way of happening. One fellow's misfortune
comes about piecemeal, by degrees; another's overtakes him by
leaps and bounds. Mine had a sweet and pleasant beginning,
and I considered it not a misfortune but the greatest luck. I
had hardly spent a week with my beloved bride when, dressed
in my hunter's outfit and armed with a gun, I took leave of
her and her friends in order to pick up what I had left in
Cologne for safekeeping. I got there without mishap because
all the roads were well known to me; in fact, not a soul saw
me until I came to the toll gate at Deutz, across the Rhine
from Cologne. I, on the other hand, saw many people; I especially remember a peasant in the duchy of Berg who was
the spitting image of my knan in the Spessart, and his son was
just like me. This boy was herding the pigs when I tried to
sneak past him; because the hogs heard me and started grunt-
ing, the boy cursed them and wished aloud that the devil
might fetch them and a hailstorm strike them. The hired girl
heard him and she hollered at him to stop cursing or she'd

tell his father. The boy answered that she could kiss his backside and spit on her mother. Now his father had heard him
too, and he came out of the house with a cat-o'-nine-tails,
shouting, "Wait, you so-and-so of a rascal. I'll teach you how
to swear!" And grabbing him by the scruff of the neck, he
beat him like a dancing bear, and with every stroke he said,
"There, you bad boy, I'll teach you how to cuss; you go plumb
to hell; I'll kiss your backside; I'll teach you to spit on your
mother," and so on. This sort of education reminded me of
myself and my knan; but I was not honest or grateful enough
to thank God for removing me from such darkness and ignorance and giving me knowledge and better insight. Why
shouldn't the good luck I was enjoying every day last forever?

When I got to Cologne I stayed with my Jupiter, who was
quite rational at that time. When I told him why I had come,
he said right away that I was probably on a wild goose chase;
the merchant to whom I had entrusted my money had declared himself bankrupt and skipped the country. True, my
effects were under official lock and key, and the merchant had
been ordered to return, but he wasn't likely to come back
because he had taken the most valuable part of his assets
with him, and a lot of water would flow down the Rhine before the matter was settled. Anybody can imagine how much
I liked hearing this news. I swore worse than a trooper, but
what was the good of that? It did not produce my property,
and there wasn't much hope I'd ever get it back. Since I had
taken along only ten thalers to spend on the journey, I could
not even stay as long as the business required. Moreover, there
was another danger in staying, for since I was attached to a
hostile garrison, someone was sure to turn me in, and I would
not only lose my treasure but get into even worse trouble. Was
I to turn around without doing anything, leave my fortune
behind with nothing to show for my trip? That too seemed
inadvisable. I decided to stay until the bankruptcy came up
in court and to tell my bride about it by letter. So I went to
an attorney, told him my situation, and asked him to set a

fee for helping me; I would pay him an extra bonus for hurrying the proceedings. Since he hoped I would be good for quite
a haul, he eagerly accepted my case and let me board at his
house. The next day he went with me to the man in charge
of bankruptcies, handed in a notarized copy of the merchant's I O U, and produced the original; then we were informed that we would have to wait till the case came up in
court, for some of the goods were missing.

Being sure now of considerable leisure, I wanted to see what
life in a big city was like. My landlord was, as I said, an attorney and counselor at law, but on the side he kept half a
dozen boarders, and in his stable there were always eight
horses, which he would hire out to travelers. He also had a
German and a French stable boy, either of whom he used for
driving or riding and to take care of the horses. With these
three, or three and a half, occupations he made not only a
living but also a good profit. Since Jews were not allowed
in town, he was able to keep a lot of money-making irons in
the fire.

During the short time I spent in his house I learned a lot
from him, particularly how to diagnose many diseases. And
that is the most important part of medicine, for they say that
when a disease is correctly diagnosed the patient is already
half cured. To my landlord goes the credit for my acquiring
this knowledge, for he taught me to observe first his and then
other people's complexions. I found that many people are sick
unto death without knowing it; others, even the doctors, consider them to be in perfect health.

I found some who were sick with anger, and when the disease came over them they made faces like the devil, roared
like lions, scratched like cats, clawed about them like bears,
bit like dogs, and—worse than savage animals—like utter fools
threw away everything they could lay hands on. They say this
disease is caused by the gall bladder, but I think it comes
about when a fool gets stuck up. Therefore, if you see an
angry man roaring, especially if it is over a trifling matter,
you can be sure he has more pride than sense. From this ill-

ness springs much unhappiness, for both the patient and others. One ought not to call those suffering from it "patients," for patience is exactly what they don't have.

I found that stuffing and swilling is also a disease. It is a trouble caused by habit rather than by opulence. Poverty helps but is not a complete cure, for I saw beggars living in luxury and rich misers suffering the pangs of hunger. It carries its remedy on its own back; it is called "want," if not of money then of bodily health, so that in the end these patients grow healthy of their own accord—that is, when because of poverty or other diseases they can no longer stuff themselves. I also found that laughter is a disease. Philemon died of it, Democritus was infected with it till he died, and to this day some of our ladies say they like to laugh themselves to death. Some think it originates in the liver, but I rather think it is caused by a plethora of silliness, and excessive laughter is not an indication of a rational human being. No medicine is needed against it, for it is a jolly disease and many times it stops before the patient wants it to.

Of other diseases, like envy, gambling, pride, curiosity, laziness, vindictiveness, jealousy, frailties of love, and other such illnesses and vices I shall not write at this time. For one thing, I don't *intend* to write about them; for another, I want to get back to my landlord, who caused me to think about such imperfections, for he was possessed by greed to the ends of his fingernails.

CHAPTER 24: *The Hunter catches a coney in the middle of the city*

This fellow, as I said, had various and sundry ways of accumulating money. He lived off his boarders, not they off him. He could have fed himself and his family well for what the boarders paid him, if he only had used the money for that purpose. But he fed us poorly and held back on everything. In the beginning I ate with his children and the hired help, because I didn't have much money with me. The tiny morsels we received seemed altogether too diminutive for my stomach, which was used to Westphalian helpings. We never got a good piece of meat on the table, only the leftovers of what had been served a week ago to the boarders. It had been gnawed at here and there and was hoary with age like Methuselah. His wife (who did the cooking, for he wouldn't hire a maid) poured a dark, sour gravy over it and deviled it up with pepper. We licked the bones so clean that you could have made chessmen out of them, but even then they hadn't been utilized well enough. They were put in a special container, and when a certain quantity had accumulated they were broken up and all the fat boiled out of them. I don't know whether it was used to flavor soup or to grease jack boots.

On fast days—there were plenty of them, and they were all meticulously and solemnly observed, for our host was very scrupulous on this point—we had to gnaw on stinky smoked herring, river salmon spoiled by too much salt, rotten kippers and other fish, all superannuated. He bought everything cheap and went to the trouble of visiting the fish market in person to pick out with his own hands what the fishmongers were about to throw away. Our bread was usually black and stale; our drink, a thin, sour beer that cut my insides to ribbons, though the landlord said it was good, aged bock. The German hostler told me that in the summertime things were usually even worse; the bread was moldy, the meat full of maggots, and their best dish was a couple of radishes at noon and a mess of lettuce at night. I asked him why he didn't quit the niggard. He answered that he was away on trips most of the time and was counting more on tips from the travelers than wages from the moldy miser.

One time the skinflint brought home six pounds of beef tripe for soup and put it in the pantry cellar. To their delight, his children found a window open, tied a fork to a long stick, and with this contraption helped themselves to the tripe, boiled it in a hurry, and ate it half raw. They told him the cat must have eaten the mess. But this parsimonious skinflint did not believe them. He looked all over for the cat, weighed it, and found out that with hide and hair it was not so heavy as the tripe that vanished! He wasn't at all ashamed of these cheap maneuvers but thought that he was very clever and ought to be admired for the inventions his greed taught him.

Since he acted so shamelessly, I asked to be transferred to the boarders' table and never mind the cost. The food was slightly better, but that didn't do me much good, for it was only half cooked. This saved the landlord money in two places —in fuel and in the quantity eaten. Nobody could digest much of it. Then, too, he counted every bite we put in our mouths and looked miserable when we ate well. His wine was watered and did not aid digestion; the cheese served at the end of the meal was hard as a rock; the Dutch butter was so salty that no one could use more than an ounce at a meal; fruit was carried in and out till it got soft and ripe; and if anyone grumbled, he started a terrific row with his wife so that we could all hear it. But secretly he told her not to change a thing.

His house was always clean, though. And when he found the smallest sliver of wood or piece of paper under foot, he would carry it to the kitchen personally and say, "Many a mickle makes a muckle"; but what he really meant was, "A lot of toothpicks make me a roaring fire."

One time, one of his clients had brought him a rabbit. I saw it hanging in the pantry and thought we would soon enjoy a piece of game, but the German hostler told me we'd never sink our teeth into it. If I went to the Old Market that afternoon, I would see the rabbit for sale there. I cut a little piece out of the rabbit's ear, and at noon, while our landlord was out of the room, I told the boarders that our skinflint had a rabbit he wanted to sell and that I would cheat him out of it. If they would go along, we would not only have some fun but get the rabbit to eat as well. They all agreed to join me, for every one of them would have been glad to play a trick on our landlord.

Therefore, in the afternoon we went to the place where the

hired man had said the landlord used to stand whenever he sold something through an agent, and where he would be watching lest he get cheated out of a penny. We saw him there, talking to some people of importance. I had employed a fellow to say to the salesman, "Mister, that rabbit is mine. It disappeared last night from my window, and I am taking it along as stolen goods. If you want to, you can take me wherever you want to go, but at your risk and at your expense." The seller answered that he would find out what to do; the rabbit had been given him by a gentleman who doubtless had not stolen it. And while the two were arguing, a crowd quickly gathered. When our tightwad noticed what was going on, he motioned to the salesman to let the rabbit go, for on account of his many boarders he was afraid he'd be the talk of the town.

The man I had employed made a big show of producing the piece of ear and fitting it in the notch of the rabbit's ear, and the crowd was satisfied that it was his rabbit, and that he was in the right. Now I and my company approached as if we just happened to come along. I sauntered up to the man with the rabbit and started haggling with him over the price. When we had agreed, I sent the rabbit to our landlord, asking him to take it home and have it prepared for our table. The fellow I had employed got a tip worth two mugs of beer and nothing for the rabbit. And so, against his will, our curmudgeon had to serve the rabbit, and he could not even say a word about it, while we had a good laugh. If I had stayed longer in his house, I would have played more such tricks on him.

End of the Third Book

✐ Book Four

CHAPTER 1: *How the Hunter was spirited off to France, and the reasons therefor*

Trying to put too much edge on a blade spoils it, and drawing a bow too far makes it break. I wasn't satisfied with the coney trick I had played on my landlord, but I continued to punish my host for his monstrous avarice; I taught the boarders to soak the salty butter in water in order to remove the excess salt and to grate the hard cheese like Parmesan and moisten it with wine. These practical jokes were like stabs at the heart of the miser. By a special trick I removed the water from the wine on the table, and I made up a song comparing a miser to a hog, from which no good can come until it is dead and hanging in the butcher shop. I sang this song to the sound of my lute and caused him to repay me quickly with the following dirty trick—for, after all, I was ill advised to play tricks on the man in his own home.

Two young noblemen who lived at my landlord's received a check and orders from home to go to France in order to learn the language. But the German servant was away, and our landlord did not dare trust his French servant abroad with the horses. He said he did not know him well enough for that, and he was afraid he might forget to come back, thus robbing him of the horses. So he asked me to do him the great favor of taking the noblemen to Paris. My case would not come up for at least a month; and if I would give him power of attorney, he would see to my affairs as diligently as if I were present in person. The noblemen begged me to go; my own desire to see France also urged me on, since I could now do so without any cost to myself; in Cologne I'd be idle for at least another month and would have to spend money for room and board. And so I took to the road as the coachman for these young nobles.

On the way, nothing worth writing about happened. But when we got to Paris and the noblemen cashed their letters of credit at our landlord's agent, not only was I arrested and the horses attached by court order, but also the agent, who said my landlord owed him a large amount of money, had the horses sold—with the approval of the local magistrate and in disregard of my protests. So I sat there like a shorn lamb and didn't know what to think, much less how to retrace the long and (at the time) dangerous road home. The two nobles expressed their sincere sympathy for me in my predicament, gave me a generous tip, and said they did not want to dismiss me until I found a good job or got back to Germany. They rented a room and I stayed with them for a few days and looked after one of them who had become indisposed from the long, unaccustomed journey. And since I had done a satisfactory job, he gave me his hand-me-down clothes when he bought a suit tailored in the latest fashion. They advised me to plan to stay in Paris for a few years and learn the language. My money in Cologne would not run away, and our landlord would take care of it in his usual pedantic way.

While I was still making up my mind about what to do, the doctor who came in daily to visit the sick nobleman heard me playing the lute and singing a German song. This pleased him so well that he offered me a good position and free board if I would give music lessons to his two boys. He knew my predicament better than I and was sure I would not refuse a good job. Since both noblemen recommended me highly and advised me to take the job, we soon agreed on the particulars. But I would hire myself out only for three months at a time.

This doctor spoke Italian as if it were his mother tongue and German as fluently as I did. That was another reason why I went to him. When I ate the farewell supper with my noblemen, he was there too, and my head was full of all sorts of thoughts—about my newly wedded wife, the troop promised me, the treasure in Cologne, and the fact that I had been persuaded to leave all this behind me rather irresponsibly. When the conversation got around to our former landlord's avarice, it suddenly occurred to me—and I blurted it out across the table—that he might have gotten me out of the way on purpose so that he could claim my property in Cologne and keep it. The doctor thought this might well be, especially if the landlord considered me a man of low station. "No," said one of the noblemen, "if he has been sent out of the country to stay, it it because Simplicissimus always nagged and twitted him with his avarice." The sick one now thought he knew an even better reason; he had overheard the French hired hand complaining in broken German to our landlord that the Hunter had tattled on him to the landlady for not tending the horses well. But the jealous skinflint must have misunderstood the Frenchman's language; for he had assured the man that he should stay, while the Hunter would be gotten rid of. Since that day he had looked at his wife askance and had had more arguments with her than before.

The doctor said, "Whatever the reason, I am sure there was a plan to get the Hunter out of Germany and keep him out. But don't let that get you down. I'll see to it that you find a way back. Just write him to take good care of your treasure or he'll have to answer for it in court. What makes me suspicious is that the presumed creditor is a good friend of your landlord and his local agent. I rather think that you handed him the paper by virtue of which the horses were sold."

CHAPTER 2: *Simplicius gets a landlord who is better than the previous one*

Monseigneur Canard (that was the name of my new employer) offered to help me in every way to hang on to my money in Cologne, for he saw how sad I was. As soon as I came to his house, he wanted me to tell him about the state of my business, so he could think up ways of helping me. I imagined I wouldn't be worth much if I told him where I

came from. So I told him I was a poor German nobleman who
had lost his father and mother and who only had a couple of
relatives in a fortress occupied by the Swedes. I said I had
been forced to keep this from my landlord and the two noblemen who were of the imperial party, lest they seize my property for their own use as something belonging to an enemy. I
intended to write to the commander of the fortress (the one
who had promised me the position of junior officer) and tell
him not only how I had been spirited out of the country, but
also that he should be good enough to take possession of my
money and give it to my friends for safekeeping until I had a
chance to get back to the regiment.

Canard was all for it and promised to expedite my letters,
even if they were addressed to Mexico or China. Accordingly,
I wrote to my dear wife, to my father-in-law, and to Colonel
de St. André, the commander at Lippstadt. The letter said
that I'd be back as soon as possible if only I had the means to
make the long trip. I addressed the envelope to him and enclosed the other two letters. I asked both my father-in-law and
the colonel to try and seize my money by military force before
the matter was forgotten. Incidentally, I detailed how much
there was in gold, silver, and jewelry. These letters I wrote
in duplicate, one copy being sent by Monsieur Canard's
messenger, the other by mail; in case one did not get there,
the other would surely arrive. Thus I regained a joyful outlook and instructed my employer's two sons the more gladly.
They were being brought up like young princes because
Monsieur Canard was very rich and very proud, and he
wanted to show off. He had caught this malady from great
men, for he was daily associating with princes, as it were, and
aping them in everything. His house was like the household of
a count, and nothing was lacking save the title of "Your Excellency." And his fancy was such that he dealt with a marquis
who happened to call on him no better than with his own
kind. To be sure, he also treated little people, but he never
accepted modest fees. He would rather charge nothing just
to have the reputation of generosity. Because I was a bit unusual and since I knew he liked to show off with me when I

accompanied him (along with other servants) on his sick calls, I helped him when he made up medicine in his laboratory. That's where I got to know him better, for he liked to practice his German on me. I asked him once why he did not call himself by the name of a valuable estate he had bought near Paris for twenty thousand crowns, and why he wanted to make doctors of all his sons and made them study so hard. Wouldn't it be better, I asked, since he already was a member of the nobility, if he bought them some offices (as was done for other cavaliers), and so let them become full-fledged noblemen? "No," he said, "when I come to a prince, he says 'Doctor, sit down'; but to a nobleman he says 'Wait your turn.'" I continued, "You know well that a doctor has three faces: an angel's when the patient sees him coming; a god's when he helps him; and a devil's when the patient is well again and has to pay the bill. A nobleman has greater honor from standing at the door for his prince than a doctor has from sitting down, because he is always waiting on his prince and has the honor never to be far from him. Besides, the other day I saw you taste something of the prince's—I'd rather stand up waiting for someone for ten years than try the taste of someone else's feces, even if I were asked to sit on roses." He answered, "I didn't *have* to do that. I did it in order to prove to the prince how much trouble I was taking to diagnose his case—and so that I could charge a larger fee. You talk of these matters like a German, and if you were of another nationality, I'd say like a damn fool!" I swallowed this because I saw he was about to get angry, and in order to sweet-talk him, I begged him to excuse my ignorance and started discussing something more pleasant.

CHAPTER 3: *Simplicius consents to being used as an actor, and he gets a new name*

Dr. Canard had more venison to throw out than some folks with game preserves of their own have to eat. Since more meat was given to him than he and his family could eat, he also had many hangers-on, and it almost looked as if he were keeping a free table for everybody. One time the king's Master of Ceremonies and other prominent court personages were eating a princely collation provided by the doctor, who knew where to make his friends—namely, among those who were around the king every day and who were in favor. To show these people his goodwill and to keep them entertained, he asked me to do him the honor of singing a German ditty to my lute.

I was glad to oblige, for I was in the mood for it and tried hard to give them something special. Consequently, I pleased those present so well that the Master of Ceremonies said it was a shame I didn't know French. Otherwise, he would commend me to the king and queen. But my employer, who feared he might lose me, told him I was a nobleman who did not want to stay long in France and who probably did not care to hire himself out as a musician. Then the Master of Ceremonies told him he had never before seen such perfection of form and voice and such skill on the lute—all in one person. A play was soon to be given in the Louvre, for the king. If I could act in it, he hoped to give me a part in which I could make a great impression. Monsieur Canard translated this and I replied that if I were told the character I was to act and given the songs beforehand, I could learn the words and melodies by heart, as pupils are required to do when they sing and act in Latin. When the Master of Ceremonies saw that I was willing, he asked me to come to the Louvre next day for a tryout. So I presented myself at the appointed hour.

I played the melodies of the different songs directly from the printed music. When I received the French words and the melodies to learn by heart, the texts were translated for me so that I could make the appropriate gestures. None of this was difficult, and I could do it in a short time—and so well that not one in a thousand would have thought I was anything but a native Frenchman.

I never had a more satisfying day than the one on which the

opera was performed. Monsieur Canard gave me something to make my voice even clearer, but when he tried to enhance my beauty by means of *oleum talci* and to powder my naturally curly black hair, he found that this only detracted from my appearance. I was crowned with a laurel wreath and had to wear a turquoise-colored toga that left bare my neck, the upper part of my chest, arms up to the elbow, and my legs. Around me I wore a flesh-colored cloak of taffeta that looked more like a baldric. In this outfit I wooed my Eurydice with a pretty song, implored the goddess Venus for support, and finally carried off my beloved in a scene in which I had to sigh and cast loving glances at her. But when I had lost my Eurydice, I dressed in a black gown that was made like the other one, except that my white skin shone like snow because of the contrast. In this costume I lamented the loss of my wife, and I got so absorbed in the act that I started crying in the middle of my sad songs, and for a minute I didn't know if I could go on. But I managed to carry it off until I appeared before Pluto and Proserpine in hell, where I begged them to return Eurydice to me. After I was granted my wish, I turned so happy in song and expression that the audience was quite astonished. But when I lost her a second time, I imagined the greatest dangers a man could get into, and I grew so pale and miserable that I almost fainted. After that, I sat down on a rock and lamented my loss with pitiful words and a sad melody, and I called on every creature for sympathy. All sorts of tame and wild animals, trees, mountains, and so on, came to listen to me. This scene looked as if magic had been used. Nothing went wrong until the end, when I had renounced women and been thrown into the water by fauns, and a dragon was supposed to eat me. (I stood behind some scenery and only my head was visible to the audience.) Now the fellow who was inside the dragon, working it, couldn't see and so his monstrous mouth nibbled and nuzzled some greenery that was next to my head. This struck me as so funny that I couldn't help laughing, and some ladies who were watching me noticed it.

Besides generous and general praise, I received not only a considerable cash honorarium but also a new name; from now on the French called me by no other name than "Beau Alman." [1] Since it was the carnival season, more such operas and ballets were given, and I was in several of them. But finding that I curried too much favor with the spectators, especially the ladies, and that I made too many enemies, I gave up acting, particularly after I had been battered and beaten more than is customary on stage, while, in the role of Hercules, I was fighting with Achelous for Dejanira.

CHAPTER 4: *Beau Alman is led against his will into the mountain of Venus*

But through my acting I became acquainted with persons of quality, and it seemed that Fortune was again smiling on me. I was even offered a job in the king's household, something that doesn't happen every day, even to the big shots. One time while I was working in the laboratory, a uniformed servant came, spoke to Monsieur Canard, and handed him a letter for me. (Because I was interested in pharmacy I had learned from my employer how to sublimate, coagulate, calcinate, filter, precipitate, wash, and so on, as was required in the alchemical method by which he prepared his medicines.) "Monsieur Beau Alman," Canard said to me, "this letter concerns you. A gentleman wants to know if you are willing to give his son lessons on the lute. He is asking me to use my influence with you, so you won't refuse this request." I answered that I would do my best to be of service if I could thereby please Dr. Canard. He asked me to dress up a little better and go along with the servant. Meanwhile, he would have something prepared for me to eat, for I'd have a rather long way to go and could hardly get to my destination before evening. So I got dressed fairly well and hurriedly bolted some

---

[1] Grimmelshausen probably did not know the rule according to which he should have nicknamed Simplicius "Le bel Alman."

of the snacks that had been prepared, including a couple of delicious little sausages which—it seemed to me—tasted a bit medicinal. Then I proceeded with the servant by curious, roundabout ways, until after about an hour we reached a garden gate that was not quite closed. The lackey pushed it open, and when I had entered after him he banged it shut, bolted the night latch, which was on the inside, and led me to a pleasure pavilion inside the garden. After we had walked to the end of a fairly long passage, he knocked on a door that was at once opened by a noble old lady. She greeted me very politely in German and asked me to step inside. The lackey, who knew no German and whom I thanked with a nod of my head, stayed behind and bade me good-by with a deep bow.

The old lady took me by the hand and led me into the room, which was covered with precious tapestry and beautifully appointed. She asked me to sit down and rest while I found out why I had been taken to this place. I was glad to obey and sat down in a easy chair she had placed by the fire, which was burning because of the cold. She then sat down opposite me in another chair and said, "Monsieur, if you know anything about the power of love, which overcomes and dominates the bravest, strongest, and wisest of men, you will not be one whit surprised that it also assumes mastery over members of the weaker sex. It wasn't your lute (as you and M. Canard were persuaded to think) for which you were called, nor did a man call you. It was your unsurpassable handsomeness and the most excellent lady in Paris that brought you here. She is expecting to die should Fortune deny her the happiness of beholding your divine form and of refreshing herself thereby. That is why she ordered me to inform you (as my fellow countryman) and to beg you more ardently than Venus ever begged Adonis to come to her tonight, so that she may take her fill of looking upon your beauty. This, she hopes, you will not deny a noble lady." My answer was, "Madame, I don't know what to think, much less what to say in reply to this. I don't claim to be such that a lady of high quality should desire my humble company. Moreover, as I think of it,

if the lady who wants to see me is so excellent and noble as
you, my dear fellow countrywoman, mentioned and conveyed
to me, why didn't she send for me earlier in the day, instead
of having me brought to this forsaken place so late at night?
Why didn't she ask me to come straight to her? What do I
have to do with her garden? May you forgive me, my dear
compatriot, if, as a stranger in a strange land, I become suspicious of being betrayed, especially since I was told to see a
gentleman, and everything seems topsy-turvy. The minute I
notice foul play I am going to use my blade." "Soft, soft, my
dear fellow countryman! Forget these uncalled-for thoughts,"
she interrupted. "Women are unconventional and cautious in
their plans. A man can't understand them at first. If the lady
who loves you more than anything in the world had wanted
you to know who she is, why, she would not have let you come
here first, but straight to her. There's a hood," and she
pointed to a table, "which you must put over your head when
you are taken to her, because she does not want you to know
where or with whom you have been. May I beg and pray of
you to behave with this lady in a manner befitting her exalted
position and the inexpressible love she bears you. Otherwise,
you may expect to find out that she is powerful enough to
punish your pride and your disdain of her. But if you treat
her as she deserves, you may rest assured that every step you
have taken in her behalf will be rewarded."

Meanwhile, it had become dark, and all sorts of worries and
fearful thoughts plagued me so that I sat there like a graven
image. I imagined vividly that I would not leave this place
except by consenting to everything I was asked. So I said to
the old lady, "All right then, my dear compatriot, if it is as
you told me, I'll entrust myself to your inborn German
honesty, in hopes that you will not permit any treachery to
befall a guileless German. Go ahead and do what you have
been told to do with me. The lady you mentioned probably
won't kill me by looking at me." "Heavens, no," she said,
"it would be a shame if such a well proportioned body—one
that might be called the pride of our nation—were to perish

so soon. You will find more pleasures than you have ever dreamed of."

The minute she had my consent she called for Jean and Pierre, who stepped out from behind a tapestry, each wearing a large shiny cuirass and armed from head to foot with halberd and pistol. I was so taken aback that I turned white. The old lady noticed and said with a smile, "A man ought not to be so frightened when he's on his way to a lady." She then told the men to take off their cuirasses and to light the way for me, with only pistols in hand. She slipped the black velvet hood over my head, took my hat, and led me out by the hand. I noticed that our way led through many doors and along a cobbled street. After perhaps ten minutes, I had to climb a short stairway, and a narrow door opened; I walked along a paved passage, up a winding staircase, then down a few steps; and finally, about six steps farther on, another door opened. When I had stepped through it the old lady pulled off the hood and I saw that I was in a room decorated in exceedingly good taste. The walls were hung with paintings, the buffet sparkled with silverware, and the bed, which stood off to one side, was trimmed with hangings of brocade. In the middle of the room stood a table, luxuriously set, and by the fireplace was a bathtub that looked nice enough—but a little out of place, I thought.

The crone said to me, "Welcome, countryman; do you still think you are being trapped? Put aside your suspicion and act as you did on stage the other day when Pluto returned your Euridice to you. Let me assure you, you'll find a prettier one here than you lost there."

CHAPTER 5: *How Beau Alman fares there, and how he comes back out*

From these words I gathered that I was supposed to do more in this place than allow myself to be looked at. So I told my old compatriot that a thirsty man gets little comfort from sitting by a forbidden well. She said that French people weren't so grudging as to forbid the water, especially when there was plenty of it. "Well, madame," I answered, "such talk is easy, but I am a married man!" "Fiddlesticks!" replied this sinful woman. "Nobody will believe you tonight. In the first place, married noblemen seldom go off traveling in France, and even if it were so I don't think you are such a simpleton to die of thirst rather than drink from a stranger's well, particularly if the stranger's is perhaps even jollier and holds better water than your own."

This was our conversation while a lady in waiting, who was tending the fire, took off my shoes and stockings, which had gotten dirty on the way over, for Paris is a dirty town. A minute later an order came that I was to be given a bath before supper. (The little lady in waiting was running in and out, preparing the bath and carrying in perfumed soap and towels of cambric cloth trimmed with the finest Dutch lace.) I was ashamed and did not want the old girl to see me naked, but there was no help for it; I had to undress and she washed me all over. The maid had to step outside for a while.

After the bath I was given a soft undershirt; I had to put on a purple taffeta housecoat and a pair of silk hose of the same color. My slippers and night cap were embroidered with gold thread and pearls, and after my bath I sat there resplendent as the king of hearts. While the old lady was drying and combing my hair—she treated me like a prince or a baby—the above-mentioned maid brought in the food, and when the table was moved over, there entered three statuesque young ladies whose alabaster-white breasts were considerably visible, but whose faces were completely masked. All three seemed to be perfect beauties; but still, one was much more beautiful than the others. I silently bowed very deeply to them; they curtsied to me in turn. These ceremonies looked, of course, as if a number of mutes were trying to act like speaking characters. The three of them sat down at the same time so that I could not guess which one took precedence, much less which one I was to oblige. The conversation opened with the question of whether I could speak French. My compatriot said no. Then one lady asked her to tell me please to sit down. When this had been done, the third asked the interpreter to sit down too. Again I could not figure out who was the foremost. The crone and I sat exactly opposite the three ladies, and there's no doubt that I looked twice as handsome beside that old bag of bones. All three looked at me with grace, love, and goodwill, and I could have sworn they sighed a hundred times. Because of the masks I could not see the sparkle of their eyes.

My old dame—she was the only one who could talk to me—asked me which one of the three I considered most beautiful. I answered that I couldn't really see them, but as much as I could see of them, none of the three was ugly. The ladies at once wanted to know what the crone had asked and I had replied. She interpreted it and added the lie that I had said the lips of each were worth kissing a hundred thousand times (for from my seat I could very well see their mouths under their masks, especially that of the one who sat right across from me). With this fib the crone got me to consider my vis-à-vis as the noblest, and I looked at her more eagerly from then on. This was all of our table conversation, and I carefully pretended that I knew not one word of French. Since it was so quiet and a quiet meal is not much fun, we quit all the sooner. The ladies then bid me good night and were on their way. I could not accompany them farther than the door, which the crone immediately bolted after them.

When I saw that, I asked where I was to sleep. She answered that I would have to make shift with her in the bed in this room. I let her know I did not mind the bed if only one of those three were in it. "Well," she said, "you won't have any of them tonight." While we were bantering like this, a beautiful lady who lay in the bed drew back the curtain a little and told the crone to quit chattering and go to bed. I picked up the candle and tried to see who was in the bed. But the old hag blew it out and said, "If you want to keep your head on your shoulders, don't you dare to look at the lady! Just lie down, and let me assure you if you make a serious effort to look at this lady against her will, you will never leave this place alive." With these words she left and locked the door from the outside. The maid, who had been keeping up the fire, extinguished it completely and left the room through a door hidden by an arras.

Now the lady in bed said, "Allez, Monsieur Beau Alman, go to bed, my sweet 'art come to mee!" The crone had taught her to say that much in my language. I advanced to the bed, to see how the situation might be handled, and as soon as I got there she was on my neck, welcomed me with many kisses, and for ardent desire almost bit off my lower lip. In fact, she started unbuttoning my housecoat and almost tore off my shirt. She pulled me down to herself and from unrestrained love acted in such a way that words fail me. She only knew one other phrase, "Come to mee, sweet 'art!" The rest she let me know by gestures.

Certainly, I thought of my dear wife at home, but what good did that do me? Unfortunately, I was a man, and with such a well proportioned creature, so full of loveliness, I would have had to be a clod to try and get off chaste. Moreover, the sausages the doctor had given me began to take effect, and I could not help behaving like a veritable billy goat. In this fashion I spent eight days and eight nights in the place, and I think the other three also slept with me, because they didn't all talk like number one and didn't act so crazy, either. And because I was fed the same kind of sausages here, I came to believe that Monsieur Canard had prepared them and had known about this business right along. Though I was with these four ladies for more than a week, I was never permitted to see the face of any of them except through veils, which they wore except at night when it was dark. When the time was up, I was deposited in a coach with the windows closed and the curtains drawn. On the way the old lady untied my eyes, and after letting me out at the house of my employer, the coach drove off quickly. My honorarium was two hundred pistoles, and when I asked the crone whether to give any tips from this money, she said, "Absolutely not. If you did that, it would hurt *les dames*. In fact, they would think you imagined you had been in a whorehouse, where one has to pay for everything." Later I had a few more customers like these, and some of them asked so much of me that I got depleted with this sort of foolishness and couldn't do it any longer, particularly as the medicated sausages weren't helping much anymore. I began to think of Dr. Canard as no better than a pimp for preparing them.

CHAPTER 6: *Simplicius takes French leave. He thinks he has the French disease but learns better*

Through these activities I amassed so much money, from payments in cash and in kind, that it frightened me. I was no longer surprised that women take to brothels where they make a trade of their bestial lust—it's good business. But I got to thinking—not from piety or pangs of conscience, but from worry that one of these days I'd be caught in one of these escapades and get my comeuppance. For that reason I tried to get back to Germany, and especially when the commander of Lippstadt wrote me, first, that he had captured a number of merchants from Cologne whom he would not set free unless my property were given back to me, and secondly, that he was still holding the troop whose command he had promised me. He was expecting me before spring; if I were not back then he would let someone else fill the vacancy. My wife also sent along a little letter in which she gave loving assurance of her great longing for me. If she had known about my fine style of living, she would have whistled a different tune.

I could easily imagine that Dr. Canard would hardly consent to letting me go. Therefore, I planned to take French leave as soon as an opportunity arose. It soon did, much to my sorrow. One day I ran into some officers of the Weimar army. I told them I was an ensign in Colonel de St. André's regiment, had been in Paris on private business, and wanted to get back to my troop. I requested permission to join them on the way home. They told me the day of their departure and were glad to have me go with them. I bought myself a nag and outfitted myself for the trip as secretly as possible, packed up my money—about five hundred doubloons, all of which I had earned from shameless hussies, by sinful work—and without Canard's leave departed with the officers. On the way I wrote him, but I dated the letter from Maastricht, so that he would think I had headed for Cologne. I said farewell to him and told him that it had been impossible for me to stay longer; I just couldn't take any more of his aromatic sausages.

On the second night out of Paris I felt like someone who had caught the plague. My head hurt so frightfully that I couldn't possibly get up. We were in a godforsaken village where no doctor was available, nor was there anyone—and this was worse—who might nurse and help me. Early in the morning the officers started on their way to Alsace and left me behind like a sick dog, not caring what happened to me since I was not of their party. But before leaving, they commended me and my horse to the innkeeper and left word with the mayor to look after me because I was an officer in the king's service.

So I lay there for a few days and lost consciousness of myself and the world; I was raving like a madman. They brought the priest, but he couldn't get anything sensible out of me. And when he saw he couldn't cure my soul, he considered helping my body. He had me bled, prepared a sudorific, and had me put in a warm bed for sweating. This did me so much good that I regained consciousness that night and recalled where I was, how I had gotten there, and how I had become ill. Next morning the priest came back and found me in black despair, not only because all my money had been stolen, but also because I thought I had the French disease. I had this coming to me, I thought, rather than so many pistoles, and now I was spotted all over like a tiger. I couldn't walk, stand, sit, or lie. I had no patience, for as I couldn't believe God had wanted me to keep the lost money, now I was so mad that I said the devil had stolen it. I cursed a blue streak; in fact, I acted like a man out of his mind with despair, and the good minister had his work cut out cheering me up, for my shoe was pinching badly in two places at the same time. "My friend," he said, "even if you can't be a pious Christian, act like a reasonable human being in your misfortune. What are you doing? In addition to losing your money, do you also want to lose your life, and, what's more, your eternal soul?" I answered, "I don't give a hoot for the money, if only I didn't have this damned horrible disease. I wish I were in some decent place where I could get a doctor and be cured!" "You must have patience," answered the divine. "Consider the poor little children in this village, of whom more than fifty are sick." When I heard that children had the same disease, I immediately took heart, for I could easily figure out that children wouldn't get the awful disease I thought I had. So I went through my knapsack to see what I might find. Except for some shirts and underwear there was nothing valuable but a little box with a lady's portrait, the frame studded with rubies. Some beauty in Paris had given it to me. I took the picture out, sent the frame to the clergyman, and asked him to sell it in the nearest town so that I might have something with which to buy food. I realized less than a third of the frame's value, and since the money was soon spent, I had to sell my horse next. The money from it barely lasted me till the scabs started forming and I began to feel better.

CHAPTER 7: *Simplicius thinks over his life so far, and learns to swim when the water comes up to his mouth*

What a man sins with, he is usually punished with. My case of smallpox changed me so much that henceforth women left me severely alone. My face was so pitted that it looked like a barn floor where they'd been threshing peas. In fact, I got so ugly that my nice, curly hair, which had captured many a damsel, became ashamed of me and dropped out of sight. In its place grew something like pigs' bristles, and I was forced to wear a wig. And just as there was no beauty left in or on my skin, my lovely voice also left me, for the pox had been in my throat too. My eyes, until lately never without the fire that could inflame a lovely woman, now looked inflamed themselves and watered like those of an octogenarian hag with cataracts. And to top it all, I was abroad in a foreign land, unknown to man or beast, did not know the language, and hadn't a penny.

Then I started thinking back and regretting the many wonderful opportunities for advancement that I had let slip by me through carelessness or indolence. Looking back, I realized that my extraordinary good luck in the wars and the treasure-trove had been no more than the cause and preliminaries of my misfortune. I could never have fallen so low if good luck had not previously smiled on me so falsely and elevated me so high. I even felt that the good I had encountered, and had considered truly good at the time, was evil and had led me to extreme disaster. I had no hermit, anymore, who wished me well, no Colonel Ramsay to give me a home in my misery, no parson to advise me—in short, there wasn't a single soul who would lift a finger for me. They had all said that when my money was gone, I would go too, and look for a chance elsewhere, even if I must herd the swine like the prodigal son. Only now I remembered the parson's advice to use my time and money for a university education. But it was much too late to clip the bird's wing with those shears, because the bird had flown the coop. Oh, quick and unexpected change for the worse! A month ago I had been a man who had moved princes to admiration and women to love; to the common people I had looked like a masterpiece of nature, like an angel, even; now I was so ugly and misshapen that the dogs would pee on me.

I evolved a thousand and more different ideas about what to do next, for the innkeeper wanted to get rid of me, and was urging me to leave, since I had run out of money. I would have been glad to join an army, but the recruiters wouldn't have me, for I looked like a molting scarecrow or a starveling weaver. I couldn't take a job because I was still too weak and —what's worse—had never become used to regular work. Was I to become a herder as in the days of my childhood? Or even beg? Of this I was ashamed. My best consolation was that summer was coming, and in a pinch I could sleep behind a hedge when no one wanted to put me up inside his house. I still wore the good suit of clothes I had ordered for the trip, and my knapsack was full of good underwear, but nobody wanted to buy this from me for fear of catching my disease. So I buckled on my knapsack, took my sword in hand, and started making tracks. The first place I came to was a small town, barely big enough to have an apothecary shop. That's where I went to have an ointment made to get rid of the red splotches on my face. And since I had no cash I gave the apothecary's clerk a nice shirt for it, and unlike the other fools who wouldn't have my clothing, he wasn't afraid to take it. My thought was to get rid of the splotches first, in hopes of getting rid of my bad luck later. And when the apothecary told me that I'd look almost all right except for the deep marks the pocks had eaten into my skin, I felt much encouraged. It was market day just then, and a medicine man was making lots of money with his show, though he sold the people only useless goods. "You fool," I said to myself, "why don't you start that kind of business? You've been with Dr. Canard long enough, and if you haven't learned by now how to cheat a simple peasant and make a living by it, you are a stupid beetle-brain."

CHAPTER 8: *How Simplicius becomes a huckster and a quack who cheats people*

At that time I was as hungry as a horse, and my stomach demanded more of me than I could give it. I had left only a single gold ring with a diamond, worth about twenty crowns.

Having disposed of it for twelve, I could easily figure out that that wouldn't last very long, since nothing more was coming in. So I decided to become a doctor. I bought the ingredients for a common theriac [2] and made it up for sale in the villages and market towns. For the country people, I took some juniper jelly and mixed it with leaves of oak and willow and other bitter drugs. Then I made a green ointment out of all sorts of herbs, roots, butter, and a few unguents; it was good for all sorts of sores on men and horses. From calamine, pebbles, crayfish eyes, emery, and pumice I mixed a toothpowder. From lye, copper, sal ammoniac, and camphor I made a blue liquid for the scurvy, bad breath, toothache, and sore eyes. I acquired plenty of small containers of tin and wood, paper sacks, and glass jars in which to package my merchandise. In order to give me the proper airs, I had a French handbill printed, which told what all and sundry were good for. When, in about three days, this work was finished, I had invested not quite three crowns for drugs and containers. I packed up my goods and left town, intending to make my way by peddling my wares from one village to the next, as far as Alsace. In Strasbourg, a neutral city, I hoped to board a merchant ship for Cologne and from there to grope my way back to my wife. My intention was good, but I failed miserably.

At first I offered my quack remedies in front of a church, but the take was small, because at that time I was much too shy. I didn't speak the barker's blatant language yet, and I saw at once that I'd have to do better if I wanted to dispose of my rubbish and make money. I took my merchandise to an inn, where I heard from the innkeeper at the bar that in the afternoon a group of people would be meeting under the linden in front of his house. If my stuff were any good I might sell a lot of it. But the country was full of cheats, and the customers were not spending anything unless they could see that the theriac was unusually good.

---

2 Theriac, theriaca: In old medicine, an antidote to poison. The best kind was made in Venice and contained 64 ingredients. "Electuary" is a synonym for "theriac."

When I had found out what the trouble was, I bought half a glass of good strong gin, caught myself a toad of the kind called "moamy," the sort that sits and squawks in shallow puddles in the spring and early summer; they are gold or almost orange colored, speckled black underneath, and no beauties to look at. I put one of these in a wine glass full of water and placed it among my merchandise on a table beneath the linden tree.

When the people had gathered in droves about me, some thought I would pull teeth with a pair of tongs I had borrowed from the innkeeper's kitchen. But I started orating: "Messieurs et mes amis," (my French wasn't very good yet), "I do not weesh to pull ze teeth. But I have much good liquor for ze eyes, for curing discharge from red eyes." "Ho-ho!" said one heckler. "Look at your own. They glow like two will-o'-the wisps!" I answered, "Zat is true, but if I had not used my liquid on zem, zey would have become blind. Usually I don't sell the liquor. I sell ze theriac, ze powder for white teeth and ze ointment for sores. The liquid I give you free. I am no charlatan, and I desire not to chit ze people. I offer ze theriac. I prove eet is good, but if you don't like, eet is not necessary that you buy." Then I had one of the bystanders select one of my theriac jars; I put a small quantity of the medicine—about the size of a pea—into the gin glass, which the people thought was full of water, and stirred it well. With the tongs I lifted the moamy out of the water glass and said, "Look here, good peoples, if this poisonous toad drink my theriac and not die, then eet is no good and you better not buy it." With these words I stuck the poor toad—born and bred in water and incapable of tolerating alcohol—into the gin, covering the glass with cardboard so the beast couldn't jump out. Then the creature started kicking wildly and acting up worse than if I had thrown it on red hot coals, for the gin was much too potent for it. And after it had carried on like this for a while, it croaked and gave up the ghost.

The farmers were struck dumb when they saw this certain proof and started buying wildly. As far as they were concerned, there wasn't a better theriac in the whole world, and I could hardly wrap the stuff in handbills and collect the money for it fast enough. Some bought three, four, five, even six jars, so that they might not be without such precious medicine in an emergency; they even bought for friends and relatives who lived elsewhere! Though it wasn't even market day, that evening my reckless method of selling brought in ten crowns—and less than half of my stock was sold. That same night I moved on to the next village, for I was afraid some peasants might get curious and try out the theriac by putting a toad in water, and when the experiment failed I'd get my back thrashed.

In order to prove the excellence of my electuary in still another way, I prepared two poisons: a yellow arsenic from flour, saffron, and gall; and sublimate of mercury from flowers and vitriol. In order to present my proof, I put two identical glasses full of fresh water on a table before me. The water in one of these was mixed with a lot of *aqua fortis,* or spirits of vitriol; into this glass I put a little of my theriac. Into both glasses I sprinkled enough of my two poisons to make the water that contained no theriac (and no *aqua fortis*) as black as ink. The other glass stayed perfectly clear because of the *aqua fortis.* "Aha!" said the people, "This is a strong theriac indeed, and for so little money." When I poured the two glasses together, the water became clear again. After such proof my good farmers untied the strings of their purses and bought. This not only helped my hungry stomach, but also it put me on a horse again and yielded a neat little penny for my trip; and so without mishap I got back to the German border. Therefore, my dear peasants, do not trust these foreign mountebanks. They'll cheat you, for they don't care a rap for your health—only for your money.

CHAPTER 9: *The "Doctor" gets a musket and practices starvation*

While passing through Lorraine I ran out of merchandise, and since I was afraid of garrisoned towns I had no chance to replenish my stock. So I had to do something else until I could

make more theriac. I bought two quarts of brandy, colored it
with saffron, filled some half-ounce vials with it, and sold it as
a precious goldwater, good for fever. This brandy netted me
thirty guilders. When I was almost out of vials, I heard of a
glass factory near Fleckenstein, and there I hoped to replenish
my supply. But while I was going there on a byway, I happened to be picked up by a raiding party from Philippsburg
that was quartered in Castle Wagelnburg. So I lost everything
I had obtained on my trip by cheating the people; and because the peasant who was showing me the way said I was a
doctor, to give the devil his due, I was taken for a *real* doctor
in Philippsburg.

There I was questioned. I wasn't a bit shy about telling
them who I was, but they didn't believe me and wanted to
make more of me than I possibly could have been. They
wanted to make a doctor of me! I had to swear that I had
belonged to the imperial dragoons at Soest, and under oath
I told everything that had happened to me from then until
now and what I intended to do. They said the emperor
needed soldiers in Philippsburg as well as in Soest, and they'd
keep me until there was a chance to send me on to my own
regiment. If I did not like this suggestion I would have to
be satisfied with living in the stockade. Until they let me go
again they'd treat me there like a medical man, since they
had caught me for one.

Thus, I came down off my high horse onto a jackass and
had to be a musketeer, though it all happened without my
cooperation. This was a hard nut for me to crack; for one
thing, they were keeping a lean larder there, and the bread
rations were frightfully small. I say "frightfully" on purpose,
for it frightened me every morning when I received my loaf,
because I knew it would have to last all day, though I could
have eaten it at one meal. Truth to tell, a musketeer is a
miserable creature who has to live this way in a garrison and
who has to get by on dry bread—and not half enough of that.
He's no better than a prisoner who is prolonging his poor life
with the bread and water of tribulation. In fact, a prisoner is

better off, for he does not have to stand watch, go the rounds, or do sentry duty; he stays quietly in bed and has just as much hope as a sad garrison trooper of getting out of his prison in time. There were a few who, by various means, had it a little better; but none of these ways of getting a bite more to eat were to my liking. In their misery, a few troopers took on wives (some of these formerly were two-bit sluts) who could increase their income by such work as sewing, washing, spinning, or by selling second-hand clothing or other junk, or even by stealing. Among the women was a female ensign who drew her pay like a corporal! Another was a midwife, and she was given many a good meal for herself and her husband. Another took in laundry and ironing; she washed shirts, socks, nightshirts, and other apparel for the bachelors among the officers and men, and she had quite a reputation. Others sold tobacco and furnished pipes for those who needed them. Still others sold brandy; it was generally thought that they were adulterating it with water distilled by their own bodies—but that didn't change the color of the liquor in the least! Another was a seamstress who was able to earn money through hemstitching and embroidery. Still another could pick a living off the field; in the winter she dug up snails, in spring she picked salad herbs, in summer she took the young out of birds' nests, and in fall she could gather hundreds of other tidbits. Some sold kindling wood, which they carried to market like donkeys; others peddled still other merchandise. To earn my keep that way was not for me, since I already had a wife. Some of the men made a living by gambling (which they could do better than professional sharps), and by means of false dice and cards they got what they wanted from their simple-minded fellow soldiers. I despised such a trade. Others worked at building fortifications or at other odd jobs; for this I was too lazy. Some carried on a trade, but I had learned none. If a musician had been needed I could have served, but this starvation district got along on pipes and drums. Some took over others' guard duty and stood watch day and night. I would rather have starved than wear out my body that way. Some made both ends meet by going on raids, but I wasn't even permitted to step outside of the gate. Some could "organize" things better than a general; I hated such actions like sin. To make it brief, no matter where I turned, I could pick up nothing with which to fill my stomach. And what made me maddest was having to take it when the gang said, "You're a doctor and yet don't know how to cure starvation?"

Finally, necessity made me juggle a couple of good-sized carp out of the moat into my hands as I stood on the rampart; but as soon as the colonel heard of it I was in dutch and he forbade further prestidigitation on pain of hanging. At last, others' misfortune turned out to be my luck. Having cured a few cases of jaundice and fever—these patients must have had special faith in me—I was allowed to wander out of the fortress to gather (so I said) medicinal roots and herbs. But instead I set snares for rabbits and was lucky to catch two the first night. These I took to the colonel and he gave me not only a thaler as a present but also permission to go out after rabbits when I was off duty. Since the country was rather deserted and nobody was catching these animals, which had multiplied over the years, I had grist in my mill again, especially as it seemed that rabbits turned up everywhere or that I could charm them into my snares. When the officers saw that they could trust me, I was allowed to go raiding with the others, and I resumed the life of Soest, except that I could not be in charge. For that, one had to know all the roads and byways and the course of the Rhine.

CHAPTER 10: *Simplicius survives a miserable bath in the Rhine*

I want to tell a few more stories before I let you know how I was saved from carrying a musket. One story deals with danger to life and limb, from which I escaped by the grace of God; the other, with danger to my soul's salvation, in which I did not fare so well. I want to conceal my vices no more than my virtues, not only because I want the reader to know the whole story, but also so that he knows what strange characters populate this world—characters who give little thought to God.

As I said toward the end of the previous chapter, I was allowed to go on raiding parties along with the others, and this is something granted not to every stumblebum but only to good soldiers. One time nineteen of us were moving through the country above Strasbourg to wait for a ship from Basel said to be carrying contraband and some Weimar officers. Above Ottenheim we got hold of a fishing boat to put us on an island where oncoming vessels could be forced to land. Ten of us had already been taken across, but when one of the remaining nine, who was a good oarsman, was rowing the rest across, the boat suddenly capsized and we were in the river before you could say Jack Robinson. I didn't worry much about the others but saw to my own safety. And though I made every effort and used all the tricks of good swimmers, the stream played with me as with a bundle of rags, throwing me helter-skelter now to the bottom, now to the surface. Struggling heroically, I managed to come up for breath frequently, but if it had been a little colder I could not have survived. Time and time again I tried to swim ashore, but the eddies that carried me from one side to another would not let me land. When I had passed the country beyond Goldscheur and had already resigned myself to taking the Rhine bridge at Strasbourg either dead or alive, I noticed a big tree whose branches were sticking out of the water not far from me. The current went right in that direction and I did my best to reach it. Luckily I succeeded, and through the force of the water and my own exertion I managed to cling to the largest branch (which I thought at first was the whole tree). But the current and the waves were constantly twisting and turning the tree and moving it up and down. My stomach became so upset from this motion that I wanted to spit out liver and lights. I was barely able to hold on, but I was beginning to faint and would have been glad to slip into the water again, except I felt I wouldn't have the courage to endure a hundredth part of the misery I had just been through. So I hung on, hoping for an uncertain rescue that God might chance to send me if I were to get off alive. But in regard to this hope, my conscience furnished me scant comfort; it reproached me for having foolishly rejected God's gracious help over the last few years. Yet, now I hoped for the best and started to pray as fervently as if I had been raised in a monastery; I resolved to live more piously and made several vows: I renounced the life of a soldier and promised never to go raiding again; I threw away my pack and ammunition and let on that I wanted to become a hermit once more, to repent of my sins, and to thank God's mercy for my hoped-for salvation until my dying day.

After I had spent two or three hours on the branch, thus between hope and fear, the ship I was to have helped capture came down the Rhine. With a piteous cry in the name of God and doomsday, I called for help, and since they had to sail right by me and saw my plight, everyone in the ship was so moved to pity that they made for shore and deliberated over how to rescue me. Because of the eddies around me and the many roots and branches, no one could safely swim to me or come close by with a boat, and thus it took a long time to decide how to rescue me. You can easily imagine how I felt all this time. Finally they sent two stout men in a boat, who floated a rope toward me from upstream. They held on to one end while I managed to tie the other around my middle. Like a big fish on a line, I was then pulled into the boat and taken to the ship.

Having thus escaped death, it would have been well for me to fall on my knees and thank divine mercy for my rescue, and also to start leading a better life, as I had sworn and promised in my utmost misery. But far from it! When they asked me who I was and how I had gotten into this trouble, I lied like a dog to these fellows, for I thought if I told them that I had wanted to rob them, they'd throw me back into the Rhine. So I said I was an organist, driven out of my village because of

the war and now on my way to Strasbourg in order to look
for a job in connection with schoolteaching or anything else.
A raiding party had picked me up, robbed me of everything,
and thrown me in the Rhine, which had deposited me in the
tree. And since I spieled off these lies without the least em-
barrassment and swore I was telling the truth, they believed
me, gave me food and drink, and showed me every kindness—
all of which I needed badly.

Most people went ashore at the customs office in Strasbourg,
and so did I, once again thanking all. In the crowd I noticed
a young merchant whose walk and gestures made me think
that I had seen him before, but I couldn't remember where.
His way of talking made me think that he was the officer who
had previously captured me, but I couldn't figure out how
such a brave, young soldier had turned into a merchant, particularly since he was a born cavalier. My desire to find out
whether my eyes and ears were deceiving me made me go to
him and I said, "Monsieur Schönstein, is it you or isn't it?"
He answered, "I am no von Schönstein, but a merchant."
Then I said, "In that case I am not the Hunter of Soest,
either, but an organist, or rather a roving bindle stiff."
"Brother," he said, "what in the devil's name are you doing
here? Where are you keeping yourself?" I said, "Brother, if
heaven has destined you to preserve my life (as now has happened a second time), my fate requires me to be fairly close
to you." We embraced each other like two good friends who
had previously promised to love each other till their dying day.
I had to come to his lodgings and tell him everything that
had happened to me since I had left Lippstadt for Cologne to
collect my treasure. I did not conceal from him how I and
my fellows had planned to ambush the ship and how things
turned out. But I did not breathe a word about how I had
carried on in Paris, for I was afraid he might gossip about it
in Lippstadt and my wife would make my life miserable.

He in turn confided to me that the Hessian general staff
had sent him to Bernhard, Duke of Weimar, to report on matters of great importance relating to the war and to confer

about future plans and the coming campaign. He had accomplished this, and now he was returning in the guise of a merchant. Incidentally, he told me that my beloved wife had been with child when he left and that she and her relatives had been in good health. He also said that the colonel was still holding the troop for me, and he teased me that the pocks had so spoiled my looks that neither my wife nor the other ladies in Lippstadt would recognize me for the Hunter, and so on. Finally we agreed that I should stay with him and take this opportunity of returning to Lippstadt, which was just what I wanted. And since I had only rags to wear, he advanced me money so I could buy some clothes to make me look like a salesman.

But they say that if a thing is not to be, it won't happen. I found this out when we were traveling down the Rhine and the ship was searched at Rheinhausen. The Philippsburgers recognized me, picked me up, and returned me to Philippsburg, where I had to tote the musket again. Though this hurt my good ensign as much as me, he could do little for me; he had a hard enough time getting away himself.

CHAPTER 11: *Why preachers should not eat rabbits that were caught in a snare*

The gentle reader has heard in what physical danger I had been; concerning the danger to my soul he must know that as a musketeer I was an awfully crude being who didn't give a damn for God or Holy Writ. No meanness was beyond me; all grace and kindness received from God was forgotten; I prayed for matters neither temporal nor eternal but lived unreformed, like a beast. No one would have believed that a pious hermit had brought me up. I seldom saw the inside of a church, and I never went to confession. And as the salvation of my soul was nothing to me, so I troubled my fellow men all the more; wherever I could trick someone, I did—and boasted of it! Almost no one was exempt; and I often got my comeuppance and was threatened with whippings and the strappado, but this did no good. I persisted in my godless way as if I were rushing straight to hell. And though I committed no crime worthy of hanging, I was so dastardly that (aside from witches and sodomites) no worse man could be found.

Our regimental chaplain took note of this, and because he was quite a zealot, around Easter time he sent for me to find out why I hadn't come to confession and communion. After he had finished his well-meaning admonitions, I treated him like the minister in Lippstadt, and the good man could do nothing with me. Concluding that Christ and baptism had been wasted on me, he summarized: "Alas, you miserable man, I thought you were going astray through ignorance, but now I know you are continuing to sin from evilness and intention. Do you think anyone will have pity on your poor, damned soul? As for me, I protest before God and the world that I have no part in your damnation; I have done—and shall gladly continue to do—all that's needed for the salvation of your soul. But, presumably, when your poor soul leaves its damned abode, I won't have to do much more than have your body taken to the place where the dead animals are buried or where the godforsaken and desparate are put aside."

This serious admonition did no more good than previous ones, simply because I was afraid to go to confession. What a great fool I was! I would often tell my knavish exploits to the assembled company, and lie to boot, but now that I was to repent and humbly confess my sins to a single person, in lieu of God, in order to receive absolution—now I was stubborn and silent as a stick. I use the word "stubborn" deliberately; I stayed stubborn, for I said to the chaplain, "I am serving the emperor as a soldier, and should I die like a soldier it won't surprise me if—like other soldiers, who are not always buried in holy ground but must make shift in the fields, in a ditch, or in the stomachs of wolves and ravens—I'll have to get along outside the churchyard." So I left the parson, who with all his anxiety for my soul deserved only this of me: I refused to give him a rabbit that he wanted very much; I said

that the hare had hanged himself by a rope, and since one
who died by an act of desperation could not find rest in holy
ground, he couldn't have it.

CHAPTER 12: *To his surprise, Simplicius is saved from toting
the musket*

Thus, no change for the better was seen in me; rather I became worse as time passed. The colonel once told me he'd like
to kick me out like a rogue, for I was no good. But as I knew
he didn't mean it, I said he could dismiss me but he should
send the executioner along. So he kept me, for he could easily
see that if he sent me away I'd take it as a favor rather than
as punishment. Accordingly, I stayed a musketeer against my
will and suffered the pangs of hunger far into the summer.
But Count von Götz approached with his army, and so did
my deliverance; for when Götz had his headquarters at Bruch-
sal, the general staff sent my good friend Heartbrother (to
whom I had given financial help, in the camp at Magdeburg)
with some orders to our fortress, where he was treated with
great honor and respect. I happened to be on sentry duty before the colonel's quarters, and although Heartbrother wore a
black velvet coat, I recognized him at first sight, but I didn't
have the heart to address him then. I was afraid he'd be
ashamed of me (as things go in this world) or even refuse to
recognize me, because by his wardrobe he appeared to be a
man of high rank and I was only a lousy musketeer. After I
had been relieved, I asked his servants about his name and
rank, so that I wouldn't perhaps address the wrong man; and
yet I didn't have the courage to speak to him. Instead, I wrote
him this letter, which I had his valet deliver in the morning:

Monsieur, etc.

If it should please my gracious master through his overwhelming
influence to rescue one whom he previously delivered out of fetters
and bonds through bravery in the battle of Wittstock—if it should
please him to rescue him now from the most wretched state in the

world, a state to which he came as a plaything of fickle Fortune—
this act would cost him little and would make a lifelong servant of
his faithful, now most forsaken and deserted,

                                        S. Simplicissimus.

As soon as he had read this, he asked me to come to his
room, and he asked, "Fellow countryman, where is the man
who gave you this letter?" I answered, "Sir, he is a prisoner in
this fortress." "All right," he said, "go to him and tell him I
will help him even if the noose is already around his neck."
I replied, "Sir, there's no need to bother going; I am Simplicius,
and I have come to thank you for my rescue at Wittstock, as
well as to ask you to rid me of the musket that I am forced
to carry against my will." He didn't let me finish my sentence,
but showed me by an embrace how much he wanted to help
me. He did everything a true friend can do for another; and
even before he asked me how I had been placed in this fortress
and in such bondage, he sent a servant to a Jewish haberdasher
to buy me a horse and clothing. Meanwhile, I told him how
I had been since his father had died at Magdeburg. When he
heard that I was the Hunter of Soest (of whose exploits he had
heard so much), he regretted not having known this before,
for he might well have been able to help me to a company.

When the dealer arrived with a whole pack of soldiers'
clothing, he picked out the best pieces, let me put them on,
and together we went to the colonel. "Sir," he said, "in your
garrison I've found this man, to whom I am so greatly obliged
that I cannot leave him in his present state (even though he
doesn't deserve better). I beg you, therefore, to do me the
favor either of promoting him or permitting me to take him
along, so that I can get him such advancement in the army as
there may not be a chance for here."

Upon hearing me praised the colonel was so dumbfounded
that he made the sign of the cross and answered, "Worthy
sir, forgive me if I believe that you are only testing my willingness to serve you as you deserve. If this is so, please demand
anything that is in my power and you will see me ready. But
as to this fellow, he belongs not to me but—as he says—to a

regiment of dragoons; and besides, he's such a devil that he has given my provost more trouble than a whole company. I think water would refuse to drown him!"

But this wasn't enough for Heartbrother; he asked the colonel to condescend to invite me to his table, and his wish was granted. He did this so he could tell the colonel about me in my presence what so far he had heard only as a rumor in Westphalia, from Count von der Wahl and the commander at Soest. He told it in such a way that all listeners had to think of me as a good soldier. All this time I behaved so modestly that the colonel and his officers (who knew me well) could not help thinking that I had put on a new man with my new clothes. And when the colonel asked how I had come by the title of Doctor, I described my whole trip from Paris to Philippsburg and my method for cheating the peasants in order to have something to chew. This made them laugh hard. Finally, I openly confessed that I had wanted by all sorts of deviltry to irritate and wear down the colonel to the point of dismissing me from his garrison so that he might live in peace and hear no more complaints about me.

After that, the colonel related all sorts of dirty tricks I had played since the day I had come into the garrison: how I had poured lard on top of boiled peas and sold the potful for pure lard; how I had sold, as salt, sacks partly filled with sand; how I had made a monkey of practically everyone; and how I had composed satirical verses about people. Throughout the meal they were talking only about me. But if I hadn't had such an influential friend, my exploits would have been worthy of only one thing—punishment. This showed me what happens at court when a rogue gains the prince's favor.

When the meal was ended, the dealer did not have a horse that Heartbrother thought good enough for me. And since Heartbrother enjoyed so much esteem and the colonel wanted his favor, the colonel gave him one of his own horses, with saddle and bridle. And while milord Simplicius, together with his friend Heartbrother, joyfully rode out of the fortress, some of his comrades shouted after him, "Good luck to you! Good

luck!" But others, moved by envy, hollered, "The worse the
s. o. b., the better his luck!"

CHAPTER 13: *Dealing with the Order of the Marauding
Brothers*

On the way Heartbrother and I agreed that I should pretend
to be his cousin. So that I might have more status, he would
get me another horse and a servant and put me in the Neuneck
regiment where I could stay as a volunteer until an officer's
position became vacant; then he'd help me get it. Thus, in no
time at all, I turned into a man who resembled a good soldier.
But during that summer I engaged in few exploits except
helping to steal a couple of cows in the Black Forest; besides,
I got to know the Breisgau and Alsace pretty well. But again,
I wasn't very lucky, for when men of the Weimar army captured my servant and horse at Kentzingen, I had to use my
other horse all the harder and when he gave up the ghost, I
joined the Order of the Marauding Brothers—that is, I robbed
on foot. My friend Heartbrother would have gotten me another mount, but since I had done away with the first two
horses so quickly, he did not exactly rush ahead but left me
up in the air in order to teach me a lesson. I didn't press him,
either, for my companions were such a pleasant gang that I
did not even want to change until it was time to move into
winter quarters.

Now I'll tell what sort of people the Marauders are. There
are doubtless some people, especially those who are ignorant of
war, who don't know about them. Neither have I yet run into
an author who treats of their habits, wonts, rights, and privileges, though it is a matter well worth knowing, not only for
our generals but also for the peasants. Concerning the name
of the group, when a certain gentleman brought in a newly
recruited regiment, the men were so weak and debilitated that
they could hardly march or stand up under the hardships of
soldiering. When they were found hiding behind fences and

hedges and were asked what regiment they belonged to, they would answer, *"Merode"* (which is French for sick, out of order).[3] From this sprang the custom of calling "Merode Brothers" all those who trot along behind and out of step, even if they are not sick or wounded. One can see them in droves behind hedges, in the shadow or in the sun or about a fire, being lazy and smoking, while an honest soldier under his flag has to endure heat, thirst, hunger, cold, and other miseries. Ahead of the army, alongside, and behind it, the marauders pick up everything they can lay hands on, and what they can't use they spoil, so that the regiments moving into camp or quarters often can't find a good drink of clean water. When they are forced to stay with the baggage train, it becomes more numerous than the army proper. When they are together or marching in gangs, they have no sergeant major, no color sergeant or corporal who keeps order; they live like masters and are scot-free. They do not keep watch, they do not labor at digging trenches, they do not attack, they are found in no battle line —and yet they make a living! Well, I was one of these brothers, and I stayed one till the day before the battle of Wittenweier. At that time I went with some pals of mine to steal oxen and cows, and we were caught by Weimar troopers. They knew what to do with us; they put us under a musket and distributed us among the various regiments. I was assigned to Colonel Hattstein's regiment.

CHAPTER 14: *A perilous fight for life in which both contestants escape death*

At that point I came to see that I was born only for misfortune. About a month before the battle, I heard some of General Götz's officers discussing the war; one of them said, "This summer there's sure to be a battle. If we beat the enemy,

[3] Grimmelshausen is here pulling his readers' collective leg. The word comes from the French *marauder*, "to plunder." After the spurious explanation, this translation uses the spelling "marauder."

we'll have to spend next winter taking Freiburg and the forest
cities; but if we get beaten we'll have winter quarters just the
same." I drew the correct conclusion from this prophecy, and
I said to myself, "You will drink the good wines of the Neckar
or of Lake Constance, and you will enjoy whatever is coming to
the Weimar troops." But I was badly mistaken. Because I was
a Weimar man myself now, I was predestined to help lay siege
to Breisach, and such a siege was undertaken full tilt right
after the battle of Wittenweier.[4] Like the other musketeers I
had to stand guard duty and dig trenches day and night. This
only taught me how to get at a fortress by way of trenches—
something to which I had paid no attention at Magdeburg. As
for the rest, I was in lousy shape: two or three of us lived in a
tiny room; my purse was empty; wine, beer, and meat were
rarities; apples and half rations of bread had to do for steak.

This situation was hard to bear and gave me reason enough
to think back to the fleshpots of Egypt, that is, the Wesphalian
hams and knockwurst in Lippstadt. I no longer thought of my
wife except when I lay in my tent and was stiff from frost and
cold. Then I often said to myself, "Alas, Simplici, don't you
think it would serve you right if someone did to you just what
you did in Paris?" And such thoughts worried me, as they
would any cuckold, though I knew my wife was faithful and
virtuous. At last I became so impatient that I told my captain
how my personal affairs stood. I also wrote to Lippstadt;
through letters from Colonel de St. André and my father-in-
law, I arranged to receive my dismissal from the Prince of
Weimar, and my captain had to give me a passport and let
me go.

A few weeks before Christmas I was walking down the Breisgau, carrying a good gun; I was hoping to receive twenty
thalers that my brother-in-law had deposited to my credit in
Strasbourg. There I would join some merchants and travel
down the Rhine, where there were a number of imperial
garrisons. When I had just passed Endingen and came to a

4 Breisach fell on December 19, 1638; the battle of Wittenweier took
place on July 30, 1638.

single house, someone shot at me and the bullet tore a hole in the brim of my hat. That instant a big burly fellow came running toward me, shouting that I should drop my gun. I answered, "Not to please you, I won't, country cousin!" and I cocked the gun. He whipped out an object that looked more like an executioner's sword than a dagger and rushed toward me. When I saw that he meant business, I let him have it, hitting him in the forehead so that he spun around and finally fell down. Taking advantage of his position, I twisted the sword out of his hand and tried to run him through. But the sword wouldn't pierce, and he jumped unexpectedly to his feet again and grabbed me by the hair. I did the same to him. I had already thrown his sword out of reach, and now we began to wrestle so hard that the embittered strength of both of us showed plainly. Yet neither could get the better of the other. Now I was on top, now he; now both of us got on our feet again, but not for long because each tried his best to kill the other. Since he was so grimly after my blood, I gathered up what was oozing from my nose and mouth and spit it in his face. This was a help because it kept him from seeing. That way we worked on each other in the snow for about an hour and a half. This exercise was so tiring that it seemed that one's exhaustion could not completely overcome the other's weariness, at least not by the use of fists; nor could one kill the other without a weapon.

Wrestling, which I had learned at Lippstadt, came in very handy; otherwise, I should have come out on the short end, for my enemy was much stronger than I, and sword and bullet-proof besides. Finally, when we had almost worn each other out, he said, "Brother, stop; I yield to you." I said, "You should have let me pass by in the first place." "If I die, what good will it do you?" he asked. "And if you shot me dead, what good would it have done you, since I haven't a penny in my pocket?" Then he begged my pardon, and I gave in and let him get up. But first he had to swear solemnly that he would not only keep the peace but also be my faithful friend and servant.

I would never have believed or trusted him, however, if I had known his previous irresponsible actions.

When both of us had gotten up, we shook hands and agreed that all these events should be forgotten. Each was surprised to have found his match, and the other fellow thought me just as big a rascal as he. I did not disillusion him, lest he try again once he recovered his gun. He had a big bump on the head from my shot; I had lost a lot of blood; and we both complained about our necks, which had been so ill-treated that we couldn't carry our heads upright.

Since evening was approaching and my opponent told me I would not meet a cat or a dog, much less a human being, on my way as far as the river Kintzig, I was persuaded to go with him. He said he had good drink and some food in his house, not far from the road. On the way he sighed many times and assured me he was sorry to have hurt me.

CHAPTER 15: *How Oliver thinks he can justify his criminal sylvan doings*

What a stupid ox is a resolute soldier who risks his life or sets a low value upon it! Among a thousand men, not one would have had the courage to go to an unknown place with a ruffian who had murderously attacked him only a short time before. On the way, I asked him what army he belonged to. He answered that for the time being he belonged to none, but was warring on his own account. Then he asked me the same question. I told him I had been one of the Duke of Weimar's men, had been dismissed, and was on my way home. He asked for my name and when I answered "Simplicius," he turned around (for I had him walk in front of me, because I didn't trust him) and gave me a hard look. "Aren't you also called Simplicissimus?" "Yes," I answered. "Whoever denies his own name is a rogue. But what's your name?" "Alas, brother," he answered, "I am Oliver, whom you remember from the days of Magdeburg." With these words he threw down his gun, fell on his knees to ask my forgiveness for having wanted to hurt me, and told me that now he imagined he'd never have a better friend in the world than me, since according to old Heartbrother's prophecy I would courageously avenge his death. For my part, I continued to express surprise at our strange meeting. But he said, "That's nothing new; mountain and valley don't run into each other. What's strange is how we two have changed: I've turned from a secretary into a fisherman of the woods, a footpad; and you, from a fool into a brave soldier! Let me tell you, if there were ten thousand of us, we'd relieve Breisach tomorrow, and in the end we'd be masters of the whole world."

With such talk we came at dusk to a small, out-of-the way hut that might have belonged to a day laborer, and though I did not approve of such boasting I said he was right, particularly because I knew his false and roguish mind. Though I did not trust him in the least, I followed him into the little house, where a peasant was just heating up the room. Oliver asked him whether supper was ready. "No," said the peasant, "but I still have the cold leg of veal that I brought from Waldkirch today." "Well, then," said Oliver, "go and get what you have and bring along the small keg of wine."

When the peasant was gone, I said to Oliver, "Brother," (I called him this in order to be on the safe side) "you have a willing host." "May the devil thank the rogue!" he said. "I take care of him and his wife and children. On top of that, he does all right with his own booty. I give him all the clothes that come my way, to use as he sees fit." I asked where the fellow's family was. Oliver explained that he had taken them to Freiburg, where he visited them twice a week. From there he brought back food and powder and shot. Moreover, Oliver told me that he had been in this freebooter's trade for a long time; he liked it better than serving a master, and he was not about to stop until he had lined his purse well. I said, "Brother, you ply a dangerous trade; if you got picked up for robbery, what do you think would happen to you?" "Ha," he

said, "you are still the same old Simplicius. You don't have
to tell me that I am running a risk; on the other hand, they've
got to catch me before they hang me. My dear Simplicius,
you haven't read your Machiavelli yet. I am an upright man,
and I carry on my trade openly and without subterfuge. I
fight, I risk my life like the heroes of old; and since I am
risking my life, it follows undeniably that to carry on this
handicraft is meet and proper."

I answered, "Assuming that robbery or theft are permitted
(or are not), I nevertheless know they are against the law of
nature, which wants us to do to others as we would have them
do to us. Such iniquity is also against worldly law, which says
that thieves should be hanged, robbers beheaded, and murderers broken on the wheel. And finally it is against God, and
that's most important, for he leaves no sin unpunished." "It
is as I told you," replied Oliver. "You are still the Simplicius
who hasn't studied his Machiavelli. If I could set up a mon-
archy in my own way, I wonder who would preach against
me then?" We would have argued longer, but the peasant had
returned with food and drink. So we sat down together and
fed our stomachs, for I was hungry as a bear.

CHAPTER 16: *Oliver interprets Heartbrother's prophecy to his
own advantage and thus loves his worst enemy*

Our food consisted of the finest bread and a cold leg of veal;
we drank good wine and sat in a warm room. "You have to
admit, Simpli," said Oliver, "that this is better than the slit
trenches at Breisach." I said that was true—if only one could
enjoy such life with a certain amount of safety and honor.
This made him explode with laughter. "Are those poor devils
in the trenches safer than we? They have to worry every moment about a sudden attack. My dear Simpli, I see you have
put aside your fool's cap, but you have kept your foolish head,
and you can't tell good from bad. If you were anybody but
the man who, according to old Heartbrother's prophecy, is

to avenge my death, I'd make you admit that I lead a nobler life than a baron." I thought, What will come of this? I'll have to think up something different; otherwise, with the help of the peasant this brute will exterminate me. So I said, "Who ever heard that the chicken is smarter than the hen? Brother, if your life is as happy as you say, let me share in your happiness—I need it." Oliver answered, "Brother, I love you as I love myself; why should I refuse you anything? Stay with me if you like; I'll take care of you. If you want to leave, I'll give you a nice sum of money and accompany you where-ever you go. And to prove that these words come from my heart, I'll tell you why I think so much of you. You remem-ber how true old Heartbrother's prophesies were. At Magde-burg he said to me, 'Oliver, look at our fool any way you like; he will frighten you by his bravery and play the worst trick on you. And you will cause him to do it at a time when you don't recognize each other. But not only will he spare your life; after a while, he will come to the place where you will have been slain, and there he will avenge your death.' On account of this prophecy I am willing to share the heart in my body with you, dear Simplici; for as one part of the pro-phecy has been fulfilled, I don't doubt the rest will also come true. From your revenge I must conclude, dear brother, that you are a good friend. If you were not, you wouldn't under-take it; and that's how I feel about it. Now tell me what you intend to do." I thought, May the devil trust you, not I! If I accept money you'll kill me on the way; if I stay with you I'll be drawn and quartered too. I resolved to trick him and said that if he liked me I'd stay with him for a few days in order to see how I'd get used to that kind of life. If I liked it, he'd have a faithful friend and a good soldier in me; if not, we could part in kindness any time. After that he plied me with drink, but since I didn't trust him I pretended to be drunk before I really was, in order to find out whether he would hurt me when I couldn't defend myself.

Meanwhile, those big, sturdy lice I had brought with me from Breisach started acting up; in the warmth of the room they crawled from my rags to look for a good time outside. Oliver noticed and asked if I had lice. I said, "Sure, more than I'll ever have ducats in all my life." "That's no way to talk," said Oliver. "If you stay with me, you'll probably get more ducats than you now have lice." My reply was, "That's as impossible as getting rid of the lice right now." "No, it isn't," he said, and he ordered the peasant to bring me some clothes that were hidden in a hollow tree not far from the house. He brought a gray hat, a jerkin of elk skin, a pair of red breeches, and a gray coat. He would give me shoes and stockings tomorrow, he said. When I saw this generous gift, I trusted him a little more and fell asleep happy.

CHAPTER 17: *When Simplicius goes out robbing, his thoughts are more pious than Oliver's in church*

In the morning, toward daybreak, Oliver said, "Get up, Simpli; let's see what in God's name we can pick up." O my God, I thought, am I to rob in thy holy name? Heavenly Father, how I have changed! What will become of me if I don't turn to thee? Check my course, for I'll go to hell if I don't repent. With these thoughts I followed Oliver to a village in which there was not one living creature. To get a better view, we climbed up on the steeple. There Oliver had hidden the shoes and stockings that he had promised me the night before, and also two loaves of bread, several pieces of smoked meat, and half a keg of wine. With these rations a man might survive for a week. While I was putting on my gift shoes and stockings, he told me that he used to watch from this hiding place whenever he thought something good was coming along. He mentioned that he had several other places stocked like this one, so that if one produced no loot he might try at another. I praised his wisdom, but I let him know that I disapproved of defiling a consecrated building. "What?" he said. "Defile? If churches could talk they'd say that what I do in them is nothing compared to the vices committed there by others. How many people who step into a church under the pretext of serving God come only to show off their new clothes, their beautiful figures, their worldly positions, or something similar? Here is one strutting like a peacock in front of the altar, and yet he acts as if he would pray the leg off a saint; there is one in the corner sighing like a publican in the temple, but the sighs are meant for his sweetheart, whose face he is staring at and for whom he came to church in the first place. More than one man could not carry on an illicit affair if the church didn't help him. Many a loan shark who hasn't taken time all week to figure out new angles does so during the sermon. Some only sit there and sleep as if they had hired the place for it. I won't mention the stories I have read, but I must bring up one more thing: people not only make a mockery of churches while they are alive, but they fill them with vanity and foolishness even after death. As soon as you enter a church you see gravestones and epitaphs of people whom the worms have eaten long ago. When you look up you catch sight of shields, helmets, weapons, swords, flags, boots, spurs, and such. Small wonder that, in this war, in some places the peasants made fortresses out of churches to defend their possessions. Why shouldn't I make a living by the church that so many people live on? Had I known of your scruples about lying in wait in a church, I would have thought up a better answer than this, but until I give you a better one, put this one in your pipe and smoke it."

I would gladly have told Oliver that those other folks who besmirched the church were as dishonorable as he and would get their reward. But because I did not trust him and did not want to get into another argument, I agreed with him. After a while he asked me to tell him how I had been doing since we parted at Wittstock, and why I was wearing jester's clothes when I arrived in the camp before Magdeburg. But since a sore throat made me miserable, I asked to be excused and requested that he tell me his life (which presumably was full of strange wrinkles). He agreed and started to recount his heinous life, as follows.

CHAPTER 18: *Oliver tells about his family and his youth, and particularly about his deportment in school*

"My father was born of simple people, not far from Aachen. Because his folks were poor, as a young man he had to work for a rich dealer in copper goods, who taught him to read and write and figure, and put him in charge of his whole business, as Potiphar did Joseph. This was to the advantage of both parties, for as time went on the merchant became richer by way of my father's industry and foresight; because of his success my father became more and more proud so that he grew ashamed of his parents and despised them. They often deplored it, but in vain. When my father had passed his twenty-fifth birthday, the merchant died, leaving behind his elderly widow and an only daughter. The latter had run into bad luck, having become pregnant by a shop clerk, but the child soon followed its grandfather. When my father saw that the daughter had lost her father and her child, but not her money, he did not hold it against her that she could never again wear virgin's white. He considered her wealth and got next to her, an arrangement that her mother gladly permitted, not only because her daughter's honor would be restored, but also because my father knew the trade inside out and was a sharp business man who never lost sight of Number One. Through this marriage my father became a rich merchant overnight, and I his heir. Because of his wealth I was well brought up; I was dressed like a gentleman, fed like a baron, and as for all the rest, treated like a count. All this I owe to copper and brass rather than to silver and gold.

"Before I was eight, my mettle already showed (for even small nettles can sting and the sting gets worse). No deviltry was too big for me, and whenever I could pull a nasty trick on someone, I did. Neither my father nor my mother would discipline me. With my fellow hoodlums I wandered up and down the streets picking fights, sometimes even with boys who were bigger than I. When I took a licking my parents

would say, 'It's a shame for a big bruiser to beat up our child!'
But if I got the better of my enemy—I used to scratch and bite
and throw rocks—they said, 'What a scrappy boy our little
Oliver is turning out to be!' This encouraged me. I was still
too small for prayers; but when I cursed like a fishwife, they
said I didn't know what it was all about. So I grew worse,
until they sent me to school, where I readily performed what
the other bad boys had thought up but did not dare to do
themselves. When I had ruined or torn my books, my mother
bought me new ones, lest my stingy father get excited. I was
a pain in the neck to my teacher; he didn't dare handle me as
I deserved because he received many valuable gifts from my
parents, and he knew they were spoiling me.

"In summer I caught crickets and released them in school,
where they chirped and sang. In winter I stole sneezing powder and scattered it in the room where the boys were being
whipped. Whenever a stubborn soul kicked up some dust, my
powder made everybody happier by causing everybody to
sneeze. After a while I felt above such ordinary jokes, and I
specialized in the following trick: I stole something from
somebody and put it among the belongings of somebody else,
whom I wanted to get in trouble. I did this frequently and
was almost never caught. I don't want to go into detail about
the gang wars we had; I usually was a leader, and my face
was often bleeding from scratches, and my head full of bumps
and bruises. People know what boys are up to, and from what
I have told you, you can easily imagine what else I did in my
childhood."

CHAPTER 19: *Oliver as a student at Liége and his experiences
there*

"As my father's wealth every day increased, there were more
and more freeloaders and parasites around, who praised my
intellectual abilities. They kept mum about my vices (or at
least found excuses for them), for they rightly suspected that

neither my father nor my mother wasted much friendship on anybody who did otherwise. So my parents took great joy in me and hired a private tutor to accompany me to Liége. I was sent there more to learn French than to engage in formal studies, for they wanted to make me into a merchant rather than a theologian. The tutor had orders not to be strict with me, lest I develop a servile attitude. He was to introduce me to other students and see to it that I did not become shy or monklike, for they wanted me to develop into a man of the world who knows what's what.

"My tutor, being bent on all sorts of devilment himself, didn't need these directives. Why should he forbid me anything *he* was doing or reproach me for a small fault when he was to blame for greater ones? He was particularly fond of drinking and whoring; I preferred fighting and scuffling. So we went roaming the streets together at night, he and his gang and I; and in a short time I learned more lechery than Latin from him. In my studies I relied on my good memory and native wit and let the work slide, but I was saturated with vices, roguery, and knavishness. Even then my conscience was so wide that a wagonload of hay could have passed through it. It caused me no qualms if, during the sermon in church, I read Berni's lewd love stories or Burchiello's comic poems or Aretino's licentious sonnets.[5] The words I liked best in all of the service were, 'Ite missa est.' [6]

"At this time I made a point of dressing in the latest fashion. Since every night was Mardi Gras for me, and since I carried on like a nobleman and spent not only my father's generous allowance but also the extra money my mother secretly sent me, the ladies were paying attention to us, particularly to my tutor. These females taught me to play around, to neck and pet. I had known how to fight before and my tutor did not keep me from gorging and swilling, because he enjoyed it too. This jolly life lasted a year and a half before

[5] Francesco Berni (d. 1536), Burchiello (d. 1448), and Pietro Aretino (d. 1556) were Italian writers of humorous or licentious works.

[6] "Go now: Mass is over."

my father found out about it from his agent. The latter received orders to watch us more closely, to dismiss the tutor, to pull my reins tighter, and to keep down my expenses. This discouraged us considerably, but though the tutor had been fired, the two of us still were together day and night. Since we couldn't spend so lavishly as before, we fell in with a gang that robbed people of their overcoats at night or even drowned them in the Meuse. What we picked up in this desperate way we squandered on our whores. Our studies were practically forgotten.

"One evening when, as usual, we were loitering about in order to snitch the overcoats from students, we were pounced upon, my tutor was killed, and I was arrested along with five others who were regular thieves. The next day when we were questioned I mentioned my father's agent, who was a man of importance. He was summoned, and I was released on his bond, but I had to stay in his house under arrest. The tutor was buried; the other five were punished as thieves, robbers, and murderers. My father, who had been sent a report on my troubles, hurried to Liége and smoothed over everything with money. He lectured me on the distress I was causing him and assured me that my mother had been brought to the brink of despair by my actions. Then he threatened to cut me off with a shilling and to send me straight to hell if I didn't mend my ways. I promised to do better and rode home with him. That was the end of my university days."

CHAPTER 20: *The good student's return and farewell, and how he sought advancement in the war*

"When my father had me home again, he found out that I was a rotten apple. I had not become a respectable gentleman, as he had hoped, but a wise guy and a windbag who thought he knew it all. I had hardly gotten warm at home when he said to me, 'Listen, Oliver, the more I look at you the more I see you are a jackass. You are too old to learn a trade, too

impertinent to serve a master, and not good enough to take
over my business. All the money I have spent on you, and
what's become of you?! I hoped to make a man of you and be
happy about you, but I had to buy you out of the executioner's hands. Oh, the shame of it! Maybe I should put you
in a treadmill until you sweat blood and vinegar, or until
your luck changes after you have done penance for your sins.'

"I had to listen to such lectures every day, until I got tired
of them and told my father that I was not the only one to
blame; it was his fault and that of the tutor who had misled
me. It was only fair for him to be unhappy with me because
his parents hadn't been happy with him either, for he had
practically let them go begging and starve to death. He was
about to reach for a stick to pay me for telling him the truth,
but instead he swore long and loud and said he'd send me to
the penitentiary in Amsterdam. This was more than I could
take; that night I went to a farm he had recently bought,
watched for my chance, and rode off to Cologne on the best
stallion in his stable.

"I sold the horse and again joined a group of con men and
thieves, similar to the ones I had left behind in Liége. They
recognized me at once by the way I gambled, and I recognized
them: both of us had the professional touch. I joined their
gang at once and helped them make their nocturnal hauls
wherever and whenever I could. But when, after a while, one
of us was caught in the Old Market relieving an old lady of
her heavy purse, and when I saw him standing for six hours
in the pillory with an iron collar around his neck, and his
ear was cut off and he was whipped, I decided to change occupations and become a soldier. Our colonel, the one under
whom we served at Magdeburg, was recruiting for his regiment, and I became one of his boys. Meanwhile, my father
had found out where I had gone. He wrote his agent to get
in touch with me, but when he did I had already taken the
king's shilling. The agent reported this to my father, who ordered him to bail me out, no matter the price. When I heard
that, I was afraid of the penitentiary again, and for once I did

not care to be free. The moment my colonel found out I was a rich merchant's son, he raised the price so high that my father left me where I was. He thought he'd let me kick around in the wars and maybe I'd improve.

"It didn't take long for the colonel's secretary to kick the bucket, and I was asked to take his place, as you remember. At that time I raised my sights and hoped to advance step by step, perhaps to become a general. From the regimental secretary I learned how to behave, and my ambition to become important made me act like a man of honor and reputation—in contrast to my previous behavior. But I did not succeed very well until the secretary died. Then I tried to get his position: I spent money where I could, for when my mother found out that I was doing better, she secretly sent me money again. But because young Heartbrother was the colonel's favorite and was preferred, I tried to get him out of the way, particularly when I noticed that the colonel was about to give him the appointment. When I was not promoted, I became so impatient that I had myself made bulletproof by our provost so that I might provoke a duel with Heartbrother and dispatch him. But·I could never find a way of getting at him. The provost was not in favor of my plan, either. 'If you get rid of him,' he said, 'it will hurt you more than it will help you, because you will have murdered the colonel's favorite man.' Instead, he suggested that I should steal something while Heartbrother was present and conceal it on him; then the provost would see to it that Heartbrother lost the colonel's goodwill. I followed this suggestion. At the christening I stole the colonel's gold-plated cup, gave it to the provost, and with it he got Heartbrother out of the way. You remember how, in the colonel's big tent, he made puppies crawl out of your clothes."

CHAPTER 21: *How Simplicius fulfilled Heartbrother's prophecy about Oliver while neither recognized the
other*

When I heard out of Oliver's own dirty mouth how he had
done in my best friend, I saw red. Yet, I could not take revenge and had to suppress my desire for it. I asked him to tell
me how he had fared after the battle of Wittstock.

"In that battle," said Oliver, "I acted not like an inkslinger
who was only paid to write, but like a regular soldier. I was
well mounted, absolutely bulletproof; and since I was not
assigned to a squadron, I showed off my bravery as an individual who is determined to advance by his sword or die. I
scurried about our brigade like a hurricane, partly in order to
warm up, partly to show that I was better suited for fighting
than for writing. But it didn't do any good. Luck ran in favor
of the Swedes, and I had to share in the misfortune of our
side, for I had to ask for quarter, which a little while ago I
had not been about to give anybody.

"So, like other prisoners of war, in order to recuperate I was
shoved into an infantry regiment garrisoned in Pomerania.
Since there were many new recruits and I gave indications of
great courage, I was made a corporal. But I had no intention
of sticking around. I wanted to get back to the imperials,
whom I liked better, though I would have advanced faster
with the Swedes. I arranged my escape this way: I was sent
with seven musketeers in order to extract contributions in
some of our out-of-the way places. When I had received more
than eight hundred florins, I showed the money to my men
and aroused their desire for it. We agreed to divide it among
ourselves and to go A W O L with it. When we had done so,
I persuaded three of them to help me shoot the other four.
Having killed them, we divided the loot—two hundred florins
each. With this we started out for Westphalia. On the way I
persuaded one of the three to help me kill the other two, and

when we were supposed to divide the money once more, I strangled the last one. With this money I arrived happily at Werle, where I joined the army and lived the life of Riley.

"Although I wanted to continue to live high off the hog, my money was running low; then I heard a lot about a young soldier at Soest who was making wonderful booty and acquiring quite a reputation. I was encouraged to follow his example. On account of his green clothing they called him the Hunter. So I, too, had a green suit made for myself, and under his name I robbed and committed atrocities on our side as well as on his, so much that both of us were about to be forbidden to go on raids. The other fellow stayed home, but I carried on in his name as much as I could. For this reason he challenged me, but—it would have required the devil to fight with him. (They told me the devil really was in him and showed in his hair.) In that case, how could I be sure of being bulletproof any more?

"But I was not able to escape the Hunter's wiles, for with the aid of a servant he got me and my fellows into a sheepfold where he tried to force me into a fist fight in the moonlight, with two real devils looking on. But because I wouldn't fight, they made me do the most foolish thing in the world. And when one of my friends spread the news of this thing, I was so ashamed that I took French leave and went to Lippstadt, where I let the Hessians recruit me. But since they didn't trust me I trundled on and joined the Dutch army. The pay was good, but their war was not my cup of tea; we were kept like monks and were supposed to live lives as chaste as nuns'.

"Since I dared not show my face among either the imperials or the Swedes or the Hessians—unless I wanted to get into trouble, having deserted from all of them—and since I could no longer stay with the Dutch because I had gotten a girl into trouble (having criminally assaulted her, an offense that would soon become known), I thought I'd take refuge with the Spaniards. From them I hoped to go home and see what my parents were doing. But when I was about to do that, I got my directions mixed up and landed among the Bavarians. With them

I marched among the Marauding Brothers from Westphalia
to the Breisgau and lived on gambling and stealing. When
I had something in my pocket I spent my days gambling, my
nights in the taverns. When my pockets were empty I stole
what I could lay hands on. Some days I stole two or three
horses, either from the pasture or out of the stables. I sold
them and gambled away what I got for them. Then at night
I'd slip into people's tents and relieve them of their possessions even if they kept them under their pillows. When we were
marching I kept a sharp eye on the knapsacks that the soldiers'
wives carried. In some narrow pass I'd cut these off their
backs; and so I got along until the battle of Wittenweier.
There I was taken prisoner, once more shoved into an infantry regiment, and thus made a Weimarer. But because I
didn't like the camp at Breisach, I quit after a short time and
went off to fight my own war, as you see me doing now. Let
me assure you, brother, that I have laid to rest many a proud
man. I have prospered with a load of money, and I don't intend to stop until I see there's nothing in it for me any more.
And now it is time you told me of your own life."

CHAPTER 22: *What happens when a person has doggone and
cat-gone bad luck*

When Oliver had finished his story, I could not help marveling at Divine Providence. I saw how the good Lord not
only had protected me like a father from this monster, while
I was in Westphalia, but even had made him shun me in terror. Only now did I see what a trick I had played on Oliver.
To be sure, old Heartbrother had foretold it; but Oliver had
interpreted the prophecy differently, much to my advantage,
as may be seen from chapter 16. For if this beast had known
that I was the Hunter of Soest, he would have done the same
to me as I had done to him in the sheepfold. I also considered
how wisely and ambiguously Heartbrother had worded his
prophecies, and I weighed in my mind the fact that it would

be difficult for me to avenge the death of a man who deserved to die by hanging and the wheel, though Heartbrother's prophecies usually came true. I also considered how healthy it had been for me not to tell him the story of my life first, for that way I myself would have told him how I had insulted him. While I was letting these thoughts run through my mind, I noticed on Oliver's face a number of scratches that he hadn't had at Magdeburg. I imagined that these scars were the mark of Jumpup, made when he, in the shape of a devil, had scratched Oliver's face. So I asked him where these scars came from, adding that I might infer that by this omission he had withheld the best part of his life's story. He answered, "Alas, brother, if I were to tell you *all* my tricks and dirty dealings we'd both get bored. But in order to show you that I don't want to conceal anything from you, I'll tell you the truth, even though it seems the joke is on me in this case.

"I firmly believe that from my mother's womb I was pre-destined to have a marked face, for as a child other boys al-ways scratched me up when I fought with them. One of the devils attending the Hunter also scratched the hell out of my face; I felt his claws for more than six weeks! But all that healed up nicely. The stripes you see now have a different origin. When I was still with the Swedes in Pomerania, I had a pretty mistress. I made my landlord and his wife give up their bed so we could lie in it. But the cat, which also used to sleep there, came every night and bothered us no end. She didn't want to give up her regular place so easily as the bed's owners had done. This made my mistress so mad—she couldn't stand cats anyway—that she swore she wouldn't do a thing for me until I got rid of that cat. I wanted to enjoy her favors a while longer, and by pleasing her I wanted to get even with the cat, but in such a way that I'd have a little fun along with it. So I put the cat in a sack, called my landlords's two sturdy dogs (they did not like the cat, either), and went to an open pasture for a bit of enjoyment. I thought the dogs would chase the cat around in the pasture like a rabbit; there was no tree to which she could retreat, and this would be fun to watch. But dammit! My luck was not only doggone bad (as they say) but even cat-gone lousy (as they would say if more people had had my experience). When I opened the sack, the cat saw only the open field with two strong enemies and no high place to which to retreat for safety. That was no reason for the cat to give up and have her skin shredded. She took to my head, that being the highest place far or near. When I tried to remove her I lost my hat, and the harder I tried to drag her off, the more firmly she fastened her claws in me to hold on. The dogs couldn't look on idly for long. They too got into the act, and with open jaws they jumped at me to get at the cat—in front, behind, and on the sides. The feline did not care to budge; she hung on as best she could by clawing into my face or any other part of my head. And if by chance she took a swipe at a dog with her thorny-gloved arm, I got *that* for sure, too. Since occasionally she also hit the noses of the dogs, they tried their best to paw her down with their front legs, and that way I got many unfriendly pawings in the face. When I tried to reach for her with my hands to get her down, she bit and scratched for all she was worth. So the cat and the dogs together waged war on me, scratching and abusing me so frightfully that I hardly resembled a human being any more. But worst of all was the danger of splitting my nose or an ear, or losing it, when the dogs were snapping at the cat. My collar and coat looked as bloody as a blacksmith's stall when he is bleeding horses on St. Stephen's Day. I had to think up something altogether new to get out of this fix. Finally I dropped to the ground so that the dogs could get at the cat and my fine head would no longer be a battleground. To be sure, the dogs strangled the cat, but I did not have half the fun I had hoped for, only mockery and a face like the one you are looking at. I was so mad I shot both dogs and beat up my mistress, who had caused all this foolishness. She left me, probably because she could not love my face any more."

CHAPTER 23: *An example of the trade that Oliver plied, of which he was the past master, and to which Simplicius was to be apprenticed*

I would have been glad to laugh at this story of Oliver's; yet I had to show sympathy. Just as I was beginning to tell him my life story, we saw a coach accompanied by two horsemen coming up the road. So we descended the steeple and sat down in a house that was close to the road and very convenient for attacking passers-by. I kept my loaded gun in reserve, but before they even noticed us Oliver had killed a horseman and his horse with one shot. The other horseman immediately fled, and while, with my gun cocked, I made the coachman stop and get off, Oliver jumped on him with his broad sword and split his head down to the teeth. Right after that he wanted to cut down the women and children who were traveling in the coach and who already looked more like corpses than people; but I absolutely wouldn't let him and told him if he wanted to do it, he would have to strangle me first. "Ah, you foolish Simpli!" he said. "I would never have believed that you are as hopeless as you let on." I answered him, "Brother, why do you want to butcher innocent children? If they were men who could defend themselves, that would be something else." "Hoity-toity!" he said. "Scramble the eggs and they won't hatch. I know these exploiters well enough. Their father, a major, is a regular slave driver and the worst tyrant in the world." After these words he was about to kill some more, but I kept him from it until he finally gave in. There were a major's wife, her maids, and three pretty children whom I pitied with all my heart. To prevent them from giving us away, we locked them in a cellar where there was nothing to eat except some dried fruit and turnips. We were hoping somebody else would let them out. Then we searched the coach and with seven beautiful horses rode off into the thickest part of the woods.

When we had tied them up and I was looking around a little, I saw someone standing quietly by a tree not far off. I pointed him out to Oliver and wondered if we hadn't better beware. "Stupid!" he said. "That's a Jew; I tied him to the tree, but the rogue croaked long ago and is frozen stiff." He went to him, patted his chin, and said, "Ha! You old dog, you brought me many nice ducats!" And when he moved the jaw of the corpse, several doubloons dropped out of his mouth. The poor fellow had kept them even after death. Then Oliver reached into his mouth and fished out twelve more doubloons and a precious ruby. "Simpli," he said, "I owe this booty to you." And he gave me the ruby, while he pocketed the money and went to get the peasant. He told me to watch the horses and not to let the dead Jew bite me. That was his way of telling me that he had more courage than I.

While he was away, I worried about the dangerous situation in which I was living. I decided to take one of the horses and be gone, but I was afraid Oliver would catch me and shoot me, for I figured that this time he was only testing my good faith and was standing by to watch me. Then I thought I'd run off on foot, but I had to consider that I could not escape the peasants in the Black Forest (who had, at that time, the reputation of being hard on soldiers), even if I got away from Oliver. If you take all the horses, I thought, so that Oliver has no means of pursuing you, and if you are caught by the Weimar troops, then you will be broken on the wheel as a convicted murderer. In short, I had no assurance of getting away, particularly as I was in a wild forest where I knew neither the highway nor the trails. Then my conscience began to bother me because I had held up the coach and been a cause of the coachman's pitiful death, and also a cause of the women and innocent children's being locked in the cellar, where they might starve and die, like the Jew. In turn I tried to console myself with my innocence, saying that I was being kept by Oliver against my will. But my conscience reproached me: for the evil deeds previously committed, this inveterate murderer and I deserved being delivered into the hands of justice. Now I'd get my due reward, and perhaps it was God's just will to have me punished in this way. Finally, having regained some measure of confidence and hope, I prayed to God in his kindness to deliver me from this troublesome situation; and when this pious mood came over me, I said to myself, "You fool, you are not tied down or locked in. The whole wide world is open to you. Don't you have horses enough for flight? Or if you don't care to ride, your legs will carry you away quickly enough."

While I was still in doubt and torment and could reach no decision, Oliver and our peasant came along. He took us to a farm where we fed the horses and took turns sleeping for a few hours. After midnight we rode on and by noon we reached the Swiss border, where Oliver was well known, and where we had a big meal served. While we were enjoying it, the innkeeper sent for two Jews, who bought the horses for something like half their value. Everything was arranged so neatly and precisely that few words were exchanged. The horse-traders' biggest question was whether the horses had been imperial or Swedish. When they heard they came from the army of Weimar, they said, "We have to take them to the Bavarians, not to Basel or Swabia." I was amazed at their easy familiarity with these things.

We had a royal banquet and I greatly enjoyed the fresh trout and excellent crayfish. When dusk came we started back. Our peasant was loaded like a donkey with roast meat and other food. So we arrived next day at a single farmstead where we were welcomed and put up in a friendly way. Because of a storm we stayed a few days. After that, having used lonely roads through the woods, we reached the same little house where Oliver had taken me when I first met him.

CHAPTER 24: *Oliver bites the dust, and so do six more*

While we were sitting there feeding our faces and resting, Oliver sent out the peasant to buy food, shot, and powder. When he had left, Oliver took off his coat and said to me,

"Brother, I don't care to haul all this damned money around with me any longer." So he untied a couple of rolls or sausages of it, which he was carrying on his bare body, threw them on the table, and continued, "You will have to be satisfied with this until I quit the business, and then both of us will have enough. That cockeyed money has chafed and galled me." I replied, "Brother, if you had as little as I, it would not irritate you." "What?" he interrupted. "What's mine is yours; and whatever we earn from now on, we'll divide fifty-fifty." I picked up both rolls and found them good and heavy, for the coin was solid gold. I told him it was not so well packed as it might be, and if he liked, I would sew it up in such a way that wearing it would be little or no trouble. When he agreed, I went with him to a hollow oak tree where he kept scissors, needle, and thread; and from a pair of trousers I made a scapular or shoulder garment for each of us and sewed up many a gold penny in it. And since we wore the scapulars under our shirts, it was just as if we were armed with gold in front and back. When I wondered why he had no silver coin, he answered that he had more than a thousand thalers deposited in a tree. From this he let the peasant pay the household expenses and never asked for an accounting, because he didn't care for such sheep droppings.

The money having all been sewn up, we went to our lodgings and cooked all night and stretched out in the warmth. About an hour after daybreak, when we were least prepared, six musketeers with their corporal came into the hut, their guns cocked and ready to fire. They burst through the door and shouted for us to surrender. But Oliver (who, like me, had his musket always ready for action and his sharp sword by his side—he was sitting behind the table, while I stood behind the door by the stove) answered them with a couple of bullets that knocked down two of the men. I got the third one and wounded the fourth with another shot. Then Oliver whipped out his trusty sword (which was as sharp as a razor and could be compared to Caliburn,[7] King Arthur's sword in England) and split the fifth man from shoulder to belly so

[7] In English, King Arthur's sword is better known as "Excalibur."

that his entrails fell to the ground and he dropped down next to them. Meanwhile I hit the sixth over the head with the butt end of my gun, so *he* didn't move much any more. But Oliver received the same kind of blow from the seventh. It was so severe that Oliver's brain was splattered all over, but I returned the favor in kind, and so number seven joined his comrades in the dance of death. When the man whom I had in the beginning injured with a shot noticed these blows and saw that I was coming at him with the butt of my gun, he threw his musket away and started running as if all hell were after him. The whole skirmish took no longer than it takes to say the Lord's Prayer; in this short space of time seven brave soldiers bit the dust.

Seeing that I was the sole surviving master of the field, I checked Oliver to see if there might still be life in him. When I found him completely without breath, it seemed downright foolish to leave all that gold on a body that couldn't make use of it. So I skinned off the gold jacket that I had finished only last night and put it on over my own. Because I had broken my musket, I picked up Oliver's; for emergencies I also took his sword, and I made tracks down the road by which our peasant would have to return. I sat down in a quiet place to wait for him and to consider what to do next.

CHAPTER 25: *Simplicius comes out rich, but Heartbrother shows up as a pitiful specimen of mankind*

I had not been waiting half an hour when the peasant came toward me, running and wheezing like a bear. He did not notice me until I was upon him. "What's the hurry? What's up?" I said. He answered, "Get out of here quick! A corporal and six musketeers are coming to raid the place. They have orders to bring you and Oliver dead or alive to Lichteneck. They caught me in order to use me as a guide, but I managed to break away. I am warning you." I thought at once that the rogue had squealed on us, in order to get the money Oliver kept in the hollow tree. But I did not let on that I suspected anything, for I wanted him to show me the way. I told him that Oliver and the party of soldiers that were supposed to capture him were dead. But when the peasant did not want to believe it, I took the trouble to go back with him and let him see the awful sight of seven corpses. "The seventh soldier," I told him, "I let escape, and I wish to God I could bring these back to life." The peasant turned white with fear and asked me what to do. I said, "My mind is made up. You have a choice of three alternatives: either you take me by safe trails out of the forest to Villingen; or you show me Oliver's money that's hidden in the tree; or you die here and keep these present corpses company. If you take me to Villingen, you can keep Oliver's money for yourself; if you show me the money, I'll divide it with you; if you do neither, I'll shoot you and go where I please." The peasant would have liked to run off, but he was afraid of my musket. So he fell on his knees and asked to guide me out of the woods. We started at once and hurried on that day and all the following night, which, as luck would have it, was bright; nor did we stop for food and drink or for rest, until toward daybreak we saw the town of Villingen before us; and there I dismissed the peasant. His reason to hurry was fear of death; mine, the desire to get out of there with my money. I can almost believe that gold gives a man great strength, as they say, for though it was heavy enough to carry, I did not feel especially tired.

I took it for a good omen that when I reached Villingen the gates were just being opened. The officer of the watch looked me over, and when he heard that I was a volunteer trooper of the same regiment to which Heartbrother had appointed me while he was at Philippsburg, and that I was coming from Weimar's camp at Breisach (by whose men I had been captured at Wittenweier and made to serve), and that now I wanted to get back to my regiment among the Bavarians, he assigned me a musketeer and had me taken to the commander. He was still asleep, for military affairs had kept him awake more than half the night, and I had to wait about an hour and a half in front of his quarters. The people just returning from early Mass crowded around me, and civilians and soldiers wanted to know how things were going at Breisach. The noise awakened the commander, and he ordered me to come in.

He started to question me and I answered just as I had done at the city gate. Later he asked me about some special points concerning the siege, and I confessed everything: how I had stayed about two weeks with a fellow who had also deserted; how we had held up and robbed a coach, hoping we'd get enough booty from the Weimarers to buy mounts, in order to return well equipped to our regiments; how we had been surprised and attacked by a corporal and six men sent to arrest us; how my comrade and six enemies had been killed; how the seventh had escaped as well as I; and how each had gone to his own party. But I said nothing about having intended to go home to my wife in Westphalia or about my wearing the two well-padded scapulars; nor did it bother my conscience to conceal this information, for it was none of his business. He didn't even ask about it, but he was amazed and almost wouldn't believe that Oliver and I had slain six men and chased off the seventh, though my partner had not survived. In this conversation I had occasion to mention Oliver's sword, which I praised and carried with me. He liked it so well that I had to let him have it in exchange for another, for I wanted to get out of there with a passport.

When he dismissed me (having ordered a passport made out for me), I went to the nearest inn, but I did not know whether to sleep or eat first. I needed to do both. I decided to appease my stomach first and ordered something to eat and a drink. Then I worried about how to arrange matters in order to get safely back to my wife in Lippstadt with all my money, for I intended as little to find my regiment as to break my neck.

While I was thinking about this, a fellow came limping into the room; he walked with a stick, his head was bandaged, one arm was in a sling, and the clothes he wore were so ragged that I would not have given him a penny for the lot. Immedi-

ately on seeing him, the waiter wanted to kick him out because he smelled bad and there were enough lice crawling on
him to populate the Swabian moors. The fellow begged that
he be allowed, for God's sake, to warm himself a little, but
he got nowhere with the waiter. When I took pity and put
in a good word for him, he was grudgingly allowed to sit by
the stove. It seemed to me he watched me with great appetite
and concentration while I ate eagerly. He let out a sigh or
two, and when the waiter went out to get me a piece of
roast, he sidled up to my table and extended a little earthen-
ware crock to me, so that I could easily imagine why he had
come. I took his pot and filled it from my can before he had
a chance to ask for wine. "Oh, my friend," he said, "for Heartbrother's sake, give me something to eat, too." When he said
that, I felt a stab in my heart and I knew it was Heartbrother
himself. I almost fainted when I saw him in such misery; but
I managed to embrace him, asked him to sit with me, and
then we both started crying, I for pity, and he for joy.

CHAPTER 26: *The last chapter in this book, for none follows
after*

The unexpectedness of our meeting almost took away our
appetites; we only asked each other how the other had been
since our last meeting. But since the innkeeper and the waiter
were constantly coming and going, we could tell each other
nothing of a confidential, private nature. The innkeeper was
surprised that I put up with this lousy individual, but I told
him that in wartime this was the custom among honest soldiers and comrades in arms. When I found out that Heartbrother had been in the hospital and was now living on alms,
and that his wounds were badly cared for, I rented a separate
room in the inn, put Heartbrother to bed, and sent for the
best surgeon in the place. I also let a tailor and a seamstress
dress him properly and thus snatched him out of the jaws of
the lice. In my purse I happened to have the doubloons that

Oliver had knocked out of the dead Jew's mouth. I threw them on the table, and within hearing of the innkeeper I said to Heartbrother, "Look, brother, this is my money. I'll spend it on you; we'll use it up together." That made the innkeeper more attentive. I showed the barber-surgeon the ruby, which also came from the Jew and which was worth about twenty thalers, and told him he could have it if he would cure my friend completely. He was satisfied and went diligently to work.

So I cared for Heartbrother as for another self and had a good suit of grey cloth made for him. But first I went to the commanding officer on account of the passport. I told him I had met a badly injured comrade from the same regiment and wanted to wait until he had completely recovered; with due regard for my regiment, I did not want the responsibility of leaving him behind. The commander praised my loyalty and gave me permission to stay as long as I wished, and he offered to give each of us a valid passport as soon as my friend could travel.

When I returned to Heartbrother and sat alone with him, on the edge of his bed, I asked him to tell me frankly how he happened thus to come down in the world. I imagined that he might have lost his former position of dignity on account of some important cause or omission. But he said, "Brother, you know I was Count von Götz's factotum and his dearest, most intimate friend. On the other hand, you also know well what rotten luck he had in his last campaign. Not only did we lose the battle of Wittenweier, but we couldn't raise the siege of Breisach either. Since on this account there is all manner of nasty talk going around (especially now that Count von Götz has been summoned to Vienna to answer charges), I voluntarily live in this humble way, partly from shame and partly from fear. Often I wish I could die in this misery, or at least keep myself concealed until the count's innocence has been proven. As far as I know, he has always been loyal to the Holy Roman Emperor. And I imagine the absence of good luck last summer is to be attributed to Divine Providence (who parcels out victories where he pleases) rather than to the count's incompetence.

"When we were to relieve Breisach and I saw that on our side everything was done listlessly, I armed myself and proceeded to the pontoon bridge as if I expected to accomplish the whole business by myself; and yet, at that time, it was neither my responsibility nor my job. I did it as an example for the others and because we had achieved nothing all summer. My luck (or rather misfortune) had it that I was one of the first men on the bridge to see the whites of the enemy's eyes. There was heavy fighting, and as I had been among the first to attack, I became one of the last when we could not resist the violent defense of the French.[8] I fell into the hands of the enemy, and I was shot once in the right arm, and again in the thigh, so that I could neither run away nor use my sword any more. And since the narrowness of the place and the heat of the skirmish did not permit much talk about giving or receiving quarter, I took a blow on the head that sent me sprawling to the ground. Being well dressed, I was robbed of my clothes and thrown into the Rhine for dead. In this trouble I cried to God and left all to his holy will, and after making several vows, I received his help. The Rhine washed me ashore, where I stanched my bleeding wounds with moss. And though I nearly froze to death, still I felt in myself a strange strength that made me crawl away. With God's help—though I was badly wounded—I reached some Marauding Brothers and soldiers' wives who took pity on me although I was a complete stranger to them. They all despaired of the relief of Breisach, and that hurt me worse than my wounds. They dressed and refreshed me near their fire, and before I could bandage my wounds, I saw that our people were preparing for a shameful retreat and giving up their cause for lost. This hurt me so much that I resolved to tell no one who I was, lest I incur mockery. For this reason I joined some

[8] Shortly after the death in 1632 of King Gustavus Adolphus of Sweden, the French, under policies devised by Richelieu, entered the Thirty Years' War on the side of the Protestants.

wounded men of our army, who had a surgeon with them. I gave the surgeon a gold cross, which was still around my neck, and for that he has bandaged my wounds until now.

"Dear Simpli, this is the miserable life I've lived lately. Nor do I intend to reveal my identity until after Count von Götz's difficulties have been resolved. Your kindheartedness and faithfulness have been a great consolation to me and are a sign that God has not yet forsaken me. When I came from early Mass this morning and saw you standing in front of the commander's quarters, I imagined that God had sent you instead of an angel to help me in my poverty." I consoled Heartbrother all I could and confided to him that I had even more money than the doubloons he had seen and that all of it was at his service. Then I told him of Oliver's death and how I had been forced to avenge it. This so revived his spirit that his body also benefited, for every day his wounds got better.

End of the Fourth Book

Book Five

CHAPTER 1: *How Simplicius becomes a pilgrim, and how he goes on a pilgrimage with Heartbrother*

After Heartbrother had regained his strength and his wounds were healed, he confided to me that in his deadly peril he had vowed to make a pilgrimage to Our Lady of Einsiedeln. Because he was so close to Switzerland, he wanted to make it now, even if he had to do it by begging along the way. This was music to my ears, and I offered him my money and company; in fact, I wanted to buy two nags and make the trip on horseback. Of course, it wasn't devotion that impelled me; I wanted to see the Swiss confederacy, because it was the only country still inhabited by beloved peace. Then, too, I was glad of the chance to wait on Heartbrother during this trip, for I loved him almost more than myself. But he turned down my help and my company, saying that a pilgrimage had to be made on foot and on peas. If I were his companion, I would not only prevent his devotion but also expose myself to a lot of discomfort on account of his slow and laborious gait. He said this only to rebuff me, because to live during such a pious trip on money obtained by robbery and murder was against his conscience. Furthermore, he did not want to involve me in too much expense, and he told me frankly that I had already done more for him than I owed him, or than he could hope to repay. At this point we got into a friendly disagreement, which was so pleasant that I have never heard such a sweet argument. Each merely reminded the other that he had not yet given all that friendship demanded—had not, in fact, half repaid the other's favors. But this exchange did not move him to put up with me on the pilgrimage. Finally I realized that Oliver's money and my godless life were equally disgusting to him. So I lied a little, telling him that a desire to lead a better life prompted me to go to Einsiedeln. If he were to keep me from this good work, and I were to die, he would hardly be able to answer for it. My arguments persuaded him to let me visit the holy place in his company, particularly when I displayed great remorse (also a lie) about my past life and told him that I, too, had imposed on myself the penance of walking to Einsiedeln with peas in both shoes.

This dispute had hardly ended when a new one arose, for Heartbrother was too scrupulous; he objected to my asking the commander for a passport made out to my regiment. "What?" he said. "Don't we intend to become better Christians by journeying to Einsiedeln? And you want to start out with a falsehood; you want to pull the wool over people's eyes? If all the martyrs and witnesses of Christ had done that, there would be few saints in heaven. Let us, in God's name and under his protection, go where our pious intention and desire call us. God will lead us where our souls will find peace." I rebuked him saying that it was prudent not to tempt God but to go with the times and make use of the inevitable, especially since making pilgrimages was an unusual activity among soldiers; that if we told of our journey, we would be treated as deserters rather than as pilgrims; and that this would plunge us into trouble and danger; and that the Apostle Paul (to whom we could not well compare ourselves) had made wondrous use of the customs of his time. Heartbrother finally allowed me to get a passport for traveling to my regiment. With this document and a reliable guide we left town, just as the gate was being locked, and started out for Rottweil. After a short distance we turned into byways and crossed the Swiss border that night. Next morning in a village we equipped ourselves with long, black coats, pilgrim's staves, and rosaries, and having paid the guide well, we sent him back.

In comparison with other German lands, the country appeared very strange to me—as if I were in Brazil or China. I saw country people trading and going about their business in peace. The barns were full of cattle; in the farmyards chickens, geese, and ducks were plentiful; the roads were safe and used by many travelers; in the taverns sat customers who enjoyed life. Nowhere was there fear of the enemy, no terror of looting, and no anxiety of losing one's goods, life, or limb. Everyone lived securely under his vines and fig trees and—unlike other German districts—in pure joy and delight, so that I considered this country an earthly paradise, though by nature it was harsh enough. All along the way I did nothing but gape, while Heartbrother counted his beads. For this he reproached me; he wanted me to pray continuously, but I couldn't get used to it.

In Zurich he found me out and very smartly told me off. At Schaffhausen, where we stayed over night, my feet hurt badly from the peas. Next morning I was reluctant to walk on peas again, and I had them boiled and put back into my shoes; and that's how I got to Zurich without sore feet. But my friend acted very nasty and said to me, "Brother, by the great grace of God you have walked well in your shoes despite the peas." "Yes," I replied, "my dear and honored Heartbrother, I had them boiled. Otherwise I couldn't have done so well." "Alas," he answered, "may God have pity on you. What have you done? It would have been better to forget your vow entirely than to make a mockery of it. Forgive me, brother, for using plain language with you and telling you in brotherly love that the salvation of your soul is in utter jeopardy unless you change your ways before God. I gladly confess and speak the truth when I say that I love no one in the world more than you. But I also do not deny that unless you change, continuing that love would burden my conscience." I was struck dumb and could not recover my breath for a while. Finally I openly confessed that I had not placed the peas in my shoes from reverence but only to please him, so that he would take me along on this trip. "Alas, brother," he said, "I see you are a long way from holiness, peas or no peas. May God help you to improve, for otherwise our friendship cannot endure."

From this point on, I followed sadly after him, like one being led to the gallows. My conscience started bothering me, and I thought of all the mean tricks I had ever played in my life. It was then that I first lamented the loss of the innocence which I had brought with me out of the woods and which I had frittered away on so many occasions. My sorrow was increased by the fact that Heartbrother would no longer talk much with me. He only looked at me and sighed, and that struck me as if he knew I was damned, and pitied me.

CHAPTER 2: *After being frightened by the devil, Simplicius gets religion*

We arrived in Einsiedeln and stepped into the church just as a priest was exorcising a man possessed by an evil spirit. That was new and strange to me. So I let Heartbrother kneel and pray all he wanted, and I went over to watch this sight. I had hardly approached when the spirit cried out of the poor man, "Oh-ho, my friend, does bad luck bring you here? I thought I'd find you with Oliver, at home in hell, when I got back; but I see you are here, you adulterous, murderous whoremonger. You think you can escape us? Oh, you priests, do not accept him; he is a hypocrite and a worse liar than I. He is only fooling himself and making a mockery of God and religion." The priest ordered the spirit to be silent because he was an archliar and would not be believed.

"Yes, indeed," he answered, "just ask this runaway monk's traveling companion. He will tell you that this atheist did not shrink from boiling the peas on which he promised to walk here." When I heard this and everybody looked at me, I didn't know which way my head was screwed on. But the exorcist punished the spirit and made him cower in silence; yet he could not drive him out that day. Meanwhile Heartbrother

came over, just when I looked more like a corpse than a live
person and was so terrified that, between hope and despair, I
did not know what to do with myself. Heartbrother comforted
me as best he could and assured the bystanders (and especially the fathers) that I had never been a monk but rather
was a soldier who had probably done more good than evil.
He added that the devil was a liar who had exaggerated the
incident of the peas far beyond what it was. I myself was so
bewildered that I already seemed to feel the pain of hell upon
me, and the priests had quite a time calming me. They advised me to go to confession and communion, but once more
the evil spirit cried from the man possessed, "Take heed, he
will make a fine confession. He does not even know what
confession is. And what will you do with him? He is a heretic
and belongs to us. His parents were Anabaptists, not Calvinists," and so on. The exorcist again ordered the spirit to be
still and said to him, "It will dishearten you all the more
then if the poor lost lamb is snatched out of your jaws and
numbered among the flock of Christ." Hearing this, the spirit
started to roar so savagely that it was terrifying to hear him.
Yet I derived my greatest comfort from this repulsive outcry,
for I thought the devil would not rant so if I had already lost
God's grace.

Though I was not at that time prepared for confession (it
had never entered my mind until then, and I had always been
as afraid of it as the devil is of the holy cross), still I felt such
remorse about my sins, such a desire to do penance and to improve my vicious and godless life, that I asked for a father
confessor. Heartbrother was altogether glad at this sudden
conversion and improvement, for he knew that so far I had
not joined any church. There and then I publicly embraced
the Catholic faith, went to confession, and after absolution
partook of the Eucharist. After this I felt so relieved and
easy about my heart that I cannot express it. The most remarkable thing, however, was that henceforth the spirit in
the possessed man left me in peace, though before confession

and absolution he had reproached me specifically with various
misdeeds, so that I suspected he had been ordered to do nothing but watch my sins. But, he being a liar, the bystanders
did not believe him, particularly because my honorable pilgrim's garb presented me in quite a different light.

We spent all of two weeks in this town, which abounded in
grace; I thanked God for my conversion and looked at the
miracles that took place there. All of this induced in me a
mood of considerable reverence and piety. But it lasted only
a short while, for since my conversion had not sprung from a
love of God but rather from fear and dread of damnation,
by and by I turned lax and lukewarm, because I gradually
forgot the terror the fiend had struck into me. After we had
sufficiently beheld the relics of the saints, the vestments and
other sights of the church, we went to Baden to spend the
rest of the winter.

CHAPTER 3: *How the two friends spent the winter*

There I rented us a cheerful parlor and bedroom, which
in the summer were usually occupied by visitors to the baths,
mostly rich Swiss who go there more to show off and have a
good time than to improve their health. I also arranged for
our board, and when Heartbrother saw that I was living it up,
he advised me to be economical and reminded me of the long
winter ahead of us. He was afraid my money would not last:
I might need my resources in the spring when we had to leave;
even a large sum of money would soon be gone if a person
only spent it and added nothing to it. Money disappeared like
smoke, he said, and so on. After such well-meaning counsel
I could no longer conceal from Heartbrother how well-lined
my pockets were. I also told him that I wanted to spend the
money for our benefit, especially since I had acquired it in a
way so unworthy of God's blessing that I did not intend to
buy a farm with it. And even though I did not want to invest

it just to entertain my dearest friend on earth, it was only
fair that he, Heartbrother, enjoyed Oliver's money, in order
to make up for the insult he had received from Oliver at
Magdeburg. When I knew we were in a safe place, I peeled
off both my scapulars, took out the ducats and pistoles, and
told Heartbrother that this money was at his disposal; he
should invest it or spend it as he thought might profit us best.

When he realized that, along with my trust in him, I had
so much money that I could have been quite an important
person regardless of him, he said, "Brother, as long as I've
known you, you have always shown me love and trust. But
how could I ever repay you? It is not only money with
which you put me under obligation—that might in time be
repaid, perhaps; it is your love and trust and especially your
absolute confidence in me, all of which are beyond material
values. I blush for shame that I would never trust a person
as much as you have trusted me. I assure you, brother, that
this proof of your true friendship binds me to you more than
to a rich man who might give me thousands. However, I beg
you, brother, yourself to stay the master, keeper, and disburser
of your money. For me, it is enough if you are my friend."
My answer was, "What strange words are these, dear Heartbrother? You assure me with words that you are obliged to
me; yet you warn me not to spend our money for nothing."
And so we talked back and forth—foolishly, almost, for each
was intoxicated with love for the other. And Heartbrother
became simultaneously my steward, treasurer, servant, and
master. During this leisurely time he told me of his life: how
he had become known to Count von Götz and how he had
been advanced. Then I told him how I had fared since his
late father died. Until now we had never taken the time to do
this. And when he heard that I had a young wife in Lippstadt
he reproached me for running off to Switzerland with him
instead of going to her first, as was my duty. My excuse was
that I could not have left him, my very dearest friend, alone
in such utter misery. He persuaded me to write my wife and

let her know that I would come to her at the earliest opportunity. I wrote and begged her pardon for not returning
earlier: all sorts of untoward events prevented me, though
I had wanted to come back before this.

Now when Heartbrother found out from the newsletters
that Count von Götz was doing well—particularly, that he
would succeed in vindicating himself before his imperial majesty, would be released, and would even get back the command of an army—he wrote to Vienna concerning himself,
sent for his equipment, which was still with the Bavarian
army, and began to hope that his own luck would improve.
On account of these developments we decided to part next
spring, he to go to his count, and I to my wife in Lippstadt.
In order not to spend the winter idly, we learned from an
engineer to build—on paper—more fortresses than the kings
of Spain and France combined could have erected. Furthermore, I got acquainted with some alchemists who suspected
that I had money and wanted to teach me how to make gold,
if only I'd pay for the apparatus and supplies. I think they
would have talked me into it if Heartbrother had not shown
them the door. He said that whoever knew *that* art wasn't
likely to go around like a beggar asking others for money.

Though Heartbrother received a favorable reply and excellent promises from his count in Vienna, I never got a single
line from Lippstadt, though on some mail days I wrote in
duplicate. That disgusted me so much that I did not go to
Westphalia in the spring. I got Heartbrother's permission to
go with him to Vienna, where I would join in his expected
good fortune. So with my money we equipped ourselves like
cavaliers, with clothes, horses, servants, and weapons, and proceeded by way of Constance to Ulm, where we took a boat on
the Danube and after a week reached Vienna safely. On the
way I did not observe much except that the women who lived
on the banks did not answer the oral greeting of passers-by
in kind, but rather gave them visual proof of their femininity
by hoisting their skirts behind. That way some men gained
deep insight.

CHAPTER 4: *How Heartbrother and Simplicius enter the war*
once more, and how they get out of it again

Strange things happen in his changeable world. They say
that a man who knew everything would soon be rich. I say
that the man who could always make use of his chances would
soon be great and powerful. Many a skinflint or curmudgeon
—these titles are bestowed on misers—soon gets rich because he
knows how to use one or two advantages. But for that reason
he is not great; rather, he receives (and will always receive)
less respect than he had when he was poor. On the other hand,
riches closely follow the man who knows how to make himself
great and powerful. Fortune, which is accustomed to granting
might and riches, looked at me with a winsome smile, and
after we had been in Vienna for a week, she gave me several
chances to climb up the ladder of importance. But I didn't
do it. Why? I suppose because my fate had decided on something else, namely, that to which my fatuousness led me.

Count von der Wahl, under whose command I had previously distinguished myself in Westphalia, happened to be in
Vienna when Heartbrother and I arrived. He was having a
banquet with Count von Götz, several imperial councilors,
and others, when the conversation turned to all sorts of unusual characters, soldiers, and famous raiders. They mentioned
the Hunter of Soest, and several of his daring exploits were so
well told that some were amazed that so young a fellow could
have achieved them. Others deplored the fact that the sly
Hessian colonel, de St. André, had framed him with a wife so
that he would have either to lay aside his sword or to join the
Swedish army. Count von der Wahl said he had found out
how the colonel had tricked me. My beloved Heartbrother,
who happened to be present and who wanted very much to
see me advance, requested permission to speak. He said he
knew the Hunter of Soest better than any other person on
earth. The Hunter was, he continued, not only a good soldier,

used to the smell of powder, but also a good horseman, a perfect swordsman, an expert in artillery and musketry, and, in
addition, one who could outdo any engineer in building fortifications. He had left behind in Lippstadt not only his wife
(with whom he had been so shamefully saddled), but also everything he owned, and had sought imperial service again; for in
the last campaign he had been under the command of Count
von Götz, and when captured by Weimarers, he had wanted
to return to the imperials. He and his friend had killed a corporal and six musketeers who had pursued them in order to
bring them back; he had made excellent booty and was now
in Vienna and willing to take up arms once more against the
enemies of his imperial majesty, but only under conditions
commensurate with his reputation, for he no longer wanted to
serve as a common soldier.

By that time, those present were so inspired with drink that
they wanted to satisfy their curiosity by seeing the Hunter,
and Heartbrother was sent out by coach to bring me. On the
way he instructed me how to behave in the presence of these
illustrious men, for my advancement and future depended on
it. When I arrived, I answered their questions briefly and to
the point, so that they began to take notice of me as one who
said nothing without necessity and who used a clever emphasis
when he spoke. To put it in a nutshell, I made a pleasant
impression on everybody, and besides, Count von der Wahl
had already praised me as a good soldier. After a while I got
tipsy too, and perhaps in that condition I showed how little
I really knew of life at court. The upshot of it all was that an
infantry colonel promised me a company in his regiment, and
I didn't refuse. I thought, To be a captain, that's something!
But the next day Heartbrother rebuked me for being too
easily pleased; if I had held out I could have bettered my rank.

And so I was presented as their captain to a company which,
though complete with officers (including me), counted no
more than seven soldiers for sentry duty. My N C O's were for
the most part such decrepit codgers that I could only shake
my head and scratch myself behind the ears. So, in the next

engagement (in which Count von Götz lost his life and Heart-brother's testicles were shot away), we were miserably beaten, though I was only slightly wounded in the thigh. For a cure we went to Vienna, where, incidentally, I had deposited my money. Besides our wounds, which healed soon enough, Heart-brother found himself in a dangerous condition, which the doctors could not diagnose at first: he became paralyzed in his extremities, like a choleric person who is bothered by his gall. And yet he was not in the least inclined to that complexion, nor to being angry. Still, he was advised to take the waters, particularly those at Griesbach in the Black Forest.

This is how our luck changed overnight. Only recently Heartbrother had wanted to marry a young lady of quality and have himself made a baron, and me a count. But now he had to think of something else, for he had lost the where-withal to propagate a new generation; and since, in connec-tion with his paralysis, he was threatened with a lengthy ill-ness (during which time he needed good friends), he made his will and declared me the sole heir of all his property, chiefly because he saw that for his sake I was throwing my own for-tune to the winds and giving up my company in order to go with him to a health resort, where I would stay until he re-gained his health.

CHAPTER 5: *Simplicius pretends to be a messenger and, being addressed as Mercury by Jove, learns what the great Numen has in mind concerning war and peace*

When Heartbrother was able to ride again, we exchanged our cash (for now we kept but one purse between us) for a letter of credit on a bank in Basel. We bought horses, hired servants, and rode up the Danube as far as Ulm and, since travel was pleasant in May, proceeded from there to the spa. We rented rooms, and I continued to Strasbourg, in order not only to cash the check we had had transferred from Basel, but

also to look for experienced doctors who could prescribe medicines and work out a schedule for taking the waters. Several
of these doctors came with me and found that Heartbrother
had been poisoned. But since the poison had not been strong
enough to kill him immediately, it had gone into his arms
and legs, from whence it had to be removed by drugs, anti-
dotes, and steam baths. Such a cure would take from one to
eight weeks. Then Heartbrother recalled when and by whom
he had been poisoned, namely, by those who would have liked
to have had his position in the army. And when he heard
from the various doctors that his illness would not require his
visiting a spa, he firmly believed that his field surgeon had
been bribed by his rivals to get him this far out of the way.
However, Heartbrother decided to complete his cure at the
resort, since the air was salubrious, and the other guests
pleasant.

I did not want to waste my time, and since I had a hearty
desire to see my wife sometime, and Heartbrother did not
need me especially, I disclosed my plan to him. He approved
and advised me not to procrastinate but to go, the sooner the
better. He gave me some precious jewelry, which I was to
give to my wife; also I was to beg her pardon, on his behalf, for
delaying my return. So I rode to Strasbourg, and there I not
only provided myself with money, but also inquired about
the safest way of making my trip. I found out that it could
not be done on horseback and alone, for raiding parties
sent out by the garrisons of the two enemies made the roads
unsafe. I hired a courier, obtained a passport for him, and
wrote up several letters to my wife, her sister, and her parents,
which I asked to have delivered in Lippstadt. Then I pretended to change my mind, got the courier to give me his
passport, returned my horses and the servant, disguised myself in a red and white livery, and took a boat to Cologne,
which was then neutral.

There I went first to see my old Jupiter, in order to find
out about my sequestered property. But at that time he was
totally unhinged in his mind and disgusted with the human

race. "Oh, Mercury," he said, when he saw me, "what news do you have from Münster? [1] Do these humans think they can make peace without me? Never! They had it; why didn't they keep it? Weren't all the vices flourishing when they induced me to send them a war? And why do they deserve peace now? Have they improved since then? Haven't they rather become worse and rushed into war as if they were going to a fair? Or did they repent because of the famine I sent, in which many thousands died of hunger? Or did the savage epidemics that cut down so many millions terrify them, so that they became better? No, no, Mercury, the survivors who see the misery and distress with their own eyes are not only unrepentant; they have grown much worse than they ever were. If they have not changed after so many severe penalties, but continue their godless life amid wretchedness and vexation, what will they do if I were to send them delectable, golden peace? I should have to worry that they would take it upon themselves to deprive me of heaven, as the titans did before. But I will prevent such insolence betimes and let them linger woebegone in war for a long time to come."

Because I knew how to treat this god if one wanted to put him in the right frame of mind, I said, "Alas, great god, all the world is moaning for peace and promising to mend its ways. Why should you withhold it from them any longer?" "Indeed, they are moaning," answered Jupiter, "but not for my sake, only for theirs. They don't want to praise God, each under his vines and fig trees, but merely to enjoy the fruits of them in peace and lechery. The other day I asked a louse-ridden tailor whether I should give them peace. But he answered, what did he care?! He would keep as busy in war as in peacetime. I got a similar answer from a foundryman. He told me that if he did not cast church bells in peacetime, he'd cast cannon and mortars in wartime. A blacksmith said, 'If I don't have plows and farm wagons to work on in peacetime, I have plenty of artillery horses to shoe and army wagons to take care of in wartime. I can do without peace.' Look, dear Mercury, why

1 Preliminary peace negotiations at Münster started as early as 1644.

should I grant them peace? Surely there are a few who want it, but only for the sake of their bellies and their convenience. There are, however, also some who want to keep the war going, not because it is my will, but because it is to their profit. And just as the masons and the carpenters want peace so that they can get rich by rebuilding and repairing the burnt-out towns, so others, who do not believe in earning an honest living by manual *labor*, wish a continuation of the war in order to have a better opportunity for manual *theft*."

Since my Jupiter was concerned only with these affairs, I took it that he could give me no news about my family. Therefore, I told him nothing, but proceeded resolutely on familiar byways to Lippstadt and asked for my father-in-law as if I were only a messsenger. But I found out at once that he and my mother-in-law had departed this world half a year ago, and that my beloved wife, after she had been delivered of a boy (who was with my sister-in-law) had also passed away right after his birth. I handed my brother-in-law the letters that I had written myself to my father-in-law, my dear wife, and to him, my brother-in-law. He offered me lodging so that he might find out from me—the messenger—how Simplicius was. For the same reason my sister-in-law talked a long time with me about myself, and I spoke of myself and told her as many pleasant things about me as I knew, for the pockmarks had so changed and marred me that no one recognized me any more, except Herr von Schönstein; [2] but being an old, trusted friend, he kept still.

When I told my sister-in-law in great detail that my master Simplicius owned many fine horses, had numerous servants, and was a man of importance, wearing a black velvet coat adorned all over with gold, she said, "Indeed? I always thought that he was of better descent than he admitted. By

[2] Von Schönstein was the cavalry officer who had captured Simplicius and taken him to Lippstadt (Bk. III, chap. 14). Later he had been on the boat that rescued Simplicius from the tree in the Rhine. Though von Schönstein had tried to get Simplicius out of the imperial army, he failed because he was on a secret mission (Bk. IV, chap. 10).

definite assurances, the commander here persuaded my deceased parents that the marriage between him and my late sister, who was a virtuous girl, was a profitable match; but I never saw any good in it. Nevertheless, he made a good impression and promised to go into Swedish—or rather Hessian—service, here in this garrison. For this purpose he wanted to go to Cologne and bring his assets here. But the matter was delayed and he, having been deceitfully sent off to France, left my sister (who was hardly married a month to him) and perhaps a dozen burghers' daughters pregnant. One after another, they all gave birth to boys; my sister was last.

"Since my father and mother are dead, and my husband and I expect no children together, we have adopted my sister's child, and we expect to make him heir of all we own. With the help of our commander here, we have collected his father's assets in Cologne—amounting to perhaps three thousand florins —so that this youngster, once he is old enough, will have no cause to complain of poverty. My husband and I love the child so much that we wouldn't give him to this own father, if he should come by to pick him up. Moreover, he is the handsomest among all his stepbrothers and resembles his father as if he were cut from the same pattern. I know that if my brother-in-law knew what a handsome son he has here, he couldn't deny himself the pleasure of looking at the little darling, even though he might not relish running into his other children, the bastards."

These and many other matters were brought up by my sister-in-law, and I could easily see that she loved my child, who was skipping about in his first pair of breeches and making my heart glad. For that reason I rummaged through my pockets for the jewelry Heartbrother had given me to present to my wife. "My master Simplicius," I said, "asked me to give these jewels to his beloved wife as a greeting; it is only fair to leave them for his child." My brother-in-law and his wife received the gift joyfully and concluded that I was not living in want, but rather that I must be a man different from the kind they had imagined before. So I asked permission to go back, and

when I was given leave, I begged for the favor of kissing the
young Simplicius in the name of the old one, so that I might
tell his father about it as a token. When this was done (with
my sister-in-law's permission), both my nose and the child's
started bleeding. My heart was about to break, but I concealed
my emotions; and in order not to have much time to think
about the cause of this sympathetic event, I left at once, and
after two weeks of much trouble and danger arrived in Sauer-
brunn as a beggar, for I had been stripped bare on the way.

CHAPTER 6: *A practical joke that Simplicius played in the spa*

Upon arriving, I noticed that Heartbrother had gotten
worse rather than better, though the doctors and druggist had
plucked him cleaner than a fat goose. He seemed to be childish
and could hardly walk upright. I cheered him up as best I
could, but he was in poor condition, and the way his strength
was failing he probably suspected that he would not last long.
His greatest comfort was that I would be with him when he
closed his eyes.

I, on the other hand, enjoyed life and sought my old accustomed pleasures where I could find them, but in such a
way that Heartbrother missed none of his care. And since I
knew I was a widower, leisure and youth again induced me to
run after women; I had already forgotten the fright I received
at Einsiedeln. At the resort there was a very beautiful lady [3]
who let it be known she was of nobility, but as I figured it
she was even more *mobilis* than *nobilis*. I busily paid court
to this man-trap, for she seemed to be a good dish. After a
short time I received free access not only to her house, but
also to any other privilege I might have wished and hoped for.
But from the beginning I was disgusted with her easy ways

[3] This is the adventuress Lebushka, who tells her life story in the
Simplician writing *Trutzsimplex or the Life of the Arch-picara Courage,*
a book that inspired Bertolt Brecht's *Mother Courage, a Chronicle Play
of the Thirty Years' War* (1939).

and wondered how to get rid of her without trouble, for she seemed to be more interested in fleecing my purse than in marrying. Whenever I was with her she showered me with loving, ardent glances and other manifestations of her fiery affection, so that I was ashamed for both myself and her.

There was also a rich Swiss nobleman at the spa. Not only had his money been stolen, but also his wife's jewelry, consisting of gold, silver, pearls, and precious stones. Now since it is as unpleasant to lose such things as it is hard to come by them, the Swiss sought all the counsel and help he could in order to recover them. He sent for the famous devil-conjurer of the goatskin, who by his conjuring so troubled the thief that he personally had to return the stolen goods to their proper place. For this service the magician received ten thalers.

I would have been happy to confer with this sorcerer; but I was afraid it could not be done without loss of dignity (for at that time I thought I was a big wheel). So, having heard that he was a great toper, I asked my servant to drink with him that evening in order to become acquainted with him, and perhaps I could find out a thing or two that would come in handy; for the stories told about him were so strange that I could not believe them unless I heard them from him in person. Having disguised myself as a traveling quack who sells ointments, I sat down at his table, intending to find out whether he could guess (or whether the devil would tell him) who I was. But I did not notice anything peculiar about him, for he just kept pouring wine down his throat, and he thought I was what my clothes indicated. He even drank to my health a few times, and he showed more respect to my servant than to me. He told him in all confidence that if the man who robbed the Swiss had thrown the least little part of the loot into running water, thus giving the accursed devil his share of it, it would have been impossible to name the thief or to recover the loss.

Hearing these silly things, I was amazed at how the sly, deceptive fiend can get his clutches into poor humans by means

of such insignificant trifles. I could easily imagine that this
was part of the pact made between the conjurer and the devil,
and that such a trick would not help the thief if another conjurer were called in, one whose pact did not contain this pro-
vision. So I ordered my servant (who could steal more skillfully than a gypsy) to get the fellow good and drunk, steal his
ten Reichsthalers, and throw a few pennies of it into the river
Rench. The man did as he was ordered. When the conjurer
missed his money next morning, he went to a wild part of
the Rench, there, no doubt, to confer in this matter with his
familiar. But he was so mishandled that he came back with a
black eye and scratches all over his face. I felt so sorry for the
poor rascal that I had his money returned to him with this
message: Seeing what kind of evil and deceptive guy the
devil was, he might henceforth quit his company and service,
and return to God. But for me this admonition turned out
like the grass that the dog eats; from this time on I had nothing but bad luck. Soon afterward my two fine horses dropped
dead from sorcery. And what could have protected me? I lived
as godless a life as an epicurean and never commended my
possesssions unto God's protection. Why should this sorcerer
not have taken revenge on me?

CHAPTER 7: *Heartbrother dies, and Simplicius starts pitching
woo again*

The longer I stayed in the resort the better I liked it; for
one thing, the number of guests increased daily, it seemed; for
another, the place itself and the style of living there struck me
as pleasant. I became acquainted with the jolliest people and
started using courteous phrases and compliments, the existence
of which I had never noticed before. I was thought to be a
nobleman, for my servants called me captain, and soldiers of
fortune do not commonly attain that rank at my age. For that
reason the rich fops sought not only my acquaintance but also
my sworn friendship, and I theirs. All manner of entertain-

ment, gambling, gluttony, and drinking were my greatest worry and concern. They took away many a pretty ducat without my noticing it especially or worrying about it, for my purse was still heavy enough from Oliver's legacy.

Meanwhile, Heartbrother's condition went from bad to worse, so that he finally had to pay the debt of nature: the doctors had left him after extracting their share from him. He confirmed his last will and testament and made me the heir of what he expected to receive of his late father's legacy. I had him buried in great style and dismissed his servants, after buying them mourning clothes and giving them a sum of money.

His death was a painful blow to me, particularly since he had been poisoned; and though I could not change that, it changed me, and I grew sadder from day to day. I stayed away from all parties and sought only solitude, there to meditate upon my sad thoughts. For this purpose I would sometimes hide in a thicket, there to contemplate not only what a friend I had lost, but also the fact that I would never again find one like him. In this connection I also made plans for my future life, but without deciding anything definite. Now I wanted to get back in the army; but then I considered that the lowliest peasants in this part of the country were better off than a colonel, for no raiders ever came into these hills. I could hardly imagine what an army would have to do in order to ruin this part of the world, where all the farms were still standing, well built, as in peacetime, and all the stables were full of cattle—though in the plains there wasn't even a cat or a dog left in the villages.

One time I lay down in the grass under a big shade tree between the road and a creek. I wanted to listen to the nightingales, whose song was likely to cheer me most in my sadness. I listened to their lovely melody not casually but with great attentiveness, and as it were, daily from habit, I wondered how such a bright, high voice and pleasant sound can proceed from such a small pipe or throat. For some time I had been enjoying myself listening to the prettiest songs of the bird and thinking that the nightingale was fascinating the other birds

by the loveliness of its song, when on the other bank, there
approached a beauty who moved me more than a well-dressed
demoiselle could have done, though she wore only the dress
of a farm girl. From her head she took a basket in which she
was carrying a roll of fresh butter that she hoped to sell in the
spa. She put it in the water so it wouldn't melt in the hot sun.
Then she sat down in the grass, took off her hat and kerchief,
and wiped the perspiration from her face. So I had plenty of
time to look at her and to satisfy my curious eyes. It seemed to
me that in all my born days I had not seen a prettier girl: the
proportions of her body appeared to be faultless and beyond
reproach, her arms and hands white as snow, her face lovely
and pert, her dark eyes full of fire and exciting glances. She
was wrapping up the butter again when I shouted across to
her, "Ah, maiden! To be sure, with your pretty hands you
have cooled the butter in the water; but with your bright eyes
you have set my heart on fire." As soon as she saw and heard
me, she ran away as if chased, leaving me behind speechless
and filled with all those foolish notions created by an enam-
ored fancy to trouble us.

My desire to have this sun shine upon me did not let me
stay in the solitude I had sought, but made me regard the
song of the nightingale as no better than the howl of wolves.
For that reason, I too trotted toward the spa, sending my page
ahead to talk to the country girl and haggle with her until I
arrived. He did what he could; and after arriving, I did what
I could. But I found a heart of stone and such reserve as I
would never have thought possible in a farm girl. But this
only increased my ardor, though as one who has been around
I could have told myself that she would not be one who was
easily fooled.

At that time I should have had either a bad enemy or a
good friend: an enemy who would have forced me to concen-
trate my thoughts on him and to give up my foolish love; or
a good friend who would have advised me differently and
kept me from the folly I was about to commit. But, alas, I only
had Heartbrother's money to dazzle me, my blind desires to

mislead me because I did not restrain them, and my own rash-
ness to ruin me and drive me into misfortune. Fool that I was,
I should have judged from the black color of our clothing (an
evil omen) that her love would be my misery. Since Heartbrother and the girl's parents had died, both of us were dressed
in mourning when we first saw each other. What joyfulness
could there have been in our courtship? In a word, I was
caught in a fool's snare, and therefore I was blind and without reason, like the boy Cupid himself. And as I did not dare
to satisfy my animal urge in any other way, I decided to marry
her. "Heck!" I said to myself, "you are only a peasant boy
and will never own a castle. This is a noble part of the country
which, in comparison to other places, is enjoying wealth and
prosperity. Anyway, you still have enough money to buy the
best farmstead hereabouts. You ought to marry this honest
Fanny from the country and get yourself a peaceful gentleman's place among the farmers. Where would you find a
jollier home than near the spa, where you can see a different
world every six weeks—on account of the guests, who come
and go. On the basis of this you can imagine how the world
changes from one century to the next." This and a thousand
other thoughts went through my head, until I finally asked for
the hand of my beloved in marriage and received her consent,
but not without a struggle.

CHAPTER 8: *Simplicius contracts a second marriage, meets
his knan, and learns who his parents were*

I ordered a big wedding, for I was in seventh heaven. And
I not only bought the farm where my bride was born, but I
improved it with many new buildings, as if I wanted more to
hold court than keep a courtyard. Before the wedding I
bought thirty head of cattle and put them on the place, for
that was the number the farm could support throughout the
year. In brief, I arranged everything in the best possible manner, including the most expensive furniture my folly could

select. But the bubble burst quickly, for when I thought I had set my sail for Angel-land I only got to Hell-land and then— much too late—I found out why my bride had been so reluctant to marry me. And what hurt me the worst was that I could not weep on anybody's shoulder about this shame of mine. It was fair for me to have to pay for my sins, but this knowledge did not make me a bit more patient or pious. Rather, because I found myself so cheated, I planned to cheat my cheater and started grazing where I could find greener pasture. Thus, I was more often in pleasant company in the spa than at home. In short, I let my household go to rack and ruin.

On the other hand, my wife was just as slovenly: a beef that I had slaughtered she salted down like pork; she wanted to roast trout on a spit and grill crayfish! By these few examples one can easily see how she kept house. She liked to drink wine and shared it with others, and that was a sign of my approaching disaster.

Once I was promenading down the valley with some people of fashion to visit friends in the lower baths. There we met an old peasant leading a goat that he wanted to sell. And because I had a feeling that I had seen this person before, I asked him where he was coming from with the goat he was leading on the rope. He took off his hat and said, "Sir, I dasn't tell ya." I said, "Well, surely you didn't steal it?" "No," he said, "I come from the town down in the valley, the one I dasn't mention to the gentleman because we are talking in the presence of a goat." [4] This made everyone laugh, and because I got white as a sheet they thought I was annoyed or ashamed that the peasant answered me so neatly. But my thoughts were elsewhere, for by the big wart which the peasant had in the middle of his forehead, like a unicorn, I was assured that he was none other than my knan from the Spessart. So I decided to act the prophet before I told him who I was and presented him with a son who was fully grown and as well dressed as

[4] The town is called Gaisbach, and *Geiss* (a variant spelling of *Gais*) means "goat." The peasant is pretending that the goat should not hear this word lest her feelings be hurt.

I was at that time. I said to him, "My good old man, don't
you come from the Spessart?" "Yea, sir," answered the peasant.
I continued, "About eighteen years ago the troopers looted
and burned your place." "Yes, God ha' mercy," answered the
peasant, "but it isn't quite that long ago." I continued asking,
"At that time did you not have two children, a grown-up
daughter and a young boy who herded your sheep?" "Sir,"
replied the peasant, "the daughter was my child, but the boy
was not. I wanted to raise him as my own." From this I
gathered that I was not the son of this coarse yokel. This
made me partly glad, but it also saddened me, because it occurred to me that I might be a bastard or a foundling. So I
asked my knan where he had gotten the boy, and why he had
wanted to raise him as his own child. "Alas," he said, "that
was strange: the war gave him to me and the war took him
away." Now I was getting worried that some unpleasant fact
about my birth might come out, and I turned the conversation
back to the goat and asked him if he had sold it for meat to
the lady who kept the hotel. That would be strange, for the
guests in the spa didn't usually eat old goat meat. "Ah, no,
sir," answered the peasant, "the lady has plenty of goats and
won't pay me much for anything. I am bringing it for the
countess who is taking the waters. Dr. Busybody has pre-
scribed some herbs that the goat must eat. The doctor then
takes her milk and adds some medicine to it. The countess,
she has to drink the milk and get well from it. They say
there's something wrong with her insides, and if the goat can
cure her, she can do more than the doctor and his gravedig-
gers combined." During this conversation I wondered how I
could continue talking with the peasant, and I offered him
one thaler more than the doctor or the countess would pay for
the goat. He agreed at once (for a slight profit quickly per-
suades most people), but with this proviso: that he would first
tell the countess of my higher offer. If she should raise her
bid to equal mine, she was to have preference; if not, he
would bring the goat that evening and tell me about the deal.
So my knan went on his way, and, I, with my company,

went mine. But I could not, and did not want to, stay with the group any longer. I turned aside and found my knan still with his goat, for the others would not give as much for it as I (which surprised me in such rich people, but their niggardliness didn't make me more stingy). I took him to my newly-bought farm, paid for the goat, and after I had got him half drunk, asked him where he had got hold of the boy we had been discussing today. "Well, sir," he said, "the Mansfeld war gave him to me and the battle of Nördlingen took him away again." I remarked that that must be a good story and asked him to tell it, since we had nothing else to talk about. He began, saying, "When the Mansfelders lost the battle at Höchst, the defeated troops scattered far and wide, for they did not know where to retreat. Many came to the Spessart, where they wanted to hide in the woods. But after escaping death on the plains, they found it with us in the hills, and since both warring parties considered robbing and killing each other, on our grounds, as fair play, we reached out for them, too; at that time hardly a peasant went abroad without his shooting iron (for we couldn't always stay at home with our plows and hoes). In this hubbub in the tremendous, wild forest not far from my farm, I had heard several shots. Shortly afterward I noticed a beautiful, young noblewoman on a stately horse. First I thought she was a man, for she rode like one; but when she raised her eyes and hands to the sky and I heard her call on God in a pitiful voice, in French, I lowered and uncocked my gun, for her gestures and her prayer assured me that she was a woman in distress. We approached each other, and when she saw me, she said, 'Alas, if you are an honest Christian, I beg you, in the name of God and his mercy, to take me to some good woman who, with God's help, will aid me in delivering me of my body's burden.' These words, together with her way of speaking and her sad but exceedingly beautiful and graceful figure, moved me to pity; I took her horse by the reins and led her through hedges and bushes to the very densest thicket, where I had concealed my wife and child, the hired hands, and my cattle. There, in less than half an hour, she was delivered of the boy we were talking about today."

My knan took a drink, indicating that the story was ended. I offered him more wine, and when he had emptied the glass, I asked him what had happened to the woman. He answered, "When she had given birth, she asked me to be the boy's godfather and to have him baptized as soon as possible. She also told me her name and that of her husband, so they could be recorded in the baptismal register. She opened her satchel, which contained some precious things, and gave my wife and child, the maid, and another woman so much that they might well be satisfied with her. While she was thus busy, having told us of her husband and commended the child to our care, she died on our hands. There being so much confusion in the country that no one could stay at home, we could hardly find a parson for the funeral and the christening. But when both were done, our mayor and our parson ordered me to raise the child to manhood; for my trouble and expense I was to keep the woman's legacy, except several prayer books, precious stones, and some odds and ends, which I was to hold in trust for the child. So my wife raised the boy on goat's milk, and we were glad to keep him, thinking that when he grew up we'd give him to our daughter in marriage. But after the battle of Nördlingen we lost the girl and the boy and everything I owned."

I said to my knan, "You have told me a nice story, and yet you forgot to tell me the most important part: you didn't tell the names of the woman or the husband or the child." "Sir," he answered, "I didn't think you wanted to know. The lady's name was Susanna Ramsay, her husband was Captain Sternfels von Fuchshaim, and since my name is Melchior, I had the boy baptized Melchior Sternfels von Fuchshaim, and that is how he's recorded in the register."

From this story I found out that I was the son of the hermit and Governor Ramsay's sister, but much too late, for my parents were both dead; and about my Uncle Ramsay I could learn only that the people of Hanau had sent him and his

Swedish garrison packing, and that this had made him madder than a hornet.

I completely drowned my godfather in wine, and the next day I sent for his wife. When I made myself known to them, they did not want to believe me until I showed them the hairy birthmark on my chest.

CHAPTER 9: *How Simplicius suffers childbirth pains and becomes a widower once more*

Not much later I rode down into the Spessart with my godfather, in order to get definite information and to obtain documents concerning my birth; these were given to me without trouble, on the basis of my godfather's statements and the entry in the baptismal register. I also stopped to see the parson who had been in Hanau and taken care of me there. He gave me a written testimonial concerning the place where my father had died, the fact that I had been with him until his death, and finally, that for a while I had been with Mr. Ramsay, the governor of Hanau. In fact, I collected various statements from witnesses and had my life history written up and certified by a notary public, for I thought that one never knows where it will come in handy. This trip cost me more than four hundred thalers, for on the way back we were caught and robbed by a foraging party, and my godfather (or knan) and I, having lost our shirts, barely came away with our lives.

Meanwhile, matters at home were getting worse, for when my wife found out that her husband was a nobleman, she not only played the great lady but also let the household go completely to pot. Since she was pregnant, I put up with it in silence. Moreover, some cattle disease had killed off most of my best animals.

I could have taken all this in my stride; but Jupiter Pluvius, it never rains but it pours! When my wife had been delivered, the hired girl was also brought to bed with child.

Her baby looked like me, to be sure; but the one my wife bore was the image of the hired man. On top of that, the same night the lady mentioned above [5] deposited a baby at my door, with a written message saying I was the father, so that all at once I had three children on my hands, and I expected more to come crawling out of the corners. This gave me a lot of gray hair; but that's how it is when one leads a godless and despicable life, as I had done by yielding to carnal desires.

What could be done? I had to have the children baptized and, in addition, pay the fine for adultery. And because the Swedes were in command at that time and I had served under imperial colors, I was fined much more heavily. Yet, all this was only a prelude to utter ruin, which was approaching. Though these many unfortunate accidents troubled me profoundly, my darling wife made light of them; in fact, she joked day and night about the handsome gift that had been laid at my door, and about my having been fined a pretty penny. If she had known about me and the hired girl, she would have treated me worse. But that good creature was nice enough to let me (and an amount equal to the fine I would have had to pay) persuade her to designate as the father of her child some dandy who, about a year ago, had been at my house for the wedding, but whom she otherwise hardly knew. Still, she had to leave the house, for my wife suspected what was on my mind concerning her and the hired man. But for all that, she could not say anything; for otherwise I could have reproached her, telling her that I could not have been with her and the hired girl at the same time. However, what worried me was the fact that I should bring up the hired man's child, while my own would not be my heir, and, moreover, that I had to keep still and be glad that no one else knew about it.

Every day such thoughts tormented me, while my wife was swilling wine at all hours, for since our wedding she had become so used to drink that she seldom was without it and

[5] As Courage tells it, the pseudo-elegant Simplicius was a deceiver whom she deceived: the child she deposited at his door was not hers at all; her maid had obtained the baby from a total stranger.

never went to bed sober. This soon caused her child's death and inflamed her bowels so much that she died, making me a widower a second time. I took this so much to heart that I almost laughed myself sick.

CHAPTER 10: *What the peasants tell about the weird Mummelsee*

When I saw myself thus restored to pristine freedom—but with a purse almost empty of money and a household burdened with many head of cattle and servants—I adopted my godfather Melchior as my father; my godmother, his wife, as my mother; and the bastard Simplicius who had been placed at my door, for my heir. To these two old folks I handed over my house and lands and all property, except a very few gold coins and jewelry, which I had saved up for emergencies. Since my bad experiences with them, I so loathed the company and cohabitation of women that I made up my mind never to get married again. But the old couple, who were hard to equal in farm experience, immediately rearranged my household: they got rid of those hired hands and animals that were no good. My old knan and mither spoke of better things to come and promised (if I let them manage) always to have a good horse in the stable for me and to earn enough to allow me to sit down over a bottle of wine with any honest man. I noticed right away what kind of people were running my farm: my godfather and the hired hands did the field work—he was sharper than a Jew when he sold cattle, timber, or resin; and my godmother knew how to get dairy money and hold onto it better than ten wives of the sort I had had. Therefore, after a short time, my farm was stocked with everything necessary, including animals small and big, and it was soon considered the best in the country. Meanwhile, I went walking for pleasure and indulged in all sorts of meditations, for when I saw that my godmother realized more from the bees, through wax and honey, than my wife used to get from beef, pork, and such, I was satisfied that she would not be caught napping in other matters.

One day I went to the spa, intending more to take a drink of fresh water than to get acquainted with the dandies (as I used to do), for I had begun to imitate the economizing of my old folks, who advised me against associating much with people who wantonly waste their parents' substance and their own. Just the same, I fell in with a group of middle-class people, because they were talking about a strange subject, to wit, the Mummelsee, a bottomless lake located on one of the highest mountains in the vicinity. They had sent for some old-timers who were telling strange things they had heard about this unusual body of water. Listening to their stories gave me great enjoyment, though I considered them no more than old wives' tales, and some sounded as mendacious as the stories of Pliny.

One said that if an odd number of items—peas or pebbles or something else, it didn't matter what—were tied in a handkerchief and dipped in the water, the count was changed to even; likewise if one dipped in an even number, an odd number would come out. Someone else (and almost everybody with him) asserted, and confirmed by examples, that if one rock or several were thrown in, no matter how serene the sky had been before, immediately a severe thunderstorm would arise, with frightful rains, hailstones, and gusts of wind. From this topic they proceeded to all sorts of stories of strange happenings at this lake: fantastic appearances of earth spirits and water sprites, and what they had said to people. One man told how once, while some herders were grazing their cattle by the lake, a brown ox had come out of the water. He had mixed with the other cattle, but a little man had come after him to drive him back into the water; and when the ox did not want to return, the little man had wished all the troubles of mankind on him. Then the ox and the little man had gone back into the lake. Another said that once when the lake was frozen over, a peasant had driven across his ox team and a load of timber without a crack appearing in the ice; but when his dog came after him, the ice broke and the poor dog went down and was never seen again. Still another asserted as true the story of a hunter who, following the tracks of his quarry and passing by the lake, had seen a water sprite sitting on the surface with a whole lapful of gold coins, which he was playing with. When the hunter had been about to fire at the sprite, the latter had ducked down and shouted, "If you had asked me to help you in your poverty, I would have made you and your family rich."

I listened and laughed at these and similar stories, which sounded like fairy tales for entertaining children, but I did not believe even that such an abyss could exist on a high mountain. But there were others, old and trustworthy peasants, who said that in their own and their fathers' memories, august, princely persons had gone up to see the lake: one ruling duke of Württemberg had had a raft built, on which to go out on the lake and measure its depth. After the measurers had dropped a plumb with nine thread-nets (that's a length of yarn, about which the peasant women in the Black Forest know more than I or any surveyor) and still had not hit bottom, the raft had started going down—contrary to the nature of wood—so that those on board had had to give up their undertaking in order to save themselves by swimming to shore. In commemoration of this event, one could still see pieces of the raft on the lake shore, and the Württemberg arms and other designs carved in stone there. Still others proved through many witnesses that an archduke of Austria had wanted to drain the lake, but many people had tried to dissuade him, and the petitions of the country people had thwarted his plan; they were afraid the whole countryside might perish and drown. Furthermore, an Austrian archduke had put several barrels of trout into the lake, but all of them had died within an hour, right before his eyes, and had floated out the mouth of the lake, regardless of the fact that the river in these hills contains such fish and the outlet of the lake flows into the same river.

CHAPTER 11: *Unheard-of gratitude from a patient almost causes Simplicius to have holy thoughts*

The last story almost made me believe the earlier ones, and my curiosity was so aroused that I decided to have a look at this miraculous lake. Concerning its name, those who had been talking gave different and contradictory opinions. I said the German name "Mummelsee" meant that the lake wore a mummery or disguise, as at a masquerade, so that not everyone could fathom its true nature or depth (which had never been fathomed, even though important personages had tried). Then I went to the place where, a year ago, I had seen my late wife and drunk for the first time the sweet poison of love. I lay down once again in the shade and the green grass, but I no longer paid any attention to what the nightingales were piping; rather, I contemplated the changes I had suffered lately. I considered that at this very place I had begun to turn from a free man into a slave of love; that since then I had changed from an officer into a peasant, from a rich widower into a husband, from a husband into a cuckold, and from a cuckold back into a widower; and that likewise I had turned from a peasant's son into the son of an honest soldier, and again into the son of my knan. I pondered how, since then, fate had robbed me of Heartbrother and replaced him with an aged couple. I thought of my father's blessed life and death, of the pitiful death of my mother, and of the various changes to which I had been subjected all my days, and I could not keep from crying. And while I was thinking of all the money I had gotten and squandered during my life (and regretting it), along came two old topers or drunks (they were taking the waters for their palsy) and sat down near me, finding this a good place to rest. They were telling each other their troubles, for they thought they were alone. They were disgusted with their doctors, but I won't go into that, for the doctors might not like me if I did, and next time they might give me a purge that would expurgate my soul. I mention this only because one of these oldsters was thanking God for not having more money. That expression of gratitude removed from my mind all the sadness I felt at the time. I resolved to strive neither for honor, nor for money, nor for anything else the world loves. I resolved to take up philosophy, to endeavor to live a life that would please God, and especially to repent of my recalcitrance and try, like my late father, to climb the highest rungs on the ladder of virtue.

CHAPTER 12: *How Simplicius travels with the sylphs to the center of the earth*

My desire to see the Mummelsee increased when my godfather told me that he had been there and knew the way. But when he heard that I had set my mind on seeing it, he said, "What good will it do you to go there? You and I will see nothing but the image of a lake that's located in the middle of a great forest. And when you have paid for your present enthusiasm with laborious disenthusiasm, you will have regrets and tired feet (for one can't ride there), and the trip down for the trip up. Nobody could have dragged me there if I had not been forced to hide there when Dr. Daniel (he meant the Duc d'Enghien [6]) was marching down from Philippsburg." But my curiosity and I paid no attention to his advice, and I found another guide to take me there. Now, when he saw I was serious, he said that since the oats were in and there wasn't much to do on the farm, he would go with me to show the way, for he loved me and did not want to let me out of his sight. And because the people in the neighborhood believed I was his own son, he liked to show off with me

[6] Philippsburg was captured in succession by the Swedish, the French, the imperials (under von Götz), and again by the French in 1644. The Duc d'Enghien is Louis II, the Great Condé, who commanded French armies with Turenne.

and behaved toward me and others as might a common poor man whose son has become a great man solely through Fortune and without the father's help and furtherance.

So we hiked together over hills and valleys, and before we had been gone six hours we came to the Mummelsee, for my godfather walked like a beetle and was as fit as a youngster. There we ate the food we had taken with us, because the long way and the climb had made us hungry. Having finished, I looked at the lake and saw lying in it several pieces of hewn timber that my knan and I recognized as parts of the Württemberg raft. I surveyed the extent of the lake by means of geometry, since it was very difficult to walk around it and measure it by paces or feet. I entered its dimensions in my notebook and made a sketch of it in reduced scale. And when I had finished with that, I wanted to find out if it were true that a thunderstorm came up whenever a rock was thrown in: the sky was clear, and the air still and warm. I had already found by the mineral taste of the water that no trout could live in the lake.

In order to start work on my experiment, I walked along the left-hand side of the shore to a place where the water, which is crystal clear otherwise, appears to be pitch black, because of the depth of the lake. For this reason it looks so frightening that the very sight terrifies a person. Here I started throwing in rocks so big I could hardly carry them. My godfather or knan not only refused to help me, but also warned me as much as he could and asked me to desist, but I busily continued. Rocks that were too large and heavy to carry I rolled toward the lake until I had thrown in about thirty. Then black clouds began to cover the sky and violent thunder was heard. My godfather, who stood on the opposite shore by the outlet and deplored my work, shouted to me to find a safe place lest the rain and the storm or even worse misfortune overtake us. But I answered him, "Dad, I want to stay and see the end of this, even if it rains pitchforks." "You," answered my knan, "behave like all these reckless brats who don't give a damn if the world goes to pieces."

While listening to his grumbling, I did not turn my eyes away from the deep part of the lake, so that I might notice if bubbles or air rose from the bottom, as usually happens if one throws rocks into deep water. But I saw nothing of the kind. Rather, far away in the direction of the abyss I saw several creatures fluttering about in the water. Their shape reminded me of frogs, and they flitted about as sparks fly from a rocket that's rising into the air. And as they approached me more and more closely, they seemed larger and taller and shaped more like human beings. I first felt great amazement and then, because they were so close to me, terror and repugnance. Moved by horror and wonder, I said to myself, yet so loud that my knan, standing on the opposite shore, could hear me above the thunder, "Alas, how great are the creations of our Maker, even in the bowels of the earth and the depths of the water!" I had hardly finished speaking when one of these sylphs appeared on the surface of the water and answered, "Behold! This you acknowledge before you have seen anything of it. What would you say if you were in the center of the earth and saw our dwellings, which your curiosity has disturbed?" Meanwhile, similar watermen emerged like ducks bobbing up. They all looked at me and returned the rocks I had thrown in. This amazed me. The first and foremost among the sprites, whose dress glittered with gold and silver, threw me a sparkling stone the size of a pigeon's egg, green and transparent like an emerald, and said, "Take this jewel so that you have something to tell about us and this lake." I had hardly picked it up and put it away when I felt as if the air was suffocating or drowning me. I could no longer stand up but reeled about like a yarn spool and finally fell into the lake. No sooner was I in the water than I recovered, and by virtue of the stone I used water instead of air for breathing. Like the little waterman, I could easily locomote in the lake and moved with the sprites into the deep part. The whole thing reminded me of a flock of birds descending in curves from the uppermost parts of the air to the ground.

My knan, having seen this marvel in part (namely, the part

that took place above the surface), together with my sudden fit, took off from the lake and headed for home as if his head were on fire. There he told the whole sequence of events, but particularly how, during the thunderstorm, the sprites had brought up the rocks I had thrown into the lake and put them in their old places; and how, in turn, they had taken me down with them. Some people believed him, but most thought it was a cock-and-bull story. Still others suspected that, like a second Empedocles (who jumped into the crater of Mt. Etna), I had drowned myself in the lake and asked my father to spread these tales so that I should gain notoriety, because they had noticed that for some time I had been in melancholy humor, almost desperate, and so on. Others wanted to believe that my adopted father had murdered me (except I was stronger than he), so that the old miser would be sole owner of my farm. So, at this time the conversation in the spa and the surrounding countryside was about nothing but the Mummelsee, about me, my departure, and my godfather.

CHAPTER 13: *The prince of the Mummelsee tells of the sylphs' life and origin*

[Summary: The prince of the Mummelsee takes Simplicius down to the center of the earth, a distance of 4,500 miles. On the way they talk, and the prince tells him that lakes have a threefold purpose: first, to fasten the oceans to the earth, as with nails; secondly, to allow the water sprites to distribute the oceans' waters to the earth through wells, creeks, lakes, rivers, and so on; and thirdly, to permit the sprites to live in them like reasonable creatures of God, attend to their business, and praise the Creator. If the sprites were to cease working, the world would perish and regenerate itself through a fire started by the heat of the sun. They are mortal creatures who rank below human beings (the scale being: angels, humans, sprites, and animals), for Christ has not redeemed them. They know the will of God, are always healthy

and therefore long-lived, free, knowledgeable in sciences and
arts, not sinful and hence not subject to punishment or God's
anger. Simplicius is bursting with questions: How can the
sprites be free if they have a king? How are they born, and
how do they die? Female sprites, he is told, conceive without
pleasure and bear without pain; death to a sprite is painless—
as if a light has gone out. Their freedom is unimpaired, for
they can traverse fire, water, air, and earth without effort and
without fatigue. Simplicius concludes that the sprites must be
happier than men, but he is corrected: men have souls; they
are able to aspire to eternal bliss and to look upon the face
of God. In his sight men enjoy in one moment more happiness than the whole tribe of the sprites has had or will have
from the beginning of creation till doomsday.]

CHAPTER 14: *What Simplicius discussed with the prince en*
route, and the strange and marvelous things
he heard

[Summary: Simplicius is informed by his companion, the
"little prince," that the rocks which people throw into lakes
have to be removed so that the communication of one body
of water with another is not impeded; and in order to discourage human beings from needlessly throwing in rocks, the
sprites stir up thunderstorms.

[In answer to Simplicius' question about the difference in
waters, the prince explains that the waters assume different
qualities as they pass through metals or semi-elements like sulphur, salts of various kinds, vitriol, alum, antimony, and so
on. Fire in the earth warms the water. Much of this information is provided in great detail.

[Simplicius asks if he could leave by a different outlet than
the Mummelsee. "Of course," is the reply. Ancestors of the
sprites guided some Canaanites to America: they had escaped
the sword of Joshua and in despair had thrown themselves
into a lake. When Simplicius is amazed by this, the little

prince is astounded at his amazement, and Simplicius asks whether the sprites don't find humans astonishing. "No," he says, "the only thing amazing about humans is the way they throw away their chances of eternal bliss. If only the sprites had this human privilege of proving themselves worthy in the sight of God." Toward the end of this discussion Simplicius and the little prince are approaching the king's court.]

CHAPTER 15: *What the king discussed with Simplicius, and Simplicius with the king*

[Summary: In contrast to royal courts on earth, the king of the sprites keeps a simple household. Yet all the princes of the various lakes and seas are present, and all are dressed in their national costumes; it's like a picture book. The king asks why Simplicius created a disturbance in his realm and is astonished to learn that the culprit has already resigned himself to dying for the offense. The king then asks Simplicius why humans persist in vice, though the millenium is reported to be near. If the earth must perish by fire, the sprites will also suffer death. As a Christian, Simplicius may have more precise information than that which is available to the sprites and sylphs. Simplicius pleads ignorance of such high matters; nevertheless, the king urges him to tell what he knows about conditions on earth.

[In obvious satire, Simplicius describes the priests, rulers, merchants, doctors and pharmacists, craftsmen, and others, as they should be, not as they are. On earth, he says, pride, envy, anger, lechery, debauchery, laziness, and so on, are unknown. Wars are caused only by excessive zeal in God's behalf.]

CHAPTER 16: *News from the depths of the bottomless sea called Mare del Sur*

[Summary: Simplicius goes on a sight-seeing tour through the subterranean realm. A delegation is just leaving for the

Mare del Sur,[7] and Simplicius joins them. On the way he is to think of a keepsake he would like to take back to earth.

[On the bottom of the South Sea he marvels at coral growths as big as oak trees. From these the sylphs gather food. He also sees giant snails, and pearls big as hens' eggs—and just as edible. The ground is strewn with emeralds, turquoise, rubies, diamonds, sapphires, and other precious stones, many as big as the rocks one finds in mountain streams on earth. Projecting cliffs are inhabited by strange crawling, stationary, or walking creatures, and the fish that swim about remind him of birds. Since it is night, he can see the full moon, the stars, and the antarctic pole. The various water inhabitants are dressed in different national costumes, but all speak German and understand Simplicius perfectly. This easy communication is possible because the sprites had nothing to do with that terrestrial aberration, the Tower of Babel. Thus they have been spared the consequences thereof.]

When my convoy had picked up enough food, we returned through another shaft from the ocean to the center of the earth. On the way I said to someone that I thought the center of the earth was hollow and that the Pygmies [8] were running around in it, as on a treadmill, and thereby turning the earth so that all of it received the rays of the sun (which, according to the opinion of Aristarchus and Copernicus, stood still in the middle of the heavens [9]). I got the horselaugh for this idea and was told to consider the opinions of the two scholars quoted, plus my own notion on the subject, as no more than a silly dream. Instead I should think of the gift I wanted from their king, lest I return empty-handed to the shores of earth. I replied that the marvels I had seen up to that point had so confused me that I could think of nothing at all, and I asked to be advised about what I might request from the king. My

7 The Pacific Ocean.

8 Dwarfs of Greek mythology.

9 Aristarchus of Samos (ca. 250 B.C.) was the first to maintain that the earth moves around the sun, a theory that Copernicus confirmed in 1530. The water people have not yet heard of it.

own idea was to ask for a well with medicinal properties, to be located in my own back yard, for wasn't their king the ruler of all the fountains in the world? The regent of the Pacific Ocean and its abysses replied that to grant this would be beyond the king's power, and even if he could do it, and wanted to please me, such fountains never lasted long. I asked him the reason for this. He answered that throughout the earth there are empty pockets which gradually fill up with all sorts of metals generated there by various exhalations. Sometimes water from the center seeps into these pockets, where it stays many centuries and assumes the noble virtues and medicinal properties of the metals. As the water presses on from the center and seeks and finds an outlet on the surface, that part of the water which was enclosed by the metals for so many hundreds, even thousands, of years gushes out first and acts on human bodies with the miraculous effects observed in newly discovered spas. But as soon as the metallically charged water has flowed off, common water follows. To be sure, it too has come through the same passages, but in its rapid flow it cannot take on the virtues and powers of the metals, and thus it cannot be as effective as the first liquid. I thanked him for this information and told him I'd like nothing better than to own such a well. This would help my fellow humans, would bestow honor on their king, and would enhance my name and keep me in eternal remembrance. The prince then answered that if this was what I wanted, he would support my request, though their king paid no attention whatever to the reputation he might enjoy on earth, be it good or bad. Now we had come again to the center of the earth and within the king's court, where he and his courtiers were about to eat. It was a light meal, at which neither wine nor strong drink was used; the guests consumed pearls that had not yet hardened like so many raw or soft-boiled eggs. These provided good nourishment and strength.

I observed that the sun shone on one sea after another, sending its rays all the way down into these abysmal depths, so that the sylphs were never without light. The sun shone at this distance as brightly as on earth, and the shadows were sharply outlined. For the sylphs, the seas are like windows through which they receive both light and heat. And if the sun does not come through directly (some seas being rather bent and crooked), reflection takes over, for nature has placed whole rocks of crystal, diamonds, and garnets in such a way that they convey the light downward.

CHAPTER 17: *Return from the earth's center; strange notions, castles in Spain, the making of schedules, and a reckoning without the host*

Meanwhile the time for my departure was approaching, and the king ordered me to let him know how he could do me a favor. I spoke up and said he could do me no greater favor than sending a regular mineral spring to my farm. "Is that all?" answered the king, "I would have thought that you might have brought along several large emeralds from the American sea and asked permission to take them with you to earth. Now I see that there is no avarice among you Christians." And with these words he handed me a stone of strangely varying color and said, "Put this in your pocket. Wherever you deposit it on earth, it will begin seeking the center. It will proceed through the most convenient minerals until it returns to us. We shall then send you a medicinal fountain of the first water, which will enhance and advance you to the extent that you have merited by revealing the truth to us." Then the prince of the Mummelsee asked me to follow him, and together we returned through the same passages by which we had come.

This return trip seemed much farther than the journey down, because the prince and I did not talk much, except for his telling me that the sprites got to be three, four, or five hundred years old and lived all that time without illness. Moreover, in my mind I had already become rich through my mineral spring, and I was occupying all my sagacity and thought in wondering where to locate it and how to make the most of it. I was already drawing up plans for the substantial buildings which would be needed to accommodate the guests and which would enable me to charge dearly for lodgings. I was thinking of the palm grease by which I would persuade the doctors to prefer my new miracle spa to all others (even the one at Schwalbach [10]), so that I'd have crowds of rich guests. I was already moving whole mountains in order that people arriving or departing would not complain about bad roads. I was hiring clever factotums, frugal cooks, circumspect house-maids, watchful hostlers, neat attendants of baths and foun-tains. I was thinking of a place right in the middle of wild mountains, not far from my farm, where I would create a beautiful, parklike garden with all sorts of rare plants, a place in which foreign guests and their ladies could promenade, where the sick could find recreation, and the healthy could delight in games and outdoor exercise. For a fee, the doctors were to compose an eloquent brochure concerning my water and its precious qualities; then I'd have a picture of my farm drawn in outline, have the whole thing printed, and any pa-tient who hadn't yet arrived could read himself half well and hope for the best. I sent for all my children in Lippstadt and let them learn all sorts of trades and professions that would be of use in the new resort. But none of them needed to learn how to be a bloodletting barber-surgeon; I'd do all the blood-letting myself—if not of bodies, then of purses.

Being absorbed in such multifarious thoughts and overly happy with planning, I returned to the air, for the prince put me ashore, at the edge of his Mummelsee, in completely dry clothes. I had to put away the jewel he had given me when he first called for me, or I would have either drowned in air or have had to put my head under water to breathe. When he had taken the jewel back, we took leave of one another as people do who will never see each other again. He ducked

10 Langenschwalbach, not far from Wiesbaden.

under the water and returned with his retinue to the deep; but I, happy about the stone that the king had given me, walked away with it as if I had carried off the Golden Fleece of Colchis.

But, alas, my joy, which was based on a nonexistent constancy, did not last very long. For I had hardly left the miraculous lake when I got lost in the large wood, because when my knan brought me there I had not paid enough attention. I had walked quite a distance before I noticed my predicament, for I was still hard at work planning the spa and getting rich without working too hard. In this manner I got farther and farther away from the place to which I wanted to go, and—even worse—I didn't notice it until the sun was down, and I didn't know what to do next. There I stood, Henry Helpless in the middle of the wilds, with nothing to eat and no gun, either of which would have been good to have as night fell. But the rock I had brought from the bowels of the earth consoled me. I said to myself, "Patience, patience, Simpli; this rock will repay you for all your suffering. Rome was not built in a day, and great enterprises are not developed without work and sweat. Otherwise, without puffing and without mopping his brow, any fool could produce such a wonderful spa as you are carrying in your pocket."

When I had thus encouraged myself, I felt better and used my feet faster, though night had already come. There was a bright, full moon, but the fir trees kept out the light better than had the deep sea earlier that day. Still, I made headway, and around midnight I noticed a fire in the distance and I went straight for it. I knew it was peasants who had something to do with resin, and though such fellows can't be trusted at all times, necessity and my own inclination made me address them. I sneaked up on them and suddenly said to them, "Good night or good day, good morning or good evening, gentlemen! First tell me the time, so I'll know how to greet you." All six of them stood or sat there shaking and didn't know how to answer. Because I am rather tall and was in mourning on account of my wife's recent death, and because I carried a frightening cudgel on which I was leaning like a wild mountain-man, I appeared like a terror to them. "What?" I said. "Does no one want to answer?" They still kept quiet for some time. Finally one had sufficiently recovered to ask, "End who ish the chentleman?" I gathered that he was a Swabian (they are often considered doltish, though for no good reason), and I said I was a traveling scholar who had just now returned from the Mountain of Venus, where I had learned a heap of strange tricks. "Ho-ho!" said the oldest peasant. "Now I think I'll live to see the time of peace return, for the students are beginning to travel once more."

CHAPTER 18: *Simplicius plants his spring in the wrong woods*

So we entered into conversation, and they asked me politely to sit down by the fire with them. They offered me a piece of bread and some cheese made of skim milk, both of which I accepted. In the end they became so friendly that they asked me, as a student, to tell their fortunes. And since I have some knowledge of palmistry and physiognomy, I started pulling their leg, telling each what I thought he would like to hear, lest I lose face among these wild men of the woods, with whom I did not feel altogether comfortable. They also wanted to learn smart tricks from me, but I put them off till next day, saying that I wanted to sleep a while first. I went aside a little and lay down, more to listen to them and to find out what they thought of me than to sleep, though my appetite for that was great enough too. The louder I snored, the more watchful they were. They put their heads together and took turns guessing who I might be. They didn't think I was a soldier because of my black dress; and they didn't think I was a burgher because I dropped in on them like a fly in the soup at such an unusual time and so far from civilization. They finally agreed that I must be a journeyman who had at one time been a college student, because I could soothsay so well. "But," said one, "he didn't know everything. I think he's a soldier in disguise who wants to spy on us and drive off our cattle. I wish we knew; we'd rock him to sleep so he'd forget to wake up!" Another quickly said that he thought I was something else. Meanwhile I lay there, keeping my ears pricked, and thought, If these hayseeds attack me, two or three of them will have to bite the dust before they lay me out.

While the peasants were deliberating and I was agitating my mind, I suddenly felt as if someone had peed in bed, for the spot where I lay got all wet. Oh, horrors! Then I realized that noble Troy and all my marvelous plans were lost, for by the smell I knew it was my mineral spring. Anger and chagrin put me into such a rage that I almost went after the six peasants in order to beat them up. "You goddamn louts!" I shouted, jumping up and shaking my cudgel at them. "This mineral spring's coming up here, in the place where I was sleeping, will tell you who I am. For two cents I'd skin you alive and let the devil take you to hell with him. You and your evil thoughts!" The ghastly expression on my face terrified them all. But soon I came to and realized the folly I was committing. No, I thought, It is better to lose the mineral spring than to lose my life; and that would be easy to do if I attacked these yokels. So I spoke kindly to them once more, and before they could think of something, I said, "Get up and try the wonderful mineral spring that, from now on, you and all the other forest workers will be able to enjoy because I was here." They couldn't make head or tail of what I was saying and were looking at each other like animated stockfish, until they saw that I—sober as a judge—took the first drink of water from my hat. Then one after the other got up from the fire around which they had been sitting, looked at the miracle, and tried the water. But instead of being grateful for it, they started cursing and saying they wished that I and my mineral spring had gotten lost somewhere else, for if their master found it out, the whole county of Dornstedt would have to do forced labor and build roads, and that would be a great inconvenience to them. "On the other hand,"

I replied, "you will all benefit. You can sell your chickens, eggs, butter, beef, and so on, at better prices." "Naw," they said, "the master will put a manager here, and he'll get rich while we must take the short end and keep up the roads and trails; and we won't even get a 'thank you' for it."

After a while they disagreed; two of them wanted to keep the spring, and four wanted me to get rid of it. If it had been in my power I would have done the latter, even without their suggestion, whether they liked it or not.

Since daylight had come and I had nothing else to do there, and since, moreover, there was the risk of a fight if the argument went on, I said, "If you don't want all the cows in the valley of Bayersbrunn to give red milk so long as the mineral spring is running, you had better show me the way to Seebach." They agreed and sent two fellows along with me, for one man alone with me would have been too frightened.

So I left, and although the whole region is infertile and bears nothing but pine cones, I felt even more like cursing it, for I had lost all my hope there. But I went quietly off with my two guides until I came to the highest place in those hills, from which I could tell approximately where I was. There I said to them, "Gentlemen, you can make a good thing out of your new mineral spring. Go to your lord and announce the discovery, and he'll give you a good reward. The prince will develop it as an ornament and an asset to his land, and he'll have it made known to the whole world, in order to increase his emoluments." "Well," they said, "what kind of fools do you think we are? Shall we offer him the rod with which to strike us? We'd rather you go to hell with your mineral spring. You heard why we don't like it."

I answered, "Oh, you hopeless drips, I ought to call you lazy beggars because you leave the ways of your rugged ancestors so far behind. They were so loyal to their prince that he could boast he might lay his head in the lap of any of his subjects and sleep there in safety.[11] But you lazybones are far

---

[11] Duke Eberhart im Barte (1445–1496), who was held in high esteem by his people, made this claim.

different, just because you are afraid of a little work, for which
in time you will be repaid, and which all your descendants
would amply enjoy. To disclose the presence of this spring
would be in the interest of your prince, and to the benefit and
health of many suffering sick people. What's the difference if
each of you spends a few days at forced labor?" "What?!" they
shouted. "We'd rather kill *you* with forced labor, so that your
mineral spring stays unknown." "You crazy birds," I said,
"that would require more of you than there are!" And, swing-
ing my cudgel, I chased them off in the name of St. Velten.[12]
Then I went downhill, and after much trouble I got back to
my farm about nightfall. Thus I found out what my knan had
told me before, namely, that I'd have tired legs from this
pilgrimage, and the trip down for the trip up.

CHAPTER 19: *A short chapter on the Hungarian Anabaptists
and their manner of life*

After my return home I kept to myself. My greatest joy was
to pore over books, of which I acquired many. I studied
all sorts of subjects, especially those demanding thought and
reflection, but I soon tired of what the schoolmasters and
pedants know. Arithmetic also bored me, and music became
as hateful as the plague: soon I smashed my lute to bits. I put
up with mathematics and geometry, but as soon as they led me
into astronomy, I gave them up and pursued astronomy and
astrology. For some time I enjoyed these, but then they appeared so false and uncertain that I no longer wanted to
trouble about them. Now I reached for the *Ars magna* of
Raymundus Lullus,[13] but I found it to be a lot of hot air and

12 St. Velten is a euphemism for the devil.

13 Ramon Lull (*ca.* 1235–1315) was a Catalan philosopher who invented
the *Ars magna*, an arrangement in which the letters of the alphabet
designate basic concepts, while their interrelation is indicated by geo-
metrical figures. *Topica* is the title of one of Aristotle's works. It deals
with the various general forms of argument employed in probable, as

little substance; and because I considered it a *topica* I soon gave it up and got busy with the Hebrew cabbala and Egyptian hieroglyphics. In the end I found that among all the arts and sciences none is better than theology so long as it teaches a person to love God and serve him. According to its precepts I devised for people a kind of life that could be more angelic than human. A group of married as well as unmarried men and women would have to join together and, under a wise leader, earn their living by manual labor like the Anabaptists; the rest of the time they would exert themselves in the praise of God and the salvation of their souls.

In Hungary I had seen this kind of life on the Hutterite farms.[14] I would have joined them if these good people had not become mixed up in, and dedicated to, a false and heretical doctrine contrary to the general Christian church. At least I considered their life the most blessed on earth, for they appeared to me in their activities very much like the Essenes described by Josephus and others.[15] First of all, they had treasures laid up and more than enough to eat; yet they wasted nothing. One heard no grumbling or cursing among them, not even unnecessary words. I saw craftsmen working in their shops as if they were doing piecework. Their schoolmaster taught the children as if they were all his own. Nowhere did one see men and women mixed; each sex was doing its assigned work in its assigned place. I saw lying-in rooms where

distinguished from demonstrative, reasoning, and the sources from which arguments may be derived or to which they may be referred.

14 The Hutterites have practiced their form of Christian communal life since the time of the Reformation. Their enemies called them Anabaptists, and after some excesses on their part under Thomas Münzer at Münster, they were violently persecuted in Germany. Their Hungarian community flourished until, under Maria Theresa's direction, all Hutterites were forcibly converted to Catholicism. Many of them escaped to Russia; and when pressure there drove them out, they came to Canada, the United States, and Paraguay. At present, communities exist in Manitoba, Alberta, Ontario, South Dakota, Montana, and near Primavera.

15 The Essenes, a Jewish sect described by Josephus in his *Jewish War* (II. 119–161 and elsewhere), in many ways resembled the early Christians.

there were only young mothers, who were well taken care of—
as were the babies—by other young mothers, without the interference of husbands. Other special rooms contained nothing but babies in cradles; women fed the babies and kept
them clean and cared for them. The mothers came in only
three times a day in order to breast-feed the infants. Only
widows were used as children's nurses. In another hall women
were working at more than a hundred spinning and carding
wheels. Some women were exclusively laundresses, some bed-
makers, cattle-feeders, waitresses, in charge of china or linen,
and so on; each had her job and knew how to do it. Similarly,
the men had their assigned activities. If a person got sick, he
or she had a special nurse; and there was a doctor and phar-
macist for the group, though because of good food and healthy
living hardly anyone was ill. I saw many an old person living
quietly to an extreme age among them, and that is seldom
found elsewhere. They had their appointed hours for eating,
for sleeping, for working, but not a single minute for play
or for promenading, except for the youngsters. After each
meal, for the sake of health, the youngsters went walking for
an hour with their teacher. During this time they also had to
pray and sing hymns. There was no anger, no zealotry, no
vengefulness, no envy, no enmity, no worry about worldly
goods, no pride, no regret. In short, there prevailed such
lovely harmony as seemed to purport nothing but the honorable increase of the human race and of God's kingdom. No
man saw his wife except when he met with her at the appointed hour in their bedroom, which contained nothing but
their well-made bed plus a chamber pot, a washbasin, a
pitcher filled with water, and a white towel, so that he could
fall asleep and go to work next morning with clean hands.
They all called each other "brother" and "sister," and yet
such familiarity never caused lewdness.

I thought that if I could initiate such a commendable Christian way of life, under the protection of my sovereign, I'd be
a second St. Dominic or St. Francis. Oh, if only I could con-

vert the Anabaptists so that they might in turn teach our
fellow Christians their way of living, how blessed I would be!
Or if only I could persuade my fellow Christians to lead such
a (seemingly) Christian and commendable life as do the Anabaptists, what an achievement I would have to my credit! To
myself I said, "You fool, why do you bother about other people? Become a Capuchin monk; you are through with women
anyway." But then I considered that tomorrow I might feel
differently, and who knows what means I might require to
walk rightly in the way of Christ. Today I inclined to chastity;
tomorrow I might burn.

For a long time I went around with such thoughts; I would
have been glad to dedicate my farm and my entire fortune to
such a Christian association, and I would gladly have been a
member of it. But my knan frankly predicted that I'd never
assemble such a group.

CHAPTER 20: *An entertaining promenade from the Black
Forest to Moscow in Russia*

That autumn, French, Swedish, and Hessian armies were
approaching our part of the country in order to recuperate
there and at the same time to keep blockaded the neighboring
imperial free city of Offenburg. Therefore, everybody fled
with his cattle and his most precious belongings into the deep-
est forests. I followed my neighbors' example and left my
house quite empty. A retired Swedish colonel was quartered
there, and he found a few books in my room, for in the general hurry I had not been able to get everything out of the
way. Among these were mathematics and geometry handbooks, some on the theory of fortification (such as engineers
use), and he concluded that the house couldn't belong to an
ordinary peasant. So he made inquiries and tried to meet
me. By a mixture of courteous invitations and threats he got
me to come to my own farm, where he treated me quite po-

litely and ordered his people not to destroy or to ruin anything of mine wantonly. Through such friendliness he got me
to tell him of my background, particularly about my family
and descent. He was greatly astonished that I was living
among peasants right in the midst of the war, that I was willing to look on while someone else tied his horse to my fence
rail since it behooved me to tie mine to someone else's. He
said I should take up the sword once more and not let the
gifts that God had bestowed on me languish behind the stove
and the plow. If I were to take Swedish service, he vouched
that my qualifications and my knowledge of the science of war
would soon advance me. I played it cool and said that advancement was rather an uncertain thing—unless a person had
friends who helped him by their influence. He repeated that
my qualifications would make friends and assure my advancement. Moreover, I would doubtless meet relatives in the
Swedish army, for there were many Scotish noblemen in the
Swedish forces. Torstensson [16] had promised him a regiment
and when the promise was made good (as it doubtless would
be), he would make me his lieutenant colonel. This and similar speeches made my mouth water. And since there was no
hope of peace, and additional soldiers would surely be quartered on my farm, so that I would be ruined, I decided to join
up once more. I promised the colonel I'd serve under him if
he would keep his promise and give me the lieutenant-
colonelcy in his expected regiment.

Everything was settled. I sent for my knan (or godfather),
who was with my cattle in Bayrischbrunn, and deeded the
farm to him and his wife. After their death my natural son
Simplicius, the one who had been placed at my doorstep, was
to inherit the farm with all appurtenances, since no legitimate
offspring were on hand. Then I got my horses and what I still
owned in money and jewels, and after I had settled all my
affairs and arranged for the education of my bastard son, the
blockade was suddenly lifted and we had to start for the main

[16] Lennart Torstensson (1603–1651) was general of the Swedish forces
from 1641 to 1646.

army sooner than expected. I acted as a steward for this colonel: I maintained him, his servants, his horses, and the entire household by stealing and robbing. In military parlance this is called "foraging."

General Torstensson's promises, of which the colonel had boasted on my farm, were not half so great as he had pretended. As far as I could see, the colonel was rather looked down upon. "Ha!" he said to me, "I wonder who the dirty dog was that slandered me at headquarters. I won't stay here long." And since he suspected I would not stay long with him either, he made up some letters, according to which he was ordered to recruit a new regiment in Livonia, where his home was. He thus persuaded me to embark at Wismar and go to Livonia with him. Once we were there, everything ended in smoke, for not only did he have no regiment to recruit, but he also was a shoestring kind of nobleman, and what he owned was his wife's.

Though I had twice been deceived and let myself be dragged so far off, I fell for him a third time: he showed me letters he had received from Moscow in which (as he said) high military positions were offered him (that's how he translated the letters for me), and he boasted of excellent and regular pay. Since he immediately started out with his wife and children, I thought he could hardly be going on a wild goose chase. So, full of high hopes, I joined him, since for the present I had neither ways nor means of returning to Germany. But as soon as we crossed the Russian border and met some discharged German soldiers, particularly officers, I became alarmed and said to my colonel, "What in the devil's name are we doing? Are we moving away from the seat of war and going to a peaceful country where soldiers are discharged and considered a nuisance?!" But he reassured me, saying that I should let him worry; he knew what to do better than these fellows of no account.

When we arrived safely in the big city of Moscow, I saw immediately that everything was wrong. My colonel had daily conferences with the magnates, but more with high church dignitaries than with important noblemen. This seemed Greek to me and caused me a lot of worry, for I could not figure out what he was up to. Finally he notified me that the war business had fallen through and that his conscience was urging him to embrace the Greek Orthodox religion. He advised me most sincerely to follow his example, since he could no longer help me as he had promised. His majesty the czar had already received good accounts of my personal qualifications and would graciously condescend—if I embraced the Orthodox faith—to invest me as a cavalier with a sizeable estate and many serfs. This most gracious offer could not be refused, for it was better to have, in this grand monarch, a gracious lord than an offended prince.

I was quite perplexed and did not know what to answer. In another place I would have given the colonel an answer he could have felt rather than heard; but being practically a prisoner, I had to whistle a different tune, so I was silent a long time while I thought of an answer. Finally, I said that at his suggestion I had come to serve his majesty the czar as a soldier. If my military service was not needed, I could not help that; nor did I blame my long journey on the czar, for he had not summoned me. But that the czar so graciously deigned to show me his favor, that was something to boast to all the world rather than to accept, for at this time I could not decide to change my religion. I wished, rather, to be back on my farm in the Black Forest, where I'd be no trouble to anyone. The colonel answered that I should do as I liked; however, he did think that if God and good fortune smiled on me I should be properly appreciative. But if I did not want to be helped nor yet to live like a prince, he hoped I realized that he had spared no effort on my behalf. After this speech he made a low bow, turned on his heel, and left me holding the bag. He wouldn't even let me accompany him to the door.

While I was sitting there dazed and wondering about my condition, I heard two Russian carriages in front of my lodgings. When I looked out the window I saw my good colonel and his sons getting into one, his wife and her daughters boarding the other. The carriages and servants were the czar's;

some priests were also present, and they showed their good will by practically waiting on this family.

CHAPTER 21: *Further news of Simplicius in Moscow*

From now on I was shadowed by several guardsmen of the czar, but I was not even aware of it. I no longer saw my colonel or his family, and I did not know where they were. At that time I developed strange notions and sprouted a lot of grey hair. I became acquainted with the German merchants and craftsmen who ordinarily live in Moscow, and I complained to them of how I had been spitefully deceived. They gave me advice and instructions on getting a ride back to Germany, but as soon as they heard that the czar was determined to keep me in Russia, they all clammed up; they completely ignored me and I had a hard time finding room and board, for I had already eaten up my horse, plus saddle and bridle, and I was taking the ducats one by one out of the lining of my suit, where I had cleverly sewed them up. In the end I also turned my ring and jewels into money, in hopes of surviving until I had an opportunity to return to Germany. Meanwhile a quarter of a year went by, at the end of which time my colonel and his family were baptized for the second time in their lives. Then he was given a fine country estate with many serfs.

At that time a law was passed, equally applicable to natives and foreigners, that no idlers were to be tolerated under pain of severe penalty. Foreigners who did not want to work had to leave the country within a month, the city within twenty-four hours. So about fifty of us banded together for the purpose of traveling by way of Podolia to Germany, with God's help. But not quite two hours' distance from the city we were overtaken by several Russian cavalrymen who informed us that his majesty the czar was displeased because so many of us had banded together and were traveling through the country at our own pleasure and without passports. Moreover, the czar could send us to Siberia for our crude behavior. On the way back to town I found out how matters stood with me, for the leader of the troop told me that the czar did not want me to leave the country. His well-meant advice would be to conform to his majesty's most gracious will, to change my religion as the colonel had done, and not to spurn a nobleman's country estate. He assured me that if I refused, declining to live like a lord among them, I'd be forced to work like a serf. His majesty the czar would be a fool for allowing a man so experienced as the colonel had pictured me to leave the country. I belittled myself and said the colonel had probably ascribed more arts, virtues, and sciences to me than I was actually capable of. Certainly I had come into the country to serve his majesty the czar and the great nation of all the Russians against their enemies, even at the cost of my lifeblood; but I could not yet make up my mind to change my religion. Nevertheless, if I was able to serve the czar in any way without burdening my conscience, I would not hesitate to do my best.

I was separated from the others and lodged at the house of a merchant, where I was openly watched but also provided daily with excellent food and drink from the court kitchens. A number of people called on me and occasionally invited me to their houses. There was one especially who, no doubt, was ordered to look after me. He was a smart man who every day conversed with me in a friendly way (for I had already learned quite a bit of Russian. He mostly discussed mechanical arts with me: war machines and others, the theory and practice of fortification, artillery, and so forth. Finally, after he had hinted several times that I should take up the czar's suggestions (but I had given no hope that I would change my mind), he wanted me—in honor of the great czar—to communicate and impart something of my knowledge to his nation, even if I did not want to become naturalized. The czar would acknowledge my willingness with imperial grace. I assured him that it had ever been my intention to serve the czar; that's why I had come. My intention had never changed, though I noticed that I was virtually kept prisoner. "Oh, not at all," he answered. "Rather, the czar loves you so much that he would not like to do without you." "But why," I said, "am I being watched?" "Because," was the answer, "the czar is afraid something bad might happen to you."

When he had clearly understood what I was willing to do, he explained that the czar wanted to have saltpeter produced and gunpowder manufactured in his own country. But since there was nobody among them who could handle the matter I would do the czar a great service if I set up the factory. I would be given enough money and workers, and he for one wanted to make sure I did not turn down this proposition, for their information indicated that I was the man who could do it.

I answered, "Sir, I say now as I said before: If I can serve the czar in anything (provided he leaves me alone in matters of religion), I shall do my best." Now this Russian, who was one of the most exalted nobles, became so merry that he drank more toasts with me than any German ever did.

Next day two noblemen and an interpreter came from the czar to draw up a contract. They brought along an expensive Russian wardrobe for me. A few days later I started looking for a saltpeter mine and taught the Russians assigned to me how to separate the saltpeter from ordinary dirt and how to refine it. Then I drew up a plan for a powder mill and taught others how to prepare the charcoal. And after a short time we made considerable quantities of the best powder for muskets and ordnance. I had plenty of workers and my personal servants besides, who were to wait on me (or rather, to keep watching me).

When things were going so well, the colonel, dressed in Russian clothes and magnificently attended by many servants, came to me; it seemed that all his flashiness was to persuade me to be rebaptized too. But I knew well enough that the clothes came from the czar's wardrobe and had only been lent to him to make my mouth water, for that's the usual thing at the czar's court.

And in order to make the gentle reader understand how that was handled, I want to give an example. Once I was busy working in the powder mill I had built out of town by the river. Suddenly an alarm was sounded because the Tartars on a hundred thousand horses were devastating the country only twenty miles away and were advancing steadily. I and my people had to go to court immediately, and there we were given arms and horses from the czar's armory and stables. Instead of a cuirass I wore a quilted breastplate of silk, which might have stopped an arrow but not a bullet. I was given boots, spurs, a princely headgear with a heron's plume, and a sword all decorated with gold and jewels and sharp enough for splitting hairs. I had never seen, let alone ridden, a horse like the one given me from the czar's stables. I and the horse's gear glittered with gold, silver, precious stones, and pearls. By my side hung a steel mace which shone like a mirror and was so well made and so heavy that I could easily kill anybody merely by tapping him with it. The czar himself was not better mounted or equipped. I was followed by a white flag with a double eagle, and from all the nooks and crannies people flocked to it, so that we numbered forty thousand horse before two hours had passed and sixty thousand after about four hours. With these we advanced against the Tartars. Every quarter hour I received oral orders from the czar, but they were always the same: Having passed myself off as a soldier, I was to prove one today, for then his majesty could consider me so and recognize me as one. Our army was increasing every moment: people of major and minor importance, individuals as well as groups, were joining us. But amid all this hurry and confusion, I could not see a single man who would take charge of the mob and direct the battle.

Well, I don't want to go into too much detail because the encounter is not very important for my story. I only want to say that we suddenly came upon the Tartars in a valley or low-lying area. They were burdened with loot, their horses were tired, and they did not expect us. We attacked them from a number of places and scattered them in a few moments. At the time of the first attack I shouted to my followers in Russian, "Come on! Everybody do like me!" They all shouted this to each other while I rode toward the enemy at full speed. First I ran into a prince's son (called a *mirza*), and I bashed his head in, so that the brain stuck to my steel mace. The Russians followed my heroic example; the Tartars could not withstand their attack and turned in general flight.

I acted like a madman, or rather like one who is desperately seeking death and cannot find it. I clubbed down everyone I met, Tartar or Russian, and those whom the czar had ordered to watch me were so close behind me that my back was protected at all times. The air was buzzing with arrows, as if bees or hornets were swarming, and I caught one in the arm, for I had rolled up my sleeves—all the better to kill and maim with sword and mace. Before the arrow stuck in me, my heart had laughed at the bloodshed; but when I saw my own blood flowing, laughter turned to blind rage. When the savage enemy was routed, some noblemen ordered me to report to their emperor as to how the Tartars had been vanquished. Therefore, on their authority I turned back with about a hundred horsemen. I rode through town to the royal palace, and everyone received me with rejoicing and congratulations. As soon as I had finished my report (the czar already knew everything), I had to take off my imperial clothes. They were immediately returned to the czar's wardrobe, though like the horse's trappings, they were spattered and soiled with blood, and as good as ruined. I thought the clothes and the horse should have been given to me as a reward for fighting so bravely in this battle. But from this indication I could well imagine how the Russians, like my colonel, managed their elegance of dress. All these goods were borrowed from the czar; they, like everything else in all of Russia, belonged to the czar.

CHAPTER 22: *The short and jolly journey back home to his knan*

While my wound was healing I was treated like a prince: I walked around in a gown made of gold brocade and lined

with sable, though my injury was neither mortal nor dangerous. In all my days I never enjoyed food so rich as what I ate
there. But this was the only reward for my labors, except the
praise of the czar, and that was spoiled by the envy of some
nobles.

When I had completely recovered, I was sent down the
Volga by boat to Astrakhan in order to set up a powder mill
there, just as I had done in Moscow, because it was not always
possible for the czar to supply these border fortresses outside
of Moscow with fresh, usable powder, which had to be shipped
by water at great risk. I was glad to be of use, for the czar
had promised to return me to Holland after the completion
of my business, and to give me a sum of money commensurate
with his majesty's gratitude and my just deserts. But alas!
when we think we are most assured and safe in our hopes and
in the ideas we have conceived, unexpectedly there comes a
wind that blows down all the unsubstantial trumpery we have
been building up over a long time.

The governor of Astrakhan treated me as if I were the czar
himself, and in a short time I had everything going nicely: I
remade, as it were, his stale, ruined ammunition, which was
spoiled and no good, in much the same way that a tinner
makes a new spoon from the metal of an old one. At that
time among the Russians, this process was unheard-of; and
because of this and other tricks I knew, I was considered by
some as a sorcerer, by others as a new saint or prophet, and
by still others as a second Empedocles or Gorgias Leontinus.[17]

One night, when I was in the middle of my work in a
powder mill outside the fortress, I was kidnaped by a gang of
roving Tartars. They took me (and others) a long way into
their country, and there I not only saw the sheep-plant bora-
metz,[18] but I was even permitted to eat of it. The Tartars
traded me for Chinese merchandise to some Tartars of Nuichi,

[17] Greek philosophers, living in Sicily in the fifth century B.C., who
were given credit for unusual skills.

[18] Legendary plant mentioned by contemporary travelers. It is essentially cotton to which mutton has been gratuitously added.

who gave me as a special present to the king of Korea, with whom they had just concluded an armistice. In Korea I was valued highly because there was no one like me in fencing, and because I taught the king how to hit the bull's-eye with the gun over his shoulder and his back to the target. For this he liked me a lot, and on my most humble petition he gave me my freedom and sent me by way of Japan to the Portuguese in Macao; they, however, paid little attention to me. For this reason I moved among them like a sheep that has strayed from its own flock. At last I was captured in a strange manner by Turkish or Mohammedan pirates, who, after carrying me around for about a year among strange foreign peoples that populate the East Indian islands, sold me to some traders from Alexandria in Egypt. They took me, along with their merchandise, to Constantinople, where the Turkish emperor was readying several galleys against the Venetians. And as oarsmen were needed, many Turkish merchants had to give up their Christian slaves (for indemnity, though). Being a strapping young fellow, I was drafted and so had to learn how to row; but this slavery did not last more than two months. Our galley was taken in the Levant by the brave Venetians, and I and all my fellow slaves were released from the power of the Turks. The galley was brought to Venice with rich booty and several Turkish captives of high rank, and I was freed. Since I wished to make a pilgrimage to Rome and Loreto, in order to see these places and to thank God for my liberation, I easily obtained a passport and a considerable sum of money from honest folk, particularly Germans; and I was able to start on my journey equipped with the long staff of the pilgrim.

I went to Rome by the shortest route, and there I was lucky, for I received good alms from important as well as plain people. After staying there for about six weeks, I joined other pilgrims (among them Germans, and particularly several Swiss who were going home) for the trip to Loreto. From there, by way of the Gotthard Pass and Switzerland, I returned to the Black Forest and my knan, who had kept the farm for me. I did not bring anything special home with me except a beard, which I had grown abroad.

I had been away for three years and several months, during which time I had crossed several oceans, seen many nations, but generally had experienced more evil than good. I could write a whole book about it. Meanwhile the German peace [19] had been proclaimed, and I was able to live in quiet and ease with my knan. I let him worry and manage, while I sat down to my books again, which were both my work and my delight.

CHAPTER 23: *This chapter is nice and short: it only concerns Simplicius*

I once read that when a Roman delegation had asked how to govern their nation in peace, the oracle of Apollo had answered, "Nosce te ipsum," that is, "Everyone should know himself." This made me reflect, and now, having nothing else to do, I demanded from myself a reckoning of my past life. I said to myself: Your life has been no life but a death; your days have been a heavy shadow, your years a bad dream, your desires grievous sins, your youth a phantom, your well-being an alchemist's treasure that goes up the chimney and is gone before you are aware of it. Through grave danger you ran after the wars, where you experienced much good luck and much bad; you have been now up, now down; now great, now small; now rich, now poor; now joyful, now sad; now well-liked, now hated; now honored, now despised. But, my poor soul, what did you gain from all this journey? This much: I am poor in possessions; my heart is heavy with care; I am loath to do good, lazy and corrupt; and, what is worst, my conscience is burdened and fearful. But you, my soul, are weighed down with sin and horribly befouled. My body is weary, my reason confused; my innocence is gone, the better part of my youth is frittered away, precious time is lost, there

19 The Peace of Westphalia, 1648.

is nothing that gladdens me, and I am an enemy to myself. When I entered the world after my blessed father's death, I was simple-minded and clean, upright and honest, truthful, humble, diffident, modest, chaste, shamefaced, pious, and devout. But soon I became mean, false, lying, proud, restless, and godless in every respect. And all these vices I learned without a teacher. I guarded my honor, not for its own sake, but for my advancement. I became conscious of time, not so that I might use it well for my salvation, but in order to profit my body. I exposed my life to danger many times, and yet I never exerted myself to improve it so that I might die comforted and blessed. I only looked to the present, to my worldly profit, and never once thought of the future, let alone that I would someday have to render an account of myself in the sight of God.

Such thoughts tormented me every day, and just then several books by Guevara [20] came to my attention. From these I must quote here, because their sentiment was powerful enough to make me disgusted with the world.

CHAPTER 24: *This is the very last one. It tells how and why Simplicius leaves the world once again*

"Farewell, O World, for you cannot be trusted, nor is there anything to be expected of you. Within your house the past has disappeared, the present is vanishing under our very hands, and the future has never begun; the most constant is falling down, the most powerful is breaking to pieces, the most eternal is coming to an end, so that you are a corpse among corpses, and within the course of a century you hardly let us live an hour.

[20] Antonio de Guevara (*ca.* 1490–1544), Spanish moralist and court preacher to Charles V, died as bishop of Cadix. The extensive quotation, which is of central importance to *Simplicius*, comes from the *Menosprecio de corte*, in the German translation of Aegidius Albertinus (Munich, 1598, and later).

"Farewell, World, for you take us captive and do not release us; you tie us down and never loosen our bonds; you sadden us without consoling us; you rob us without restoring; you accuse us without cause; you condemn us without a hearing, so that you may kill us without sentence and bury us without waiting for our death! With you there is no joy without sadness, no peace without discord, no love without suspicion, no rest without fear, no fullness without want, no honor without strain, no possession without a bad conscience, no occupation without complaint, and no friendship without falsehood.

"Farewell, World, for inside your palace promises of gifts are made without the intention of giving; people serve without pay; they caress in order to kill, elevate to cast down, help in order to cut down, honor in order to dishonor, borrow in order never to return, punish without pardon!

"May God bless you, World, for in your house great lords and favorites of princes are hurled down; unworthy creatures are preferred; traitors, looked upon with favor; faithful men, made to stand in the corner; evildoers, left unimpeded; the innocent, condemned; the wise and qualified, dismissed; bunglers, given great rewards; crafty men, believed. Plain and honest men gain no credence; each does what he pleases, not one as he ought.

"Farewell, World, for in your domain no one is called by his right name: the headstrong are called bold; the fainthearted, careful; the willful, diligent; and the negligent, peaceful. A wastrel is called magnificent; and a miser, self-sufficient; a crafty tattler and prater, eloquent; the quiet man, a fool or visionary. An adulterer or despoiler of virgins is called an amorous blade; a person with a dirty mind, a courtier; a vengeful one, a zealous partisan; a gentle mind, a dreamer. You are selling us the usual for the unusual, and the unusual for the usual.

"Farewell, World, for you mislead every one: you promise honor to the ambitious, change to the restless; to the climber, the favor of princes; to the easygoing, offices; to the miser, great treasure; to gluttons and lechers, gorging and venery; to enemies, revenge; to thieves, secrecy; to youths, long life; to court favorites, unwavering princely favor.

"Farewell, World, for within your palace neither trust nor truth can find lodging; whoever speaks with you is made shameless; whoever trusts you is cheated; whoever follows you is misled; whoever fears you is most badly mistreated; whoever loves you is rewarded with evil; and whoever relies on you absolutely is ruined absolutely. You repay no gift that is given to you, no service shown to you, no kind word spoken to you, nor faith nor friendship kept with you; rather, you deceive, cut down, put to shame, besmirch, threaten, devour, and forget everyone; for that reason everyone cries, sighs, laments, complains, and is undone; and everyone comes to an end. In your house one sees and learns only to hate to the point of strangulation, talk to the point of lying, love to the point of despair, overreach to the point of stealing, beg to the point of cheating, and sin to the point of death.

"God be with you, World, for while one follows you, one idles away one's time in forgetfulness, one's youth with running, racing, jumping over fences and across paths, roads, and lanes, over hill and dale, through woods and wilderness, across lakes and oceans, in snow and rain, heat and cold, wind and weather. A man's strength is worn down with mining the ore of metals and smelting it, with cutting and shaping rocks, clearing land and building, planting and cultivating, with thinking, scheming, and longing; with advice, arrangements, cares, and troubles; with buying and selling, quarreling, feuding, warring, lying, and cheating. Old age is spent in misery and care: the spirit grows weak, the breath begins to stink, the face becomes wrinkled, a straight body bent; eyes grow dim, limbs tremble, the nose begins to drip, the head grows bald, hearing deteriorates, the sense of smell grows insensitive, and taste leaves us. A man sighs and complains, is lazy and weak; in sum, he has nothing but misery and labor until his death.

"Farewell, World, for within your bounds no one wants to

be pious. Every day murderers are executed; traitors drawn
and quartered; robbers, thieves, and holdup men hanged; slay-
ers beheaded; sorcerers burned; givers of false testimony punished; and rebels exiled.

"God be with you, World, for your servants have no other
job or pastime than that of being lazy, of irritating and
scolding one another, courting virgins, waiting on beautiful
women, making eyes at them, playing cards and dice, dealing
with pimps, making war on neighbors, gossiping, thinking up
new schemes, going after profit, inventing new fashions, orig-
inating new tricks, and introducing new vices.

"Farewell, World, for within your bounds no one is satisfied or contented. If a man is poor, he wants more; if rich, to
be considered a great personage; if lowly, to rise high; if
insulted, to avenge himself; if in favor, to lord it over others;
if full of vice, to be in a happy mood.

"Farewell, World, for with you nothing is constant. High
towers are struck by lightning; mills are carried away by
water; wood is eaten by worms, grain by mice, fruit by cater-
pillars, and clothes by cockroaches; cattle grow worthless with
age, and mankind with disease: one man has scabies, another
cancer; a third has lupus; a fourth, syphilis; a fifth, arthritis;
the sixth has gout; the seventh, dropsy; the eighth, kidney
stones; the ninth, gravel; the tenth, consumption; the eleventh, a fever; the twelfth, leprosy; the thirteenth, epilepsy;
the fourteenth is insane! Within you, O World, one person
never does what the next does, for when one is crying the
other is laughing; one is sighing, the other is joyous; one is
fasting, the other is stuffing himself; one is having a feast, the
next is starving; one is riding, the next is walking; one is
talking, the other is silent; one is playing, the next is working;
and when one is born, another is dying. Nor does one live
like another: one is the master, the other is the servant; one
is a pastor of men, another is pasturing his hogs; one follows
the court, another the plow; one is sailing across the seas,
another is journeying over land to the weekly markets or
annual fairs; one is working in fire, another inside the cool

earth; one is fishing in water, another is catching the birds of the air; one is hard at work, another lives off the land as a robber or thief.

"May God bless you, O World, for within your house one cannot live a holy life, or suffer death uniformly. One person dies in the cradle; another, in his youth in bed; the third, by the rope; the fourth, by the sword; the fifth is broken on the wheel; the sixth is burned at the stake; the seventh dies in a wine glass; the eighth, in a watery river; the ninth suffocates in a pork barrel; the tenth is killed by poison; the eleventh dies suddenly; the twelfth, in battle; the thirteenth, through witchcraft; and the fourteenth drowns his poor soul in an inkwell.

"May God keep you, O World, for your conversation disgusts me; the life you give us is a miserable pilgrimage, an inconstant, uncertain, hard, harsh, fleeting, and unclean life full of poverty and error; it is to be called death rather than life; for we all die in it every moment, through the many imperfections of inconstancy and through death's various approaches! You are not satisfied with the bitterness with which you are permeated and surrounded; but in addition you cheat most people by your flattery, your incitements and false promises; from the golden chalice that you hold in your hand, you dispense bitterness and falsehood and make people blind, deaf, drunk, and insensitive. Oh, how happy are those who reject your community, despise your sudden momentary joys, spurn your society, and refuse to be lost in the company of such a malicious impostress; for you make of us a dark abyss, a miserable clod of dirt, a child of anger, a stinking carrion, an unclean vessel in a dung pit, a vessel of putrefaction full of stench and abomination; for after you have long harried and troubled us with flattery, caresses, threats, beatings, tribulation, martyrdom, and pain, you surrender the worn-out body to the grave and deliver the soul to an uncertain chance. For although nothing is more certain than death, a man is never sure how, when, and where he will die, and—what is most pitiable—where his soul will go and how it will fare. But woe unto the poor soul that has served you, O World, has obeyed you and followed your luxuries and lusts; for after such a poor, sinful, and unconverted soul has departed its miserable body in a sudden and unexpected fright, it is not surrounded by servants and acquaintances (as was the body, while alive), but it is led to the judgment seat of Christ by a drove of its most ghastly enemies. Therefore, O World, may God be with you, for I am sure that in time you will forsake me, not only when my poor soul must appear before the face of the severe judge, but also when the most frightful sentence of all is delivered and pronounced, 'You who are condemned, go to the eternal fire,' and so on.

"Farewell, World, you vile and wicked world, O you stinking, miserable flesh; for because of you, and because the ungodly unrepentant followed you, he is condemned to eternal damnation where, in all eternity, nothing is to be expected but suffering without solace, in exchange for all the pleasures enjoyed; thirst without quenching, for all the drinking; hunger without fulfillment, for all the gluttony; darkness without light, for all the magnificence and splendor; pain without alleviation, for all the voluptuous pleasures; howling, gnashing of teeth, and complaints without surcease, for all the domination and triumph; heat without coolness, fire without extinction, cold without measure, and misery without end.

"God be with you, World, for instead of your promised joys and lusts, evil spirits will lay hands on the unrepentant and condemned soul, and they will rush it to the pit of hell where it will see and hear nothing but the frightful shapes of the devils and the condemned, unrelieved darkness and smoke, fire without brightness, cries, howls, gnashing of teeth, and blasphemy. Then all hope of grace and forgiveness is past; there is no respect of persons: the higher a man climbed or the harder he sinned, the deeper he is cast down, the greater is the pain he must suffer. Much is asked of him to whom much was given; and the more one made himself to shine within your bounds, O vile and wicked World, the more torment and suffering is meted out to him, for divine justice requires it thus.

"God be with you, World, for although the body stays awhile with you in the ground and decays there, yet it will rise on doomsday, and according to the final judgment there will be eternal hellfire. Then the poor soul will say, 'World, be accursed! For through your blandishments I forgot God and myself, and I followed you all the days of my life in voluptuousness, evil, sin, and shame. Accursed be the hour when God created me! Accursed be the day when I was born into your domain, you evil and wicked World! O you mountains, hills, and rocks, fall on me and hide me from the grim anger of the Lamb, from the countenance of him who sitteth in the seat of judgment. Ah, woe is me, and woe again in all eternity!'

"O World, you unclean world! For these reasons I pray, I beg, I ask, I admonish you, and I protest against you. May you have no part of me any more. I, for my part, do not desire to place any hope in you, for you know I have determined to put an end to care. Hope and fortune, farewell!"

All these words I pondered diligently and constantly. They caused me to leave this world and become a hermit once more. I would have liked to live near my mineral spring, but the peasants of the neighborhood did not want me, though the lonely woods suited me well. They feared that I might give away the secret of the spring and get their lord to build trails and a road to it, now that peace had come. Therefore, I went to another wild place and resumed the life I had led in the Spessart. It is not certain that I, like my late father, shall keep it up until the end. May God grant us all the favor of obtaining from him what is of greatest value to us, namely, a blessed

End.

ℐ Book Six:
Continuation and Conclusion

O motion wondrous strange, O most inconstant rest!
A man who thinks he stands is straightway onward
    pressed.
O most elusive rest, so restless in repose.
Our downfall rushes in, descent we never chose,
Even as death itself. Inconstancy that took
Great toll of me is found described here in this book
Inconstancy doth lurk within each moment's gladness;
Inconstancy alone outlives our very sadness.

CHAPTER 1: *A little preface and a brief report on how the
new hermit's life agreed with him*

If anybody imagines I am relating my life story merely to
while away the time or to make people laugh (as jesters
and mountebanks do), he is greatly mistaken. Too much
laughter is disgusting to me, and whoever kills that noble,
irreplaceable asset, time, badly wastes the divine gift which
is granted us that we may work out the salvation of our
souls. Why should I help anybody to such vain foolishness
and, without being asked, become other folks' Secretary of
Entertainment? As if I didn't know that by doing so I would
participate in other people's sins? Dear reader, I consider myself above such business; and whoever wants a fool, let him
buy two and he'll have one to spare. The reason I am present-
ing my story with a dash of humor is that some delicate

tenderlings can't swallow pills that are good for them unless they have been coated with sugar and gilt, not to mention the fact that even the most sober-sided of men will put down a serious book, whereas they keep reading one that makes them smile ever so little every once in a while.

If I am charged with making satirical attacks, I plead "Not guilty." Many folks would rather see general vices berated and scored in a general way than have their own deficiency of virtue corrected in a friendly way. Unfortunately, Mr. Everybody (to whom I am addressing my story) does not enjoy the theological style either. One can see how mountebanks and medicine men nowadays draw more of an audience when their clown begins to shout and caper than can the most enthusiastic minister of the gospel who is calling his flock together, by having all the church bells rung three times in a row, so that he may deliver a wholesome sermon.

Be that as it may. Let me protest to the world that I am innocent if someone takes offense at my having dressed my Simplicissimus in the fashion demanded by the people themselves, when they want to be taught something useful. If here and there a reader is satisfied with the husks and disregards the kernel which is hidden underneath, he will have a jolly story to content him, but he will miss by far that which I had really wanted him to get. So I'll start where I left off at the end of the fifth book.

There the gentle reader learned that I became a hermit once more, and why. Now I must tell how I behaved in this state. The first few months, while my ardor was still strong, everything went well. From the start I easily put a damper on my carnal desires (better called "lust"), to which I had been dedicated, for since I no longer worshiped Bacchus and Ceres, neither did Venus care to visit me anymore. I still was not perfect; I had my temptations, a thousand every hour. For instance, when, in order to make myself remorseful, I thought of the practical jokes and tricks I had played on people, the lust of the flesh which I had enjoyed came back at the same time. That wasn't always good for me, nor did it help my spiritual progress. I have since concluded that idleness was my greatest enemy, and freedom (for I was not subject to a clergyman who would minister to me and watch me) was the chief cause of my failure to persist in the life I had determined to lead.

I lived on a high mountain range called the Moss, a part of the Black Forest that is covered by a somber stand of firs. I had a beautiful view east into the Oppenau valley and its branches, and south into the valley of the Kinzig and Geroltseck County, where the lofty castle rises among the neighboring heights like a kingpin in a game of ninepins. To the west I could see upper and lower Alsace, and to the north in the direction of lower Baden, down the Rhine, where the city of Strasbourg, with its high cathedral tower, stands out like the heart enclosed by its body. I spent more time looking at the beauty of the view than praying: my telescope, which I had not resigned myself to putting away, was a powerful encouragement in this. After dark, when I could no longer use the glass, I picked up the instrument I had invented for the reinforcement of hearing and listened through it, for instance, to dogs barking several hours away or some game stirring closer by. This is the kind of foolishness in which I engaged, and in time I neglected work and prayer, two activities by which the old Egyptian hermits had maintained themselves physically and spiritually.

In the beginning, while I was still new, I went about the neighboring valleys, from house to house, looking for alms in order to keep alive. I took no more than what I barely needed, and I especially shunned money, an attitude that my near neighbors viewed as a great miracle, even as a kind of apostolic holiness. But as soon as my abode became known, everybody who came into the woods brought me something to eat. These people bragged about my holy and unusual life, so that folks from farther away, driven by curiosity or veneration, also came to see me. Thus I suffered no scarcity of bread, butter, salt, cheese, bacon, eggs, and other vittles; I even had too much! But that did not make me any more

blessed. Rather, the longer I lived, the worse I became, growing lazier and less charitable. I could well have been called
a hypocrite or a holy faker. For all that, I did not give up
thinking about virtues and vices and considering what I
would have to do if I wanted to go to heaven. But I did this
thinking without system, without good counsel, and without
the firm resolve to be as serious as my condition and the
amount of desirable improvement would have required of me.

CHAPTERS 2–18: *Summary*

[Simplicius, asleep, reports a vision or dream: The Prince
of Darkness receives word that the Thirty Years' War is ended
and that peace on earth is greeted with the joyous singing
of "Gloria in excelsis" and "Te deum laudamus." This news
drives Lucifer almost insane with rage. He lashes out at various devils for having wasted their chances through laziness.
But Belial points out that peace also produces a respectable
crop of vices and that all is not lost. Lucifer's fury has attracted many other spirits of hell, who are now lectured by
their prince and promised rewards if they redouble their
efforts.

[The pep talk over, a dispute arises between Extravagance,
a gorgeous female, and Avarice, a ragged old man, concerning who can serve hell better. Instead of receiving a verdict,
they are sent out into the world to substantiate their respec-
tive claims. Extravagance is assigned to a rich, young English
lord; Avarice, to his steward. The lord wastes a fortune,
while the steward fraudulently amasses one. In the end they
join the army of Charles II and after his defeat become robbers. After their capture, the master is beheaded, the servant
hanged. Thus the quarrel remains undecided. Simplicius
wakes up from his sleep.

[On a walk through the woods Simplicius finds a life-sized
statue. It looks like an old German hero; and when he tries
to turn it over, it begins to speak, saying its name is "Soon-

different," who has always been with him and who will not leave him until he dies. It gives Simplicius a recipe for conversing with lifeless objects and, as if for fun, changes into about a dozen different shapes, but always remains its own true Soondifferent self. Having changed into a bird, it flies away.

[Simplicius feels that he is not really serving God or man; and after reading some saints' lives he decides to make another pilgrimage. His dress and hairy appearance get him an easy living, but he is hardly better than a hobo: in Schaffhausen a rich burgher gives him a night's lodging, and in turn he tells fanciful tales about his travels and gives the burgher a foolproof coded recipe against being hit by bullets: "Stand where no one is shooting and you will be safe." His conscience bothers him, however, and in order to keep the man from a false sense of security, he informs him by letter that he has played a hoax on him.

[Along his way, Simplicius tells the most egregious and fantastic lies. He has culled them mostly from ancient writers like Pliny, but he leads his listerners to believe that he has personally seen and experienced everything.

[In a castle owned by a former acquaintance, Simplicius exorcises a ghost. For this service he is offered valuable gifts, which he refuses. He only accepts a lining for his threadbare old cloak. However, the owner secretly sews pieces of gold into it.

[In another burst of humility and devotion Simplicius visits the holy places of Loreto and Rome, and when he discovers the gold coins in his cloak, he decides to journey to Jerusalem. In Genoa he takes a boat for Alexandria, where war prevents further progress. While sight-seeing in Egypt—in Cairo he sees pyramids, and mummies, and machines that raise chickens without hens—he is captured by Arabian robbers and taken to the Red Sea. But whereas the other Christians are sold as slaves, Simplicius is exhibited as a wild and woolly cave man from Arabia Deserta. Under threat of death he is to keep silent while on exhibit. Simplicius doesn't mind his life too much, but in a large commercial city, before an audience consisting partly of Europeans, he blurts out in Latin that he is being held against his will and would appreciate being rescued. A riot ensues, and the local ruler decides Simplicius must be freed; his former masters are sentenced to become galley slaves, and part of their confiscated money is to go to Simplicius in payment for damages. Simplicius renders thanks to his European rescuers and wonders what to do next.]

CHAPTER 19: *Simplicius and the carpenter come away with their lives and, having suffered shipwreck, are provided with a land of their own*

My fellow countrymen advised me to buy a new set of clothes, and because I had nothing else to do I sought the acquaintance of all the Europeans; they liked to have me about, both for reasons of Christian charity and because of my unusual experiences. Since there was little hope that the Damascene war in Syria and Judea would soon end, enabling me to resume and complete my journey to Jerusalem, I changed my mind and decided to go home via Portugal in a large Portuguese galleon that was ready to leave. Instead of the pilgrimage to Jerusalem, I would make one to St. James at Compostela, and then I would retire somewhere and use up what God had granted me.

In order to sail without special expense (for as soon as I had plenty of money I started pinching pennies), I made an agreement with the head merchant on the galleon: he was to take over all my money and use it to his advantage; he was to return it to me in Portugal, but instead of interest I was to receive free passage and food; furthermore, I was to do all sorts of jobs aboard ship and ashore, as occasion and necessity required. But I reckoned without my host, for little did I know what the good Lord had in mind for me. I undertook this long and dangerous journey all the more eagerly because the previous trip across the Mediterranean had gone so well.

When we had boarded the ship and moved with a favorable wind out of the Gulf of Arabia (or the Red Sea) into the ocean, we set our course for the Cape of Good Hope and sailed for several weeks, enjoying weather that could not have been any better. When we thought we were roughly opposite the island of Madagascar, there suddenly arose a storm so violent that we hardly had time to take in sail. The storm grew worse, and as time passed it got so bad that we had to chop off the mast and abandon our ship to the capricious force of the waves. They took us up almost to the clouds and in the next moment dropped us down into an abyss, where we stayed for as long as half an hour. This very effectively taught us how to pray. Finally the waves threw us on a hidden rock with such violence that the ship broke to pieces with a horrible crash, and a pitiful cry arose all around. The rocks were instantly strewn with boxes, bales, and parts of the ship. On the crests and in the depths of the waves woeful human beings were clinging to objects which they had happened to grasp in their predicament. With ghastly screams they deplored their end or commended their souls to God.

A carpenter and I were lying on a large piece of the ship, a sort of raft held together by beams. We clung to them and encouraged each other. Gradually the cruel storm subsided, and little by little the raging waves grew calm and smooth. But pitch-dark night came, bringing with it a sudden shower. It now appeared that in the middle of the ocean we were to be drowned from above. The rain lasted till midnight, and we suffered greatly. Then the sky became clear again, so that we could see the stars; and by them we could tell that the wind, coming from Africa, was drifting us out to sea in the direction of unexplored Australia; and that gave us quite a shock.

Toward daybreak it got dark again so that we couldn't see each other, though we were not far apart. We continued drifting in this dark and miserable state until we suddenly noticed that we had run aground and stopped. The carpenter, who had a hatchet in his belt, probed the depth of the water and when he found it was less than a foot deep on one side we were greatly relieved; we had hopes that God had helped us to reach land. When we recovered, we noticed a fragrance of flowers, indicating the same thing. But because it was so dark and the two of us were so tired, we did not have the heart to look for shore, though we thought we could hear birds singing (as, in fact, we could). As soon as day broke in the east we saw close by in the dim light some land and bushes. So we dropped off into the water, which became shallower as we waded, until, overjoyed, we finally stepped onto dry land. There we fell on our knees, kissed the earth, and thanked God in heaven for preserving us like a father and guiding us to this shore. And that's how I came to this island.

At first we did not know whether we were in an inhabited or an uninhabited country, or only on an island. But we noticed right away that the soil must be very fertile, for every square foot of it was so covered with bushes and trees that we could hardly get through. When it was completely light and we had made our way through the undergrowth for about a quarter of an hour without seeing even the slightest trace of human habitation, we concluded that we must be on an unknown but very rich island. Many strange birds approached us without fear; we could even catch them in our hands. We found lemons, oranges, and coconuts—fruits we enjoyed very much. When the sun rose we came to a plateau that was full of palm trees (from which palm wine can be made). This delighted my comrade no end, for he loved to drink. There we rested in the sun and dried our clothes, which we had taken off and draped over some bushes; meanwhile, we walked around in our underwear. My carpenter struck his hatchet in a palm tree and found that it was full of cider. Unfortunately we had no vessel in which to catch it, for we had lost even our hats in the shipwreck.

When the sunshine had dried our clothes, we put them back on and climbed to a high, rocky peak, located on the right

side, toward the north, between the plains and the sea. Looking around, we found that we were not on a large mass of
land but on an island no bigger around than an hour and a
half's walk. And when we could see no other land far or near,
but only water and sky, we both became sad and lost all hope
of ever seeing human beings again. On the other hand, we
were consoled that God's kindness had sent us to this safe and
fertile place, and not to a barren spot inhabited by cannibals.
Then we started to consider what we would have to do in
order to survive. And since we had to live together on this
island almost like prisoners, we swore each other eternal
loyalty.

On the mountain we had climbed were many and various
birds, and their nests were so full of eggs that we could hardly
stop marveling. We ate some raw and took a supply with us to
a spring of sweet water, which flowed toward the sea with
enough volume to drive a small mill wheel. Again we felt
joyful and decided to build our house near this spring. For
our new household the two of us had no other equipment
than one hatchet, one spoon, three knives, one fork, and a
pair of scissors. There was nothing else. To be sure, my comrade had some thirty ducats that we would gladly have spent
for a lighter if we had only known where to buy one. But the
money was of absolutely no use to us; in fact, it was worth less
than my powder horn, which was filled with tinder that had
become soft and gooey. I dried this tinder in the sun and put
part of it on a flat stone; over it I spread some easily com-
bustible material, of which there was plenty—moss and fibers
from the coconut trees. Then I ran my knife through the
powder and struck a fire. This made us as happy as our rescue
from the sea. If we had only had salt, bread, and a drinking
cup, we would have considered ourselves the luckiest fellows
in the world, though twenty-four hours before we could have
been counted among the most unfortunate. Such is God's
faithfulness and mercy toward men. His be the honor in all
eternity. Amen.

We caught some of the birds that were all around us, killed,

plucked, and washed them, and stuck them on a wooden spit.
I turned the roast while my comrade brought in timber and
started building a hut to protect us from rain (which is rather
bad for health in this part of the world). To make up for the
lack of salt, we seasoned our food with lemon juice.

CHAPTER 20: *They hire a pretty cook, and with God's help*
they get rid of her

This was our first meal on the island; having finished it, we
collected dry wood to keep up our fire. We would have liked
to explore the whole island; but because of exhaustion, sleep
pressed in upon us and we slept without interruption until
early next morning. Then we followed the brook to the place
where it pours into the sea, and we saw with great amazement
that a vast number of fish, all the size of medium salmon or
large carp, was moving up the sweet water of the little river.
It looked like a large herd of hogs crowding ahead. When we
also found some bananas and sweet potatoes—both good eating—we thought we had struck it lucky, though we missed
four-legged animals and wished we had company to help us
enjoy the fruits, fish, and fowl of this island. But we could not
find a single sign that men had ever been there.

We were walking along the shore, wondering how to arrange our household and especially how to get pots and pans
for cooking, and for fermenting and keeping palm wine so
that we could really enjoy it, when out at sea we saw drifting
something that we could not make out at that distance,
though it looked bigger than it turned out to be. When it
came closer and drifted ashore, it turned out to be a half-dead
woman. She lay on a box and her hands were stuck through
its handles. Christian compassion caused us to pull her ashore;
and when we figured out from her clothing and other indications that she must be an Abyssinian Christian, we were all
the more anxious to bring her around. Observing the pro-
prieties, as is becoming with honest women, we held her, head

down, until a considerable quantity of water had run out of her. And though we had nothing save lemons with which to revive her, we squirted under her nose the oil contained in the peel, and shook her until finally she began to move and speak in Portuguese. As soon as my comrade heard this, and after a little color had returned to the woman's face, he said to me, "This Abyssinian woman sailed in our ship as the maid of a great Portuguese lady. I knew both of them well. They embarked at Anacao and were headed for Annabon." [1] When the woman heard this, she showed great joy, addressed the carpenter by name, and not only told about her trip but also spoke with amazement at their both being still alive and meeting here, ashore and out of danger. The carpenter asked what might be in the box. She answered that it contained some Chinese cloth, some weapons, and several pieces of china (which had been bought from her mistress' husband as a gift for a great prince in Portugal). We were very glad, because we needed all of these things badly.

After that she asked us to be kind enough to keep her with us: she would cook for us, do the laundry, and generally act as our maid—even be like a slave to us—if only we would protect her and provide her with the necessities of life, as much as good fortune and the nature of this country permitted. With much difficulty the two of us carried the chest to the place we had chosen for our house. There we opened the chest, finding in it goods so practical that, in our present shape and condition, we could not have wished for anything better. We unpacked and dried them in the sun, and our new cook proved very helpful and diligent. After that we butchered poultry, which we boiled and fried. Meanwhile, the carpenter went to get palm cider, while I walked to the nearby mountain to gather eggs, which we used hard-boiled in place of our daily bread. On the way I thankfully contemplated God's gifts and benefices, which his providence had lovingly furnished us and would continue to provide. I prostrated myself and thanked the good Lord with outstretched arms and a

[1] Opposite Cape Lopez on the coast of Guinea.

heart gratefully uplifted. Then I gathered as many eggs as we needed and returned to our hut, where the evening meal was already set out on the very chest that we had fished out of the sea and were now using as a table.

While I had been away getting eggs my comrade (who was twenty-odd years old, while I was over forty) had made an agreement with the cook which was to turn out badly for both him and me. Being alone together, they had talked of old times and the fertility and abundance of this island, which could be called truly blessed; and they had become so close that they were considering marriage. But the Abyssinian girl would not hear of it unless my comrade, the carpenter, got me out of the way and made himself the sole ruler of the island. She said it was impossible to have a happy, peaceful marriage if a single man were around; and she made him consider how suspicion and jealousy would plague him if an old fellow were talking with her every day, though he might never even intend to deceive him. "But I have a better plan," she said. "If I should ever marry and increase the human race on this island, which can easily support a thousand or more people, let the old fellow marry me. Then it's only a matter of some twelve or fourteen years until we'll have a daughter whom you can marry." He would still not be as old as I, and the firm expectation that one would become the other's father-in-law (or son-in-law) would prevent any ill feeling or danger, into which he might otherwise enter. Of course, she would rather have a young man than an old one, but under the circumstances they would have to act as necessity required and play it safe for the sake of herself and the children to be borne by her. This conversation was far longer than I write it here. But it and the quick movements and apparent beauty of the Abyssinian (who looked much more impressive by firelight) so captivated and deluded my good carpenter that he did not mind promising to throw the old fellow—meaning me—into the ocean, for he would sooner ruin the island than give up such a lady as she. That's when they made the agreement I mentioned before. But he was to kill me with his ax while I was unaware or sleeping, for he was afraid of my strength and

my cane, which he himself had made for me, in the shape of
a Bohemian earpick.

After such conniving the woman showed my comrade a
good bed of clay not far from our hut, and promised to make
beautiful pottery from it—just like that of the Indian women
who live on the shores of Guinea. She also made all sorts of
suggestions as to how she would advance both them and their
children, feed them on this island, and provide a peaceful,
enjoyable life for a hundred generations to come. She could
hardly stop enumerating all the good she would get from the
coconut trees; for example, from their fibers she wanted to
make clothing for them and her children and grandchildren,
and so on.

And now I, poor man, returned, being completely in the
dark about their evil agreement and foul business. I sat down
to enjoy what had been prepared, and according to Christian
custom and praiseworthy tradition I said grace. But as soon
as I made the sign of the cross over the food and my table
companions and asked for divine blessing, box and cook disappeared with all that had been in the chest. Left behind was
a stench so strong that my comrade almost fainted.

CHAPTER 21: *How they dwelt on the island, and how they
became accustomed to such a life*

As soon as he had recovered a little and come to his seven
senses, he knelt down in front of me, folded his hands, and
for perhaps ten minutes repeated nothing but the words, "Ah,
father! Ah, brother! Ah, father! Ah, brother!" And while he
repeated these, he cried and sobbed and could not utter a
single sensible word. I was beginning to think that fright and
stench had deprived him of reason. When he did not stop but
kept on asking my forgiveness, I demanded, "Dearest friend,
what shall I forgive you? You never hurt me. Tell me how
I can help you." "I ask your forgiveness," he replied, "for I
have sinned against God, against you, and against myself."
And then he repeated again and again his previous lament,

until I told him that I knew of nothing sinful in him, but if he had indeed done something that weighed on his conscience, not only would I forgive and forget from the bottom of my heart (as far as it concerned me), but I would also join him in calling on God's mercy and forgiveness. At these words he embraced my legs, kissed my knees, and looked at me so sorrowfully that I fell silent, for I neither knew nor could guess what was the matter. But when I had cheerfully taken him into my arms, embracing him and begging him to tell me what was on his mind and how I might help, he reported in great detail his conversation with the pseudowoman from Abyssinia and the resolve he had made against me, in defiance of God and nature, of Christian love and the oath of true friendship solemnly sworn. And he uttered this with words and gestures that definitely indicated true repentance and a contrite heart.

I consoled him as best I could by saying that God had probably sent us this as a warning so that in the future we might better resist the devil's snares and temptations, and live in constant fear of God. After I had talked with him in this way, he was consoled a little, but he was not satisfied and begged me most humbly to impose a penance for his crime. In order to restore his downcast soul as much as possible, and because he was a carpenter and his ax was still good, I asked him to erect a cross near the place on the shore where we— and the diabolical cook—had landed. This deed would not only be a penance pleasing to God, but in future would also prevent the fiend (who shuns the sign of the holy cross) from invading our island so easily. "Alas!" he answered, "I shall build and erect not only one cross on the plain but also two on the heights, if only I may regain your grace and favor, O father, and may hope for God's forgiveness." He went to work eagerly and did not stop until he had finished the three crosses. We erected one on the seashore, the other two separately on the highest peak of the mountain. The inscription read: *To honor God and in defiance of the enemy of mankind, Simon Meron from Lisbon in Portugal, with the advice and aid of his faithful friend Simplicius Simplicissimus, a Ger-*

man, has made and here in Christian intent erected this token of the passion of our Saviour.

From then on we lived a little more religiously than we had before, and for a calendar I carved a notch in a stick for each day and a cross for Sunday. To keep the Sabbath and celebrate it, we sat together talking of holy and divine matters. I had to use this method of keeping track of time because I had not yet thought of how to record anything verbal without the use of paper and ink.

In concluding this chapter I want to reminisce about something that happened on the evening after our good cook's departure. The first night we had not noticed it, for because of exhaustion and fatigue we had fallen asleep at once. The new event that frightened and distressed us was this: We still had vividly in mind how the accursed fiend, in the guise of the Abyssinian, wanted to destroy us by a thousand sly tricks, and we could not sleep. We lay awake a long time; mostly, we prayed. As it grew dark we saw innumerable lights hovering about us in the air. They shone so brightly that we could tell the difference between leaves and fruit in the trees. Thinking that this might well be another temptation of the devil, we fell silent and kept very quiet. But in time we found that it was a kind of firefly or lightning bug (as we called them back home), which comes from a special sort of rotting wood that is found on the island. These bugs are so bright that they can be used in place of candles. Later I wrote long passages of this book by their light. If they were as common in Europe, Asia, and Africa as they are here, the candlemakers would lose a lot of business.

CHAPTER 22: *Further consequences of such events; how Simon Meron quit life and the island, and how Simplicissimus remained its only master*

Since we saw that we had to stay where we were, we also arranged our housekeeping differently. My companion made hoes and shovels out of a black wood that becomes almost as hard as iron when it dries out. We used them, first of all, to dig holes for the crosses. Then we made ponds for sea water, in which salt could form (as I had seen in Alexandria, Egypt). Third, we started a pleasant garden, for we considered idleness the beginning of the end. Fourth, we channeled the brook, so that we could direct it as we liked, enabling us to dry up the old bed and thus pick out, with dry hands and feet, so to speak, as many fish and crayfish as we wanted. Fifth, we found extremely good potter's clay next to the brook, and though we had no potter's wheel, or a drill and other tools with which to build one, and though we had never learned this skill, we figured out a way of making what we needed. After we had kneaded and prepared the clay we made it into sausages about as long and thick as British tobacco pipes. We stuck these coils on top of each other like snails and so made pottery vessels—large and small crocks and dishes for cooking and drinking. After the first firing turned out well, we had no more cause to complain about any lack of supplies. And though we had no bread, we had plenty of dried fish, which we now used in its place. In time the scheme of producing salt also succeeded, and then we really had nothing to complain of—we lived like people of the golden age.

Little by little we learned how to make a delicious cake from eggs, dried fish, and lemon peel, by grinding the last two ingredients between two stones to make a tender meal and baking it with grease from the so-called dodo. My partner learned how to make palm wine by gathering the juice in large jars and letting it stand for a few days until it had fermented. Then he drank so much of the stuff that he staggered, and toward the end he did this almost every day, regardless of what I said about it. He argued that the cider turned to vinegar when you let it stand too long; and there's truth in that. When I asked him not to make so much at once, only a sufficient quantity, he answered that to despise God's gifts was sinful; the palm trees had to be tapped, or they would choke on their own juice. I had to let him run the gamut of his desire, or he would have reproached me for grudging him what we had in abundance.

And thus, as I said above, we lived like the first men in earth's golden age, when without the least labor a bountiful heaven produced everything that is good for man. However, as no life in this world is so sweet and happy that at times it is not made bitter by the gall of suffering, so it happened to us, too. Insofar as our household improved daily, to that extent our clothing deteriorated from day to day until it rotted on our bodies. Fortunately, until now we had never noticed any winter, not even the least cold, though at the time at which we began to go naked, we had been on the island more than a year and a half, according to my tally. At all times the weather was like that of Europe during May and June, except that about August or a little earlier we had hard rains and thunderstorms. From one solstice to the other the length of days never varied more than an hour and a quarter. Although we were by ourselves on the island, still we did not want to go naked like brute animals but wished to be clothed like European Christians. If we had had quadrupeds, we could have used their skins for covering; lacking them, we skinned large birds, like penguins and dodoes, and made ourselves trousers. But because we had neither the tools nor the necessary chemicals to prepare the skins, they turned hard, became uncomfortable, and deteriorated before we knew it. The coconut palms furnished us with enough fibers, but we could not spin or weave them. My pal, who had been in India for several years, showed me a spine like a sharp thorn on the tips of leaves. If it is broken off and pulled along the stalk of the leaf (more or less as is done with string beans), then there remains connected to the thorn a thread as long as the leaf which can be used in place of a needle and thread. This gave me an opportunity to make trousers from leaves, which I sewed together with thread from their own growth.

While we were living together in this manner and had progressed to the point where we had no reason to complain about overwork, waste, want, or trouble, my comrade daily drank his palm toddy, as he had become used to it, until finally his liver and lights became inflamed; and before I knew it he quit me, the island, and the palm wine by reason of an early death. I buried him as best I could, and while contemplating the inconstancy of human beings and similar topics, I made him the following epitaph:

> The reason I am here and not at sea,
> Nor yet in hell, is that there fought for me
> Three things: the first was raging ocean;
> The second, mankind's fiend, hell's cruel Satan.
> These two I did escape with help of God;
> But palm wine put me underneath the sod.

Thus I became the sole master of the island, and once more I began the life of a hermit. For this I had not only ample opportunity but also a stubborn will and determination. To be sure, I made use of the gifts and goods of the place (for I was grateful for God's mercy and omnipotence that had granted me such abundance); but I also tried my best not to misuse these riches. I often wished that some of those honest Christians who had to suffer want elsewhere might be present to enjoy the bountiful gifts of God; but since I knew well that it would be easily possible for God (if that were his will) to transport any number of human beings to this place, by means more miraculous than the one by which I had come here, I humbly thanked him and his divine providence for caring for me like a father and placing me in this serene situation ahead of thousands of others.

CHAPTER 23: *The hermit concludes his story and makes an end of these six books*

My comrade had not been dead a week when I noticed a spook near my abode. All right, Simplicius, I thought, you are alone. Why shouldn't the Evil One dare to trouble you?

Don't you imagine this malicious mischief-maker enjoys making life hard for you? Why do you let him disturb you, when God is your friend?

For a few days I walked around with such thoughts; they helped me considerably and made me more pious. I was expecting an encounter with the evil spirit, but this time I was mistaken; for one evening when I heard something suspicious I stepped out of my hut, and there by a rock wall, near the largest spring of the brook that runs from the mountain into the sea, I saw my comrade standing and scrabbling with his fingernails in the cracks of the cliff. I was considerably frightened, but I took courage, made the sign of the cross, commended myself to God's protection, and went to the ghost. I thought that since I would have to do it eventually, today was as good a time as any. I used words that are customary on such occasions, and I soon found out that while still alive my late companion had hidden his ducats there, thinking he'd get them out and take them with him when, sooner or later, a ship came to the island. He also gave me to understand that he had relied on this amount of money more than on God for getting home. This was why he had been punished with restlessness after death and been forced to cause me trouble, for which he was sorry. At his request I took out the money, which I valued at less than nothing. (Since I could use it for nothing, one may easily believe me.)

This was my first fright while alone. Later, ghosts other than this one troubled me, but I want to say nothing of that. With God's help and mercy I got to the point where I no longer noticed any enemy except my own thoughts, which were most variable, for thoughts are hard to control, being scot-free; yet in time a reckoning even of these will have to be made.

In order to have my account less heavily charged with sin, I tried to avoid what did not improve me, but I also assigned myself a daily physical task, which I had to do along with my usual prayers. For just as man is born for work (as a bird for flight), so idleness causes illness of body and soul and, in the end, when one least expects it, death. Therefore, I made a garden, though I needed it less than a wagon needs a fifth wheel, since the whole island could justly have been called a lovely pleasure-garden. Nor was my work good for anything but introducing a more complete order here and there, though many a person would have considered the natural disorder of the plants far more charming. But as I said, it did away with idleness.

Oh, how often I wished for books of spiritual instruction; after I had tired my body and needed rest, I wished to console, edify, and delight myself. But books were not to be had. Now, since I had read in some holy author that the whole wide world is a great book, in which he recognized the wondrous works of God and through which he was encouraged to praise him, I remembered the crown of Christ when I saw a thorny bush; when I saw an apple or a pomegranate, I thought of the fall of our first parents and mourned it; when I drew palm cider from a tree, I imagined how my Saviour had mercifully spilled his blood for me; when I saw a mountain or the sea, I recalled the miracles our Lord had worked in these places, or his experiences there; when I picked up a rock to throw, I visualized how the Jews wanted to stone him; when I was in my garden, I thought of the anxious prayer on the Mount of Olives or of Christ's grave and how he had appeared to Mary Magdalene in the garden, after the Resurrection, and so on. Such thoughts were my daily occupation: I never ate without thinking of the Last Supper, and I never cooked my food without reminding myself of the eternal pains of hell.

At last I found that I could write very well on large palm fronds with the juice of lemons mixed with that of Brazil wood (of which tree there are several kinds on this island). This greatly delighted me, for now I could take notes and write down prayers. While regretfully considering my entire life, all the nasty tricks I had played since the days of my childhood, and how a merciful God, disregarding all my coarse sins, had until now not only preserved me from eternal damnation but even granted me the time and the chance to better myself, to convert, to ask his forgiveness, and to thank him for his kindness, I wrote down everything that came to my mind in the book that I made from palm fronds. This, together with my comrade's ducats, I put in a place where people who might sometime come here would find it and be able to tell who had previously inhabited this island. If someone should find the book and read it (sooner or later, before or after my death), I beg him not to take offense if he should find words in it unbecoming to the mouth, not to mention the pen, of a person bent on improvement. Let him remember that the telling of easygoing stories requires easygoing words. An honest Christian reader will marvel all the more, and praise God's mercy, when he finds out that, for all this, such a rogue as I received enough of God's grace to withdraw from the world and live in such condition that he may hope to find eternal glory and by the sufferings of our Redeemer to attain everlasting bliss and a blessed

End.

CHAPTERS 24–27: *Summary*

[The last four chapters constitute a report written by John Cornelissen, a Dutch sea captain from Haarlem for a friend in Germany:

[On the way from the Moluccas to the Cape of Good Hope, bad weather separates Cornelissen's ship from the others in the fleet. While looking for St. Helena, Cornelissen sights an island marked by two crosses on its highest point, though the maps show no land at all in that part of the ocean. A boat, sent to investigate, returns with water, fresh poultry, and quantities of fresh fruit. The only inhabitant of the island has retreated into an inaccessible cave. He is thought to be an outcast and probably insane. Further exploration reveals that pious messages, mottos in various languages, and crosses are attached to trees or carved into their bark. When a grave and a third cross are found, the sailors call the place the Island of the Crosses.

[A number of sailors now start behaving like madmen, and the captain determines to speak with the hermit in the cave. The second attempt to penetrate into the cavern is no more successful than the first: flares and torches go out, and only when the men are at the point of complete frustration does the hermit shout at them. The invaders, he tells them, are welcome to everything the island offers, but after what happened yesterday he is afraid for his safety. It turns out that the first group of sailors had looted and destroyed Simplicius' hut and threatened his life. The ship's chaplain apologizes and asks advice on curing the madness of the sailors. The hermit assures the captain and his men that he is ready to repay evil with good, and after he has been promised that he will not be taken off to Europe and that the location of the island will not be revealed, he appears, shakes hands all around, and guides them out of the cave. The light he uses comes from dried specimens of big lightning bugs, which he has fastened all over himself.

[The madness among the sailors has increased so much that now hardly a sane man is left. They are given the kernels of the plumlike fruit that induced the madness in the first place, and within the hour all are normal again. The chaplain calls the men together and gives them a stern lecture on looting. Thereupon the sailor who has stolen Simplicius' most precious possession, the palm-leaf book, returns it together with the thirty ducats in cash which he had also taken. Simplicius gives the book to Captain Cornelissen as a personal gift and asks him to distribute the money among the poor of Haarlem.

[Simplicius is very skillful in treating and nursing the ship's sick. His help is as much appreciated as he enjoys giving it, but to show their gratitude, the officers invite him to a sumptuous meal. Unlike any German Cornelissen had known, Simplicius eats only the plainest food and drinks water instead of wine. He states his reasons for refusing to return: When he left Europe the place was filled with war, arson, murder, pillage, rape, and fornication. But when God took away these evils, removed plagues and famine, and once more sent noble peace to profit the poor people, there arose all sorts of vices such as voluptuousness, gluttony, drinking, gambling, whoring, sodomy, and adultery which drew the whole swarm of the other vices after them. The worst of it is that there is no hope of improvement because every one thinks he is a good Christian when he goes to church once a week at best and to communion once a year. Simplicius is afraid that God who had shown him the grace of putting him on the island would treat him like Jonah if he tried to leave it after dwelling there for fifteen years. On the island he has freedom from want and vain desires. When the captain asks him whether he is not afraid to die there alone, he answers that the absence of men does not disturb him so long as God is with him.

[After all the sick have recovered and supplies have been taken aboard the merchantman, Cornelissen sets sail on the sixth day and rejoins his fleet at St. Helena. Before leaving, the ship's carpenters rebuild Simplicius' hut and the captain gives him a burning glass which he has requested for making fire from the rays of the sun. They also leave behind an ax, a shovel and a hoe, two bolts of cotton cloth, a dozen knives, a pair of scissors, two copper pots, and a pair of rabbits, to see if they will multiply on the island.]

The End

The Library of Liberal Arts

AESCHYLUS, Prometheus Bound

D'ALEMBERT, J., Preliminary Discourse to the Encyclopedia of Diderot

AQUINAS, ST. T., The Principles of Nature, On Being and Essence, On Free Choice, *and* On the Virtues in General

ARISTOTLE, Nicomachean Ethics
On Poetry and Music
On Poetry and Style

ARNAULD, A., The Art of Thinking (Port-Royal Logic)

AUGUSTINE, ST., On Christian Doctrine
On Free Choice of the Will

BACON, F., The New Organon

BARON and BLAU, eds., Judaism

BAUDELAIRE, C., The Prophetic Muse: Critical Essays of Baudelaire

BAYLE, P., Historical and Critical Dictionary (Selections)

BECCARIA, C., On Crimes and Punishments

BERGSON, H., Duration and Simultaneity
Introduction to Metaphysics

BERKELEY, G., Principles, Dialogues, *and* Philosophical Correspondence

Principles of Human Knowledge
Three Dialogues Between Hylas and Philonous
Works on Vision

BOCCACCIO, G., On Poetry

BOETHIUS, The Consolation of Philosophy

BOILEAU, N., Selected Criticism

BOLINGBROKE, H., The Idea of a Patriot King

BONAVENTURA, ST., The Mind's Road to God

BOSANQUET, B., Three Lectures on Aesthetic

BOWMAN, A., The Absurdity of Christianity

BRADLEY, F., Ethical Studies

BURKE, E., An Appeal from the New to the Old Whigs
Reflections on the Revolution in France
Selected Writings and Speeches on America

BURKE, K., Permanence and Change

BUTLER, J., Five Sermons

CALVIN, J., On the Christian Faith
On God and Political Duty

CATULLUS, Odi et Amo: Complete Poetry

CICERO, On the Commonwealth

Cid, The Epic of the

CROCE, B., Guide to Aesthetics

DESCARTES, R., Discourse on Method
    Discourse on Method *and* Meditations
    Discourse on Method, Optics, Geometry, *and* Meteorology
    Meditations
    Philosophical Essays
    Rules for the Direction of the Mind

DEWEY, J., On Experience, Nature, and Freedom

DIDEROT, D., Encyclopedia (Selections)
    Rameau's Nephew and Other Works

DOSTOEVSKI, F., The Grand Inquisitor

DRYDEN, J., An Essay of Dramatic Poesy and Other Essays

DUNS SCOTUS, J., Philosophical Writings

EPICTETUS, The Enchiridion

EPICURUS, Letters, Principal Doctrines, *and* Vatican Sayings

ERASMUS, D., Ten Colloquies

EURIPIDES, Electra

FEUERBACH, L., Principles of the Philosophy of the Future

FICHTE, J., The Vocation of Man

GOETHE, J., Faust I and II (verse)
    Faust I (prose)
    Faust II (prose)

GRANT, F., ed., Ancient Roman Religion
    Hellenistic Religions

GRIMMELSHAUSEN, J., Simplicius Simplicissimus

GROTIUS, H., Prolegomena to The Law of War and Peace

HAMILTON, C., ed., Buddhism

HANSLICK, E., The Beautiful in Music

HENDEL, C., Jean-Jacques Rousseau: Moralist
    Studies in the Philosophy of David Hume

HERDER, J., God, Some Conversations

HESIOD, Theogony

HOBBES, T., Leviathan I and II

HORACE, The Odes of Horace *and* The Centennial Hymn

HUME, D., Dialogues Concerning Natural Religion
    Inquiry Concerning Human Understanding
    Inquiry Concerning the Principles of Morals
    Of the Standard of Taste, and Other Essays
    Philosophical Historian
    Political Essays

JEFFERY, A., ed., Islam

KANT, I., Analytic of the Beautiful
    Critique of Practical Reason
    First Introduction to the Critique of Judgment
    Foundations of the Metaphysics of Morals
    The Metaphysical Elements of Justice, Part I of *Metaphysik der Sitten*
    The Metaphysical Principles of Virtue, Part II of *Metaphysik der Sitten*
    On History
    Perpetual Peace
    Prolegomena to Any Future Metaphysics

KLEIST, H., The Prince of Homburg

LAO TZU, The Way of Lao Tzu

Lazarillo de Tormes, The Life of

LEIBNIZ, G., Monadology and Other Philosophical Essays

LESSING, G., Laocoön

LOCKE, J., A Letter Concerning Toleration
Second Treatise of Government

LONGINUS, On Great Writing (On the Sublime)

LUCIAN, Selected Works

LUCRETIUS, On Nature

MACHIAVELLI, N., The Art of War
Mandragola

MARCUS AURELIUS, Meditations

MEAD, G., Selected Writings

MILL, J., An Essay on Government

MILL, J. S., Autobiography
Considerations on Representative Government
Nature and Utility of Religion
On Liberty
On the Logic of the Moral Sciences
Theism
Utilitarianism

MOLIÈRE, Tartuffe

MONTESQUIEU, C., The Persian Letters

NIETZSCHE, F., The Use and Abuse of History

NOVALIS, Hymns to the Night and Other Writings

OCKHAM, W., Philosophical Writings

PAINE, T., The Age of Reason

PALEY, W., Natural Theology

PARKINSON, T., ed., Masterworks of Prose

PICO DELLA MIRANDOLA, On the Dignity of Man, On Being and the One, and Heptaplus

PLATO, Epistles
Euthydemus
Euthyphro, Apology, Crito
Gorgias
Meno
Phaedo
Phaedrus
Protagoras
Statesman
Symposium
Theaetetus
Timaeus

Commentaries:
BLUCK, R., Plato's Phaedo
CORNFORD, F., Plato and Parmenides
Plato's Cosmology
Plato's Theory of Knowledge
HACKFORTH, R., Plato's Examination of Pleasure
Plato's Phaedo
Plato's Phaedrus

PLAUTUS, The Haunted House
The Menaechmi
The Rope

POPE, A., An Essay on Man

POST, C., ed., Significant Cases in British Constitutional Law

QUINTILIAN, On the Early Education of the Citizen-Orator

REYNOLDS, J., Discourses on Art

Roman Drama, Copley and Hadas, trans.

ROSENMEYER, OSTWALD, and HALPORN, The Meters of Greek and Latin Poetry

RUSSELL, B., Philosophy of Science

Sappho, The Poems of

SCHILLER, J., Wilhelm Tell

SCHLEGEL, J., On Imitation and Other Essays

SCHNEIDER, H., Sources of Contemporary Philosophical Realism in America

SCHOPENHAUER, A., On the Basis of Morality
Freedom of the Will

SELBY-BIGGE, L., British Moralists

SENECA, Medea
Oedipus
Thyestes

SHAFTESBURY, A., Characteristics

SHELLEY, P., A Defence of Poetry

SMITH, A., The Wealth of Nations (Selections)

Song of Roland, Terry, trans.

SOPHOCLES, Electra

SPIEGELBERG, H., The Socratic Enigma

SPINOZA, B., Earlier Philosophical Writings
On the Improvement of the Understanding

TERENCE, The Brothers
The Eunuch
The Mother-in-Law
Phormio
The Self-Tormentor
The Woman of Andros

Three Greek Romances, Hadas, trans.

TOLSTOY, L., What is Art?

VERGIL, Aeneid

VICO, G. B., On the Study Methods Our Time

VOLTAIRE, Philosophical Letters

WHITEHEAD, A., Interpretation of Science

WOLFF, C., Preliminary Discourse on Philosophy in General

XENOPHON, Recollections of Socrates and Socrates' Defense Before the Jury

The Library of Literature

CRANE, STEPHEN, *The Red Badge of Courage*, ed. Frederick C. Crews, 6

DICKENS, CHARLES, *Great Expectations*, ed. Louis Crompton, 2

HAWTHORNE, NATHANIEL, *The Scarlet Letter*, ed. Larzer Ziff, 1

MELVILLE, HERMAN, *Moby Dick*, ed. Charles Feidelson, 5

One Hundred Middle English Lyrics, ed. Robert D. Stevick, 7

SWIFT, JONATHAN, *Gulliver's Travels*, ed. Martin Price, 3

TWAIN, MARK, *The Adventures of Huckleberry Finn*, ed. Leo Marx, 4